NEW BREED

BY

M. A. MARRISSETTE

Dedication

To my father, Scranton C. Marrissette, may he rest in peace, who used his contacts and had my first draft reviewed by The Steve Tisch Corp. Their assessment and those of their friends inspired me to continue onward and further develop my stories.

To my husband, Christopher E. Hall, shares my vision for New Breed and many more novels to come. His business acumen and support have assisted me with this great endeavor.

To the rest of my family and loved ones, who have always seen more in me than I have seen in myself at times. They've helped me become the person I am today.

CHAPTER ONE

"This is living!" Desmony thought as she flew vicariously through the San Francisco night air. Her perception of reality was rather distorted. She swept through the air, much like an ominous storm cloud, moving in, to cause disarray and mayhem on whomever or whatever it could. If anyone had seen her flying through the steel-gray night sky, they would have seen a creature with a wing-span of at least six feet in either direction. Desmony was in every sense of the word a Vampire. She knew what she was, and she loved it. Feeding was a fact of life for her. She didn't feel remorse about it. Actually, she thrived on it. To be more accurate, she didn't feel anything much about the subject. It was a subject that bored her to tears whenever her sister, Morgana, and she discussed. She couldn't understand, for all the years she's been in company with her sibling, how the "child" could feel bad about eating! Desmony tried to explain that humans eat meat. Some even fancied themselves to be Vampires, drinking animal blood from goblets and such. It was hysterical to Desmony. Still, it wasn't enough reasoning for her melancholy sister. It didn't matter to Morgana that this was a fact of their lives. Desmony was not known for patience. It was par for the course; if patience truly is a virtue, then that alone would give her reason not to wait.

Morgana spent much of her evenings debating the issue to feed, or not to feed. Once, when Desmony actually gave the analogy of humans eating other living creatures, Morgana simply stated that humans are the most developed species. She said they can reason, love, and question their purpose for living. That, among other things, made a large difference between humans eating smaller creatures, and vampires depleting their victims of their blood supply. Discussions such as those drove Desmony to drink. Of course it wasn't alcohol. Desmony would go out on rampages, making several humans a night her feast. Morgana, on the other hand, seemed to torture herself. She never had a choice, although neither did Desmony. Morgana was born this way. If it was up to her, she would've been much happier being born, living, and dying, as all humans around her did.

Desmony couldn't identify with the "child". There were several things she couldn't understand about Morgana. For one thing, Morgana rarely fed. She drank very seldom, usually remains from a raid performed by other family members. It was almost as if she would order take out, and eat whatever was left over for a week. Desmony had to feed nightly, although she was somewhat a glutton by Vampire standards. Another thing was if they stayed out too long, which was typical for Desmony when she went out with her sister, Morgana wouldn't suffer from the rising sun as badly. Desmony could feel her skin almost evaporate as the gigantic flaming orb lifted itself upwards. Morgana would just sweat a little, seemingly more from the heat, as a human would, than the sun's power trying to annihilate her very being as a Vampire.

These traits, as well as others were a constant enigma for Desmony to figure out, usually when she would go out by herself. Desmony began to feel a little bored, as well as fatigued from her night of swooping through the sky, peering into houses and businesses. She got a thrill out of spying on people. She had caught humans doing various activities. They would be watching television, laughing, arguing, or making love. Desmony would watch for as long as she could stand it. For all of her life, she hadn't the seeming joy of giving herself to another. Locating another Vampire seemed almost hopeless. She would be damned if she ever thought to try and turn a human into a mate. She had seen that attempted, and failed. It wasn't that much of a desire to her to risk that sacrifice.

The sky was changing from a deep navy blue, to more of a cobalt blue. The sun was on the rise, which was Desmony's signal to get back to her sanctuary, the family home. The late twentieth century had its advantages, as well as its set-backs. Their home was state of the art, for a Vampire. Alloy shields protected them from the sun, which allowed them to sleep in beds, not musty rank soil from some land they had left centuries before. The blood on Desmony's chin from an earlier conquest was beginning to dry. She wiped away the flakes of crimson hemoglobin, as she looked out to the horizon that's face was changing moods quickly from gloom to optimism. Desmony had been perched on top of a sky scrapper, which gave her solitude. She leaped from her post, driving through the air at an almost supersonic pace. "I wonder what Morgana is doing?" Desmony laughed as she thought to herself, "Nothing!"

Desmony swooped into Morgana's bedroom window. She changed form into what would pass as human. Her wings melted into her back, so she had room to enter the stained glass windows that depicted the story of Morgana's existence. The fangs that assisted Desmony in retrieving blood disappeared, as did the flaming tint and black iris of her eyes. A gust of wind moved the windows as Desmony came in. Desmony tripped on a pair of shoes Morgana had lying around, which insulted Desmony's vanity. "Whoops! Almost took out your stained glass windows! That would be a terrible loss for you, wouldn't it?" Desmony tried to hurt Morgana with her words, even though Morgana had no intent to harm her sister.

Desmony smoothed out her clothes and fluffed her curly black hair as she tried to compose herself. She smiled at Morgana with a slight sneer. Morgana wasn't trying to acknowledge Desmony. Desmony stroked the floor as she walked over to where Morgana was hunched over. She hovered over her, as a scolding mother does to a brooding child. Morgana was looking quite pale, refusing to feed yet another night. The circles around her eyes proved Desmony's point without argue. Morgana needed blood, but she refused it. "This is utterly useless! Making yourself sick is not the answer. Morgana, you need to feed. You can't sustain life this way. You know you can't eat as humans do. Remember the last time you tried? You were sick for days! As much as you envy them, you can't be one of them. You aren't one of them." Desmony had a twinge of sibling sympathy and proceeded to kneel down, next to Morgana.

"I remember a time when blood was like Kool-Aid to you." Desmony began to stroke Morgana's straight ebony hair. It was so beautiful and strong, like she had once been. The blunt bundle of hair weighed heavily on Morgana's back. Morgana moved her hair forward to hide her face. In a reflex to the rejection, Desmony said, "You never did have my appetite, but you did show promise. We used to have such great adventures! Now you seem to be trying to accomplish the impossible by killing yourself. You know we can't do that!" Desmony still tried to show affection to her troubled sister, only because they were bound by family blood, more than the blood that mixed in her veins from her victims.

"Desmony, I'm so tired of it! I've been killing since the seventeenth century. It was never easy for me, you know that. I just don't feel I'm meant to survive this way. I guess somewhere along the line I developed a conscience." Morgana studied Desmony's eyes, trying to see if Desmony showed any signs of comprehension. All she saw in response was a blank stare. "It doesn't matter if they are strangers, or if they were criminals. God deals with them, right?" Still there was no sign of understanding from Desmony. "I forgot, you wouldn't know. You've been so distanced from any human influence or compassion; you just don't give a damn about them. You lived as one, once. Has it been too long for you to remember?" Morgana was hoping her words would touch Desmony. Desmony's shield deflected the message. It had been four centuries since she had seen the sun. She had no recollection of the *incident*. Her first years of life were insignificant to her now. Morgana decided to lie down, hoping that her hellish sibling would literally vanish, so she could get some rest.

The sun was almost up. Nola, the dedicated ally of the family came into the room to prepare it for their slumber. She slept as they fed. When their time for touring the night sky was over, Nola was the one to care for them. For nearly one hundred- fifty years, she looked after the family, as they had for her. They had her eternal gratitude. When Nola came into the room, she saw that the coming day had weakened both of the girls. As a habit, she came to their room last, since they were the last ones to bed down for the day. Nola reached behind the sheer curtains that framed the stained glass windows. There was a lever behind the curtains that controlled the alloy screen that protected the girls from the fatal sun. As the slab of metal came down, Nola helped Morgana under her covers. Desmony bowed out of the room. She made her own room ready for the day and lay down, over her covers.

Morgana still had thoughts about her conversation with Desmony. It outraged her that she couldn't reach her sister. Morgana had worked so hard to build up a resistance to sunlight, not being able to read the bible, and watching television evangelists on cable. She so wanted to be "normal", but no one, not even Nola knew what that was, if they ever did. For now, Morgana needed rest. She wanted to pray, but she would suffer crippling headaches if she tried. "Someday," she said, "someday." Nola knew that Morgana had tried to pray. Nola tried to as well, since that was her faith before she forfeited her mortal life. Desmony laughed from her room. She could see everything that was going on in her mind. She found the whole thing ridiculously funny. Nola touched Morgana on her brow, feeling compassion for the girl. "Night and day. Night and day." Nola thought this as she moved down the corridor to start her day.

Morgana lay on her back, trying to let sleep take her over. She was ill at ease, so sleep would not come to her. She thought about the home she was about to buy for her very own. She was going to make some changes in her life. What those changes were, she wasn't sure yet. She wasn't looking for something to obtain some sort of unspoken forgiveness from society for feasting on mankind. She wanted to fit in. She became emotional watching "Rudolph the Red Nosed Reindeer!" She could identify with the poor creature. Rudolph couldn't change himself, neither could Morgana. People were narrow-minded and cruel. With her, that point was different. Rudolph didn't prey on humans! She wanted more purpose in life than to find pleasure and to care only for her own survival.

Morgana began to sleep, but only for an abrupt time. She had been conditioning herself to lead a non-nocturnal "life". She began to stir, then to think, ultimately to remember. The beginning goes far beyond her memory. She only could go by the stories that were told to her, over the centuries. She also managed to steal a few memories from her elders. These stories spanned as far back as the fourteenth century, in England.

The sister's mother, Elsebeth Alburré was a docile being. Innocent was an understatement when describing this delicate flower. She was poor, living only with Alec, her father. Their home was extremely humble, housing only the bare necessities. Between her many domestic skills, such as sewing, cooking, and entertaining others with her music, and her father's ability to create furniture that was as beautiful as it was functional, they were able to keep food on their table. Elsebeth used her talents to aid others in town that needed help. They would pay her, modestly for her services, but it was mutually beneficial. Her mother just wasn't strong enough to endure the hardship of labor. Elsebeth had only the women in town to provide any maternal support.

Ava, Elsebeth's mother was every much as beautiful and graceful as her daughter. It was Elsebeth's sorrow that she would never know the woman that gave her life. Her only link to her mother was her father. He filled her imagination with fantastic stories about Ava. Everyone in town reinforced his boasting about his wife. When he was a young man, he pursued Ava until her family condoned marriage, probably more so out of fatigue than anything else. Fortunately, Elsebeth's mother was very much in love with the young man. Alec promised to fill her life with all the joys that the world could offer her. He tried, but time was too short. She became with child shortly after they were wed.

Ava's pregnancy was a tumultuous one, which foreshadowed Ava's imminent death. Ava's family was leery from the beginning, but there was nothing they could do about it. Ava swore to bring her first babe into the world, and kiss her brow, passing on her love to the baby. Alec tended to her every need. She could no longer be wife, and mother-to-be. She held close to the bed at all times. She had been Alec's wife just long enough to make their home a thing of beauty.

The home was modest, but manicured all the same. She would sew while she was practically pinned to the bed. She made curtains, clothes, and even several quilts, mostly for the baby. Ava dreamed of combing her child's hair, holding it, and teaching it all she knew and encouraging it to learn more, but she knew in her heart that it was not to be.

The night of Elsebeth's birth, Ava died. She did, however, get to see her reason for living. In her weakened state, she held her little girl close and whispered to her, "My love, I'll see you one day." She kissed her loving husband on the brow, closed her eyes, and began her sleep for eternity. From that point on, Alec was the only source of direction for Elsebeth. He was so proud. He raised her, on his own, keeping the dreams of Ava for her daughter foremost in his mind. He guided Elsebeth, showing her how to do simple things at first. As she grew, so did Alec's responsibility to being her guardian. She learned many things from Alec. It seemed as though her talent for sewing was established through her mother's spirit. She spent time with many of the townspeople, letting them teach her the things Alec could not. As Elsebeth grew, Alec became more of a protector than a teacher. Always, Alec was a caring father to her, never raising his voice to her, never needing to.

Elsebeth finally reached the age when her heart felt more than love for just her daddy. Young men in the village stopped chasing her to throw mud at her, or shove a frog in her face. They wanted her attention, her affection. It was a difficult lesson for Alec to teach, but he did the best he could to instruct her on how to behave as a lady when she spent time with the village boys. Once, a boy made an improper advance toward Elsebeth. Instinct and her father's teaching caused her to get away from the boy and run home, with haste. Elsebeth came home distraught one evening, and a little confused, Alec had to explain the most painful lesson he had to teach his girl. Loving someone and making love to someone is how he lost his Ava. If he could, he would've kept Elsebeth locked in the house, as every caring father would. He knew he couldn't. Alec was never sure if it was the way he explained it, or if it was the fact that she was the daughter of the wisest woman he ever knew, Elsebeth sat calmly, and understood everything.

Elsebeth was mature beyond her years. She was very peculiar when it came to men. She stayed with her father for many years after the expected age for marriage. The people closest to them understood their quandary, their fear. Alec didn't want to lose his daughter and Elsebeth didn't want to leave her father. She wanted to keep him happy, which she had done. She couldn't bring herself to be married to just anyone because it was expected. The person she left her father for had to be remarkable.

The following spring, a new family came to town. They located their home, which was an expansive structure just short of a castle, on top of a hill overlooking the village. They were quiet, mysterious, and removed. At first, no one truly noticed that they made appearances only after dusk. The townspeople watched out for one another, but most tended to their own affairs. The first one to notice was Alec. He was one of the few villagers that knew how to read. As with most common folk, he learned from the bible. Other literature was too difficult to obtain, especially in such a remote area. In Alec's brief travels as a young man, before he decided to start his life with Ava, he came across some that believed in the occult. He disregarded the first few as freaks, or witches, bound for the stake, or a good flogging. As he moved on, he observed that the stories all had common bonds. The words, the legends and myths were all around him. He made sure to remember some of the stories. Once he returned, he used his knowledge only to recite these stories to frighten children that appeared to be heading down the wrong path. Some children would go away crying. Others would run home laughing. It all depended on Alec's mood, and how he told the story.

From the cold fortress that landscaped the small mountain top where the mysterious family lived, only one tenant, other than ghostly looking servants, descended. His name was Bernard Mal. He was a tall, lean man. His eyes were dark and harsh, but his mouth was kind, almost seductive. He had long, black hair. It shinned like sable, and moved as though it was sable, still on the small beast. He kept his mane in a ponytail, tied at the nape of his neck. Even though the weather was usually cool, his complexion reflected the weather with an opalescent, almost translucent tint to it. Some noticed the drastic lack of color in his countenance, but discarded it to thin blood.

No one else existed as he walked through the village. His appearance was quite distinct. He drew attention no matter where he went. He had a sleek stride. Ironically, Bernard would buy flowers, every day. When he would reach for the flowers, his gloved, gracile fingers would stroke the hand of Lysa, the vendor. He pierced her soul with his eyes. She felt a certain magic, but she couldn't understand it. Her eyes glimmered when his glance met hers. She had to look away due to his intense beauty, and how it affected her. Bernard, even without his hyper-sensitive intuition and telepathy, could see what affect he had on the girl. He smiled as he left Lysa. He put his head down, content with himself at the set up for his bait. The flowers he brought each day became a crusty cinder, shortly after he walked away.

Shortly after that encounter, a brilliantly decorated envelope was delivered to Lysa, the flower girl. The presentation created a frenzied stir in the village. Lysa feared she would never be able to remove the smile that was etched on her face as she read the invitation. Her presence was requested at the home of Mal that evening. Lysa was so excited. Her mother and married sister helped her prepare for the evening. When all the work was done, Lysa carried the façade of a woman from royalty. Her thick blonde hair was curled in tiny ringlets. It was soft and flowed like honey. Her skin smelled of lilacs. She was tall, but fully and firmly shaped. She gave herself a last look, gathered her breath, as well as her nerve, and showed herself off to Smythe, her father. He nearly cried at the site of his baby girl. He had let one daughter go, fortunately to a good man. He hoped that he would have equal success with this match.

Prior to all the preparations, Smythe and his wife insisted that he be a part of the impending courtship. No daughter of theirs would be going unattended to a strange home, no matter who was the inviting party. Bernard accepted this stipulation, naturally. He rather expected it. Arrangements were made for two visitors, instead of just one. The sky changed its mood and hue as the carriage approached. It slowly became a somber, silver gray. The butler greeted them. He was an emotionless human being, if human was an accurate description. He looked coldly at the two enthusiastic people poised at the doorstep. Smythe disregarded it as "high and mighty" behavior. The butler showed them in, going through the motions, not really acknowledging their existence. He was, however, aware of their every move.

Even the foyer bragged of the affluence the family possessed. The furniture was of the finest craftsmanship, down to the minutest detail. The pure gold and silver metal that accented the home was tastefully done, but extravagant all the same. Tapestries hung oppressively on the walls, showing stories of battles previously fought. There was little doubt that the brother and sister actually fought in some of them. Lysa studied one of the older tapestries. Even though the faces were made from fabric, one face in particular favored Bernard in such a way that it made Lysa's flesh run.

The butler showed the two into the parlor. Music was playing softly in the background. There was no evidence of people playing the music, which made the mood more unsettling than not. "Would you care for any brandy, or some other form of refreshment, sir?" The butler's nostrils flexed as he spoke to them. It appeared as though their scent made him nauseous. The air was cool, coursing through the house. Lysa's skin turned to goose flesh as the wind swirled around her. The seduction had already begun. They waited for quite some time, but between the music and the wind, the time seemed to pass quickly. The wind, which was Bernard transformed into a clear mist, seemed to almost touch the two visitors as they sat. They were unquestionably in awe at the abundance of wealth. Smythe divulged information to Bernard's mind as he fantasized about his daughter living so nicely, as Bernard's wife. He only wanted what was best for his child.

Bernard smirked as he read The man's mind. It was wide open, like a green, grassy field, untouched by human hands and vacant of trees, or any other foliage. There was a candle sitting in its brass holder on the table near the cocktail tray. The flame shuttered, more so from Bernard's entrance than from the wind that was touring the mansion. Lysa smelled Bernard's familiar scent first. She turned to see her *prince*. He was standing there, looking over her, as he always did. The familiarity, despite the rich surroundings, comforted Lysa. Smythe saw his daughter blush as she was entranced by Bernard. Smythe stood up first, walking over to where Lysa was sitting. "My name is..." Bernard cut Smythe off. "Smythe. Don't be surprised, your daughter speaks very highly of you. We speak briefly, albeit often, when I venture into town." Bernard was warm cognac, intoxicating both parties present.

Bernard gestured for Smythe to make him comfortable once more. "I would hate for you to feel uncomfortable or anxious in my home, as long as you are here. Have you had any refreshment? Shall I pour you a drink, sir?" Bernard was on his best behavior, despite his hunger. Lysa's floral fragrance actually made him sick to his stomach. The rich wild flowers that scented her body were a covert weapon, unbeknownst to them. What saved Bernard's appetite was the blood giving life to the beautiful, hopeful girl. She was sitting there, so nervous. She hadn't been afforded the opportunity to be taught grace common in higher society, or royalty. She didn't want to disappoint Bernard. Bernard almost burst out with laughter as he caught a gleam of Lysa's anxiety. He thought she'd throw up before he ever had to!

Smythe answered politely, "Well, sir, we are quite refreshed. Thank you, for allowing us to take part in your dinner this evening. I hope we will provide sufficient entertainment for you." Smythe was truly a gentleman. Bernard thought about just how delicious they were going to be. He had to snap back to reality right away, before he gave himself away. "I'm sure you will. If you are ready, we should start for the dining room. I would be disappointed if your dinner was ruined by the cool weather." The climate Bernard spoke of was much to his liking, but just above unsettling for his two human guests.

Bernard guided Lysa and Smythe to the dining room. A crystal chandelier hung in the dining room, over a large dining table. The setting took up only a small fraction of the perfectly set table. Polished silverware and a silk cloth covered the small section, giving a touch of perfection to the room. Candles laminated a great area of the room. Some distant corners were discretely dim, giving a baroque feel to the room. Bernard took Lysa by her gloved hand and guided her to the north side of the table. Smythe was shown to the chair on the south side by the butler. Bernard took his reserved place at the west side of the table. His setting only had a silver goblet, not seemingly chilled. His butler had the goblet filled with his own blood. It was to only sustain Bernard until he could make his attack on Lysa.

Bernard promised a portion of Smythe's blood to the butler. The rest was to go to his sister, Blythe. She was slightly older, and a lot stronger than her brother. Blythe viewed the drama from her cold, lofty room. She could see the entire interaction in her mind. When the temperature was cold, her senses were heightened. She couldn't see faces, just images moving in the rooms as she knew them to be. In the room with life, Lysa fumbled with her dress, made with intricate detail until The butler entered the room again with their feast. Bernard stared at the girl until she almost lost her water. Her chest was pounding so vigorously, that she had to check her dress to see if her heart was making the dress move. Bernard smiled at her, seeming to know what she was thinking. He in fact did, but he did not let on. He just drew a smile on his face.

Bernard was becoming physically excited. It wasn't for Lysa's heaving bosom, but the blood coursing through her veins. Her arteries were moving at a marching band pace. He could smell the blood. Her pale flesh was thin, which excited Bernard even more. He pulled out a handkerchief and dabbed either side of his mouth. All of these things, the blood and its bitter-sweet flavor that he was anticipating, made Bernard drool. They both snapped back to where they should be. He seated himself, not waiting for the butler. His physical state wouldn't allow him that luxury. His movements were stealth. A fine feast was set before the two visitors. They ate well, minding their manners the entire time. They weren't scavengers or barbarians, by any means, but eating was never quite this formal or intense. The wine was sweet, as was the conversation. Bernard coated Lysa with compliments. Smythe cocked his eyebrow at the exchange of words. Lysa couldn't continue to consume all of the stress. She stood up to excuse herself for some air. Before she could leave her chair properly, she collapsed to the floor.

Bernard's non-human speed allowed him to beat Smythe to where his daughter laid. Bernard ran gallantly to her aid. As he met her, she slumped over onto his shoulder. He lifted her and carried her into his drawing room, which wasn't far from the dining room. He laid her down on a chaise lounge. The windows were opened, which let air come in to revive Lysa. Smythe edged Bernard out of the way. He held his daughter by her shoulders. Smythe shook her ever so lightly. He tried to bring her around, and shortly thereafter, she did return. The butler came in with cold compresses to aid in her recovery. After doing so, the butler took Smythe sternly by the arm and suggested that he take a short walk with him. "A young girl trying to make a good impression with her father monitoring her every move could be rather harsh on the nerves, I suppose." The butler still had to use some force to lead Smythe out into the yard.

Bernard lifted his eyes, long enough to meet with Smythe's. It may have been a telepathic suggestion that did it, but Smythe resisted no longer.

Bernard turned back around so that he might focus on Lysa. He could see so much potential in her. He could mold her into something astounding. He studied her features as he caressed her hair. He thought secondarily of how beautiful she was. Not only would she be his precious dessert, she would share his eternity. "You're fine now. You needed some air, that's all. I'm truly sorry, I had the fire too high." Bernard kissed her brow. It was moist with perspiration. That contact of flesh ignited a passion within Lysa. She had never been kissed. This was truly special. He would receive all that she had to give. Whether or not the sweat was from the fire place, or the trauma of fainting was hard to tell. A kiss on the lips followed.

The butler had showed Smythe to the stables. There were several fine horses. Their eyes shinned like fire when Smythe looked into them. They were transports for the devil, or something terribly close. There was ridding tackle hanging on the wooden walls. A pitch fork was set up against the opposing entrance. There were several other unsuspecting weapons there, none of which Smythe thought of as such or that he would need. The butler had been rambling, which was enough to drive the most docile person mad, but with whatever witch craft or spell Bernard had placed on Smythe, it appeared to be a normal conversation. It was largely one sided, but Smythe managed a few words.

Bernard's hand arched Lysa's back. She sat up, trembling. Lysa wasn't sure what was about to happen, but if it was what she feared, she was prepared to call for her father, no matter how badly she wanted this man. Being taken by Bernard sadly was the last thing Lysa had to worry about. She could feel him, pressing hard against her, but it was not a response to Lysa's bosom pressing back onto Bernard. "Sir, this is all too much for me. I have feelings of love for you, I truly do, but I must be wed 'fore anything else is to happen. Per chance, I should collect my father and be on my way. I am very grateful, but it is quite late." Bernard smiled again at her. He hushed her with his long index finger. Bernard touched her cheek, reassuring her that all was well. "My darling, don't worry. These things you fret about won't happen. I love you too, especially the life that you possess."

Before Lysa could respond, Bernard's face began to alter. His persona followed suit. Bernard's cool flesh became even colder as he pressed Lysa close to him. He didn't want her to struggle. He also didn't want her to take in enough air to scream, if she saw him change. His eyes were cruel and his mouth was fuller. His mouth was holding the fangs that were growing within. His nails were growing, right into Lysa's back. Hair burst from his pores. His back cracked as it grew into a grotesque hunch. He was hunched over Lysa, salivating, enjoying the pain the change brought him.

Lysa couldn't see what was going on to react the way she normally would have. She only got a brief glimpse of the beast that was suffocating her. The glass shattering shriek she began to emit was cut short as he stroked her throat with his fingernail. It was long and sharp. It cut her young throat, smooth and quick. He liked her, so he spared her any additional pain. He needed her blood, her life. He then used his deadly nail to cut his lip. He kissed her, one last time, before all of the life was out of her. He needed to intertwine his blood with hers to make the transformation complete. Bernard left her with just enough blood to stay alive for the transformation, to become "unborn".

CHAPTER TWO

Bernard was full of the knowledge he could choose what people would live and who would die as he met them. He had the power to choose whose life was more necessary. It wasn't his right, but he accepted it and took advantage of it whenever he needed to feed. His means of survival was crude and he knew it, but he had to live, just as everyone and everything else did. His sustenance was simply different. That is what helped him, had he a conscience. He looked down at Lysa. She was so peaceful. She looked like a lily, lying in a clear bowl, filled with water. The next time she was to wake, she would not feel her pure and giving heart pound as it once did. She would only feel the need to satisfy her hunger, with blood.

All the while, Smythe was trying to endure the self-involved butler. He was rattling off some irrelevant story that sent Smythe into a lull. Just as he was about to collapse from boredom, he heard the trail of Lysa's scream. Smythe's nightmare was coming true. His child was in danger, just as he feared. He had hoped his daughter would come running from the main house, yelling of how Bernard loved her, how he wanted to marry her. Sadly, this was never to be. Smythe came to attention, as did the butler. The butler knew that he had to stop Smythe from interfering. The evening had to go as scheduled.

The butler lunged for a sickle that was perched, out of place, in the stable. He tossed it in the air, hoping to protrude an air of confidence that would terrify Smythe. The only thing that was frightening Smythe was the echo of his daughter's scream. She was in peril, and he had to get to her. Smythe managed to get to a pitch fork that was tugging at his sleeve. He grabbed it just as the tip of the sickle was about to strike the crown of his head. The prongs of the pitch fork met with the sickle, sending a sheet of electrical sparks through the air. Smythe was under the pressure of the semi-human servant to the monster that was killing Smythe's daughter. It didn't matter. He found enough strength from God at that bleak moment to fight the emotionless creature that was before him.

Smythe pushed the butler away from him. It wasn't far, but it was enough for him to regroup. The fight was on! The butler twirled the sickle as a high school student would maneuver a tall flag, impressing himself more than Smythe. It only gave Smythe enough time to plan a strategy. Smythe approached the butler. He spun around as he came closer. The pitch fork was perched, ready to hit the butler in the belly. It was a clever plan, and well executed, but the butler had been fighting for more years than Smythe had been alive.

The butler blocked the blow with the sickle. He pushed Smythe back. A horse behind Smythe reared up and started him.

The butler seized his chance and sliced Smythe across the chest. It sheared his shirt. The butler whirled around after making the blow. He was stunned to still see Smythe standing. With all of Smythe's energy, he jabbed the pitch fork into The butler. The tool wedged itself deep into the *man*. Smythe had to shake the large fork, so that he could relieve his victim from the impaling. The butler was dead. He was sure of it. The trouble with undead servants was that they lived as long as their makers, provided they didn't sustain any life threatening injuries. They could almost live forever. Smythe threw the pitch fork to the ground and started for the house.

There were several candles sparsely located that were flickering in the night breeze. The bed was an oak canopy. A sheer silk netting covered the top and sides of this magnificent bed. Smythe had made his way back into the mansion. Smythe searched every room until he found the one that contained his Lysa. Bernard stood perched in a corner. Blythe was still observing, curious as to how the entire drama would play out. It was as if she was watching a play. When Smythe found the dimly lighted room, the bed was the first thing he saw. He could see a gentle form behind the scarcely moving silk screen. He was frozen. It was as if he knew what happened, and he couldn't face it. Smythe eased over to the bed, one of the only focal points in the bedroom, other than the fireplace and a large armoire. It was poised in the middle of the room. The armoire was angled in a corner, slightly facing the opposing window. The floor underneath him creaked as he moved closer. He knew it didn't matter if anyone heard him. It was simply a matter of time.

Smythe finally reached the curtain that covered the bed. He moved the silky screen away, which revealed his daughter. Lysa was so still, as never before. She was perfect. Her lips were perched, like she was going to kiss her father hello, just as she did every day when he came home. Now, he was never going to know that feeling again. It was now to be replaced by a deep, eternal pain that would tear into his gut for the rest of his life. How was he going to tell his wife? How was he going to tell his daughter that her baby sister was dead?

Bernard peeled himself from the thick, Bordeaux curtain that covered the vaulted window. The entire sky would have seen what had taken place, had the curtains not been there to keep the secret. Bernard had no sense of feeling a he stared at Lysa's father. It was done, and there was nothing Smythe could do, or nothing Bernard wanted to do. He couldn't and wouldn't take it back. Lysa's blood was sweet, even though the blood was actually tart, even salty. It was sweet to him. He needed it. He felt rejuvenated, as much alive as he would ever feel again. He wanted more, but he didn't want Smythe invited to the party.

"I trust you know that your child is dead. She was spared any pain, if that matters to you. You need not worry about her, however. She will be taken well care of by my family. I suppose it will be just Blythe and I, since you destroyed my servant. I'd keep you on, but I doubt that you will be willing. You will have to die, completely. Your wife and other daughter will be taken care of. I suppose that's the least I can do. I want Lysa, and you are in the way. I must say, ignorance truly is bliss. In fact, it's salvation for some." Bernard was a monster now. Smythe stood there, sobbing as he listened to this mad creature, saying these cold words to him, telling him what was to happen, so coldly. He wasn't in fear of his death as much as what had happened to his family in the name of love. He prayed for God to forgive his anger. Smythe's tears dried up as the heat from his face showed through in his flushed cheeks.

Smythe was not to be bound. He shook with rage, hurt, and uncontrollable emptiness. "All that know me know that I trust no man, no man! Not for the money he has, or the foolish look of love he may have in his eye for one of my angels. I did this favor of letting Lysa see you. You, who did this to her! Yes, I killed your butler, and now, I'm going to kill you!" Smythe was going to fight, even though he knew he was going to die. Bernard was still in his nocturnal form. Smythe charged Mal. Bernard didn't even make use of his strength, or power. Instead, he used his prowess with the sabre. He stuck the sabre, one fatal time, into the heart of Smythe. Before Smythe died, he said, "Damn you! Lysa will never conform to your ways. She was beautiful alive. She will be your undoing dead." Smythe slumped over onto Bernard. Bernard threw him to the ground, only slightly unnerved by Smythe's final words.

Bernard felt a swirl of wind at the door way. It was his sister, Blythe. She did not appear amused. "I stood around, and watched you handle this transformation. You are much too old to be given a critique. Lysa was the wrong candidate from the beginning, I told you that. We are trying to establish ourselves somewhere. You have possibly destroyed that chance for us!" Bernard didn't seem worried. He had his plan all laid out, from the beginning. It was possible he did these things just to ignite Blythe's senses.

"Sister, sister. I would not endanger our stay in this lovely town. I know how much you still like to be around humans, even though you have yet to step out of this house!" Bernard was a little snit, more times than not. " I have no intention of being snuffed out, like an animal for being different, simply because you have a wild streak! Contain yourself!" Blythe whirled around and flew upward, until she reached the railing of where she resided. "Don't worry! I'll care for the body." Bernard smiled as he picked up Smythe, so he could dispose of his body.

Usually, the butler took care of the details, like burying bodies and spooking or killing prowlers. Now, Bernard had to stoop to his level. He really had no personal interest in the butler. The butler just happened to be loyal. He seemed to have been addicted to Blythe and Bernard's world. He was in another world now, one neither sibling hoped to see. The work was difficult, but it didn't take Bernard as long as it would for a normal man. He drenched himself in water, cleansing himself so that he could be presentable for Lysa, when she awoke. It was a gesture, if nothing else He had taken off his shirt for the tedious task of digging the grave for the butler. The next part wouldn't require so much sweat. It seemed ironic that he would still sweat, even if he was undead. He was cold, but his heart did beat, with the help of his victim's blood when he fed.

Bernard lifted himself onto the stage that had brought Smythe and Lysa to their doom. He rode around to the back of the estate. They were conveniently located on a cliff, overlooking the water that made up the coast. The land before the water was not considered beach land. It was rocky. It was probably the most dangerous terrain in the area. It merely added to the mystique of the mansion. Bernard hoisted up Smythe onto the coach with him. He was not in the mood to do this sort of labor. He actually spoke to the deceased Smythe, cracking a joke or two, just to add insult to injury. He then dismounted the coach, leaving Smythe sitting on the bench. With one slap, the horse began to run. Bernard looked at the creature and then at the rocks it was balancing on. The horse, despite his will to live, lost its footing. It began to fall, then the carriage. Smythe and the horse plummeted to the rocks below. The rocks broke and tore at the horse and Smythe's body.

The place where Smythe finally rested framed his mutilated body. The rocks had distorted his entire being. Whoever was to find Smythe was going to be the terrified teller of a story that would haunt the village for a long time. Bernard had taken the precaution of bringing a piece of Lysa's dress with him. He wasn't too particular about the pattern, so it didn't seem like a loss to tear the garment. She would be wearing finer clothes from that point forward. He tossed it onto the rocks below. It would appear as though Lysa suffered a greater death than her father, being lost at sea. Her body would not be laid to rest. In reality, that story rang very true. Lysa got the poor end of the bargain. She hadn't even been interested in the deal.

Bernard started back for the house. It was going to be light soon. Lysa would sleep for a while, waking up in a night or two. Bernard had to make all the necessary preparations for her. He damned the butler for dying. The butler left him to do this menial labor. Blythe was upset with Bernard's seemingly impulsive and erratic behavior, but he was always like that, and cruel. If Bernard saw something he liked, it was soon his. This time, it was a girl with no future, or so he thought. When would he tire of Lysa? Would he tire of her? He would know when she opened her eyes for the first time, as a Vampire. She would first struggle to gain control of her body. Her very nerve endings would flow differently. She would not be able to see at first. Then, her vision would show whatever she saw in a ruddy haze. Everything would have some relation to blood. For what she saw, it was the hue of blood. Potential victims and other humans would not look the same. All Lysa would see is the blood flowing through their veins, their muscles, and bones. For what she touched, its consistency would be as light as blood. She would be times stronger than she ever was. All she was ever to taste again was blood. All else would taste rotten and spoiled.

Bernard thought of these things with a smile, as though he had done Lysa some great service. That remained to be seen. He expected a fight, some sort of struggle. That didn't worry him. This was the first mate he'd sought in many years. Blythe had never looked for companionship. She didn't require it. She had her brother. Passion and love were not things that held great importance to her. They were a hindrance. Blythe tried to teach Bernard that lesson, but his head was hard. Bernard's desires often overwhelmed him. He had saved some of Lysa's blood from earlier. He sipped it like aged cognac, near an empty fire place. He conjured a cold blue fire to take the place of the amber fire that was supposed to occupy that space.

Bernard was fully relaxed. He prepared himself for the day. His sleeping area was below the main floor of the castle. He didn't require a coffin, or anything as dramatic as that. Both siblings possessed one, for traveling purposes, or whatever the need may be as it occurred. Blythe was not far from him, in case there was an intruder. Blythe only stole away in the higher areas of the house during the early evening and morning, as if she were in a constant vigil. They slept during the day, but that didn't mean they were entranced while they slept. They could wake up and defend themselves, but not with the same strength. The day, as well as the lack of rest, made them vulnerable, but not defenseless. Bernard laid down, into his subterranean bed. It was a rectangle, cut into the floor. The border was raised. and there was soft earth making his mattress. Several fine folds of silk made a cover over the dirt. He was not going to allow his fine clothing damaged or soiled by the ground. Even the pests and vermin knew to stay away.

Bernard and Blythe slept the entire day. The town was preoccupied with the disappearance of Smythe and Lysa. Several were brave enough to venture to the front door of the castle, but when they made their presence known, there was no answer. Bernard saw the townspeople at the gate in his mind. He had concocted a scheme to explain that he and his beloved sister spent the day looking on their private property for the two, but they had no luck. The last time they had seen them was when they were leaving, after a lovely dinner and night of conversation. During the evening hours, when the few brave townspeople returned to search for the beloved members of their village, Bernard was the perfect picture of concern. He helped them look all evening. He didn't steer them towards Smythe's final resting place. He wanted it to seem like hope was almost gone, before they found him and Lysa's cloth.

Bernard led them throughout the estate, searching for the missing townsman and his daughter. "I feel so responsible. I wanted to formally introduce myself to Lysa. She is such a lovely girl. I feel very sorry for her mother and sister right now. I hope Smythe is with Lysa, safe somewhere." Bernard had his brow creased just so. The trusting and gullible people followed him, as if he were playing a flute and they were simple mice. Finally, he got tired of the drama. He brought the search party closer to the spot. One of the men was looking over by the cliff. He wanted to look there, hoping he wouldn't find anything. His hope was turned into a very bleak reality. He saw a human form, down by the rocks. He wanted to look, by himself, so he wouldn't alarm anyone needlessly. It was too dangerous. He reluctantly called for one of his friends. Smythe was a friend to most of the townspeople. The two men that were about to make a chilling discovery were among Smythe's best friends.

The two men eased gently down the cliff They made cautious and calculated movements. It was very slippery and perilous. They made it down, despite all the obstacles. Bernard could feel their presence, going down the steep mountain side. The first man reached out to the body that was clashing pale against the ebony rocks. He turned the corpse around, only to see the face of his friend, Smythe. The men dragged their heads low. They cried, to themselves, then gathered their composure. The second man called out, "We've found Smythe! He's gone." Just then, they saw the piece of cloth Bernard attached to a rock further below. "Oh dear God. We've lost them both!" The first man yelled for all the women to stay back. The men formed a human chain, with the help of ropes. They lifted their friend, along with the only trace of Lysa. Smythe was hoisted into a cart and covered. The women feared telling Smythe's wife and daughter. They were among the brightest the town had.

Bernard ran toward the cart, pretending to look for Lysa. He was on the verge of being frantic. "Where is she? Where is Lysa? She wasn't down there, was she?" He ran his fingers through his hair. It was rather theatrical, but Bernard carried it off. Bernard did anything for the class alibi. "I'm afraid she was taken by the sea, after the fall. We have lost two wonderful people. I'm not sure how the wife and daughter are going to make it." The first man that found Smythe was just distraught. The second man informed them of kin the wife had in a town, several miles from there. Bernard began to babble about the evening, but no one was listening. Everyone was handling their shock the best way they knew how. The sun had already started its ascent, once again. Bernard helped as much as he could, but the townspeople weren't sure how to react to him, since he was probably the last person to see them alive. Their suspicions were alert, but there was no proof, even if someone thought to make the accusation. They always believed the Mal family was strange, but Bernard was very convincing.

Bernard closed the door, just as the wagon was leaving the estate. People moved away with the wagon, on foot and on horseback. He pushed his back up against the huge door that kept all the bad people away. They weren't bad, but if they knew, if they knew, he would be the victim of a town lynching. Even if they did that, it wouldn't be enough. He would escape and destroy the entire town, as many people as there were. Blythe would have to help, which would be more than enough. She wouldn't want to, but she would have to, out of familial duty. Fortunately, that wasn't going to be the situation. Bernard carried himself down to his bed. Blythe stared at him as he descended the staircase. She disapproved of Bernard's actions, and possibly his motives. Lysa was a diversion from the lull Bernard had found himself in. She would at least be an addition to the family, hopefully an asset. Time would tell. He wouldn't know for sure until she awoke.

The mother of Lysa, the wife of Smythe, packed up her home and took her daughter, and her daughter's family, to the village the townspeople spoke of. Bernard tried to give the mourning family some money to help them manage without Smythe, the bread-winner. The distraught woman rejected the "gift". It seemed like an insult, although she wasn't sure why. Bernard accepted and tried not to be insulted by the refusal. It was the saddest day the town could remember. There was nothing else to do, or to say on the matter. The story was preserved in their minds, but not spoken of too often.

Lysa felt the chill of the house creeping into the bed where she lay. She moved her body, but stopped suddenly. Her memory was coming back to her. She remembered Bernard and how he looked, just before he killed her. She couldn't understand how she was alive, alert at any rate. She could feel how cold she was. She placed her hand over her chest, fearing what she would feel. Her suspicions were real. Her heart was ceasing to beat. There was barely a trace left. She wanted to scream, but she could do nothing but cry. She sobbed openly, until she her whimper became shouting, then screaming. If Bernard and Blythe weren't awake yet, they certainly should've been from the cries above.

Bernard made his way up to where the poor girl lay. She was face down, crying uselessly. Bernard peered through the transparent cloth that hung over the bed where she was. It was so full of bed linen, it seemed to float, like a cloud above a golden sunset. She moved, just a bit. Bernard felt her misery. It didn't make him feel uncomfortable, or remorseful. He wasn't capable of those emotions. He was a creature of passion. He was also egotistical enough not to let that bother him. His mind was made up. She would be a success. It was funny how he felt that he could control another human being, or creature. He was actually successful with smaller, less intelligent animals, but humans, humans were entirely too complex to control indefinitely. Once altered, changed into Vampires, there was the assumption that the ability to control the mind was greater. It wasn't known to Blythe or Bernard that certain success was only with zombie slaves, but nothing more.

Bernard pulled the curtains back as he leaned onto the bed. It was sheer heaven to sit on the bed, even if he was used to cold hard surfaces, such as stone slabs, terrain beds, and caskets. He moved to stroke her hair, to move it out of her beautiful face. She was perspiring profusely. She shivered as she felt his cold hands touch her now cool body. She wasn't completely dead, but she was well on her way. Nothing could stop the process. The blood had been exchanged. It just didn't happen overnight. A series of changes had to take place before she could be a part of the living undead. Her blood had to change its composition. Her heart had to stop beating as a human. She had to readjust to how her body reacted to all of the things she had been used to. She was never to be sick after this one last time. She wasn't to feed on warm food, unless it was raw flesh she'd tear at as she consumed her victim's blood.

So many things had to take place before she could be as powerful as her maker. As the changes took place, she became more and more certain that she didn't want it. She felt nothing. She thought of her family, knowing she couldn't see them or be with them ever again. She wouldn't want this for anyone, so changing her family was not an option, whether it was done by Bernard, or by her own doing. Bernard saw Lysa's body move up and down rapidly as she cried. He was bored quickly, looking at her. He cleared his throat, making his presence known. Lysa looked up, eyes glowing red not so much from crying as from the changes that were affecting her. She had small, almost quaint fangs. They would grow quickly, but for now, they were like rice. She was weak and completely vulnerable. If there is any time, other than during the day to destroy a vampire, it is when they are transforming.

Bernard tried kindness with Lysa. He tried firmness. Nothing seemed to spur the child. She was a motionless clot of a being. She wasn't dead, and she wasn't alive. She wasn't sure how she qualified as whatever she was. All she did know was that she hated Bernard for what he'd done to her. She was prepared to give herself to him, but not like this! He didn't want her innocence. He wanted her life-force. She felt so betrayed and deceived. Anything Bernard did from this point on was a futile gesture on his part. She felt an extra pang of spite when she became so hungry that she had to feed on him. She refused to stalk other innocent creatures for their blood. Bernard didn't mind at first, but after a few weeks, it became monotonous and tired. He began to throw her off of him after she had taken barely enough to survive. It almost made him laugh at how pathetic Lysa was. The only sadness he may have felt was the fact that he made an error in judgment.

Lysa kept herself secluded from that point on. Bernard looked in on her, really out of obligation, since he was the one that milked her, changed her, or destroyed her. Blythe wanted nothing to do with the entire situation. She avoided Lysa, more than likely because she would find herself on the wrong side of loyalty. She would stand by her brother, but the girl should've died, or been left alone. Blythe approached Bernard one month to the day Lysa and her father had been killed, or so the town thought. "Bernard, some time, short for how humans grieve, has passed. I believe we should try to break the mourning that has plagued the town. Show them you have accepted the girl's death. I feel this will be successful, because you loved her so, and wanted to make her your bride. I trust you are following my conversation, brother?" Although Blythe was socially dysfunctional, she was tactful.

"I quite understand. As a matter of fact, I think it would be wise for my recently recuperated sister to start venturing into town. You will aide me in my appeal to the folks." Bernard was younger, but his gender helped him have more influence. Fortunately, Blythe saw the logic in his conniving. She was in no rush to relocate after just short of a year. It was rather difficult to find ideal places to reside, so that their secrets stay just that, secrets.

The players performed without flaw. Once in a while, Blythe made her agreed visits into town. The townspeople could do little else except stare. Some had no opinion. Others stared simply because of her ghostly appearance. Still others used their superstition to prejudge the two queer-looking siblings. The stares didn't annoy the two. They could read into what the townspeople were feeling and thinking. If there was any change in the people's actions and feeling towards Blythe and Bernard, they would know as soon as the people did. It was easy to read several of them, if not more, simultaneously. When Blythe did venture into town, it took her several attempts to perfect her people skills. Blythe truly did seem like a fish out of water. Bernard tried to help her by describing all the people he knew. They would travel, undetected into town, as beast-dogs, so they might get a true flavor of the town. It was rare that they would shift their form. It was very difficult and painful. They left that talent to the legendary werewolves and shape shifters of other lands.

CHAPTER THREE

On one of Blythe's later visits, she came across the woman that was to be Bernard's mate. Elsebeth saw how uncomfortable Blythe was around people. She also noticed how different in appearance both Blythe and her brother were. Elsebeth was the first to initiate contact. That was the initial invitation that changed Elsebeth's life, forever. "I was quite shy when I was younger. I would run away from people, if my father would let me!" Elsebeth laughed at herself, feeling silly all over again. The story was just enough to break the ice between the two women. Elsebeth was taking her evening stroll, so that she could collect her thoughts and rest for the evening. She often thought of her mother at that time. Blythe picked up on that. It was very easy to, since her feelings were laid out for anyone to see, if they just looked. Blythe looked, and she kept looking.

Something in Blythe's being took a hold of liking this human. She couldn't understand why. She shrugged it off as to her natural desire to add on to the family. Blythe felt that she had a much keener judge of character than her brother. Elsebeth wouldn't be a mistake. Elsebeth's good nature compelled her to try and be kind to Blythe, despite her icy exterior. Blythe repaid Elsebeth's kindness by giving her expensive gifts. Once, it was a comb, made with ivory and trimmed in jade. The next time it was fine materials, to craft beautiful gowns. These gifts were in return for just simple gestures, like a smile, or defense from a cruel child's taunting. Blythe by no means needed her chivalry, but it was refreshing to see a human defend her, even if Elsebeth didn't know her true identity.

As time moved on and Blythe's relationship developed with Elsebeth, there were even more gifts. One day, Blythe struck up a conversation about fine cuisine. Elsebeth didn't know much about gourmet dishes, and blushed at the thought of being asked by sophisticates to attempt such a task. Blythe provided Elsebeth with recipes for a poor man's feast, almost good enough for royalty. Elsebeth gracefully accepted these gifts, on the condition that Blythe be her guest to dinner one evening. Elsebeth assured her that her father, Alec, wouldn't mind at all. He rarely got any company, since most of the population was either children, or elderly people in the village. All the women were either married, or too old to consider for matrimony. Blythe bonded with Elsebeth intensely. They almost behaved like siblings, or mother and daughter.

Blythe was not nervous preparing herself for her first town engagement with Elsebeth and her father. Elsebeth was a junior match maker, and Blythe knew that. Blythe was going to play the game, just to see where it would take her. Usually, she preferred to be in control, calculating every move. So far, she was still doing that. However, it was a great challenge doing that with humans. They could change on you, without any notice. Blythe thought about Bernard and his limp protégé. That would prove to be a grave mistake on his behalf. Blythe didn't want to make that error with Elsebeth. She wanted things to work out, completely. So far, Elsebeth hadn't asked why she only would see her friend after dusk. The girl was a dutiful daughter, helping her father out whenever needed. He had his farm to run, cultivating the best produce for the town. Elsebeth raised a few animals on her own, but they were really just pets. Hopefully, Elsebeth would be dutiful to Blythe and Bernard, and more of a companion than a pet to them.

Alec's home was modest, but in order. Elsebeth was quite a home maker, striving to do everything to make her father happy. The house was large enough for two bedrooms, a kitchen and dining area, and a living room. There was a fireplace in the living room and a small oven in the kitchen area. The walls were decorated with some art that Elsebeth painted on quiet afternoons when the weather was nice. Tonight, there were little metal vases with petite blooms in pastel colors throughout. The flowers created a perfume that finished the warmth started by the wood-burning fire place.

Blythe arrived one half hour after sundown, perfect for dinner. Elsebeth hurried to the front door as Blythe stood poised. "Good eve, my lady". Elsebeth was sweet, assuming Blythe was of a higher station than she actually was. In fact, Blythe and Bernard's family were modest in terms of income, but they managed to have only a slightly higher status than the hard working Alec and Elsebeth. The Mal fortune came from murder, thieving, and treachery.

Alec came behind Elsebeth shortly after Blythe entered the house. Blythe was radiant in a sapphire gown she had made in France. Alec invited Blythe to sit for a while, but she apologized as she declined. "If you please, I'd like to go directly into the dining area and start dinner. I can't stay for long. My brother is still a little under the weather. The accident at the house nearly destroyed him. He is stilled plagued with guilt over the incident. I suppose he is grieving, although his relationship with Miss Lysa was so abrupt." Blythe polished off Bernard's alibi with continued attempts to sway local opinion further into the belief that there was no foul play. Befriending Elsebeth, and subsequently Alec reassured many neighbors in the community. Their trusting nature and attraction to the brother and sister was the deciding factor. Mainly, the people were tired of hurting and being so unhappy. Efforts to strengthen shaky trust had begun.

Blythe continued to be as evasive as possible, but included truth to stories of her long gone family. She spoke of them as if they were separated by distance, not time. Alec tried to remain suspicious, but he had long fallen victim to Blythe's charms. Everything about her was so fine, so pristine. Elsebeth tried to direct their conversation so each may find out as much about the other as possible. Elsebeth tried to be coy, but the adults were fully aware of her intensions.

Blythe claimed to feel a little weary, not eating, but only drinking the wine Alec had served. "Dear lady, I hope we did not imposition you to come out on a night when you're ill". Alec came over to Blythe's seat to help her rise. It was evident she would not be staying longer. "I am sorry for turning the evening into a short one. I have learned much about your family. There is a tremendous amount of trust and good will. Alec, you are a fine father and a good man. I am proud to know you, and proud to have dined with you both. Please excuse me, good night." Blythe was escorted to the door by both father and daughter. Alec gave Blythe a lingering look and Blythe turned her obliging stare down to Elsebeth. The sensation fascinated Blythe. She hadn't held those feelings, compassion, desire, and intimacy close in a long while. Blythe mounted her carriage and rode off. Alec held his daughter by the shoulders, thinking of the young woman he had, and the woman he desired.

Blythe invited Elsebeth and Alec to the mansion finally, on an autumn evening. Both Blythe and Bernard were weak due to the heat that lingered in the air during summer. They were not as strong in warmer climates. England was a cool territory, but not so much as their last home of Finland. The population was too low there, so they tried for a compromise. Blythe acted as butler and waitress for the father and daughter. There was little mention of the last time company was had at the estate. It was thought to be in bad taste as well as bad luck. Elsebeth was quite trusting, and summed up the events that had taken place as a very unfortunate incident. The terrain was in fact rough in nature around the castle. After the previous dinner with Lysa and her father, there was little to speculate and Elsebeth wasn't trying to search for any reason not to care for her new friend.

Both Alec and Elsebeth had on what would pass as their Sunday best. Elsebeth was still in the process of using the materials that Blythe had given to her. The dress she wanted to wear wasn't quite ready. Alec was pieced together well enough, but their clothing wasn't the only thing that made them feel uncomfortable about the company with which they were mixing.

As Blythe and Elsebeth sat in the solarium, Bernard walked the lawn with Alec. They discussed local events just outside, occasionally glancing up at the two ladies. Unbeknownst to Alec, Bernard would prefer to stalk any perimeter they inhabited. This was his manner, his way. Bernard was stirring inside, feeling trapped. If he allowed his feelings to show, it would have affected his reserved demeanor. Blythe sent Bernard a mental signal not to scare her friend away. Bernard telepathically continued to taunt Blythe, pushing her to the limit. No luck. Blythe reserved herself more than anyone else could. Blythe maintained a conversation with Bernard mentally, while speaking of fluff with Elsebeth at the same time.

The hour was becoming late, so Blythe and Bernard bade good night to Elsebeth and Alec. Alec was convinced that Elsebeth was in good hands with the gentlewoman Blythe, despite the fact that his daughter was at the house where his friend and daughter died. Elsebeth's good nature was true, but unknown to others, misguided and deceived.

Blythe was tired of feeling Bernard's attitude while the girl was at the mansion. She also was concerned about Lysa's spontaneous shouts of despair. She had enough. Blythe accused Bernard of jealousy, desire, and contempt. "For your information, brother, she is my friend, not a potential conquest for you. I love her. I want her to be with me!" Blythe stroked Bernard's mane, "With us. Maybe I'll arrange it so that she will bear children for you. It is possible, but not now. She is special. Do you want her, brother? Do you?" The afterthought shook her. She was offering him something she wanted. She didn't want Elsebeth in a sexual way. That was for her brother to do. Bernard responded, "Yes, I'm anxious. I would like a success after my unforeseen failure. There is no progress with Lysa. It becomes more and more apparent that I will be forced to banish her, if her skills do not incorporate soon. Besides, you spend more time with that girl than any of your other pets, or me anymore." Bernard had an awful crease that pressed his brow. He went downstairs, down to the stables to take off for a brisk ride on his ebony mare, Chasm.

Everything was happening as it had with the girl Lysa. The only difference was that the sister was doing the seducing, not the brother. Blythe genuinely just wanted Elsebeth's friendship, but Bernard was a dangerous factor. His mind was on populating the family. Procreation was his foremost thought. Their number was too sparse for them, in his eyes. They were mighty and powerful, but they couldn't fight a town filled with angry people. If they took another victim, the townsfolk would know it was them. If the people knew that they had killed Smythe and damned Lysa's soul, there would be no stopping them.

Many dinners passed where the topic of conversation was how the Mal family shouldn't be trusted. Elsebeth had only seen how kind Blythe had been. Elsebeth knew only that the brother liked her, but decided to keep his distance. It was all true. Bernard was still too savage and bitter over Lysa. He wouldn't be kind to her if her were to take her now. He was much too hungry and had no feelings for her that would allow him to curb his ferocious behavior. He was tired of dinning on animal blood. He needed the spirit of a human soul flowing through his marrow. Alec sensed something very unnerving about the entire liaison. After some time, Blythe invited Alec and Elsebeth for another dinner at the mansion. Alec was inclined to turn them down, but he could not disappoint his daughter, without good reason.

Just in time for the occasion, Elsebeth created a fine coat for her untrusting father. From the material Blythe had given Elsebeth, she crafted a beautiful blood-burgundy and gold trimmed gown. It swept the floor as she swayed to and fro. She had also made an ascot for her father's collar, to accompany his coat. The coat was a rich Bordeaux color. The scarf was the color of sand on the sea shore. Alec had some britches that went well with the ensemble, so Elsebeth was glad. Elsebeth, to finish her outfit, had been sent some fine slippers from France. They weren't comfortable, but they were extravagantly decadent. She pulled her hair back, tying it with some fine ribbons. She then braided the entire length of her long flowing hair with her long and gracile fingers.

Alec drove Elsebeth them in his carriage to the castle. He made sure to watch every move he made, trying not to have the same thing happen to him and his lovely daughter as the previous father and daughter that ventured into the Mal lair. The terrain was quite steep, making both people very nervous. The wheels of the carriage creaked as they climbed the vaulted mountain. It seemed to take forever to scale the mountain to the castle. No doubt nerves were a determining factor in that observation. They could both see how the previous tragedy could have happened. The sky was looming over them, making them feel as ants to elephants. They were truly aware of their place in the scale of life. Elsebeth was fluttering with excitement, thinking of her second formal dinner with such a graceful and caring individual. She had complete faith and trust in Blythe, which would prove to be to her detriment.

The two finally reached their destination. The front door seemed as high as the sky. Since the butler was gone, the siblings had to answer the door once the knocker made the announcement of the guests. They had to play the help once again, to their dismay. Blythe knew every move that Elsebeth made. She had her good eye on Alec as well. She admired his tall and sturdy form. He was robust, but not in an unattractive manner. His hair was thin, but his smile was warm and inviting. It was almost as hypnotic as Bernard and Blythe's mind controlling skills. Blythe opened the door, slowly. As the door widened its arc, she began to see the face of her friend. She was so happy to see the stunning Elsebeth.

Elsebeth was met with a hug and kiss from Blythe. She cleared her throat, welcoming Alec into her home as well. Alec accepted her welcome with enthusiasm, especially after seeing her again. He was reminded of how beautiful she was. Blythe was unique in her features and she had a pale shade of bisque hue for skin. It was polished to that of fine porcelain. Had she been alive, her complexion would be significantly deeper, but what remained was enough to keep suspicion suppressed. Bernard sat alone in a room adjacent to the entry, pensive as the invasion took place. It wasn't so much that he didn't want them in his home. It was the fact that he was to stifle his passion for human blood. Alec held his daughter's arm as Blythe took the other, showing them past the foyer. The paintings that peered from the approaching rooms were remarkable. The carpet that lay under their feet was plush, and dark in color. It was difficult to make out, since night was approaching quickly.

Neither Alec nor Elsebeth took notice of the brooding Bernard. He was concealed by his large leather chair in the library facing the fireplace. He could feel their pulses racing from the excitement of being guests in such a formidable home. Blythe played the perfect hostess. She was filled with personality. Blythe hadn't cause to be so animated in a very long while. Everyone proceeded to the dining area. Drinks were offered, but not required. The fire place that reflected Bernard's gaze had an electric blue glow. It was barely enough to warm a human, but it satisfied Bernard. Bernard listened closer to the beating pulses of the couple. It began to arouse him. He removed a handkerchief from his breast pocket, so that he might dab his mouth. He then wiped his brow, deciding the fire was entirely too high. With a slashing of his arm, the fire was hushed out.

Alec sat his daughter at her designated seat. The card declaring where Elsebeth was to eat was so ornate. The wording was done in calligraphy with gold leaf. Alec sensed her tension, rubbing her shoulders before he took his seat. Even though Elsebeth was already quite familiar with Blythe, she still wanted her approval, to know that her conduct was that of a person f quality. Alec jumped over to help Blythe, but she motioned to decline his assistance. She was both hostess and cook, for this meal as well. She returned hastily with a meal rich in flavor and texture. It was not the sort of meal Elsebeth prepared for her father and herself. Blythe ate what was cleverly disguised raw meat and vegetables. She ate very little. What she consumed the most was large quantities of thick, red nectar. It seemed to please her very much, so any tension lessened with each swallow.

Bernard finally joined the small party. His disposition was snobby, at best. He remained guarded because of the previous "incident" and he sensed Bernard's reluctance to trust him. He smiled innocently at the guests. Alec smiled, but not convincingly. His attention was weaning slowly over to the flawless Blythe. However, his priority was Elsebeth, but the charm that Blythe emitted began to unconsciously work a spell on him. The same was to be said about the pending liaison between Bernard and Elsebeth. She looked up at him as he sat himself wherever he pleased. Elsebeth had just taken a small bite of food, which found its way down the wrong pipe. She choked the instant she made eye contact with Bernard. He was fabulous. Elsebeth really hadn't had an occasion to see him well at the last meeting. She was too nervous and he spent a majority of his time with Alec. The lighting was rather dim, but now with all of the radiant candles lit, she could see all of his natural imperfections. It was a pity that he was so reserved, but in a way, it made Elsebeth desire to come out of her normal self to try and win his interest.

Bernard took note of all these thoughts and emotions running through Elsebeth's mind as she was struggling. Bernard looked at the young lady. He took definite note that she was beautiful. The gown she wore was never to look as well on another. He was the first to hand her some refreshment. Alec was next to her, but Bernard's speed was astounding. Alec dismissed it to a delayed reaction, shocked that his daughter was distressed. Blythe took notice of Alec's stares and took his hand, assuring him that it was all right that his reaction was retarded. Elsebeth thanked the now intense young man. Dinner continued after the excitement died away. Alec let thoughts of his dead wife escape for anyone to catch and use. Blythe was the recipient of the thoughts and images Alec was conjuring. He remarked at how she favored Elsebeth's mother. Blythe shared many qualities with her, and that pleased him.

For a few moments, all that was heard was the clanking of silverware, glasses, and flatware. Elsebeth weaned away from her food the more she concentrated on the fasting Bernard. "Mister Mal, is there some reason, may I ask, you are not dinning with us this evening?" Elsebeth wanted to hear if his voice was as smooth as his skin and hair. It was curious that he had only tilted his head and smiled the entire time. "I don't like this kind of food. It shouldn't be a concern of yours, however. I am fine. You, my dear should take great care with this meal. It is a very important one for you." Bernard smirked as he sipped his drink. He was trying desperately to conceal his desire for the young naive. Blythe spoke through her mind into his. "Not tonight, brother. I know you are hungry, but I refuse to waste another protégé! I must know for sure she has the stuff to carry us on!" Blythe's nostrils had flared as she spoke mentally to Bernard. Alec asked her what the matter was. "I believe I've had my fill of food for tonight. When you are done, I would like you to join me out on the yard." Blythe knew that Alec was well acquainted with the land. Alec had worked much of the land as a young man. She wanted to spark conversation with him, to improve her relationship with Elsebeth.

Bernard looked at Elsebeth with indecent lust. Blythe quickly suggested that Elsebeth join Alec and her on the lawn. The night sky welcomed into its company the intimate group. Bernard stalked them, paying attention to the muffled cries of Lysa in the tower above. He thought of how she must have been laying there, like stretched leather hanging on a pole. The thought disgusted even him. It spited him more than anything. He turned his attention to Elsebeth. She was a fresh lily on a placid pond. Alec made several attempts at humor, which Blythe politely laughed. Elsebeth laughed genuinely, but stopped when she saw that she had caught Bernard's attention. She wondered how he was still unwed, without a family. Bernard listened to her thoughts and told himself that he hadn't found a qualified partner. He wondered if he finally had.

Bernard turned away quickly, so that he wouldn't betray his aloof exterior. His passion was becoming unbearable. It made him so uncomfortable, he thought about going upstairs to suck the last life out of Lysa, and try anew with Elsebeth, by force, if he had to. No matter how much he wanted to snuff Lysa's pitiful existence, he couldn't. It was simply against their nature. It was not done, not that way. Alec noticed the young man sitting on the concrete railing. He decided to try bonding with his fellow man once more. He left the two ladies to discuss idle issues, things that intrigued only them.

Each man looked at the others female blood. Alec was being charmed relentlessly. Bernard was being unwittingly swayed as well. His inner rage smothered into a deep desire for Elsebeth. The sky was becoming too dark to stay outside. It was getting too late to continue their visit and Alec's memories of the last tragedy were still pressing on his mind. Blythe turned her attention from Elsebeth to Alec. Their conversation about the grounds about them was sweet. She appreciated how much he cared for the things that were close to him. Elsebeth understood their romantic glances, and suggested everyone retreat back to the house. Bernard was the last to fall in. He wanted Elsebeth, tonight. He didn't want to wait another night. The girl had been to the house enough. She knew almost everything she needed to know about the Mal family. The last few details of their family life required some incredible show and tell.

Elsebeth walked past Bernard, feeling his stare upon her. She smiled, thinking she had made great progress. Bernard reached out, almost grabbing Elsebeth by the hair. He wanted to draw her close to him. He wanted to satisfy her by making love, and satisfy himself by changing her into what he had been for several centuries already. Blythe turned quickly so she was facing Bernard. "I don't want to do this, not now! Wait, just wait, please!" Blythe's face was truly sympathetic. Bernard owed her, so he retracted his desire, for one more night. It wouldn't take long for him to change her. He wanted to take his time with this one, but the waiting was just too difficult.

Alec spoke with Blythe a little longer about garden. It bored Bernard so that he had no choice but to lose interest in Elsebeth, at least for one night. Alec took note of Bernard's boredom. It demonstrated his fleeting social skills. Alec made a mental note to try and improve. "As much as I enjoy talking with you, it is late, and I must get my lovely girl home. I appreciate your hospitality, I truly do. You understand, don't you?" Alec took Blythe's hand, kissing it like a gentleman. Bernard moved from the rear of the group to the front. He gave a very anti-climactic departure. He simply bid them all a pleasant evening. As taken as he was with Elsebeth, he had other matters to attend. He leapt up the stairs, making his way to his hide away. Elsebeth tousled with feeling inadequate. Alec took Elsebeth by the hand. She smiled at Blythe. Blythe leaned over to kiss Elsebeth. "Don't fret my dear. The evening was a success. All that was meant to happen has." Blythe smiled at both Alec and Elsebeth.

The two walked themselves out. Blythe closed the door. She gleamed as she went downstairs, to her sheltered place from the sun. The two humans made it home, safely. They were high about the entire evening. The tension in the house was weighty, but the experience was precious for them. They were common people, with no anticipation in becoming more than what they were in their life's station. They weren't to remain the same, however. There was too much of an attraction between the four of them. Alec put Elsebeth to bed, but the thrill of the evening kept her awake for some time. Alec struggled with thoughts of his wife and Blythe. Alec fought in vain feelings that were consuming him. This wasn't due to any spell or trickery from Blythe. It was much more, more than he would admit, even to himself. So much started that night.

Some time passed before the next encounter. Elsebeth had seen Blythe on several occasions during that period, but Bernard was not to be found. Bernard was attending to the melancholy Lysa still. Blythe presented Alec with new farming tools, claiming they were compensation for teaching her more about caring for her flora and shrubbery. Alec questioned her on the late hour of her visits. Blythe responded cautiously. "I have pressing business that keeps me occupied during the day hours. I would love to visit you, but you have work of your own, don't you?" Blythe was skillful with her conversation. "Well, I suppose you are right. I don't mean to sound forward, but I just wonder from time to time how your hair would look like in the morning sun." Alec absolutely blushed as the words betrayed his rugged exterior. "It looks just as it does in the moon light" Blythe smiled a crooked grin staring at Alec, simmering with passion. Before another exchange of flirting remarks, Elsebeth wedged herself between the two.

Blythe smiled at the tall, gentle man. He tipped his hat to her and departed, fearful that he had made a beastly advance, regardless of Blythe's easy demeanor. Elsebeth politely asked how Blythe was doing. Almost immediately after the question was answered, Elsebeth prodded Blythe for information on the dashing Bernard. "My dear, he is fine. He wonders how you are doing, but he has many matters to attend to. I apologize for his negligence. I must add that you should take your time with him. He is much older than he appears, and is very experienced. There are no women around that can tell you so, but I know it to be true. Elsebeth, I care for you deeply. I want only the best for you, and now your father. Be careful, be a pure girl as long as you can. I only speak so boldly because I know of the attraction you two harbors for one another." Blythe, if she could've cried, would have at that moment.

"I will try, Blythe. He is so fine and graceful. I would like to meet with him, again, if it is appropriate. If you feel I should wait, I will. I trust you, implicitly." Elsebeth tried very diligently to make use of the vocabulary she consumed from all the educated people she came in contact with. Blythe was impressed with her progress. She wanted Elsebeth to grow, just a bit more, before she was to change her. Bernard wanted to act now, so she had to keep Elsebeth out of his reach. "Elsebeth darling, it is time for you to get ready for bed." Alec returned, tired from a long day of work. "I thank you for entertaining me. My carriage is waiting. I shall bid you good night." Blythe took Alec's hand. He raised her hand to his mouth, kissing it softly.

Days later, a mysteriously delivered note came to Elsebeth. The note was delivered mysteriously in that it just appeared. It was decorated beautifully. The envelope had a waxed seal, all the trimmings from persons of higher social status and the like. It was reminiscent of Lysa's invitation, but unbeknownst to Elsebeth, she made no connection. She had no reason to suspect any hidden agenda besides a secret romance. For several nights, Bernard would fly around their home, familiarizing himself with the entire layout. Elsebeth found the letter, posted to her bedroom window. She pulled the woven parchment out of its soft handmade envelope. It read, "Elsebeth. I didn't know what else to do. Forgive me. I am not a coward, but I am respectful of my sister, Blythe. I know she has discouraged you from visiting the house. I enjoyed your first formal visit. I've been looking forward to others, but my sister's judgment has ruled it unwise. You are a vivacious, extraordinary young woman with whom I'd like to share company with. There is some lovely country behind the house. I'd love to show it to you. If you can liberate yourself, for a short while, perhaps we could meet on the lawn, just before the woods tomorrow evening?" Bernard signed the letter "Your prince awaits". It was just arrogant, yet seductive enough to send her swooning.

Bernard was on the limb of a nearby tree, listening to her heart and mind race as she read his alluring letter. He squatted, never once losing his balance. His head leaned back, just a bit. He was smiling a sinister smile. He took off from the limb, flying towards home. It wasn't going to be that night, but soon, she would be his. Elsebeth held the dear letter close to her bosom. She had never felt that way before. She had thoughts of actually defying her father. She stayed awake, most of the night, planning her escapade. Alec was deep in thought about Blythe. He dreamt of her all evening as a result. Bernard blocked his thoughts so that even if Blythe was in top form, she couldn't pick up on his devilish scenario. She was occupied herself, charming Alec.

Bernard fasted on the evening he was to meet Elsebeth. No stray animal or foreign wanderer would be his prey. Tomorrow was to be his finest accomplishment. Bernard strolled into Blythe's chamber. She was sitting quietly, reading a book that helped her stay in touch with human society. "Dear sister, I am going to remain at home tonight. I feel rather strong. I shan't feed this eve. Would you care to spend time with your brother?" Bernard crafted his plan carefully. "I suppose that would be a good idea. We've been at odds lately. I don't like that. You are all I have in this world. We both agree that Elsebeth would be a priceless addition to our slim family, no? We are blood and soon so shall she be." Blythe placed her book on the window sill. "What of your heart, dear sister? Do you suppose Elsebeth's father would be inclined to pledge his life to us? Do you think he would care to be unborn?" Bernard loved his sister, and hoped she would follow his scheme. Blythe left the room abruptly, not replying to his inquiry. He left the topic unresolved. His sweet Elsebeth was on her way to be unborn, made into a vampire. His actions would possibly answer his question to Blythe, without her opinion.

Elsebeth felt warm inside. She had never in all her days rivaled her father's wishes. He had implored her not to pursue a relationship with Bernard, just as Blythe had. They both didn't want them to have a relationship. Alec felt that her relationship with Blythe was pure in essence, but Alec didn't trust this man. Bernard was not humble, nor did he appear to be sincere. Bernard could not cloak his true heart with a masque. Both males seemed to understand who each other was, save for Bernard's dark secret. Alec and Blythe did not want Elsebeth to fall for Bernard, at least not yet, but for different reasons. Elsebeth thought much of her father, but she had to defy him. She was in love, or so she thought. She dressed herself in another creation she had crafted with the aid of Blythe's fine fabrics. No man would refuse her anything, outfitted in such fine garb. Her hair was coiled tight. The ringlets framed her face like a portrait of a cherub, or some nymph. Elsebeth gave her bed the illusion she was asleep in it. For a virgin deceiver, she did a class job. She left her room, just for a moment. She wanted to look in on her father. Alec was sleeping peacefully. Blythe's thoughts had him in a deep sleep. Elsebeth was free for the duration of the evening. Blythe's charms were working against her wishes. She was unwittingly assisting Bernard, doing his bidding. That was the very thing she was trying to avoid

The moon helped Elsebeth navigate her way to the Mal fortress. She had been there enough times; she was confident that she could find her way. This venture would test that. Without error, Elsebeth found her way to the front of the house. She remembered she was to meet her prince in the yard, in the rear of the house. She held close to the walls of the house, as if she were without sight. The stones were cold and coarse. It tore at her delicate skin as she turned each corner. Finally, Elsebeth felt the smooth marble from the bottom of the balcony. She then crossed the yard, to the rough ground of the forests' threshold. She made it. Now, Bernard had to show up. She would be devastated if this was merely a ploy, a joke at her expense. Her eyes almost welled up with tears at the thought, but she wouldn't allow it. A yell nearly leapt from her full coral tinted lips. Bernard had crept up behind the young lady, nearly making her heart stop. Seeing his face made her heart do just the opposite. It began to beat faster and faster as she took in all of his fine features with her widely open yet clouded eyes.

Bernard looked at Elsebeth. He actually felt a soft tender sensation inside. His heart had been dead for so long, but now Elsebeth had reached his vacant soul. She sparked vitality in his being, something he thought wasn't necessary to survive. This was a sign to him that he must strike now. He couldn't let her go. Legend had it that their kind were to be barren after they were unborn. In their travels, Blythe and

Bernard met with other vampires that had proved conception to be possible, but the vampire had to be mated with the perfect match. They felt that they could find the perfect mate and they would search until the end of their being to find them. Besides, Bernard couldn't confirm for Blythe, but he still had passions of a human male. His nature would still rise, and he could still perform in love making, whether it was from want of blood, or the heaving bosom of some attractive female. It didn't happen often. He thought he felt that for Lysa, but he was sadly mistaken. In the year she had been unborn, she had yet to conceive. Bernard had no success rising Lysa's passions, and he was becoming bored with forcing himself on her. Bernard wanted his family to grow organically, not by one blood conquest after another. Lysa still had to be fed, like a babe. He tired of her, but he was responsible for her.

Bernard pushed those thoughts out of his mind for the moment. His dream was about to come true. He could see children in Elsebeth. Naturally, they wouldn't be human. They would be nurtured on mother's milk, then blood as they grew. They would be beautiful creatures, with his ebony hair, and her kind facial features. Bernard began to salivate. He felt his fangs grow. He couldn't reveal himself just yet. "Fair night, isn't it?" He was as charming as ever with his smooth and welcoming tone. Elsebeth stared at him for a moment. Once she remembered how to articulate, she began to speak. "Yes, it is quite lovely. I am so pleased you invited me to your home. The hour is late, but I am happy, none the less." Elsebeth's hand was taken by his. Bernard kissed it, softly. His lips were cool, but they warmed next to her skin. Bernard escorted her to the top of the balcony, outside of the dining room. The last time they were on those steps, a very strange feeling was upon all that were present. This time, a feeling she had never before encountered over powered her.

Bernard left her side, but only for a moment. He returned, with a goblet filled with wine. It was dark and sweet. Elsebeth drank it as if it were water. She was nervous, and didn't know what effect the alcohol would have on her. She soon felt sleepy, but was too elevated by adrenaline to fall unconscious. Elsebeth leaned over the banister overlooking the forest. The moon was full. The clouds had receded, making the sky much brighter. Bernard hoisted himself on top of the banister railing. He let his feet swing back and forth, like a child on a tree branch. His manly features and dark mood hid the fact that he was not more than a young man. Before he was unborn, he was shy, naïve, and awkward. He wasn't the suave, sophisticated, and assured male that demanded awe. That was several lifetimes ago, and he'd rather forget it than to relive it in his mind, causing him emotional pain that he wouldn't tolerate.

"Why did you summon me here, this evening? I would've been able to come during the day, while my father labors. It isn't uncommon for me to run off then." Elsebeth was becoming quickly acquainted with scheming. "Elsebeth, I have had many thoughts of being in your presence, since we last met. Of all the ways I could imagine it, I saw you best illuminated by the midnight sky. Your skin is a burning porcelain against the moon glow. May I touch your face?" Bernard was very quaint and persuasive. "I would like that very much." Elsebeth held her face out, to be touched. His touch was softer than even her delicate skin. It was as though a rain drop had dabbed her cheek. "Elsebeth, I must confess things to you. They are, and I promise this on the life of Blythe, things I can't refuse. I feel you now, in my soul. You are of a special quality. I fear that you will go away from me, and that makes me quite desperate." Bernard felt himself changing, from the inside out. He tried to suppress it a little longer.

Bernard presented Elsebeth with a small cloth sack. Elsebeth pulled out a pearl and emerald choker necklace. She was so startled that she almost dropped it. "This is incredible! What have I done to merit such a gift?" Bernard looked at her, as if she should've been ashamed to ask such a ridiculous question. "Let me put it on you." Bernard edged closer to Elsebeth. "There is something else I must give you, but that will come later." Bernard closed the choker by its clasp. It hung just right, as if it were made only for her. Bernard sat before Elsebeth. "Elsebeth, I care for you. In fact, I love you. I want no harm to come to you, but there is something I want of you. Would you do whatever I asked?"

Bernard for once in a great while had the look of tenderness on his face. Elsebeth was confused at his nervousness. He was usually so calm. She did not see herself as such a threat on his self-assurance. "Bernard, I am happy that you love me. I never thought it possible for someone, other than father, to care for me. I love you as well. I feared it was to be a secret forever, but you said the words!" Elsebeth moved to where he was.

Elsebeth surprised both Bernard and herself, kissing him. She aimed for his mouth, but reached only his cheek. Bernard smiled. He could never laugh at her. All of his negative sentiments left while he was forbidden to see her. He wouldn't crush her heart like that. "I must tell you, Elsebeth, there are many things, dark things you will need to know." Bernard was afraid she would flee in terror, but she kept her place. "Bernard, I fell in love with you for the strength you possess. Don't diminish that. Tell me what I need to know. My heart will share with no one else. I have devoted it to you, for now and always." Elsebeth's words gave Bernard ample comfort. She surprised Bernard with her loyalty. Her trust was based on misguided instinct, a quality she regarded greatly in herself. "It will be more effective, if I show you. Make your final decision then. Whatever it be, I will respect it." Bernard's skin grew pale, almost glass-like. His pupils became a hollow black which centered a luminescent glow. His teeth finally slid from behind his lips.

Elsebeth turned to Bernard. She became paralyzed with fear. Bernard tried to steady her shock with his mind, but Elsebeth trembled uncontrollably. Bernard was taking a risk, a risk that would not work on anyone but a truly remarkable woman. His desire was that Elsebeth be that woman. Bernard took Elsebeth by her shoulders, now trying physically to console her. Elsebeth found Bernard behind his horrible façade and then she became calm. Bernard took note of her renewed composure and said to her, "I'm not going to hurt you, I love you. Blythe loves you as well. That's why I am going to help you. Elsebeth, I want you to live forever, with me. I know you must be thinking of your father. I will give him the option of joining you, keeping our secret. If he doesn't want to, I'm afraid he will lose you, Blythe, and sadly go on to his glory. I suppose there is no real choice to make, but I can't help myself, Elsebeth. Help me know that this is the right thing!" Bernard was right. Elsebeth had no real choice. The decision was already made. Her mind was not her own. From that moment on, she was no longer Elsebeth Alburré.

CHAPTER FOUR

Elsebeth was without emotion. She was numb. Bernard was in total control, as he had been from the very beginning. He hovered over Elsebeth. The first thing that touched Elsebeth was Bernard's mouth on her neck. With a kiss and a pricking of her skin, he drank. His teeth sank past her soft skin, deeper and deeper, until he found her vein. He drank until he knew that Elsebeth would be as they had been for centuries before. When he was sure he had taken enough blood, Bernard completed the transformation by slicing open his wrist. He did this for Elsebeth this time, as he had done for Lysa. He was hoping that this would be the only time he would have to for her. Elsebeth let the warm fluid glide into her mouth, as if it were a natural thing. She could feel her frail body take in the foreign life force, accepting it and the changes it brought to her own chemistry.

Finally, Elsebeth collapsed on the floor. She felt herself fade, but not into death. She encountered sensations that electrified her very being. She viewed her life, as though she was dying, but it seemed more as though she were leaving an old life to start a new one, one completely unrelated to the first. There was much for Elsebeth to experience yet, but she would not begin to be aware of the internal and external changes that were to transpire for a while. Blythe walked in on the transformation. She was outraged, but kept silent. Bernard was risking the destruction of everything Blythe had been working toward with Elsebeth. Blythe wanted the process to be handled as delicately as possible. She couldn't imagine Bernard taking care with her. Blythe silently dammed Bernard for not sharing his plans with her. She felt betrayed by Bernard. Bernard was too impetuous to trust Blythe's judgment. Blythe collected Elsebeth and carried her carefully upstairs, to her new room. Blythe laid Elsebeth on the bed and folded her arms over her chest. She then kissed Elsebeth's brow. Blythe looked at Bernard and he allowed her to see how the seduction worked. She understood Bernard's true feelings and was relieved to know that his feelings were sincere. The exchange would be a success, but there still remained the question of Alec and how he would react and respond. As Blythe thought about what was to come for her new friend Alec, she flew out of the window, near the bed where Elsebeth laid. It was her turn to proposition her desired mate.

Alec awoke in the middle of the night. It was almost as if he knew what was happening. He looked around and saw that his girl was missing. He searched the small house for Elsebeth, then the yard outside. He returned inside, convinced that something terrible had taken place. He had many fears about why his daughter couldn't be found, but none of them could have horrified him as much as what was reality. "Where is she? Oh I feel as if something terrible has happened!" Alec stopped his anxiety when a knock at the door alerted him. He expected it to be his Elsebeth, but it was not. What he saw was a hairy, fanged monster with eyes flaming white lava.

With one hand, Blythe lifted Alec from the floor. She carried him across the floor. Her hunched back almost touched the ceiling. As they moved across the floor of the modest home, she said, "Your young lady is now with us, body and soul. She is Vampire. She will forever be young and more powerful than you can imagine. She has been given a rare gift, Alec. The plan was always there, but to my chagrin, it was carried out without unity. We always wanted Elsebeth, but then, I met you. I have come to desire you in my house as well. I came to you this way so that you could see the worst and be done with it. This is my worst. You have seen my best. I cannot change who I am and you will have to decide for yourself how you wish to exist. You have some brave decisions to make, Alec." Alec closed his eyes and bowed his head. He couldn't believe what he was seeing. He wanted to dismiss this all as a horrible nightmare. He thought to doubt the creature, but couldn't allow himself to ignore the facts that were presented before him.

The creature lowered him to the ground, releasing him. Tears were crawling out of Alec's eyes with resistance.

He tried to hide his fear, but it was evident. Alec began to pray for forgiveness. He blamed himself for allowing this to happen. He let his daughter, for as talented yet naive as she was, become involved with these demon-like creatures. Alec now saw Blythe for what she truly was. He saw also what Elsebeth was going to be. Alec couldn't leave Elsebeth to dwell in a horrific limbo alone. It was his duty to watch after her, no matter what. He swore that to his wife. There really was no decision to make. There was only need for him to have courage for him to do what was necessary. Alec didn't have enough time to stall for reason. He couldn't mourn the loss of his daughter, his memories of their life, or his own life.

"I vowed to my dying wife that I would care for Elsebeth all her life. I couldn't kill her, if given the chance. I know that is what I would need to do to free her soul, if the legend is true. I cannot leave her alone, so I must join your brood. I will care for her as you see fit." With that, Blythe moved toward Alec. Blythe changed her appearance to a less horrific countenance. She returned to her beautiful self, the woman Alec had fallen for. Blythe wept, inside. She could barely remember what it was like to share human compassion for anyone. She felt some remorse for placing these two lovely souls in this situation. If it were Bernard in her place, he would have chosen to kill Alec. The least resistance would be for the better. However, Bernard made a promise to Elsebeth to bring her father into this, should he decide to accept this destiny. Blythe truly cared for Alec. She wasn't sure how, but she just did. "Alec, if I could feel remorse for what I do, I'd feel it for you now. My family's survival is paramount. I do this, in the belief that you will use this cursed privilege and find ways to do well for human-kind for centuries to come. Alec, be the influence you are now, forever." Blythe leaned towards Alec. She kissed him on his lips, tenderly. She then touched the area that she was to strike with her fangs.

Blythe's spiked teeth pricked his skin, just at the throbbing vein in his throat. It didn't hurt nearly as much as the thought of never living out his life the way he was supposed to. He pondered what he had perceived to be his destiny, but he gave up, wondering if this wasn't his destiny. Blythe picked Alec up as he began to sink down, shrinking in stance. His descent was from the pain and lack of blood in his body. Blythe tore her chest, leaving a stream of blood to flow down to her breast. Alec's face fell on the blood. It came to his mouth, as if it was guided from Blythe's mind. As Alec drank, he straightened up. His strength increased, but not enough for him to pass as healthy. Blythe picked up her lover, and raised them both out of the roof of the modest home, into the sky. The noise stirred a few of the nearby neighbors. A few of the townsmen peered out into the night sky, but it was only a quarter moon. Visibility was next to nil. Blythe took Alec to his new home, to his new life.

Bernard felt Blythe's arrival with her paramour. "One too many, I suspect." Bernard lifted himself from his seat. There was a cold impression where he had sat. Blythe set Alec down, carefully on a bed. It wasn't decorated, but it was comfortable which was descriptive of Alec. Although he lacked physical strength, he feared for his daughter. He wondered where and how she was. Elsebeth was unborn longer than he was. Alec needed to know how her transformation was progressing, what he had to expect. He wanted to know that Elsebeth was all right. However, Alec hadn't the strength to find out. Blythe kissed Alec on the forehead. "I shall return. I will look in on your daughter. Do not worry, Alec. We will discuss more and I will answer your questions when you have more strength." Blythe had yet to tell Alec the life he truly had in store, not the myths that were spread from culture to culture.

Blythe walked through the still house, feeling the location of her brother. There was much to discuss. Blythe could sense the animosity that was brewing in Bernard's somewhat hollow soul. She had rather be with both Alec and Elsebeth, but it was crucial she speak with her brother. Bernard didn't want to tolerate any more reluctant offspring and he was still concerned that Alec would be a barrier between Elsebeth and him. He was aware that there was a chance that having Alec with them would make it easier for Elsebeth to fully accept what she now was. He also knew that having Alec was a desire for his sister. Blythe finally found

Bernard. He was perched on top of the fortress, near a gargoyle that was believed to protect castles such as those. He was brooding, like a spoiled infant. The cold air slapped his face. He welcomed it like a warm breeze.

Bernard had nothing to do for now, except wait for the transformation to complete itself. Much action was taken that night. Two more villagers were gone. Talk was pending the discovery of their disappearance. Their time was short. It would be no doubt that the more suspicious folk would be pounding on the Mal family's door, to inquire, or to accuse. Blythe sat next to her kin. "It had to be done." She felt she had made a sage decision. "You know, it will be more difficult for me to manipulate her with her savage father around. What were you thinking?" Bernard was perfectly nasty to Blythe. "Brother, I hadn't contemplated it that way. I thought it would make it easier for your new mate to assimilate to our life. I hope you can appreciate my philosophy, darling." Blythe stroked Bernard's hair. She pulled at the ends, allowing his thick black hair help her stand. Bernard winced with a wicked laugh.

The night faded into day. Everyone slept. Bernard and Blythe needed the rest, for lack of blood made them not as strong as they should've been. Alec and Elsebeth were apart, but their hearts were united. They would always be together, and they were happy to know that. Each of them was alarmed by the thought of where their souls would rest, or if they would at all. Elsebeth wound herself up into a tighter ball than she had been. Her skin lifted into puckered bumps as Lysa let out a periodical shriek. More blood was given to the newly unborn, so that they could assist in the abrupt relocation. It was assumed Lysa would not be of any help. Their unnatural strength made it easy for them to take their treasures along.

The time was right and necessary to move on. Too many questionable events had taken place. The household was quickly abandoned for whoever wanted, or dared to inhabit it. Alec and Elsebeth returned to their home, for the last time. They packed items that were of value, whether it was sentimental or monetary. They loaded up their wagon with their belongings and stole out of their home, their town, their loving community for all time. Alec left a note, for anyone to read. It explained how there were opportunities available for his daughter and him to take advantage in another township, far away. It was flimsy, but it was accepted by the townspeople that would have undoubtedly attempted to destroy Alec and Elsebeth if the truth were known. Alec and Elsebeth obeyed their immortal jailers, now, more so out of desire to survive and the confused feelings of love they felt for them, rather than any allegiance or threat of mind manipulation by Bernard.

The new clan of night creatures left England that night. The next stop for the creatures would be north-west

France, in Normandy. They commissioned a small boat that would take them across the water. The captain of the ship was more concerned with their currency than their story of being stricken with a skin ailment that caused them to seek refuge from the sun. The trip was mildly intolerable and none among them dared to feed. The lack of strength they had to endure caused them all to be at a physical disadvantage should any conflict arise. They finally landed and once upon shore, looked for a dwelling that would suit their immediate needs. They found a small farm house in a sparsely populated area. After inquiring, they learned that the home was empty after the owners had passed away. They were allowed to rent the residence for as long as they needed. There wasn't much land and they had no intention of working it. There were farms in the distance and just enough livestock for them to use for sustenance without drawing any unwanted attention to them.

The change in scenery and culture did them all good, except for Lysa. Her moods moved swiftly from bitter to melancholy. She would have been a slave to them, if they could have made her move. Her will was only strong enough to oppose the force that was being put forward by Bernard. He was the only one that would bother with her. Alec and Elsebeth kept to themselves, letting the blood influence their souls. It hurt less if they didn't resist. That explained the constant cringe of pain and nausea Lysa felt. Lysa hated Bernard. She would always feel a proverbial knife in her back because of him. When Lysa spoke, it was usually a roar, or some kind of ear throbbing yell that made everyone avoid her. She resolved to sit in a corner of the room in which she inhabited.

Lysa needed to feed, but she didn't have the desire or the will to kill. Any patience Bernard had for the feeble being faded with each passing night. He saw his failure in her blank stare. "It wasn't supposed to be like this." Bernard thought as his dissatisfaction turned to anger. He struck out at Lysa. Maybe, if he tried to be firm, she would snap out of her melancholy charm. "You stupid little wench! You just don't see it, do you? I did you a favor!" Bernard moved towards Lysa with each phrase. He raised Lysa up by the shoulders. He opened his cuff, then his wrist with his teeth. "Drink. I would free you, but you would surely die. It's a pity you don't possess the attribute of self-preservation." Bernard jerked away his arm from Lysa's suctioned lips. She almost fell to the ground, almost choking on the blood she was trying to swallow with such urgency.

Lysa braced her arms on her knees. She was finally able to stand. "I wouldn't have these problems, if you had just left me alone, or killed me, as you did my father". Bernard swung his hand at her face. The connection almost cracked her skin. "Be gone then, you bitch! Die, if you must! Maybe your hatred will help you live." Bernard turned his back on her shriveled form. Lysa stood up, hissed at him with her fangs, and broke through the bedroom window. She let the air flow through her wings as she ascended. She had only flown within the walls where they resided, and had only tried that a few times. She teetered through the night sky, until she mastered gliding. "You will feel my pain." She thought as she flew towards the rising moon.

Bernard was as flushed as he could be from the dialogue with his farcical disciple. Bernard breathed in, then out. He cracked his knuckles and eased his way upstairs. He wanted to forget that pathetic, ineffective, and useless girl. Elsebeth had the design of a woman. She was strangely solemn, yet delightful as well as peaceful. She had a graceful style to her. Her seemingly sad pout was settling and somehow befitting. She was charming, and the epitome of beauty. Bernard found joy in her pensive visage. Bernard wanted to set his entire focus on Elsebeth. Lysa was hindering the nurturing that Bernard wanted to give Elsebeth, but no more.

Elsebeth and her father migrated to a small room. At every possible moment, they held each other. Everything was so uncertain for them. Their hunger elevated, which brought them fear. They had been feed blood from Bernard and Blythe and understood that they were fed upon by the two. They knew what they needed to survive, but they weren't confident that they could do what was necessary. If they could commit murder, to feed, how could they live with the knowledge that they had to kill another human being in order to survive? They had never felt this conflict with hunger before.

They wanted to pray, to find guidance from their spiritual father. They couldn't pray. As each of them tried to utter The Lord's Prayer, a numbing pain invaded their heads. From that point on, they weren't sure of what they could or couldn't do. They didn't know what they wanted. They wanted peace, but that was no longer an option. As each hour passed, more of what they knew disappeared. What began to consume them was a void feeling. The knowledge of what they were was dim to them. The memories were becoming diluted, fading as their new instincts and behaviors were starting to consume them, programming them from the inside out. What they were to become was yet to be appreciated. The door to their room creaked open. Bernard popped his head in with a gleaming smile. "May I come in?" He was trying to subdue his anger from his earlier confrontation with Lysa. His entire mood appeared to have changed, but he was still hot. Alec wanted to hate him, but his mind and body were so displaced, he could not do anything except be obedient. "Yes." Alec answered in a monotone drone.

Bernard slid past the threshold, and reached gently for Elsebeth. She took his hand and quietly rose from her seat. "Don't worry Alec, the worst is over. If you believe anything, believe that. I won't hurt either of you. Blythe and I promise." Bernard ushered Elsebeth out of the room. The door closed shut and Alec lowered his head once more. Alec continued to question himself, still wondering if he had failed. It was a question that would plague him for all of his days. No matter now, this was the life both his daughter and he were destined to live.

Elsebeth drank wine in front of the fireplace. She sat on a rug made out of some smooth and plush fur. Bernard stared out the window as she drank. He wanted to do so much for her, to her. Bernard could barely look at her, for fear of falling in love with her deeper than he had already. He pulled his reserved strength, so that he could face Elsebeth. Bernard sat next to Elsebeth on the floor. He tried to soothe her fears as they talked. "You know, Blythe loves you. She has many plans for you. I hope you don't mind me being a part of those plans, Elsebeth. Your spirit is very powerful. I've been intrigued by you for some time now." After he poured Elsebeth another glass of the red nectar, he took her hand. "The more you visited, the more I wanted you. You're so sweet, and so pure. I would've scared you. Blythe wasn't sure what to do, but I persuaded her to follow my plan. I am a fierce person, but I am also complex." Bernard bent over and kissed her flushed cheek.

Bernard felt vulnerable, confessing to Elsebeth. He feared losing Elsebeth as he did Lysa. "There have been countless others, you know. I'm referring to victims as well as lovers. I needed you to bring my tame side back to life. I believe you can do that for me, I doubt that anyone else could." Bernard set his glass down, and moved close to Elsebeth. He touched her shoulder, and traced her arm with his finger until he met her hand. His other hand set her shoulder free of the material of the gown that was covering it. He softly pressed his lips on her shoulder. She flinched slightly. He held her hand. Then, they met in a kiss. He gave his heart to her in that instant. Elsebeth was confused, but she felt such love for him, she let herself be seduced by Bernard. She gave him her heart, then her virtue. They were truly bonded forever.

Their love making was sweet. It surprised Elsebeth that Bernard wasn't a savage when they made love. He truly cared for her. He stroked her arms, kissed her shoulders, and held her chin in between his two thin fingers as he smiled. They forgot about all the pain of the events that brought them to that point. The only thing that mattered at that moment was that Bernard was showing his true self, the person he wanted to be, but couldn't because of what he was. No one save Blythe and now Elsebeth understood what he was, and what he had to do to survive. Elsebeth was slowly beginning to understand as she continued to absorb his memories, feelings, and thoughts. He really saw no fault in how he brought Elsebeth over. It was necessary for him. As selfish as it was, it was done. Elsebeth tried not to think about it. It was difficult to feel the hate as he embraced her like a truly satisfied lover. She succumbed to his passion and locked her bitterness away. It was a necessary compromise to "live".

The air in the house seemed lighter without the oppressing spirit of Lysa looming around. Elsebeth felt poorly about it, still she was happy about Lysa's expulsion from their family. Elsebeth didn't feel threatened by Lysa, but it was the fact that Lysa had created such a sense of depravity, no one could adjust to all of the sudden changes made in each of their lives. Elsebeth didn't know whether to feel anger or joy about the change in her being. She had been told by Blythe, when she would visit to comfort her, that she would have incredible powers. Since Elsebeth was younger and more open, she toyed with the idea of being a superior human, but at what cost? Alec was set in his feelings of disgust, anger, and betrayal. He trusted Blythe, and she was implicated in his undoing. Right now, he was not too particular about speaking with Blythe, definitely not Bernard.

The new family made advances away from their current lair. It was more out of necessity, rather than desire or curiosity. They didn't go out too often, but enough that they could bring back blood for all of them to consume. The first to venture out was Bernard. He felt responsible for the family, so he would retrieve farm animals and stray travelers. At first, Bernard served Elsebeth and Alec their nourishment. He warned them that soon, they would inherit the instinct to hunt for their food. That wasn't the case for Lysa, but he hoped to phrase his instructions, so that his new brood would accept their new station in *life* more easily.

When the group fed, it would be isolated attacks throughout France. Occasionally, a small Belgian village would lose a family that was small in number. Their victims would inhabit remote areas, nothing that would attract too much attention. Animals were their biggest prey. Blythe and Bernard would handle the messier kills. Alec and Elsebeth became painfully aware of their stalking and hunting abilities. After time, they both became used to their means of self-preservation.

They did not destroy every human they came in contact with. It was agreed that the less attention they attracted, the better. Meeting people of great renown or importance was not a priority with them. In a short span of time, they had moved around, more than any of them had desired to. It was not a stretch to assume none of the family was interested in running the risk of being discovered. They would have been seen as demons and burned or tortured, as witches had been and would be, for centuries to come. They had kept themselves so well cloaked from human society, that they were able to walk the streets of Italy and feast on beer in Germany. The taste of the bitter brew was nowhere as sweet as the warm crimson blood they stole from "innocent" people.

The drogues and the scourge of the city were their normal prey. They never lost their ability to interact with humans. They met many different types of humans, from many different walks of life. It would have been difficult to understand how their kind could chide with humans one evening, and then dine on possibly the same individuals the following evening. Blythe and Bernard tried to help them understand the order of their existence. "I've only met a few other vampires in my time. Most of them will usually cut themselves off completely from having relations with humans. Some just no longer liked humans. Others were still too close to their human side. They worked at making that part of them so prevalent, that they would sometimes go mad, or destroy themselves wanting something they could no longer have. It is all really sad. I actually have a healthy respect for humans. I don't think any less of them, but I need them to survive. It's never personal, really. The butler we had was a protector as well as an assistant. He was a willing participant, so it was a good arrangement." Bernard for the first time stated his character so that everyone, most importantly Elsebeth could understand him. At that moment, she allowed herself to feel for him as she had in the past, before he killed her human spirit, so he thought.

Alec made peace with the violent creature, just enough so that his existence wasn't so unbearable. Alec discussed Bernard's philosophy with Blythe. It appeared that

Bernard and Blythe shared the same feelings. "Let me assure you that you weren't a piece of flesh for me to conquer. I wanted you with me, as Bernard wanted Elsebeth. My plan's outcome was not different, but Bernard was just a touch too impetuous. In your eyes, we may have misused our power, our abilities, but we had the best of intentions." Blythe was still trying to make peace for her brother and his actions. "It doesn't help me, not yet Blythe. It is true that I feel things for you that I hadn't felt for anyone since my wife. I suppose, knowing that you care for me, this was the inevitable." Alec laid his head on Blythe's shoulder. They proceeded to engage in a passionate interlude that would become their practice and secondary to the feelings they had for one another. Alec's anger was quelled by his desire for Blythe. At first, they made no contact. Eventually, the bond they had once shared was resurrected.

The new *family* was subtle, kind, and basically normal. Elsebeth was everything to Bernard. Alec and Blythe's relationship cured slowly. They existed, undetected for two centuries throughout Western Europe.

CHAPTER FIVE

Elsebeth had become an excellent cook in all the years she had been alive, as well as undead. She thought about all the dishes she prepared as a human, feeling sorrow because she couldn't prepare many of them for her new *family*. She no longer worried about burning her fingers, or checking to make sure her dish was cooked all the way through. Now, the meals were always raw, and consisted largely of meat. Wine was a staple in every meal. It never intoxicated them, as it would a human. Their body chemistry no longer reacted to the alcoholic brew. Elsebeth took special care with one meal in particular. She was a collection of raw nerves. Elsebeth had news for her family. She never had to divulge such information to anyone, ever, like this before.

The meal was a success and the family confirmed what Elsebeth already knew with their many heartfelt compliments. All the proper seasonings were used. The dining area was lit subtly with long, ornate candles. The wine was sweet. It sufficed as their dessert. Blood from the meat was the beverage of choice. The salt rested nicely on their lips. After dinner, Elsebeth played the harp Alec had made for her. The work was of the highest quality. Royalty would've paid top dollar for Alec's work. It was something that fed his ego and fantasies, but he couldn't exist with the notoriety. Being the simple man that Alec was, it didn't disturb him by not being able to draw attention to his God-given talent because of what he had become. The music relaxed everyone. Bernard was calm, yet suspicious. Elsebeth was generally a mild mannered creature that took her time to do everything as accurately as possible. Tonight, however, she was anxious and clumsy.

Elsebeth couldn't wait any longer. She laid her harp against the chaise lounge she was perched on. She stood to make her announcement. "Everyone, I have some joyous news." Elsebeth took Bernard by the hand. He had a puzzled look on his face, much like the others. Elsebeth took a deep breath. "I will be giving birth to a child in the winter." Elsebeth was smiling so wide, she could barely speak. Bernard leaped up and kissed her. He then knelt down to embrace her and the child of his she was carrying. Everyone was so thrilled for her. Blythe toyed silently with the feeling of jealousy. She wasn't the child bearing type, so she wondered why she harbored those feelings. Besides, Blythe thought of Elsebeth as her own child. Alec moved over to where Blythe was standing and placed his hands on her shoulders. A tear rolled slowly down his cheek. He was proud that his daughter could still bear children. He thought that Elsebeth possibly couldn't, by no longer being human. He then thought of his wife, and became afraid. He didn't want the same fate for his daughter, but he realized she wouldn't die. That made him especially pleased.

The family had no way of knowing, no way of understanding their vampire physiology. As long as Elsebeth lived on blood, fresh from another living creature, her organs and reproductive system still functioned, as though she were a mortal creature. No science could explain the anomaly. To them, it was a blessing, a break from the curse. It was a chance for them to multiply their numbers without having to make another human choose either eternal damnation or a gruesome demise. It mattered more for some than others, but all were mesmerized by Elsebeth's ability.

Elsebeth was spoiled with care as everyone tended to her every need. The child grew as the seasons evolved, moving from one to the next. It waited until early winter. The time was just right. The cold wasn't an issue for the family, since the more frigid the climate, the more acute their senses were. The snow came early that year. The setting was peaceful and stunningly beautiful. One day, a scream shattered the placid, rural area they inhabited. The yell broke as did her water did the same. The contractions were normal by human standards; however, Elsebeth had never experienced any pain comparable to this. Alec was the first to reach her. He found her lying on the floor, on her side. The poor girl was cradling her stomach. "Help me father, please!" She was sweating profusely.

Alec called out with a roar to the others for assistance. As he helped her to her bed, he was consumed with thoughts of his beloved wife. "Elsebeth won't die. I'm sorry dear, if I've failed you, but have I? Please help me. Darling wife, this way, you will live forever." Alec shook himself and stopped speaking to the image of his wife that he saw before him. He dabbed Elsebeth's brow as he struggled with his thoughts. The others had been out, feeding. Blythe was trying to help Bernard bring a human victim covertly to their lair. It was important that Elsebeth had strong, pure, human blood to ensure a healthy birth. Animal blood was fine, but usually was only had out of necessity. The two siblings dropped the body in the foyer. They had felt the infants' presence coming near. Blythe stood erect when she heard the scream in her mind. They tore into the bedroom where Elsebeth was literally clawing at the bed linen.

Blythe had seen much and experienced many things. She learned from humans as well as using them for sustenance. Blythe felt it important to understand the birthing process, since that is what kept her primary food source plentiful. She also was human, but as with Bernard, any memory of her first life was far beyond recollection. Blythe did the best she could. Bernard was alert, but did not fear the life of his beautiful mate. He kept Alec sane during the delivery. They found common ground in their desire to make sure that Elsebeth made it through this birthing in good health. Elsebeth's' fangs grew longer than they ever had. Her senses were at their peak. She could feel every bit of hemoglobin move throughout her body. Her screams echoed throughout the countryside. The baby was pushing itself out. It was more than Elsebeth thought she could bear. She felt her nature tear as the child broke through, into their world. It was as if it couldn't wait to get out and get on with it.

Alec was truly relieved. There were no visible signs of distress. Alec also marveled at how the torn flesh of Elsebeth healed right before his eyes. The child was pink and healthy. It was a girl and Alec cried out to everyone so they could rejoice in the grand news. The baby cried the moment all the fluid it had been submerged in was free of its mouth. Bernard eased a smile across his face. His heart didn't beat often, but his soul stirred as he looked at his beautiful daughter. When most of the excitement was over, Elsebeth held her little girl in her bosom. "You are truly beautiful. Be good darling, the best you can at whatever you do, whatever you become." Elsebeth kissed her new child on her cheek and leaned back to sleep. She was delighted, but exhausted.

Elsebeth recovered fully, something her immortality guaranteed her. Her daughter clung to her with desperation. The infant feed on her mother's milk and cried terrible fits if everyone's attention weren't on her. Alec and Blythe cared for the child, but the baby obviously preferred her parents. Bernard could care for the child without too much fuss.

Heaven help his victims, but at home, with his family, Bernard was emotionally loving and devoted. Elsebeth and Bernard played with the baby almost as if she were a doll, a fragile, soft, lovely doll. They decided on the name Desmony. The name had no real significance or meaning, it just seemed right. Now that Elsebeth had seemingly settled into her existence as a vampire and had conceived a child with Bernard, a ceremony took place. The intention was for the uniting of Elsebeth and Bernard as man to his eternal mate. It wasn't a traditional wedding by any stretch of the imagination, but it was beautiful and sacred, none the less. In the still of the night, Bernard met Elsebeth on a high hilltop nearby. They said words of love to each other. Fortunately, love for each other wasn't an emotion they had to sacrifice.

"I will follow you into eternity, I will now damn my soul to love you."

"It is noble to be corrupted for love, My destiny is dark, my love is true."

"Damn my soul."

"Damn my soul."

"A putrid thought, so gladly held, as I clutch your spirit in my heart."

"For so long, I knew not the face of who I'd love, I didn't know where to start."

"I see cupid, shooting his arrows at me through your welcoming eyes as you stare."

"I couldn't have found a love more pure, for all time now, my soul is in blissful despair."

They kissed with urgency under the moonlight. Everything was wonderful. They were truly in love. Their vows were written down and titled "Sympathy for the Damned".

As Desmony blossomed, she seemed to be of exceptional intellect. Her growth proceeded at a normal rate, in comparison to a human child. She showed no signs of craving blood, or changing into the type of creature they were, at first. "I'm assuming that won't happen until she reaches puberty. Since she was born as a human child, she must grow and mature physically and mentally before the undead part of her becomes active. I believe she will only know a human's life for a short while, before her immortal life as a vampire takes control." Bernard did not know what to expect with a child born of two vampires. Both Bernard and Blythe knew only a little from what the black hearted demon that changed their lives so long ago taught them. He didn't teach them through instruction, only by example. They were desperate to survive, but unbearably distraught by the devastating disruption in their natural lives. How long vampires existed, what their origins were, none of the fundamental information was known to either sibling. They lived by instinct and what they knew to be true. They were taken from their lives and thrown into this one without any consideration for how they were to continue to exist. Their sire was a cruel and hateful creature. Sadly, it wasn't spoken of and no one present would dare touch upon the subject, because they knew it would bring too much pain to Bernard and Blythe. Their story would have to remain unspoken for a while longer. Until then, they would all care for Elsebeth and Bernard's child, learning each step of the way.

The time between Desmony's birth, and her maturing was filled with memories of a quaint, yet curious childhood. Desmony gave subtle hints, foreshadowing the type of vampire she was to become. Desmony's behavior was wild and her senses were keen. Even while she lived as a human, she stalked and practiced hunting. Her temper was violent at times, and she would perform stunts, simply for the thrill or to make a statement about her character. When Desmony came into womanhood, she did it with a quake. She had already been very mischievous and inquisitive. There was a bit of the devil in her that was for sure. Desmony grew to be medium height, shapely, and mature looking for a young woman of seventeen human years. Her appearance was that of a woman at least twenty-four years of age. Her hair was coiled and black as pitch. Her eyes were only a few shades lighter. Her lips were full and rich, just as her mother's. All of her features were ideal, perfect to most. Desmony was aware of the beauty she had acquired, and intended to use it to her advantage.

Soon after she finished developing physically, her transformation began to take place. Bernard anticipated this when she was born and showed no signs of being born of vampire parents. Her awareness soared and her vampire instincts revealed themselves, much to her pleasure. "Finally!" Desmony yelled as her fangs grew in. She was admiring her reflection at a nearby lake when she noticed her first signs of change. Mirrors were thought to be windows to the soul. This would possibly explain why vampires had no reflection. It would definitely fit for Desmony. Desmony made it home, but she did not to seem to be in the best of health. She was engulfed in sweat and burning with fever. Her mouth was bleeding, from her fangs growing. Desmony licked the blood, almost laughing as it dripped from her gums. She was actually jovial over the experience!

The days passed with aching fatigue as Desmony's changes became apparent. Desmony's joy turned quickly into uncertainty. The family became very concerned as Desmony began to deteriorate before their eyes. The young woman's flesh became cool to the touch, and turned an ashy shade of ivory. Her breathing became shallow, then labored. Desmony was dying. The human life she had suffered through was finally ending. She winced from the pain of her organs failing her, slowly, but she never wept. Instead, she smiled, knowing that what she truly wanted was on the horizon. Elsebeth was fearful that something was wrong, that her child was dying, completely. All of the family members studied the changes, and made their unskilled prognosis. Desmony calmed all of their fears in one of her stronger moments by saying, "I feel new. Mother, don't shed tears over my soul. I never had one. Please, let this life pass. I will survive!"

Finally, her metamorphose was complete. Desmony's heart beat no longer as a human, yet she lived. She was much stronger than before. Most of the changes were internal, yet there were decisive changes to Desmony's appearance. After some doing, Desmony's wings blossomed, much like an orchid in spring, after a light morning shower. They were a fleshy, rose tinted hue. They were moist as they peeled out of Desmony's back. The bright full moon shone through each break in her wings, creating a stunning visual effect. After an hour or so, Desmony's wings became drier, or not quite as moist. Her wings were no likeness to the texture of human flesh. They weren't bird-like feathers either. They were a shimmer-like, thin, tissue. This *skin* was tight, and strong as tungsten steel. Desmony tried her wings out after they reached full span. The wind moved through them as they cut through the air. The sound of the air was like that of an oncoming twister. She giggled as she made moderate sized statues and candles fall over. As her wings aged, they became darker with each day. At the end of their bloom, they had a color of cashmere brown.

The changes that were taking Desmony over weren't necessarily enjoyable, just exciting. Desmony felt ill most of the time. She rested while she stayed holed up in a corner of the country home the family occupied. It was drafty and rather dark. She rarely came out, and deterred anyone from coming in. Her screams echoed through the area. Many nearby humans heard the noises that tore through the night sky. The family had the pleasure of instilling fear and sustaining life of the myth to every town's person. The town's fear caused them to not venture out and seek the source of the bizarre noises They stayed close to their homes and hoped that whatever caused the noises never found its way to their front doors. It provided the Mal clan with added protection.

It took some time, but Desmony reappeared. This pleased her family. Now, in her new state, Desmony was magnificent. When she surfaced, her entrance was spectacular! She experienced a moment without agility and almost fell out the window of her *changing* room, but she managed to descend gracefully. She swooped into the family room window. Her silk clothing fluttered in the air as she landed. Her wings retracted slowly when she bowed. It was as if she had just given a command performance. It was more like a vaudeville act in the eyes of her veteran audience. Never the less, she was made to feel as though it was the greatest feat ever accomplished. Elsebeth embraced her. "You are doing wonderfully, dear! I love you so much! We all do." Elsebeth kissed Desmony on the lips and hugged her beautiful daughter. A new part of Desmony's life was just beginning. It was a new part of the rest of her eternal life.

Desmony's thirst for blood proved itself to be slightly unusual. It was like filling a deep chasm. Her appetite alarmed Elsebeth. Bernard tried to soothe Elsebeth's fears. "I was much like her at the beginning, believe it or not. I've calmed down! You wait dear. It may take some time, but it will happen." "I know darling, but she drinks until she is sick. It scares me. Even if she does tame her thirst, it will still be dangerous. Someone will find her out, capture her, and let the sun, or a sharp piece of wood, end her life!" Elsebeth collapsed in her sobbing. Bernard just held her. He feared to himself that Elsebeth was voicing a premonition, not simply an isolated parental concern.

Desmony couldn't control herself, much to Elsebeth's dismay. The truth of the matter was that Desmony didn't try to control herself at all. Elsebeth tried to monitor virtually every move Desmony made. She was worse as an undead adolescent than a human toddler with uncharted curiosity! This was very much like a second childhood but this time, as a vampire. Blythe, knowing more than Elsebeth ever could about being a vampire, gave sage advice to both the mother, as well as the child, although Desmony would only pretend to listen out of respect. Alec had never experienced anything like this. He was quite uneasy about Desmony and her traits. He had seen some peculiar children, but Desmony was exceptional. Bernard kept his feelings tight. He did not want to let on just how concerned he was. He did emphasize his dislike in Desmony's careless technique. Desmony was warned numerous times, but she never acknowledged whether she learned a lesson or not. Her actions assured everyone around her that she apparently hadn't.

Desmony went out one evening, seeking flesh. Blythe had taken up the slack for Elsebeth in monitoring the child. After trying to keep Bernard in control, she was expert at it. Blythe followed the little minx out into the night. Desmony traveled a great distance. If she wasn't careful, that characteristic that would certainly be her undoing. Desmony searched the desolate countryside for a lonely house. It took her some time, but she found one. Through the windows, she saw two fairly small silhouettes. One was an adult female. The other, was a child, probably a boy. Desmony thought to herself, "That's the one. I should feed well there tonight!" Desmony licked her lips at the thought.

Blythe was never too far behind. She could feel the thoughts and emotions Desmony was feeling before she attacked. Those feelings made Blythe feel concerned and even uncomfortable. It wasn't a feeling she ever possessed throughout her life, undead, or otherwise. Regardless of Blythe's numerous kills, she still felt as though she had a sense of ethics. Children were simply off limits. Blythe enjoyed a good fight and subsequent meal just as much as any vampire, but there were parameters. She felt that was essential in maintaining some level of Integrity. It made her feel sick that her kin had such a black heart. She continued following this apparent stranger she had help bring into the world, waiting to see if she would have to intercept Desmony's feeding ritual. One thing was for sure, Desmony was in need of some guidance.

Desmony stole across the field to the house she was about to invade. The door became larger as she traversed the open field. There was not much foliage, since the cool weather of fall was upon them. Desmony looked at the door, which encased her prey. The door was well built, but fragile compared to Desmony's strength. Desmony burst through the door of the small family. They were frightened beyond words. Naturally, they screamed in absolute terror. No one was close enough to hear them. Surprised by the husband, Desmony struck the man first. It was a good tactical move on her part. His full and flabby chest was torn apart, but not enough to kill him. Blood stained his coarse hand woven shirt, but he didn't realize it. He fell unconscious for just a moment. That was long enough for Desmony to turn her attention to the wife. The woman, despite the instant shock of her husband's Impending demise, was inspirational. She displayed her maternal instinct by covering her child, which was indeed a young boy.

The young boy tried to free himself from the shield of his mother's body. Desmony could barely see the boy as he struggled. The boy wanted to protect his family. Desmony laughed at the way the wife neglected to adorn herself. She was so plain, so mundane. Desmony paced the floor, deciding what to do next. She lunged at the both of them as they moved. The boy tried to reach for a nearby knife. "Your blood will certainly be sweet. Come here!" Desmony grabbed the boy from the mother. The boy saw Desmony's eyes flame as her fangs emerged. The boy screamed as Desmony moved in to drink.

The mother passed out from the horror of it all. The husband finally came too, just in time to see his beloved son fall limp and pale to the floor. The boy wasn't to wake again. Desmony drank until the boy was dry. The man tried to yell out, but he was nearly dead himself. He struggled to his feet and pulled a sword that was above where he had fallen. Desmony was looking away, thinking of what to do with the mother. She was, however, painfully aware of the man and his thoughts and movements. "How weak," Desmony thought. Desmony's disposition was that of utter disdain for humanity. As Desmony paused for her character assessment of the pitiful family, the husband had moved upon her with the long blade when Blythe appeared. Blythe took hold of the shiny metal instrument. She broke the sword in half before he could use it, on the spoiled ass of the child Desmony, or herself. Desmony, without any real.concern for the man, just looked on at the scene. Enough life had left the man so that it wouldn't be long before he would collapse, and die. The woman, still unconscious and would've awaken to the gruesome sight of her destroyed family. Blythe took the woman by the nape of her neck. "This is how it is done." Blythe took the woman's throat to her mouth. It was not erotic by any means. It was sacred. Blythe almost seemed to apologize to the woman as she punctured her artery. She drank, but she didn't gorge.

Blythe lit a torch, with some firewood that was handy. She burned the modest house down. After she had completed that task, she took Desmony by the hand, and lifted her into the slate blue sky. "You have so much to learn, my dear. I wonder if you ever will. You are much too impetuous, and show little forethought. We will discuss this more. For now, think upon tonight. My advice is that you concentrate on your many errors. Feeding, as with anything else, requires skill and finesse. It is a talent that must be perfected, if you hope to survive." Blythe was not a favorite of Desmony's. She wasn't certain if it was from contempt at Blythe's strict criticism, or from Desmony's deep hidden fear of the powerful creature.

When the two returned, just before dawn, Bernard looked at his daughter and bowed his head. He knew what had happened by looking in his daughter's eyes. They were the doorway to her mind and black, hellish soul. "Your actions are too risky. You will not leave this house until I say so. Your wildness will destroy us all!" Bernard was outraged and embarrassed beyond words. His quietness scared Desmony, something she had never felt. Desmony did as he said. She stayed inside. Her nourishment was brought to her for several decades. Many evenings, months, even years were spent trying to optimize her technique. It continued to lack any skillful elements. Bernard, Elsebeth, and Blythe were extremely concerned by Desmony's disobedience towards their instructions. It was finally accepted that Desmony did not possess neither gratitude for the life she had been given nor an aptitude for proper feeding. What was yet to be revealed was why she had such distaste for discipline.

After time, Desmony was allowed to go out with supervision for short periods of time. This quelled her rage, somewhat. Desmony felt that she had paid her penance, but her parents were doing her a favor. They may have prolonged her life, since she was so careless. Desmony wasn't a skillful killer. She was greedy and destructive. It only took one experience, followed by continuous failures in practice for them to make that assessment. Blythe could read her soul as well. She showed no sign of change. Actually, she showed apathy for this crude form of discipline. Desmony resented this human-like punishment, but she held quiet.

Before long, an entire century had passed. Desmony had improved, but her demeanor was still dark. She was constantly cynical and crass. She was, however, undeniably beautiful. She was smart, but not wise. During this time of retreat, Elsebeth had become restless. It wasn't certain if it was from shadowing her unruly daughter, or some other well-guarded secret. Elsebeth had decided to take a short sabbatical to Spain. This decision was sudden, but accepted by the family. It was fully understandable, since she had dedicated so much time to her child. "Mother, may I go with you?" This was not a request Elsebeth wanted to hear from her daughter, yet Desmony persisted. "I've been in France far too long. I need to see more." Elsebeth's heart was bruised by trying to discourage Desmony. "Blood tastes the same, no matter where you are, dear." Elsebeth wanted and needed to be alone. "It's warmer down there!" Elsebeth laughed at her slightly amusing joke. Elsebeth knew how much Desmony hated warm weather. It made her feel weak, and she despised that.

Desmony didn't find amusement in the humor. She straightened up and asked again. Elsebeth gritted her teeth, and gave in. "All right Desmony, but you must promise me that you'll be careful." "I promise, mother." Desmony sprouted her wings, smiled, then streaked through the air.

CHAPTER SIX

The journey to Spain was bittersweet. Elsebeth and Desmony were closer to the equator than they had ever been. The climate was slightly uncomfortable for them, even at night. The rise in temperature caused the two to suffer from fatigue. It diminished their powers, to an extent. It was an inconvenience that, for the moment, was something with which they could contend. There was no present danger, no need for them to use their abilities for survival. Elsebeth made sure Desmony understood that their powers weren't to be used for any recreational circumstance. Spain bore so much natural beauty, it seemed a shame they were not able to be a part of it all. They were deprived of seeing the peaceful, stunning sunrises and sunsets. They couldn't walk along the busy streets during the day and buy fresh food from the vendors. Honestly, neither really cared about taking part of any human activities that would only bring cause for others to notice their apparent differences. Elsebeth was all too eager to avoid the scene. It only reminded her about the life that she left behind and the possibilities that there never to be. The only thing they cared about, in relation to the sun, was that it never hit their skin and that they could get their blood without raising suspicion.

Before their trip, Elsebeth made them several dresses. Their attire, as they strolled in the luminous moonlight, suggested that they were of some high social ranking. They passed easily as French aristocracy. Their pale complexion made them looked like powdered nobles. It was something Elsebeth could have done without, but the attention couldn't be avoided. They're beauty and appearance wouldn't allow anonymity. They were able to socialize by night with carefully planned activities, as they dined with the finer Spanish families. They were attracted by the social elite and as a consequence were invited to social dances, as well as operas and shows at the local theaters. Once they were out of sight, the two beauties made their lodging at a local mausoleum. It was quite stereotypical, but suited their needs. There was a hollow mountain of rock nearby. It was cool and dark at all times. Mother and daughter relocated, and made the cave their home.

Elsebeth finally got the rest she so badly deserved and craved. Elsebeth made sure Desmony and she maintained a strict diet, so they wouldn't raise any cause for questions that couldn't be answered without bloodshed. At times, Desmony's hunger would almost consume her. When it became too much, they took the chance of raiding a farmer's herd. The animal blood wasn't as good, but it helped them to survive. One evening, Elsebeth and Desmony had dinner with a noble family. Their story was that they were sisters from France, traveling to meet their family in England, but taking a short vacation in Spain before heading to their destination. They should have been accompanied by an escort, so they made up the tale that their escort was ill after eating at a common tavern. They were bored at home, so they risked the scandal of traveling without a man, ready to aid them. The family thought they were brave, but questioned their judgment and appreciation of etiquette.

One of the young men, Xavier Montez, concentrated on Elsebeth the entire night. He made no effort to hide his attraction towards her. All of his conversation was directed at her. Desmony noticed this and became very upset. The puny, pretentious human was disrespecting her father, whether he was aware of the insult or not. It wasn't difficult not to notice, but the rest of the family was accustomed to Xavier's thrill with being in love. This time was different, however. Desmony sensed that his attraction to her mother was more than lust. Xavier presented his interest so sincerely. How dare this frail, insignificant, vermin of a mortal make advances at her mother? "I should rip his throat out this minute!" Desmony thought. Elsebeth took hold of Desmony's hand. She noticed Desmony's nostrils flaring and heard her thoughts. She could also feel her rage. Desmony kept the violent fantasy of Xavier's demise, to herself, not upsetting her mother.

After dinner, coffee, and coffee, Elsebeth took a walk on the grounds. Desmony was cornered by Xavier's two younger sisters, Blanca and Lydia. They were rebellious and she liked that. Desmony knew she didn't have to worry about her mother's safety, but something else about Elsebeth being with Xavier bothered her.

Xavier sneaked up on Elsebeth, or so he thought. She smelled him coming for a long while. She showed no surprise when he came from behind, facing her. She looked troubled. He asked her what the matter was. It was such a shame to see as lovely a creature as Elsebeth look so unhappy. "Oh, I'm just wishing for things I cannot have. It's a long story, one that must never be repeated. You look so warm, so deliciously warm." Elsebeth almost let a tear fall as she looked at Xavier. A part of her wanted to feed on him, yet another hidden part of her was jealous of him. Elsebeth found herself missing mortality. She missed praying and living. She missed not fearing simple things like daylight and her old crucifix. Smiling, Xavier took her hand and placed it on his chest, right over his heart. "It is beating for you. I've never met a woman so mysterious, so alluring."

Xavier began to lose control. He held her close and stared at her. It seemed to last for hours, although it was only a few seconds. He moved almost painfully slow to her lips. Elsebeth didn't resist. He stroked her lips with his and let them settle right in the middle of her rich, supple, and tempted mouth. They kissed without arrest, for moments that would have to last an eternity. Elsebeth was intoxicated by his life force. She let a tear fall as they kissed. As the tear fell to the floor, so did their bodies. Elsebeth knew what she was about to do was wrong, but she had been so sad before, but not really not knowing why. She was not sad now. She had suppressed feelings of betrayal by Bernard for too long. She was human again, if only for the night. Xavier undressed her as though she were a fragile porcelain doll. With every move he made, he used the utmost care. She wanted to make love to this mortal. She knew it would only be this one perfect night, but she didn't care. She promised herself not to hurt him, to stay in control, no matter how great the temptation.

The love they made lasted off and on for many hours. Xavier was a wonderful lover. He had been with many young women, but never had he felt such spirit in a woman as he did with Elsebeth. Their bodies moved in absolute sync. He plunged into her, gently, but as far as he could. Elsebeth welcomed his attempt at subtle aggression. It was simply sweet to her. Xavier swept his hand over her face. He traveled the entire course of her face. His fingers wavered as he moved from her face, to her slender neck, then to her chest and hips. He pulled himself toward her, for another session in romance. Once they finished, Elsebeth dressed herself, and explained to him that she and her "sister" must leave tomorrow. Xavier was stunned by the announcement. "But why are you leaving? How? You can't tell me that you are leaving, after making love with me! I love you! My heart tells me that I do. I've never felt this way. Elsebeth, you cannot do this!" Xavier pulled up his pants as he ran to catch up with Elsebeth. She had already started for the house.

Elsebeth picked up her pace, but Xavier caught her by the arm. "No, I will not allow you to walk away from me! You may be on your way to France, or to England, wherever! I don't care! All I care about is you! Elsebeth let your sister go, but please stay with me!" Xavier was crying. He never showed his emotions, to anyone. "I'm sorry, but I must go. We aren't to be. I'm promised to another, for eternity." Elsebeth felt such shame. She didn't know what to feel bad about. She was unfaithful to Bernard, but she was in the process of destroying someone she would've spent the rest of her mortal life with. She couldn't be with Xavier, no matter what. "Do not argue with me, please! Tonight wasn't a mistake, please know that. There are too many things about me that you don't know. I must go!" Elsebeth continued her brisk stride. "I will always love you." Xavier said these words in a whisper to hold back his pain and anguish. Xavier fell to his knees, not caring if anyone saw him. Elsebeth looked back, seeing Xavier on the ground. She cursed herself for wanting what she couldn't have.

Desmony was keeping herself occupied with the two scandalous vixens Xavier lovingly called sisters. She wanted to make them as she was, but even she knew that wouldn't be the smart thing to do. They honestly would have been friends, had time and fate worked out a little differently.

Desmony flinched occasionally. She felt a strange sensation coming from Elsebeth, but she couldn't read her. Desmony hadn't really perfected that extra sense, but to try with Elsebeth on guard was futile. Elsebeth had to protect her indiscretion as long as she could. Several times, Desmony tried to get away, but the ever excited sister duo double teamed her. Finally, Elsebeth came to her rescue. Desmony was overjoyed to see her, even though she had her suspicions about her mother's late night activities. Elsebeth took Desmony by the arm, smiling at the family as she did. "I trust you are ready to take leave, my dear." Elsebeth had a terrible look of fear in her eyes. She was hoping that Desmony couldn't pick up on anything.

Desmony felt such relief when she received the decision to disperse. "This night was entirely too long! How much longer are we to be bored by these silly people?" Desmony looked at her mother again. A strange look in Elsebeth's eyes showed through. Desmony took the look as if she were beginning to worry if their secret was out. Elsebeth spoke to Desmony through her mind. Desmony could receive thoughts, without any problem. Pulling them out of people was where her weakness laid. "We must leave, and return home! We must dismiss ourselves from this country immediately!" Elsebeth offered no explanation. When Desmony requested one, silence was the response she heard.

Xavier returned to the house. He looked once more upon Elsebeth. He tried to control his true feelings. The sisters were surprised at Elsebeth's announcement. She explained that their escorts were feeling better and were ready to travel. She knew they had to leave, but she was enjoying herself so much, she couldn't bring herself to destroy their wonderful visit. "We will truly miss you. Please, if the opportunity presents itself to you to come back, you will always be welcome." Xavier cleared his throat and walked from the sitting room toward the stairs. He brushed by Elsebeth, making her tear up once again. Elsebeth's life would never be the same. In many ways, it made her a better person. She finally knew the love of a human, not just Bernard. Bernard gave her love, but he took it first, with little love in return, so she thought. Elsebeth considered that there may not have been any love involved at first, just love and the desire to conquer. Bernard said he cared, but he was still very rigid and cold at times. Elsebeth knew she was to remain with Bernard, but at least now she felt some satisfaction, some closure to her previous existence.

Elsebeth and Desmony flew faster than the wind the night they left. They had to make it home before light. Desmony was quiet the entire way home. Elsebeth knew that her secret had been discovered by Desmony. Her guilt was too overwhelming to shield from her. Desmony didn't know the entire scenario, but she filled in the voids easily enough. She knew about human nature and desire, as well as love and the art of seduction. She never used these traits out of sincerity. She had to learn how to emulate them to seduce her prey. She never thought to apply them to a lover. Learning the truth about Elsebeth disappointed Desmony, and devastated her. Desmony revered her mother so. She was the picture of grace and perfection. After Desmony starred at Elsebeth for a while, the rest of the story unfolded. Desmony was finally able to read her mother. The entire story flashed before her mind as if she were there. The images were so disturbing to her, she couldn't expect her mother to confide her horrible secret. "I won't tell, mother. I will try and understand." Desmony had no ulterior motive for calming her mother's fears with those words, although, that was how she normally operated. The sun was starting its ascent much too fast for them to make it home. They sought refuge in a small cave in the southern country of France. As the sun awoke, yawning rays of light throughout the sky, Desmony interrogated her mother about the events she believed that had taken place the night before.

"You have all but confessed to what I suspect, mother." Elsebeth nodded to Desmony's statement. "Why? Why did you betray father?" Elsebeth had a sudden streak of furry, thinking of the words Desmony had so self-righteously spoken to her. "He is your father, but we are not married in the eyes of God! I can never do that. I was human. I was supposed to live, grow up, bear children, and die. I suppose I wanted, needed to be close with a mortal!" Elsebeth calmed down a bit and tried to express herself in a less resentful manner. Her deceit between Xavier and she was unintentional, as was the hurt placed on her so long ago. Relentless desire is far from perfect. "Blythe and your father love me, I know that. It didn't seem as suck at the time, but they gave me a choice. Your grandfather made a choice, based on events that took place before he could really help me. I have lived since the fourteenth century now. You don't know what it feels like to have had a destiny, then have it altered, drastically, seemingly without permission. You also have only one century behind you. All of this is still relatively new to you. You are a vampire, completely. I was happy as a human." Elsebeth lay down to sleep. Desmony tried to understand, but she never would be able to, not really.

Desmony wanted to discuss this once human issue a little more in depth. She was perplexed by it. Where was the problem with being a vampire? To her, it was no different than being human, eating cow flesh and making knew discoveries, expanding one's mind. Humans were a less developed race in Desmony's and even Blythe and Bernard's minds. That was one of the few things they could discuss. Desmony just couldn't figure out why her mother was bitter, and why she didn't speak about it with her father. Would he really not want to discuss that subject with her? Was it that volatile? Desmony wanted sleep to come to her, but the weather was fairly warm and rather uncomfortable for her. It caused her to become confused as she tried to solve her new mystery.

Elsebeth awoke just at sundown. She nudged her daughter wake. "Wake now, child. We must be off. We've been away from home much too long." Elsebeth gathered their few items, and began to walk through the field, choosing an area so they could take flight. "Mother, can we please talk more?" Desmony was relentless with this subject, as though she were after a fine human with rich, healthy blood. "I have said all I can, child. You have to know what it is to have something you are content with, and then have it ripped away. One tends to miss such a thing, after a while. It took me longer. Maybe something significant in this sabbatical of ours triggered it, but it sent me into a seduction I won't get over too soon. It would be best if you put these details of our journey out of your mind, and choose never to try and alter my judgment with regards to you regarding these matters in the future. Do you understand?" Elsebeth was a quiet, even-tempered lady, except when she fed. However, she picked up a stone and crushed it, so that Desmony would not misinterpret her words.

Elsebeth and Desmony returned home the following evening, in silence. The sky cried tears like rain in the midst of gloom. The homecoming managed to be happy and quaint. Bernard was overjoyed to see his two women. He embraced them both and inquired about their journey. The two ladies looked at each other. "We had a wonderful time, darling. I feel much better. I think I'll be at peace for at least another century!" Elsebeth laughed a slightly nervous laugh." I hope my need to travel didn't disturb you much, Bernard." She poised her body close to his, not giving him an opportunity to think different than what she wanted him to think. "Of course it did not, my love. I just missed you. You are my heart's passion, you know?" Bernard held her with his muscular, yet lean arms. His touch did feel right, but Xavier's touch was still warm on her skin. Desmony lay across the divan and added, "Yes. We met a lot of people and got to experience many things." Desmony didn't look at her mother. She feared the daggers would pierce her eyes, if she let them meet Elsebeth's.

It took a long stretch of time before Elsebeth was comfortable with her daughter again. Bernard still was not wise to the source of their tension. It was really difficult to detect at times, yet there was an obvious change in the way Elsebeth and Desmony interacted with one another. Elsebeth took his mind away from the mystery by wooing him into sex. They made love tirelessly, more so when Elsebeth first returned. It just wasn't to quell any potential suspicion. It was due to a little guilt, as well as consummating the relationship she had chosen to commit. Elsebeth was more aggressive than she had ever been, but Bernard decided that the trip had in fact done her good. She was finally relaxing and accepting her fate.

Desmony brooded, but that was par for the course. She was still held within the borders of the house, not to leave without supervision. Once, she approached Elsebeth with the idea of letting her venture out alone. Elsebeth denied her, reminding her that she was not to test her, in any way. Desmony threatened to become sick from the lack of blood she was receiving. She seemed to require so much more. This was dismissed as a symptom of a young bred vampire. Blythe took pity on the child. They went on hunts, almost nightly. Blythe only fed occasionally on the hunting parties. Alec assisted Bernard in bartering their collected possessions, for new ones, and occasionally cash. They found themselves being entrepreneurs in the antique industry. They required some money, but rarely accepted it. Alec also used his craftsman skills to make quality furniture for the aristocrats, saying it was made by the hardest working-men underneath him. It was a therapy for him. He gave life to an alter ego that worked as he used to, and was a simple man, as he had been.

As far as Elsebeth, some time had passed before any repercussions appeared as a result of her infidelity. First, there was fatigue, then nausea, and finally some other indications that could be confused with a virus. The only problem was, as a vampire, she never became ill, by human standards. The other symptoms could in no way be confused with any virus, human or vampire. The only choice Elsebeth had after she was certain she was pregnant was to tell Bernard. She knew she couldn't tell him about the affair. She could, however, tell him about the child-to-be. Elsebeth had continued with her sexual relationship with Bernard almost every night since her return. She felt intense guilt about her mind and heart being elsewhere at first. It was obvious that Elsebeth would have to omit that it was possible the child could be half human.

Elsebeth couldn't ask anyone, nor did she know about vampire genetics. As educated as she was, no one knew the answers to those types of questions, and wouldn't for at least two, almost three centuries. What powers would the child possess? Would it have any powers at all? There was no way to find out. There wasn't even a way for her to know if the child belonged to Xavier or Bernard. Elsebeth would unfortunately have to wait and see what the outcome would be. Elsebeth took comfort in knowing that at the very least the child would have her vampire blood coursing through its veins. The stress that undermined her patience didn't help her pregnancy. Being the strong spirit that she was, Elsebeth persevered.

Elsebeth did her best to create the proper atmosphere. She had the walls of Bernard's and her bedroom dancing with the glow of a chorus of candles. A gentle breeze played with the lace curtains that untouched, would wrinkle on the floor. Dried flowers, all except nearly fatal wild roses, left a faint fragrance throughout the room. Bernard entered the room. The first thing he noticed was his beloved decorating the bed as she lay there. His mouth was dry, and it fell wide open. "I should thank someone for granting me this subconscious wish. Did you read me? I didn't feel you if you did. You look exquisite!" Bernard practically trotted to where she was. He purred a growl and slinked up on the bed. As he approached her, she held up one finger to his lips. "My love, I have something I must tell you. There's no waiting."

Bernard cradled her in his arms, rocking her slightly. She could feel the lie stinging her lips as it almost reached articulation. It bothered her heart, but as far as pleasing God, she kept reminding herself that she was already dammed. She also held onto how Bernard seduced her as well, putting her in a position that presented a tragic outcome. This lie couldn't harm her soul any more than it already was. Elsebeth began to speak. "Bernard, we will be blessed with still another child. It should arrive early spring! I hope you are happy!" She turned around and looked up at him, anxious for a response. Bernard just sat there, crying in joy. It was thought a fluke that Elsebeth became pregnant the first time, but the anomaly happened yet again! "Thank you." Bernard let those words pass before he turned Elsebeth around, so that he might bury his head in her bosom, smiling. Bernard moved his head from her quivering breasts, all the way to her moist lips. He wanted to take advantage of the time they had alone, quiet. No one else had risen just yet.

Bernard kissed Elsebeth with total concentration, for several minutes.

The kisses escalated into caresses, all along his beautiful mate's body. She encouraged every move her lover made. She responded aggressively with kisses along his body. Bernard became weak as Elsebeth mounted his body. She kissed the entire canvas of his perfect form. They laughed, honestly, and without shame. They had constantly been serious. For once, they just enjoyed each other. Bernard tossed Elsebeth on her back, obliging the position Elsebeth had. He pulled her soft silk gown down, so that it exposed her breasts. He tenderly suckled each, equally. The touch of his lips against her nipples made her nearly scream with ecstasy. For whatever reason, she wanted her man desperately that night. Her prior thoughts of Xavier faded, rather quickly to her surprise.

Elsebeth's gown tore suddenly as Bernard lost all reservation of his desire. The silk moved apart, like wet paper between his hands. Bernard breathed in Elsebeth, as he pulled himself into her. She was pained, just a little. She pretended Bernard was making her pregnant. She hoped that there would be no signs of human blood coursing through the child's veins. Bernard's joy was also Elsebeth's pain as she thought about the betrayal she had committed towards her mate. Bernard could not, nor was he trying, to read Elsebeth's mind. He didn't have the slightest notion he was unintentionally being deceived. Elsebeth took advantage of his distraction in making love. She thought these things, but briefly. Bernard would wake her from her subtle trance by thrusting himself in her yet again. He stopped, not abruptly, however. He lingered there, inside her. He retracted himself slowly, as he stared at her.

They lay next to each other, glistening in sweat. The castle had never been so quiet. Later that night, without telling anyone else their secret, they flew to a nearby province. They approached the town separately. They fed on a pair of drunken sailors each. They were deprived of nourishment, so they killed more than their normal ration. It seemed as though Elsebeth's hunger had increased, leaving her very little room for human compassion. She had been hungry like that once before, when she prepared to birth Desmony. The blood tasted different when she was with child. It was sweeter than normal. It gave her the strength to endure the changes her body underwent. The next morning, the sailors were found in an alley. Their pockets were empty with their wallets on the floor. A jagged blade was discovered not far away. The townspeople chalked it up to a random robbery and murder.

Despite the increased feedings, this gestation was much easier for Elsebeth than Desmony's. Blythe supported her, as always. Elsebeth's father was another source of strength for her. By human standards, Elsebeth was stronger than most men, if not all human men. As a vampire, however, she was highly vulnerable at that time. This pregnancy also sparked the interest of Alec when he spoke with Blythe. She responded gravely to him. "I can't bear any child. In fact, I still don't and may never understand how Elsebeth can have children. Of the few vampires I've had the occasion of knowing, none have ever conceived. I had intended for my life to play out much differently than it has. My children were to have my heart and my husband's strength. That will never be. Alec, please, don't ever ask me about this again." That was all Blythe was to ever say about the subject. If Alec was to learn more, it would be from Bernard, or some other source. The conversation made Alec very sad, but Blythe made him happy again, as they lay in her bed.

Blythe dreamed as she slept next to Alec. The current man in her life was nothing like the others of before. When Blythe was a human, just before she was made undead, she was joyfully in love with a young man, Michael Dites. He was a favorite of the community, having his choice of young maidens. His love was Blythe. She was rich in color, as well as grace. She made him laugh, not as a joke, but as a trait that wasn't acceptable for young ladies, but it was her spirit. They planned to marry, and make their home in Blythe's native land, Sweden. To Blythe's dismay, another young man had found love in Blythe's character. He was new to the land, a traveler that now had reason to settle down. His name was

Hlival. He was from another land, but learned how to communicate well, and quickly. He was a striking man, but frightfully pale. He claimed to have a harmless skin condition that restricted him to venture out only at night.

This man was able to rule the mind of Blythe's family at will, making their decision to disallow the marriage of Blythe to Michael. All were convinced, except for Blythe. She knew her heart, but Hlival was too strong. One evening, Blythe went against her parents, and confronted Hlival. She called him a warlock of some kind, and demanded that he remove whatever spell he had placed on the family and her betrothed. He responded by laughing at her. He said he would do as he wished. Blythe was amazed at Hlival's cruelty. He decided that he no longer wanted to do the honorable thing. He wanted her, so at that moment of their argument, he jerked her neck to his mouth and tore into her flesh. Before she knew it, she was no longer the pure girl she once was. She was dying, quickly. The next time she woke, she was a prisoner to a crypt as her bed and the moon was her sun. In time, after Blythe convinced him that she had accepted her fate, Hlival taught her how to survive, and she learned, well. She had no intention to remain by his side. She would learn how to beat him, destroy him.

Hlival knew that Blythe planned revenge. As a precaution, Hlival transformed Blythe's entire family. The parents were killed, outright. Bernard was made into a vengeful, hateful creature. For a century, the siblings learned what was necessary to survive. Hlival tried to change their desire to exact revenge, but he never would be able to be pardoned for his rash decision and ruthless behavior. Rather than hold to his mistake, Hlival chose to destroy his non-compliant students. Blythe and Bernard took every opportunity to try and outwit the cunning and crazed vampire. They could never succeed as they were too young and Hlival would never teach them every trick he had learned.

Early one cool morning, Hlival overtook both Bernard and Blythe. He was still so much stronger that they together. He strapped them to a sturdy rock on a lonely mountainside. They were to die there, for one last time, as an inconvenience to Hlival. Blythe, being the older of the fraternal twins, was given the duty of thinking under such great pressure. She was accustomed to this, so she planned as the sun rose. She may not have known all of Hlival's tricks, but she was very resourceful. Blythe wore a lorgnette her grandmother had given her, when she died. The light made the ropes burn as the magnifying glass intensified the heat. Just before sun break, the ties broke free.

Bernard and Blythe took to the nearest, darkest, coldest area they could find. They first tore their clothes off, so it would appear they turned to ash in the sun. Some chiseled rock sufficed as charred bone. Their plan worked.

The two found clothing nearby, at their home of old. They took one last look around. Their parents had since been buried. The house had been locked up until distant relatives could claim the family fortune. Blythe and Bernard took what they could. Hlival had left. He was off to find another family to annihilate.

Blythe stopped her nightmare, her recollection of her origins as a vampire. She was to marry, have Michael's child, and make sure Bernard matured into a strong and responsible man. All of that was robbed from her by Hlival. That was what Bernard had known, which made it no surprise when he took Elsebeth the way he did. The difference was Elsebeth wasn't promised to another. She wasn't clouded by magic of any kind. Her family wasn't murdered. Finally, she wasn't deprived the chance to say good-bye. Blythe thought so, but Elsebeth thought different. She didn't say her fare well's to being human either. That was something that would haunt her in the life of her unborn child.

CHAPTER SEVEN

Elsebeth dropped a pitcher of water as the pains struck her. She knelt down. A quiet moan was all she let out. Her intention was to try and deliver the child alone, whimpering all the while. She was afraid that a human trait would be obvious upon birth. Blythe passed where Elsebeth had fallen to the ground. Blythe ran full speed to her aid. She reached Elsebeth within seconds. Elsebeth was in hard labor, but she wouldn't accept help. She shivered with the pain that shouted through her body. "Leave me! If I do wrong and the child die, it will be best. If it lives, I may want to die!" Elsebeth looked positively wild. Blythe took her ranting as a woman in intense pain. "You have a fever! You're talking mad! Lay here, be still and I shall return. Blythe did her best. Elsebeth had been eating herself alive through her pregnancy with the guilt of betraying Bernard.

The thought of Elsebeth actually wishing for the death of her child to keep her secret terrified her, but she couldn't hold it in any longer. Fortunately, Blythe didn't take her seriously. The contractions intensified, becoming closer and closer. Her confession was dismissed, even though it was a non-comprehensible testimony, it was ignored. The delivery wasn't delayed. The baby was born, in total silence. It was born healthy, and with no initial detectable signs of its possible human influence. After she was cleaned and cared for, Blythe introduced the child that was forever to be called Morgana to the family. Elsebeth lay in her bed, in a horrible limbo. She wanted to love the child, but if Bernard ever found out! He could and with all rights would destroy her!

Bernard entered the room with the slow beauty of a flower that wakes up with the morning sun. He smiled as a blossomed flower would, because he was holding his new daughter, Morgana. "She is a true beauty, just as Desmony was, and is." Both Bernard and Elsebeth laid together on the bed, drowning in thought. Elsebeth's secret was safe, for now. Later in the evening, just before dawn, Bernard got up to prepare the room for the awakening sun. He placed large metal sheets over the eyes of the home, which were the large and open windows. The baby stirred, and began to cry. Bernard started for Morgana, but Elsebeth awoke and held Bernard back. "She needs me now. Finish the room, my dear." She suckled the child, their child. Elsebeth didn't hate the child, but her shame at first kept her quite distant. For now, she must not create any suspicion to her guilt.

Elsebeth held the babe close to her and spoke. "Mother loves you. I truly do, for many reasons. I care for your true father. I love the only father you will ever know. I can't be angry at you; it isn't your fault. You are beautiful. I'll always hold you and love as long as you want me to. I'm so sorry I wasn't happy at first. Both of my daughters will be loved, as much as each of you desire." Elsebeth lifted Morgana up and held her over her shoulder. Bernard concentrated on them both, looking slightly puzzled. "Don't love one more than the other. I see how you are looking at Morgana. Don't pay her more attention, love. Any child that is lesser loved will hate the other, or you, or both of you at worse! I won't stand for that, please." Bernard and Elsebeth reclined with Morgana and rested all day. Morgana lay with her parents, but Morgana didn't sleep.

Morgana showed no signs of being half human, as a child born of a vampire. Morgana would be visibly human, until she reached puberty, and became unborn. This realization was the only thing that held Elsebeth together through Morgana's early development. She was a particularly gentle child, playing with all the nature that surrounded her. She nurtured small animals, while Desmony teased her. Desmony played devilishly with Morgana, threatening to suck the creatures dry. Since she still was under a form of house arrest, Desmony had no choice but to feed on whatever she could, since her appetite had not subsided in her near century of feeding. Desmony managed to look after Morgana, much like an older sister would. She never hid any of her vampire habits. No one did really. It was seen as normal to Morgana. She wondered why she couldn't do the things they all did, like fly and change her appearance, among other skills. Blythe explained to her that she would do all those things and more, in due time.

Morgana laughed and played in the sun. That was her time alone. She slept at night, which kept her family from attending to her very much. This caused her to be self-sufficient, which seemed to come natural to her. However, it was difficult on Elsebeth, as her mother. She had to play with Morgana inside, behind heavy metal slabs that covered the walls. She fed her and cared for her, but it made Elsebeth very weak. She had to stay awake during her usual time of rest. She didn't remember that part bothering her quite so much with Desmony. Desmony was a restless child, but she helped Elsebeth care for Morgana when she saw Elsebeth becoming too weary. As a reward for her sibling support, she was allowed to venture out, alone. She finally began to feed more responsibly. Desmony didn't want to ruin the privilege of her loosened leash, even though it was certainly tempting. Alec shared the concerns of the others that Desmony may not have beaten her blood lust, so he took it upon himself to shadow Desmony, just to assure her safety, if nothing else. Alec wasn't an avid hunter, but he was skilled enough to remain undetected, even to Desmony who tried to discover ways to be a superior vampire every chance she had.

Morgana continued to grow into a lovely child. She was every bit as wonderful and full of life as Desmony had been, as a human, but the similarities ended there. Morgana wasn't nearly as mischievous as Desmony was. She was tranquil in her play time. Desmony wanted to be a vampire, very much. Morgana didn't inquire about what Blythe did, or why father did that. She simply didn't seem to care. She observed everything, and as she got older, knew that her instinct would ignite her interest in their world. It just wasn't a part of 'her world' yet. Morgana seemed to fear it, resist it. Desmony didn't approve of Morgana's lack of interest in becoming a vampire. It reminded her of their mother's infidelity, and how Morgana was proving to be the living flesh product of that event. Desmony's thoughts caused her to flare up at the child, for no apparent reason. "One day, I'll hurt you! Don't ever forget that! Morgana, don't ever forget, I can always hurt you more than you could ever dream of hurting me!" Desmony was a master of manipulation and control, especially if her will was stronger than her opponent.

Morgana was still so young and naïve. She didn't understand why Desmony was so cold and abrasive to her. Desmony's treatment bewildered Bernard as well. He tried his best to stay neutral, but with Desmony constantly attacking Morgana, he seldom took Desmony's side. All tried to have compassion and understanding towards Desmony, but her bitterness made it nearly impossible. Elsebeth could get in, where no one else could. Desmony and Elsebeth had a bond that went deeper than any relation Desmony had with anyone in her family. Elsebeth was the only person that could keep Desmony under control. Desmony minded her father, merely out of shame for something she had done prior. Elsebeth quickly lost patience with Desmony. Desmony continued to ruin any attempts Elsebeth made at trying to forget the past events that made Desmony as spiteful as she was and Elsebeth as remorseful as she was.

Morgana slept, peacefully, as the sun hovered lazily in the sky. Her dreams soothed her as she lay perfectly still. She lay out in the fields, not far from home while the others slept. Something awakened Morgana in her subconscious. The sun had made its appearance for the day, and was bowing out. When the first signs of dark came, Morgana began to stir. She opened her eyes, not really expecting to see anything but the budding stars. What she saw was a vicious face, staring back at her. The creature was hideous, frothing from the mouth. The fangs on this animal nearly reached its chin, which was covered with fur. Its beaming red eyes stared right into Morgana's quivering heart. When Morgana's eyes came fully into focus, she saw the creature changing. It was her sister, Desmony. She got a perverse thrill out of unnerving her sister, who was still in a state of *human-vampire* limbo. By this time, the daylight began to make her weak. For the most part, she was human. She liked being different than her family. She was emotionally sophisticated enough to deduce that she didn't want the life that they portrayed as normal.

Morgana was also beginning to feel some of her inner and outer strength coming in. She lost her human fear for the horrible beasts that surrounded her. "Damn your spiteful soul! Why do you find such pleasure in torturing me?" Morgana was livid. Desmony was weak. The sun still reflected in the pond on the west side. She needed more rest, so she declined from a confrontation with Morgana. "Oh, go back to sleep. I was just letting you know what it is you have in store. What we have is a gift. It's an extra power that we have. Don't be so in love with your human side. Despite our weaknesses, we are still superior." Desmony reclined and Morgana closed her eyes, but they soon found their way open, again.

Only a short while passed before Morgana began to really feel the change coming. She could feel the sweat surface from her very soul. The feeling of her human death made her extremely frightened. She felt intense nausea. At times, she would become violently ill without warning. The filth that surrounded her disgusted her. Her family supported her, but they really could do nothing to ease her discomfort. Her teeth became sharper as she wiped her mouth after being sick. Her tears streaked her face. She mourned her own death. She would miss what she was. Morgana wondered if she would remember any of her human childhood. The thoughts were shattered with each new pang of her vampire side awakening. Her skin became paler. Her nails grew at an unnatural rate, Morgana cried constantly. Disturbing visions intensified her fever as she absorbed the thoughts and memories of her family members.

Morgana thought about the face Desmony created and scared her with. Seeing the changes within her, being conscious of it all, was the cruelest part. Part of her wanted to stop it, if she could. There was no chance of it. There was a very small, yet a very real part of her that was intrigued by it all. "Please stop! Please go away! I can't stand it! I don't want it. Please, please, please, no!" Morgana raged and screamed, all day and all night. The fighting made her journey much more unbearable. Elsebeth tried to help her as much as possible. Then, her wings came. The power of it in the room was enough to make Desmony change. She could barely stand it. She had an intense desire to kill someone. She was excited by it to no end. Desmony stood in the hallway, just outside of Morgana's room. She actually salivated at her sister's cries of pain. 'I hope she becomes more fun. We'll finally have something in common!" She smothered her desire to feed. Desmony levitated a few inches off of the floor and floated down the hallway and then the stairs.

A few days passed before the initial attack awarded Morgana any rest. She began the recovery process. She dragged herself down the stairs. Everyone had just awakened and was conferring the providence's that each was to cover. They looked up and saw Morgana there. There was no joy or sensation of achievement in her face. Everyone responded with uncertain stares. Desmony walked over to Morgana and said, "Finally, you're one of us. I've wanted to show you this life for a long time. Come on, I'll take you out for a bite, your first." Desmony actually acted choked up with emotion. Morgana stood there, in her cotton gown, drenched with sweat. She put a lot of thought into justifying killing others, in order to sustain her life and benefit her new quality of life. "I must get ready. Take me to a port or an inn" was all Morgana said. The hunger was undeniably there, but the desire was lacking severely. It was a truth that Morgana faced prior to her descent. She was ill and blood was her only treatment.

Morgana had no desire to feed, even though she knew she must. She didn't know how she was going to pull someone to her, and take their life away. Morgana made herself presentable, with the help of Elsebeth. Elsebeth looked pitifully at her youngest daughter. She knew her heart and could recall easily when she had to make her first kill. Elsebeth thought so that Morgana could her. She gave her words of consolation and encouragement. Morgana smiled at her mother and let her new wings unfold from her back. The sensation was a little uncomfortable, but exhilarating at the same time. Morgana seemed to take to the changes instinctively, which caused her some surprise, but she grew up watching everyone do the things that she was now doing herself. Desmony bellowed a terrifying shriek and yanked Morgana's arm. Before anyone could say good-bye, or wish them well, they broke through the front door. Elsebeth watched them ascend to the sky, almost kissing the moon. "Be one of us dear. Become your destiny, your legacy. You must, or you shall die." Elsebeth closed the door and hugged Blythe.

As they searched along the river Seine, they did not steal through the night. Desmony pranced along the streets in one of the small towns. Everyone focused on her. Morgana tried to keep up with Desmony. Morgana looked very unenthusiastic and a bit awkward, not complementary to the attitude Desmony was emitting. Desmony exhaled with disgust and waited for Morgana to catch up. "Come on! There are a lot of needy, lonely, and drunk sailors covering that area. No one will miss one or two. Who knows, maybe we'll even get three!" Desmony giggled and kept her brisk pace. She could smell the blood all around her. The movement of the water was hypnotizing. The sound of blood swirling through all of the passersby veins almost made Desmony drunk herself. They arrived shortly after at the only inn the town had. Right away they were bombarded by women starved men.

"Hello. My name is Guillaume. You, my pretty, pretty lady may call me Guy. I haven't seen either of you two around here. Where are you from?" As Guy moved closer towards them, he smothered them with his intense stare. "It matters not where we are from." Morgana was behaving slightly suspicious, but it came across as nervousness. Morgana began to see rather quickly by how the women around her behaved, that she was expected to perform certain tasks, doing things that she had never done before. She had never been with a man before. It was terribly apparent that she was going to have to grow up, quicker than she ever thought. She thought about how Elsebeth taught her to pretend. She imagined herself being an entirely different person. She didn't think about what she was about to do, try to do, to that person, whoever they were. "Well, sir, it is a good thing you haven't seen us here before. We wouldn't want you to think we were used to this atmosphere. We have lost our escort and thought it would be best to seek refuge in this establishment."

Desmony eased into a chair and brushed her locks out of her face. Morgana stood behind her. Morgana was gripping Desmony's shoulders so tightly her nails almost pierced Desmony's shoulders. Desmony winced in pain and swatted Morgana hand away immediately. Morgana finally became composed and reluctantly began to play along. Morgana felt a gnawing at her stomach. It wasn't like the hunger she felt as a human. It made her feel as though she was dying. Her breathing was becoming shallow. She was beginning to perspire, but it didn't show just yet. She hid her shaking hands while she tried to look conscious. "My chum over there with the green eyes and I were looking for some companionship tonight. My previous lady friend and her cousin recently got married. It was a double ceremony. Anyway, I was hoping you would like to take a walk and have a drink with us?" Guy stroked Desmony's hand, making her all the more anxious. She had him right where she wanted him. "Let's go," was all Desmony said.

The foursome got up and followed Desmony's lead. She knew the area well enough to find the most deserted locations. Even though the city was almost pitch black, the moonlight lighted the river created a setting that would mystify most other couples. Morgana saw the beauty of the evening. All Desmony saw was the perfect setting for a feeding. Guy and his friend, *son coupain,* began to feel a little nervous, but a bit more intrigued. They traveled up across several lush mounds then they descended into a small valley. The world was asleep. The world was unaware.

They arrived in a deserted pasture. "I love the night!" Desmony was truly in her comfort zone. Guy ran to where Desmony had stopped. He offered a bottle of ale to her that he liberated from the inn. "No, I don't drink that. When I'm thirsty, you'll know." She pushed the bottle out of the way. Desmony went over to where Morgana's and Guy's friend were standing. They were both quiet. They appeared to be awkward with one another, like they were at their first social dance. Desmony moved Morgana aside. "Darling, your appetizer awaits. I'm going over that hill, there. Don't mess this up, all right? He will more than likely to try and touch you, in a way you've never been touched. Most women like that. Follow his lead, then go for his throat, as you kiss him!" Desmony stroked Morgana's flowing straight hair. "He seems nice. Must we do this to them?" Morgana was so timid. She heard every word Desmony said, but she didn't have the heart to do what was in her nature, yet she was so hungry. "You wait. They change quicker than we do." Desmony whirled around and skipped to where her *date* was. She then escorted him to what would be the place his body was to be discovered.

"I suppose I should tell you my name. It's Martin. I'm from Whales. What's your name?" He sat next to a nearby tree. "Melissa. How long have you been here?" Morgana was beginning to like him. That was what she was never supposed to do. She started to think about backing out. The only problem was Desmony. She wouldn't allow her to let one of the boys get away. It would destroy everything for them. "Well, shall we get started, love?" Martin took off his coat He smelled her hair as he moved to untie her cape. "What are you doing?" Morgana was stunned. She thought he was nice, that she should spare his life. "What comes naturally, lass." He smiled, and proceeded to undress her. "Stop this now!" Morgana tried to stand to get away from this Jekyll and Hyde creature. Morgana couldn't believe how right Desmony was. "Now listen. I want you. There's no harm in this. Trust me, you won't regret this." He pulled her back down to him aggressively.

Martin was sweating heavily from the ale, as well as from tussling with the brazen beauty. He was already panting, but smiling with the joy of the struggle that "Melissa" had put up. "You shouldn't do this. Stop it! You won't be able to do that again. I have never been with a man. I won't be with one like you. You have no honor or respect. Don't force me to hurt you!" Morgana could feel the tears rise up in her eyes. "If you don't hurt me, I won't hurt you, all right? You must forget, I'm stronger than you." Martin tried to embrace her and kiss her, but she swatted him with one blow, like a fly. Martin picked himself up from the ground. He couldn't believe the distance her strike had sent him. He lunged at her with a hateful masque on his face. She met his roar with a bigger one. Morgana's face began to change, mysteriously. Her fangs jumped out in an instantly. Her large and sympathetic eyes glowed in the dark, like a wolf.

Morgana's eyes danced as she ran towards him. He turned to run, in horror, but she caught his arm, dislocating it as she stopped him. Martin shrieked in pain. He thought the next sound he heard was his voice echoing, but it was Guillaume, dying in the distance. Desmony made it over the hill to in time to see her sister's first kill. Morgana met Martin's throat with her mouth. She hit his jugular the first time. It was very neat and clean. Morgana drank until there was no life left in him.

When Morgana finished, she ran away. She was so good at killing. It scared her that she performed so well. The hunt and the feed went as expected. The entire scene scared her. It disturbed her that she was so good at vanquishing her prey. She didn't enjoy the thought of killing "innocent" people to suit her needs. Desmony found her, grabbed her by the shoulders, and they flew home, silent, in the middle of the night. Morgana spoke to no one when they returned home. She ran to her room, in tears. She was angry at everyone. Why did she have to live like this? It was all their faults. She couldn't change it, and that frustrated her the most. "Don't mind her, she loved it. She was wonderful! I don't know why, but she seems ashamed by it all. Pity about that." Desmony hopped up the staircase, pleased with the evening. She knew why Morgana behaved the way she did. She was innocent until tonight. She had been pure. Now she was on her way to becoming jaded and depraved, like the rest of them. Desmony also hoped that her nature would change, become more on the beastly side after her first kill. Elsebeth looked at everyone bashfully and said, "I'll go and look in on Morgana. The first time can be very traumatic. She was told about everything, but to actually do it, and do it well is another story. Not every vampire enjoys their diet." Alec felt a little curious. Even he enjoyed the taste of blood.

CHAPTER EIGHT

Morgana's depression over her first kill lasted for some time. Desmony tried tirelessly to bring Morgana out of her funk, but nothing would work. Only until she was desperately weak, and had no choice, she would accompany Desmony to feed and strike quick and with dangerous accuracy. The area was becoming too small for them to feed locally. Once again, stories of devil creatures began popping up. The family was so different that they attracted attention without trying. They could not dispel any rumors that would originate from their eccentricities. They decided it was time to move on. They had seen enough of Europe through their travels and looked forward to putting some distance between their current home and themselves. Each family member knew several languages. This would make their transition much more easy. For what Morgana had not experienced, she learned from books. Women weren't encouraged to be book learned, but Morgana was not to be bound by social prejudice.

Everyone in the family could easily adapt to any culture they might experience. They were due for a change. They needed a challenge. The orient was too extreme. They debated over the location of their next home. They decided that the new land called the Americas would be their destination.

They studied the progressing American culture. It was difficult to really get a grasp on it, since the inhabitants were so diverse. The land was open, filled with people from many nations, and from many walks of life. The most prominent of the newer cultures were the English. The land was still being sought out by many people, which was too opportune for the Mal family. They studied what they could about America. They consumed every piece of information they found in books, as well as Americans traveling abroad. The family spared the people they interviewed, in exchange for the information. They found that the land was wide, spacious, and uninhabited. The move toward the west of the Americas hadn't come to pass yet. The states that were developing wouldn't be united for some time. The eastern territory was still evolving and being occupied by whatever country thought they had a right to it. Namely the new settlers from England and established themselves, building relations with the Native Americans in the north and the French and Spanish in the south. Their move would be simple, judging by the barren land that spread out before all that had settled there.

The thought of the dry winds blowing sand made Elsebeth think back to Spain. This was something she had promised herself not to do. "It'll be different, I know. I will never have that again." Elsebeth finished packing, and resumed dreaming of anything but her mortal lover.

Alec made all of the arrangements. He spoke with the captain of a vessel that was to transport some "possessions" of a well-respected family. They were in seclusion, and wished not to be disturbed by other passengers. Of course, they wanted their personal belongings to reach their new home first. They would arrive, shortly thereafter, in another ship. It was made clear no questions were to be asked, so none were. The Mal family stole onto the ship in the middle of the night., making no one aware they had stowed away. The gusts created by their flight to the ship took on the sensation of a slightly higher wind over the heads of the crew. They appeared as a large migration of birds in the new moon sky. No one was the wiser, which was best, for the crew.

The ship traveled for several months on sometimes life threatening seas. The journey, for most, was difficult. When the vessel would port, The Mal family made stray locals their victims and drained the blood so they could have a decent supply until the next time they docked. They were rather weak, due to the fact they couldn't feed very often. Killing any passengers would be foolish. The thought did cross Desmony's mind, purely for the fun and excitement of it.

Alec and Elsebeth would sit where no one would bother them sometimes and reminisce about their home in England as they moved further away from their European continent. "People only wake up screaming if they have dreams like this reality we're living." Elsebeth took a deep sigh and Alec kissed his "little girl" on the brow and thought of the lush green land he had to leave, now centuries ago. He also let a stray thought go to his wife, Elsebeth's mother. "How her heart must ache over the way our lives have developed. What we've become is beyond human comprehension. I'm afraid the shock of it all would've killed her also. She is better to not see us this way. To see her grandchildren, her legacy as creatures that feed on humans, well, it isn't what she deserved. But do not mistake me, my Elsebeth. I do love my grandchildren, as I love you. It just isn't fair, is all. It simply isn't fair." Alec rested his head on Elsebeth's shoulder as they began to sleep during the coming day. "I know, papa. I know. What can we do now? So much time has passed. Nothing can be done. We can only look out for one another, and love one another, for who we are, not what we are." Elsebeth shut her eyes, not to open them again, for quite some time.

The nights were stagnating at best. There was no change in scenery for days at a time. To make the time pass, they would stretch their wings, flying around the ship, actually helping the ship move along its course more rapidly. They discussed politics, their hopes for their new life in

America, and their lives as mortals, among lesser things. At night, everyone was lively, while the crew above slept. The crew only knew they were carrying packages and crates, not creatures that were a little more than hungry for their blood, their essence. Desmony had been controlling her desire for the human's blood that was ripe for the taking. They had nowhere to run, nowhere to hide. They were very much like the rat that kept lodging on the ship as well. During the day, as the family slept, Morgana would occasionally wake herself, craving the day, not the blood of the passengers or sailors. She was told that these temptations were not conducive to her existence, so she tried to cure them by consuming as much blood as she could tolerate, which was very little.

Elsebeth had been trying to condition Morgana since she was the one Morgana would come to about her feelings that sympathized with her more human qualities. Desmony also listened to her concerns, but neither could reveal the truth about her conception. It would destroy her, as well as her father. Morgana adored her father. She admired his strength and conviction in the purpose and survival of their family. Their relationship was rich in love. Bernard tried to tolerate her lack of blood lust because he loved her, unconditionally. It may have seemed as though they didn't have a close relationship because Bernard's reserved personality raised concern about that perception. In the family, there was no question. Morgana found that she unintentionally kept away from most of the family. She never felt as though she belonged. She was emotionally torn. She had been since she was made unborn and those feelings weren't close to being resolved. Both her parents filled her with compassion, trying to help her accept herself, love herself, as they loved her. It was difficult, but their love took the sting of her abnormality away from her mind. Desmony would counter act the subtle training Bernard and Elsebeth would give by telling Morgana to, "Love blood, no matter what else. It is your life. The daylight is your death. I don't know why you crave it so! Know what I tell you to be true, and speak no more of it!" That was all Desmony said about the subject, and no more was said about it, for a long while.

They finally reached their destination. The boat docked for its last time with them as passengers, just after dusk. They hung like the rats down below, on the beams that supported the deck and ceiling. They waited until everyone left the ship. All cargo was taken away, including the crates that were to be delivered to the Mal's new home. Fortunately, no one saw the family disembark. That would be a disaster. They would have no trouble defending themselves, but they would be unmasked. Their secret would be revealed. They couldn't afford that. They arrived shortly after all of their belongings were delivered to the new home they would occupy.

They took possession of some land on the very edge of Vermont. It was nice and cool most of the time in the eastern part of what is now the US. Later on, when the warmer months would come, they would venture further north, into Canada, west to Alaska, or further east to Greenland. Their home was a customized one, built for six. It wasn't uncommon, since large families were customary, if not expected. The more developed cities that existed in the area were very attractive to the family, but they fancied their anonymity. They stayed far enough away, so they could feed on the livestock that they had purchased, or taken. They also made brief expeditions into town, so they could acquaint themselves with the local customs, as these people were no longer restricted by laws from their former countries and were taking steps to build a government that would accommodate most, but not for all.

Desmony took on the settlers' ideals about liberation from tyranny. She was the first in the family to break the rules. She flew, one night, to a poor excuse for an inn. She took one man. Desmony seduced him, had him, and fed on him. The physical attraction the man had for Desmony was ignored. She didn't attach herself to prey that way. Using male lust had been and continued to be a tool for Desmony. She enjoyed the physical act of mating, but she really didn't know what it was to have genuine feelings for a mate. She didn't alarm herself over that fact either. That was, as it was to be. She buried the man's remains in a secluded patch of forest. She left, and returned the following night, to see if she had created a "situation". She discovered the man was an overseer. He had just returned from the Caribbean. He had "acquired" several young men and women that were natives from the islands that made up the Caribbean. The new inhabitants of the Americas would not, nor would they ever be seen as fellow countrymen. The journey was not for their betterment. They were brought to the new land to work as slaves for anyone that could afford to buy them.

After Desmony learned this, she reached far down in her soul to think that what he had been doing was unconscionable and cruel. She pretended to look as sad as the ignorant people that actually mourned his loss. As she walked off, she began to smile. She said, "no tremendous loss." That instant, while no one was watching, she grabbed at the air until she was high enough to streak through the sky, unnoticed.

When Desmony returned home, she told only Morgana of her experience. Morgana was furious, but not for the reason Desmony thought. She couldn't bear the thought of some man subjecting another human being to forceful labor, without that person being free to come and go as he or she pleased. She knew of the stories about slavery. There was slavery back in Europe. She saw it first hand, among the finer families. At times, it didn't seem too cruel, but there were other times when an owner of a slave would forget that the person they were whooping for dropping something, or whatever the reason might be, was a human, not a beast. "I

151

just can't understand it. When we make a person into a *watcher,* it's just one, and they protect us. We've never had a watcher, not since father had the butler, before we were born. We, as vampires usually don't force our subjects to help us. They come over on their own free will. It's willful submission, not being captured like a wild stallion, and broken. Slaves are forced to work, even when they can't. Our watchers aren't belittled, de-humanized, or made to represent a "lesser species". They are just like us, you know?" Morgana could've continued, but Desmony was losing interest.

Desmony snapped her fingers. She found a way for her sickly looking sister to feed, without conscience. She stayed with the conversation long enough to make a connection with her interest and her sisters. "That's it! You can feed off these bastards! Not the slaves, the people that bring them over! They're a disgusting lot that take life for granted. Their life is made comfortable while others suffer. We feed to survive. We don't strip hundreds, thousands of people of their heritage, rights, and dignity. That can kill a person slowly, if the disease and malnutrition doesn't first." Desmony had made a formidable pitch, and Morgana bought it. She was hungry and her anger made it very easy.

The rest of the family soon felt comfortable enough to feed occasionally on a lone human, rather than a stray animal. One evening, Morgana was out, primarily to just enjoy the night air. She "appeared" by a tree that was close to some servant's quarters on a nearby mansion. She witnessed one slave being thrashed for spilling a side dish on the dining room carpet. After the beating, the slave was carried off to his poor excuse of a bed. It was really just a wool blanket on the floor. Morgana fumed at what she saw. Her stomach began to growl, and she began to feel a little weak. Her eyes glowed in the night as she observed. The hunger was increasing, which allowed her subconscious desire to feed to corrupt her.

The man that was doing the beating was a hobby of Morgana's. She had become obsessed with him. He was the nastiest man to hold the position of overseer. He enjoyed the tyranny he enforced on the enslaved blacks. Morgana had feasted on a few that encouraged the institution of slavery, but not enough. She was fasting, for the man that was called Mr. Neely. She wanted him to feel all the pain that the broken people, torn away from their families felt. She knew a little about disrupted lives from her grandfather and mother. It was quite possible that her ancestry made her more sympathetic than normal. She tried not to blame her father. He was blinded by love, and was a very different person then. Morgana flicked her straight mink-like hair away from her face. "It is time, Mr. Neely. You have ruined your last life. Now, I'm going to ruin yours." Morgana rose up and hovered over Neely as he stumbled over to the women's quarters.

Mr. Neely went in briefly and came back out with a demure young woman, with flawless features. She was tattooed with bruises from a beating a few nights ago. Morgana had seen this beautiful creature, but not like this. She could see inside her. She saw the kind, gentle creature that cared for her family, before she was taken away in the Caribbean. She was tortured repeatedly by Mr. Neely. He seemed to pick on her. Possibly it was because she was so beautiful, any man, black or otherwise, would want her under more racially liberal circumstances. The girl's name was Nola. She was a strong and willful girl. She was, however, losing the struggle to fight Mr. Neely, as he sullied her, time and time again. Her friends cried and pleaded as he yanked her past the threshold. Nola was not safe any place and she knew this. She was numb to all of the terror and ugliness put upon her for the past four years. She was silent. She said nothing to him as Mr. Neely dragged her into the nearby barn.

"Come on love, you know it's better with a little noise." Mr. Neely slobbered on her frail bosom as he slurped up some ale. His touch repulsed her to no end. Mr. Neely laughed a bitter, hateful laugh. He threw the now empty bottle across the floor. It crashed up against a wall. There were a few horses in the stable. Most stirred at the shattering sound. Nola tried to close her mind to it all, but she simply couldn't. He reeked so badly. Every move he made on her caused her to crave death or some form of escape. When he exhaled on her, the smell and the whistling sound almost made her lose consciousness. The violation to Nola's senses and of her body made her wretch several times. Neely was too drunk to care. He had no ulterior motive other than to disgrace this little black slave. Morgana had seen enough. She moved in closer. Morgana landed quietly behind Neely. "You beat one and you rape the other. Neither is better." Morgana stood firmly as she spoke. Neely spun around, and Morgana gripped his bloated throat. Morgana turned her head and looked to the poor girl, wrapped up in a ball, eyes wide with fear and shivering. "Close your eyes darling. Close your eyes or I will have to deal with you as well."

Morgana stared pitifully at Nola. Nola got up and ran into a vacant stall. Morgana slid her fingers out from around Neely's throat. As her nail struck his jugular, blood sprayed the stable wall next to Nola. Morgana kept Neely standing with one hand and tilted his head with the other. She drank his blood, despite his rank body odor. The blood tasted like the ale he had been choking down. It was warm, yet his stench defeated the triumph of the feed. Morgana let his fat, grotesque body fall, like a thud, to the floor. She wiped her mouth with her ruffled handkerchief. Nola peered out from her shelter. She was terrified, but somehow intrigued. "Thank you. How'd you do that? He was over two hundred pounds!" Despite all that Nola had been through, she was glad and forced a smile. She looked at the disgusting mass of man that lay before her. She thanked her God that he was gone. Nola was spared another night of shame, pain, and humiliation.

"You must put all of this out of your mind." Morgana liked Nola from the first time she saw her. She didn't want to hurt her. Morgana's concern was that Nola had seen too much and would talk. Too much had happened for this to be covered up easily, but would anyone really believe her? There were too many people around that saw Neely take Nola, but how would she explain his death and her survival? Surely the other maids and slaves were looking to see when Nola would reappear, after her routine violation. Nola stayed on the ground. She was on her knees. She looked up at Morgana. She had to do something. She didn't want Morgana to start in on her, so she tried speaking to her. "They will blame me for this. You must help me leave, or they will kill me. I don't want to die! I don't deserve this. Please, I just don't deserve this." Nola pleaded with her, sobbing all the while. Her bottom hit the ground. She slumped down to rest her rattling bones.

Morgana paced the stable floor. Nola watched her as her life hung in the balance. The wind had picked up, swirling Morgana's straight hair all around. All of Morgana's hair swirled out, as if she were standing on an electrical conductor. The image that Morgana exuded nearly gave Nola a seizure. "You know of me. You know what I do. I can kill you too, or I can grant your wish and take you far away, or I can let you stay with me and my family. I just can't risk you to simply run away. I could try to make you forget, but I don't know exactly if I possess that skill just yet. I feel as though I can trust you, but I can't be a fool either." Morgana knelt down and studied Nola. Nola's fate was still undetermined, but there was the problem of the dead man in the barn. "What are we going to do about Neely?" Nola tried to look at him, but she was so disgusted by his memory that she couldn't. It was strange that the blood and gore that was all around her didn't bother her as much.

"This is how we will get rid of old Mr. Neely." Right before Nola's eyes, Morgana fell out of her clothes and onto all fours. Fur covered her body. Parts of her anatomy grew, while others shrank and curved. Her body pulsated, contorted, and pulled at itself. Before she knew it, Morgana was a beautiful heaving wolf-dog. She walked over to Neely and tore at his throat. Morgana then looked at Nola, who was picking up her clothes, hoping to prove herself as a useful helper. Morgana said, "Come, follow me." The words floated into Nola's head. She wasn't stunned. It was possibly being caught up in all the excitement, but she kept her wits about her. Nola followed her calmly. They left the corpse on the ground.

Many stories would be generated. The most popular was that a wild animal smelled the sex, found the two, and attacked Neely first, by chance. Then, the animal chased down Nola, who couldn't have gotten far. When she tried to escape, the animal caught her, and dragged her into the night and thrashed her small frame in the nearby river, where the current swept her body away. Nola was dead to those that knew her. Morgana made sure to tear some of Nola's raggedy dress and staged it on a river rock to help the authorities piece together the night's events.

Nola followed Morgana as they traveled through the night. They picked up the pace as they moved through the brush that surrounded the owner's land. No one would hurt Nola while Morgana was with her, no one ever.

The distance back to Morgana's home was a little more difficult for Nola to endure. Morgana remained in the beast form that she had started the journey on. It improved Nola's chances of being protected, without sacrificing Morgana's true identity. The hour was so late, that no one was about. The terrain soon became a struggle for Nola. It wasn't so much the fact that Morgana was in a form more conducive to travel. Morgana was simply stronger than Nola, or any human, for that matter. Several times, Nola fell hard to the ground. Fortunately, she didn't sustain any serious injuries. Morgana offered to change, but Nola insisted she was fine. She was running on adrenaline and the hope of freedom.

Despite all that had transpired that evening, they both took a moment out to observe the serenity of the moon that brightened the sky for a short distance. "It's so peaceful. I miss the sun I saw before the change, but this is nice also."

Morgana sounded a little wishful. There was so much about this strange creature Nola didn't understand. How could a beast that was so destructive appreciate the beauty of nature? Most would see Morgana as an abomination of nature, but Nola didn't. She was fascinated. She imagined how hated Morgana would be, if people knew the truth about her. It was always told in stories how black, evil, horrible creatures were to be feared and destroyed whenever possible. Nola only saw a person with feelings, compassion, and tolerance for things different than she. Morgana was a person that was different, due to circumstances out of her control. Nola thought about how others saw her. She felt like a freak at times. Hardly anyone that wasn't of color accepted her. They definitely didn't appreciate her. Many people would just prefer that people like Nola would be sacrificed at birth, leaving the ones that were already alive to be annihilated in mass quantities.

Nola definitely understood the sadness that Morgana displayed. Nola initiated the conversation with Morgana on how they felt like outcasts. Even though their situations were completely different, there was more to what was seen on the surface for both of them. Nola had taken for granted that being a vampire was just victimizing humans, preying on them for blood, Like the stories told to her as a girl. Now, she saw a different picture, as Morgana painted it for her. Morgana sat solemnly, and described what it was like to be such a rare form of creature. Nola smiled and they reassured each other. A bond of trust was forming at an accelerated pace.

Nola still pointed out, to Morgana's dismay the truth about Morgana being a vampire and Nola being of color. "I don't need to kill to survive. Well, other humans, I mean. If you could live without doing that, I bet you wouldn't have it so hard! I'm trapped because of my skin. People think I'm less because of it. You, you are controlled by such a force that I don't think anyone could understand your kind. It is such a shame people are so mean!" This was probably the first time Nola truly got to express herself. Morgana was really listening to her, which made her feel brilliant, for once in her life. Morgana answered Nola's observation with sage summation. "It is fear and ignorance, Nola. It would take a great power to rid everyone of that. Everyone is born with both. Some choose to change, but others never try. It will take a lot of fighting on the part of good people, such as yourself, before any changes are made. People need to realize they can't continue to teach hatred for people and things, simply because it or they are different."

Morgana began to feel as though she were speaking to a younger sister. It was nice to have an opinion, and not have it shot down by Desmony's tart remarks. Most of the family agreed with Morgana, but Nola was relatively young, as close to Morgana as any human could, at least for the time being. They were friends, and there was no turning back. Nola reached over for Morgana's hand. That was the first time Nola forgot to be afraid of Morgana. She resolved to be her friend and consoled her by saying, "I bet they'd listen to you!" Nola was silent then they broke out in a girlish giggle. Nola was the only person visible laughing, so she had to control herself. They got up and carried on until they reached both their new home.

Everyone stared in amazement as the door closed shut. Morgana walked in with her new found friend without warning. It was quite a surprise to everyone. It was as if she had brought home a puppy or something. In some ways, she had. Nola's first contact with Neely was when he and his crew captured her cousins and her at a town party one night. Nola had been separated from them for years now. She had also been raped of her family, her dignity, and then physically. They were subjected to the same harsh conditions as some other slaves that Morgana had witnessed on the ship next to hers as she disembarked. Morgana could see this as she looked into Nola's eyes. Now, Nola had a look of such hope on her face.

Nola was gripping Morgana's hand so tightly. She was walking in the proverbial "lion's den". She could sense the power in the room. Nola wanted that power. She needed it. "This is Nola, everyone. She is my friend." Morgana escorted Nola into the middle of the family room. Nola wasn't sure how these creatures were feeling inside. Their uneasiness could have been just as easily from fear than from rage. Nola's voice cracked as she spoke. "Hello. Please don't fear me, if that is even possible. I'm sure you don't. I won't tell nobody about this, not ever! If I have to serve you people for the rest of my life to survive, I will, especially if you are like Morgana. She saved me from a horrible life. If I have to live a life not by my own choosing, I'd at least like to choose who I will serve. I will protect you all, like Morgana has done for me, just help me."

Despite the sympathetic look Morgana displayed for the entire room, Nola was still unsure as to if she would be dinner or not. She continued to speak. "I am from the islands, just south of the coast with the big water. My family was destroyed when a man named Mr. Neely came and took me and my cousins away. I even had a brother. They killed him for not working hard enough. He was proud, and didn't like how he was treated. After he died, I was taken away, sold, and made into a woman fast. I was twelve then. Mr. Neely did it to me. He hated me, but he still would take me. He beat me somethin' horrible too. He beat me more than the other slaves sometimes. When he would, I'd picture myself back home, with my mama and daddy. Maybe one day, us slaves can be free, but there is no hope for me to live now. I don't think I'll ever be free, though. I'll always be dark, and judged for that, if nothing else. I can't live that way anymore. Morgana changed my destiny. My prayers were answered. Whether it was by the lord, I do not know. One thing's for sure, I'll never betray you, ever!"

CHAPTER NINE

Blythe stood up and crossed the floor to where the uncertain girl stood. "My dear, I'm sure Morgana had very good reasons to bring you here. I know you realize that if you want to "live", as it were, there is only one choice." Blythe watched her carefully to see if she was beginning to change her mind. "I know that. Do what you have to, I'm ready. I want to belong somewhere and have people around me that care for me. Morgana cares for me, so I will do what I have to so I can be with her. So far, none of you seem to hate the sight of me. That's a start." Nola looked down. She was trying very hard not to cry. She stood firm, however. Her perspiration betrayed her image of fearlessness.

"To kill, we drain you of your blood. To make you as we are, we share blood. To make you a watcher, you take our blood." Desmony's words hypnotized the eager Nola. Each family member opened a vein. They let their blood drip into an old chalice. Morgana carried the cup filled with eternal life to Nola. She enveloped the large cup in her small but chaffed hands. "May God forgive me. It's strange, though. I feel like I'm leaving hell, not going to it. I know I'm forsaking God. I'm so sorry for that. I guess I'm not a strong human being. I should have just died by 'ol Neely's hand. But Morgana changed that, so maybe this was all supposed to happen. Maybe I should've let Morgana take my life and end my suffering. She didn't want to do that. She wanted to help me. I guess I will pay my price for the choices I'm making now when my times finally comes. Maybe I can be some kind of help this way that I couldn't as a human. I don't know, but I feel like this is right. You seem like good people and I just want to help you." Nola lowered her head, and drank. Her head rose up as she took in all the contents of the cup. She drank every last drop. There was no evidence of it on her mouth when she removed the chalice from before her face.

Alec caught the chalice before it struck the ground. Nola fell blindly into the arms of Bernard. He carried her upstairs to a bathing room. The women took wet cloths to her body. They bathed her and put her in a simple but beautiful combed cotton gown. She lay on the bed they set her on, limp, for most of the night. She slept the entire following day as well. Nola became conscious for a short time during the second night. Alec and Morgana were the last to retire for the day. They looked in on Nola before they went to their shielded dark rooms. Nola's transition was significantly less painful than was anticipated. She did experience a fever and profuse sweating, as well as hallucinations. She managed to be either unconscious or semi-conscious through it all. It was a drunken slumber, so she had no control over it.

Each bed had a carpet-like layer of black material on the canopy above them. Nola's was the only exception. Her canopy had a white gauze over it. It was the same bed Lysa had occupied for a short while. "Where is she? Is she alive?" From time to time, Alec would ask these questions, but would keep them to himself. It was understood that Lysa was not a person or subject to be discussed in the house, ever. Alec reflected silently as the family and he waited for Nola to completely recover.

"Good morning my friend, how do you feel?" Morgana was able to stay up, just before the sun had made its appearance for the new day. She was trained to leave before first light, so the sun wouldn't destroy her. She didn't question her training for fear of any attempt to test her limits resulting in her demise. Morgana pulled back the sheets and gave Nola a hand out of bed. "I feel new." Nola looked around, and at herself. "This gown is beautiful!" She caressed the material and gave a look of thanks to Morgana. "There are no mirrors, so take my word that you look like a princess." Morgana hugged her as if she hadn't seen her in years. "Mirrors show flaws, and they break. They bring you bad luck. You can't see yourselves, but you can see the place you live in! It is a mess! Listen, while you rest, I'll begin work on this grand house!" Nola couldn't remember the last time she had so much energy. "As you wish, young lady but don't over work yourself, please." Morgana placed her hand on Nola's shoulder. Alec came in to greet Nola and to fetch Morgana for her rest.

Morgana and her grandfather directed themselves to their rooms. Morgana slept peacefully this day, more than she had in a long time. Elsebeth and Morgana were both drawn to Nola. They seemed to have a common bond. Nola was still freshly human, but her human scent and chemistry faded as did her mortality. Elsebeth would look at Nola and reflect on her own past indiscretion. She marveled at how Nola saw this existence as an opportunity, something better than life experience she had. Elsebeth's lust for humanity and the infidelity that followed still and forever would haunt her. Their human life experiences were completely different and Elsebeth quickly understood that their past circumstances dictated the choices and the outcome. For Morgana, it felt as though her abilities and Nola's were closer than Morgana's were to her own family. What abilities she didn't know. It was more instinctual, but fear would stop her from ever finding out.

Nola concentrated on making the house into a home. The others could only work with what they had. They couldn't patron the shops in town, since the businesses were only open during daylight hours. Nola was able to go into town, and buy provisions. The townspeople tolerated her and allowed her to shop for the family she worked for. They weren't necessarily friendly, but most people she dealt with were accommodating. It was a little different in the north and race relations weren't as strained since the political climate wouldn't change for many years. The area they lived in was remote, but not too far from what the settlers called civilization. Nola cleaned all day, also dealing with visitors as they happened by. She kept aware of anything that would pose as a potential danger for her new found family. Nola would also acquire animals and breed them so that the family would have some sustenance until they could get real nutrients from human blood. It was the blood that truly replenished them. At night, members of the family would return the favor by looking after Nola. Each family member would take turns, so the others could go out into the night. They would travel mostly, familiarizing themselves with the country they now called home. It didn't take too long for them to accomplish that task.

Acquainting themselves with the settlers was a luxury they could not afford, but they had to have some limited contact with the public in order to operate their business and make a profit. Bernard was the financier for the family. They survived by selling their wares for either currency, or new possessions. They were referred to as the antique dealers of the area, but it was a means to an end for them. Alec continued with his carpentry and furniture craft. They never professed to be of high social ranking, but they prospered with their business. They were as they appeared, well-bred art entrepreneurs. Things were beginning to change rather rapidly, and as a greater variety of merchandise became available, it caused their business to grow. The assimilation the family made was fascinating, but they had time to perfect anything they set their minds to. It seemed to be the consensus that hiding themselves from the world was crippling them, but a necessity to remain anonymous to the population. The old deserted castles that seemed abundant in Europe were not so in the soon to be United States. There was, however, plenty of undiscovered land and room to move and grow. Eventually they might have to change careers or continue to relocate so no connections could be derived by travelers that realize they were the same people in the same industry, an entire generation later.

Northward, cities evolved quickly, but they still had time. The eighteenth century did bring many advances and subsequent changes. Inventions were debuting so fast, it was difficult to maintain. Some lasted, while others didn't, but the spirit to be innovative was strong with the American People. There was still much land before the soon to be American people. It was land they assumed was for the taking. As the years passed when that wasn't the case, war was declared. Land was purchased by some of the countries, at the right price. The settlers fought the natives and other countries that wanted to dominate and prosper from the rich natural resources. Eventually, the new American nation went to war with itself. During the War of Independence, many young men, men far from home were available to the Mal family. It was a good time for them to replenish their blood supply, with so many dead and dying. They were scavengers, and acted as such as they fed on the casualties.

It was a sign of good fortune for them that the revolutionary war in France started shortly after the civil war. They closed down their home in America, so they could relocate to Europe, their old home. They would use their wealth to renovate the old small farm house as they had done with their American home. All that may have encountered them in Europe were dead for some time now. When the time was right and they returned to the states, the people around them would be gone as well. This decision was agreed upon and would allow them to continue with their preferred art and antique dealership.

Provisions were made so that the home would be untouched, unless granted by any surviving members of the Mal family. Nola delivered the documents that saved the rich and beautiful house for any of them that wanted it, or needed it, when the time came. It was assumed that she was a mere delivery person for the lawyer that truly represented the family. In truth, Nola was taught by the family and she learned very well. She studied as she watched over her family when she wasn't working on the house or hiring help for construction as ordered by her masters. She maintained the illusion that she was a servant, moderately educated and respectful of her place. She was however, skilled as a fine attorney for the time.

Once they arrived in France, they fed well. They fed so well that they almost felt alive, if that was possible. Morgana was the exception. She ate, drank to live, but something was missing. All had experienced love but she. Desmony never spoke of it, still never seeming to care about it. Morgana wanted and needed more. Nearly a century of living, and she had no romance to reminisce over.

When the family arrived at their old French country home, they were pleased to see that although it appeared abandoned, it remained as they left it. They kept to themselves in the house, making the necessary changes to accommodate their needs now that they had the income to improve. The *terror* as it was known to be, struck fear in the hearts of much nobility in France during and after the war. Many of the aristocrats that were not on the side of the rebels were subject to many horrors. Some were more gruesome than being the victim of a quick clean feed. The Mal family made the modest changes to their home, but kept a low profile for that reason. Fortunately, their home was still in a fairly remote location, away from Paris and far enough to avoid the political conflict that was raging. Their fear of being revealed as vampires was greater than the fear of any punishment a crowd of humans thought they could enforce upon them. Just as a precaution, they hid all of their acquisitions and conducted their business in a humble manner.

One cool evening, Morgana ventured out for a stroll, alone, across the country side. She looked at a berry bush during her walk that was just on the side of the road. She moved towards it, hoping she could cheat herself and eat a few pieces of the fruit. She tried to dine on the supple red berries, but they were like poison to her. She resolved to take in the aroma of some flowers that hadn't covered themselves for the night. She was safe, as long as the flowers weren't wild roses. Those flowers had a severe weakening effect on vampires. She dared not touch them, regardless. Legend and superstition were very powerful for her family and her. Suddenly, she was tackled from behind by a lone soldier of the revolution. He was on leave, and looking for a diversion. *"Bon jour, Mademoiselle. Viens à moi, maintenant!"* The soldier rolled her over and began to try and take her.

He observed her rich body. It aroused him more than the average female had. She was magnificent. *"Va t'en, couchon!"* A young, cleanly dressed officer lunged at the rogue and tore him off Morgana. "How dare you! Leave this lady alone!" The officer pulled out his sabre, to make his notice firm. The dirty, vile soldier pulled out his sabre as well, never cowering to the arrogant boy before him. Their duel was fierce, but brief. The soldier was good, but the officer was better. The officer had definitely earned his rank. A shower of flint sprayed the air as one of the sabers hit a rock. The display was formidable. At one point, the officer stumbled as he tripped on a small shrub. Morgana caught her breath, hoping that no harm would come to this valiant officer. He rallied, and with one calculating blow, he ended the battle. Satisfaction was had by the chivalric young man. The officer mounted the body of the soldier on his horse. He would return him to his regiment and recount the assault and discipline that led to his demise.

The officer ran to where the lady was standing. He had expected her to be devastated, ready to faint. She was fine. Morgana was smiling, joyous that the honorable man won the duel. She appeared as though she was watching a play or some type of tournament. *"Êtes-vous bien, Mademoiselle?* The young man was still slightly out of breath, thankful the fight didn't go the other way. *"Oui. Ça va bien, et vous?"* Morgana nearly drooled as she surveyed him. Not for his blood this time. He was an extraordinary specimen and she wanted him.

"Je me sens bien. Comment appelez-vous?" The young man dusted himself off as he looked at her, more than just to check for any injuries. He cocked his eye as he looked at her. He forgot about any pain he may have felt as he perused her body. *"Je m'appelle Morgana. Parlez-vous anglais?"* Morgana was hoping that this lovely young male had some formal education. "Yes, yes I do speak English. I'm called Victor de

Champagne. I'm so pleased that he didn't shame or harm you. What are you doing out so late by yourself?" Victor dusted her off, minding where he touched her body. "Thank you. Sleep wouldn't come to me." Morgana laughed inside. She didn't need his help, but it was refreshing to pretend. "Let me walk you home. I was on the way home myself." Victor took her hand lightly, placing it around his arm and they walked westward, to his home. "I live a little further, but I assure you that I can make it home all right." Morgana felt a strange feeling inside her. She almost felt warm, alive. "Somehow, I believe you. May I see you again? Would I be welcome?" Victor was so eager, like a little boy. "Bien sur, Monsieur. Tomorrow night, near that pond over the hill." Morgana fought to conceal her joy. "Why so secretive?" Victor smiled lustfully at her. "Respect my wishes as well sir, please." Morgana turned and walked away. Both went home, but neither slept.

The revolution had been long, and much too bloody. That very next day, news reached Victor and many others. His leave was made permanent. The war was over, finally. There was much work to do in the aftermath. So many dead, so much destruction! Victor would work to help all of the innocent people that lost so much in the war. He would also make time, however, to see his new fancy, Morgana. They both rejoiced in the knowledge that the war was over. People from all walks of life celebrated in their villages. The night the news was known to them both was truly magical for them.

They ran across the fields and danced near 'their' pond. They spent the night laughing, playing, and telling stories.

Victor's tales were detailed and very wholesome, as well as entertaining. He spoke of little anecdotes, like when he was a boy he would gather friends and play war. It was nothing compared to the real thing. He would always come out victorious. His parents would tell him that was how he got his name. They just knew that he would be a great fighter. Not just for the sake of fighting, but doing it for the good of the people. When he joined the army, it was to stop the unjustified killing of both aristocrats, and the poor. If his family still had the power they once had, he would have been able to be more than what he was. He did accomplish his goal, despite his position in society.

Morgana's stories were enchanting and interesting, but slightly vague. Times and places were skillfully omitted. Even though the truth was not fully indulged, the conversation was still vibrant. Victor hanged on every word Morgana spoke. In some ways, it didn't matter what she said. Victor found himself, more times than not, lost in her gaze, or staring at her beautiful lips. "You are unlike any woman I've ever met. You are so charming, yet mysterious. I would like to have known you as a child. Were you always like this?" Victor leaned against a tree as he became lost in her eyes again. "You couldn't have known me as a child, but I really haven't changed much in a long while. You are quite intriguing

yourself. I've waited a long time to meet someone like you."
Morgana leaned close to him, placing her hand upon his
chest.

"Not so long, my dear. You're much too young and
lovely to speak so gravely. Would it be too forward of me if I
were to kiss you?" He had that eager look in his eyes again.
"Forward? Heavens no! This courtship is at an accelerated
pace, we can't deny that. I feel that I've known you forever,
like I've read your mind and know all of your memories." In
fact, Morgana had. She was convinced that he was the one
for her. Victor's soul felt right to her. It wasn't a mere
infatuation. Morgana was praying that wasn't the case. Victor
was an honorable man. Morgana could see he was not hiding
anything. He wouldn't play with her. His pursuit was
genuine. He was no Casanova. She wanted him, but their
consummation of their apparent love would have to wait.
Dawn was on the horizon. "My love, you must kiss me now
and let me go. I must be home before everyone wakes." She
had a look of urgency that alarmed Victor. *"D'accord, mon
trèsor."* He kissed her with animated passion. A lifetime of
love was in that bonding. Morgana smiled a reassuring smile
at Victor and took off, running like a comet over the
countryside. Victor was slightly bewildered, but never the less
in love. He couldn't wait to tell Morgana how deeply he felt for
her. Victor thought sharing his feelings would be a great
surprise to her, but it wouldn't. Morgana already knew Victor
was in love with her. His emotions were shouting out form

his soul, too easy for her to detect. A female human would've known. Morgana would have to refrain from saying anything to him. It would be horribly impolite to ruin his declaration of love.

Morgana was beside herself. She had never been in love before. She wasn't sure anyone she lived with had been. They all reserved their feelings. Elsebeth, her mother and the most human of them all, save for Smythe was the most open about her feelings. Her mother always maintained a look of a woman in love. Morgana dared to speak, in confidence, with her mother about her feelings. She knew Victor was in love with her, but did she love him as well? Yes, with all her heart. She never felt the way she did when she was with Victor. "Darling, are you sure you just don't want this young man? How does he make you feel?" Elsebeth was not afforded the human dilemma of worrying about her daughter's sexuality and their reputation. Sex was something very natural for them as vampires and a very useful tool for feeding. It was part of the game, luring victims in with sexual promises. Usually, they would only tempt their victims, but it wasn't uncommon for them to use their victims for carnal pleasure. Morgana reassured her mother that she was pure. That made Elsebeth happy to know at least one daughter valued her virtue and after all of this time. "Mother, I do feel that I want to be with him, but it's more than that. He touches me here." Morgana placed her hand on her heart. It was still, but she could almost swear it beat when she was with Victor. "Well, I felt like that once. I mean, I still do. Your father forced our love, out of a girl's crush. I learned, after some time, that his love for me is pure. I love him for that." Elsebeth turned her furrowed brows to a smooth surface as she smiled at her lovely daughter.

Elsebeth touched her daughter on the cheek. "My dear, I am fairly certain that you love this young man. This is wonderful, but disheartening for me. You have a very delicate situation, loving a mortal." Morgana bowed her head down. "Yes, I know, mother. You know, I have to be honest with him. Maybe one day soon but not now. What if I lose him?" Morgana was whiter than normal with fear. "Speak the truth. That is the best thing. You know the consequences. If he doesn't understand, he must perish. If that changes your decision, then silence may be the best. If he is a strong man, he will be worthy of your love. If he is not, then his love is not deep enough. I must remind you our secret cannot be sacrificed." Elsebeth kissed her child on her forehead. She swept herself out of the room, with her robe trailing behind her. Morgana had much to consider. The one thing she knew for fact was that she cared for Victor. She decided to let things develop. She didn't want to push an unfavorable demise to their relationship. That was something she knew might happen, once she revealed the truth. No matter how she played the scenario in her mind, she could lose Victor, her first true love.

Morgana was drawn to Victor physically, but she restrained herself. She felt she should not be aggressive toward the young man. She wanted to continue to be "new" to him. Victor appreciated all her attempts at perfection. Truth be known to her, she didn't have to try so hard. He loved her unconditionally. In the following weeks, they became closer, better acquainted. With each encounter, their passion elevated each time. This was probably the only thing that scared Morgana, more than the sun, garlic, or crosses. She was so attached to him. Giving herself to him was a priority in her mind and in her heart, but there was so much that would have to happen if their union was to be complete. She wanted to be completely honest with him, as her mother suggested. She feared losing him, to induced amnesia, or worse. It was possible that her cold heart would have to turn to ice, and she would have to destroy the man that charmed her so. Even if she told Victor, showed him the truth and he accepted her and decided to become as she was, she could possibly loose him in the sense that he would no longer be the high spirited, fresh, ethical, morally strong man that made her fall in love.

One warm evening, Victor prepared a wonderful picnic for them. They fed each other fruits and cheese, with a sensual undertone, as lovers do. They drank wine. The wine was tart to her, not sweet, as Victor tasted it. She tried not to choke. Fortunately, their meal was complete after a short while. Morgana dodged around the meal and excused herself to vomit the food up when she was out of Victor's sight. When she returned, Victor laid Morgana across his chest and held her hand. "I have something for you." From Victor's pocket, he took out a folded handkerchief. "Open it." That was all he said. Morgana did as he requested. An unusually beautiful silver band was what emerged out of the cloth. It was Marcasite, a very ornate and exquisite form of silver. Victor put it on her finger. it fit perfectly. The ring was his mothers. It was one of the few things he brought with him when he left home for the war.

"It's precious! Victor, thank you! I have some beautiful pieces, some very old pieces, but they compare very little to this!" She wept silently. Victor wiped her tears and asked without warrant, "Will you marry me?" Victor's parents knew he was in love, and intended to ask Morgana to marry him. They were glad, but unhappy that they hadn't met the girl. Victor spoke so highly of her they had no choice but to fall in love with her as well. "My parents are thrilled! Please give me the answer I want." The mystical Marcasite ring sat on Morgana's delicate finger as she thought about what she was facing. It wasn't the most expensive of engagement rings, but it rivaled many rings of gold, or precious stones. Marcasite gained most of its popularity during this century, which was fortunate for Morgana. The style fit her flawlessly.

"Oh my darling, as much as I love you, I couldn't make you happy as your wife. I can't do the things you need me to. There's something I should tell you to try and excuse my refusal." Morgana was trembling. He put his cape around her shoulders. "Tell me all! As I've told you to, always! I care not what it is, I must know, I must know!" Victor was furious, but he didn't want to alarm the woman he loved so. "Before I let you love me, before you feel in your heart that you want me, I must show you the real me." Morgana backed away from Victor. Her eyes became fluorescent. Almost immediately after, her wings broke out from the back of her gown. The dress she wore so beautifully tore in the back. Her wings were moist from escaping from beneath her skin. Morgana looked up at him, her fangs reflected in the light of the half moon. They almost lit up the rest of the sky. Morgana put a shock in Victor. She frightened him so that he wanted to run, as much as he loved her. Yet, he did not move. His heart trusted her. He didn't feel that his safety was in any danger, but he couldn't believe what he was seeing. Victor felt as though he were dreaming, but his pounding heart kept him conscious and alert. His heart beat like thunder in a rain storm.

"I am what legend calls Vampire. The night we met, I could've easily made a meal of that soldier, and you. Once I looked at you, I knew I would be making a mistake. I fear religious objects, garlic, and holy water as the stories say. The sun would kill me. I can fly also. I'm stronger than a room full of you. I can change form. I can move things with my mind, not very well, but I can. I can read minds and I'm learning to manipulate them as well. I am a monster to all that see me. I am a walking plague. I am not capable of loving you as a mortal can. I can't bring you joy. I can't fulfill your dreams as your bride. I'm sorry, but you can't love me." Morgana cried fiercely as she spoke.

Victor calmed himself. He never felt threatened by her. Even after he'd seen the incredible sights before him, he still loved the Morgana that was inside the creature. After a while, all he saw was her true beauty. She truly was a sad creature. Morgana moved her form to one that Victor was more accustomed to. Victor came to her, of his own free will. Morgana couldn't believe what Victor was doing. "You are abnormal in your understanding." Morgana kissed his cheek. "I love you. You can't change your condition, and sadly I can't change mine. My family needs me. I wanted you to be with my family, but I couldn't put you in that danger. I will love you forever, only you, but we can't make this alliance work." Victor joined her in her sobbing. Morgana held victor tightly as she said, "I know. Do this for me. Don't live your life alone. The one you marry, one day, try to love her, whoever she may be. Have children with her. It would kill me if you didn't leave a legacy. Your honorable name must live on! You could never have a child with me. I'd birth you a beast, if we could even have children. I was born a vampire and it is still a mystery how I came to be. I'm so sorry." Morgana dropped her arms away from Victor. He grabbed at her arms, bring her back to him. "I will never truly love another. You know that, I'm sure."

Despite the knowledge Victor had of his love, he took her by the hand, and led her to the blanket he had brought along. "I will love you, only once. It will be the way I would have loved you all your life, if we could live it together." He took great care as he disrobed Morgana. He touched and kissed her body so softly. Despite the longevity of her life, this was her first time. He took great pride in this knowledge. He owed that to her, to himself. He prayed for them, for her sorry soul. He led her, as their bodies danced. They exercised love completely. He stroked her sleek blue-black hair as he kissed her full lips. He refused to think about what she had shown him. She was so beautiful. Her skin was placid, undisturbed by any marks. He kissed her brow, which was his sign of tenderness and love to her.

Morgana smiled as he moved his hands across her body. She breathed in deeply as he touched her chest. Her bosom was modest, but perfect in shape. He stroked her, massaged her, tenderly. Morgana arched her back as he did this to her. Making love with Victor was thus far everything she anticipated. She had destroyed any man before they had a chance to mar her self-respect. Victor continued down her lean, yet curved form. He pushed down on her hips as her kissed her with such urgency. He prayed that he could hold on as well. He didn't want to be a disappointment to her, not during her first time. Victor moved down her neck, reaching her chest. He stopped there to give each breast the attention he had given her luscious mouth.

Victor smiled as Morgana's body and breathing responded favorably to his actions. Victor didn't want to scare her, but he wanted to taste her, badly. Morgana was completely passive. She trusted him implicitly. Victor's tongue roamed below Morgana's hips. She assured him that his intention was understood, and accepted. Victor pushed his tongue inside her, gently. She was moist from all the excitement. He didn't toil within her for long, since their time was short. Victor declined asking Morgana to reciprocate, since she was inexperienced. This evening was entirely about her. He traced her body upward with his tongue, until he reached her mouth. Morgana pulled her lover to her, kissing him. She could faintly taste herself on his mouth. Morgana wanted to make him feel special, but Victor held both her arms above her head. "Allow me." Victor moved on top of his beloved.

Morgana gasped like one of her victims as he plunged himself into her. It was too much emotion for her to take. She began to sob to herself. She wanted to be selfish, to bite him, just enough, for him to be with her for eternity, but she wouldn't allow herself. She couldn't imagine wanting to feel this way and experience this with another creature, human or vampire. When they became used to each other's movements, their rhythm was totally in sync. They were perfect lovers. It was a shame they wouldn't be able to love more than this one time. Morgana's fangs began to surface. She tried to control herself, but it was becoming increasingly difficult. She growled, but it delivered like a lion's purr. Victor had his head buried in her hair. He was concentrating so hard, that he missed her beastly expression. She screamed as they climaxed. It was simultaneous, it was epic.

Victor held Morgana under the glazed full moon that made their bodies seem iridescent. The cool night air bathed their bare bodies. They studied the night, every detail of their experience. "Your secret will lay dormant with me until I am put in the ground. Don't be sad. Chance may allow us to meet again." Victor sat up. He got up slowly. He looked at her, wishing for so much he couldn't have. He helped his lady stand up. He embraced her, strongly. Both feared it was for the last time. They dressed themselves and Victor gathered the supplies for the picnic. He packed them on the horse that he brought with them. He walked beside Morgana, all the way home, this time.

"I leave tomorrow. I'm going back to America." Morgana looked at her ring. "I'll never take this off. You'll live as long as I do, in my heart and in my mind. I respect your decision. I can't say I am happy about your decision, but never the less. Just know, your memory will never leave me." Morgana touched his face, and kissed it. The time her lips touched his forehead seemed an eternity. Morgana wished it had been an eternity, could still be. "A bientôt, mon cherie." Victor kept her secret, and she kept her promise to him. Morgana kept this part of her life away from everyone. No one but her mother would ever learn about her only love, her first love.

With some urging by Morgana, they made arrangements to relocate to America as soon as possible. So many changes had taken place since they had been in Europe. The Americas were now The Unites States of America. The land was more civilized, but not so that they could keep their identity concealed. During the time it took for them to pack their belongings, Desmony was extremely moody. No one was allowed to feed. It was just too risky. One early evening, just before they were to start their journey, Desmony initiated an argument with her mother. Desmony was still being punished for her rebellious impulses from long ago. She had held her tongue for as long as she possibly could. Desmony thought she would be able to have another chance at true liberty, since they were returning to the land of freedom. "Why is it that Morgana can still go out, and I can't? She was out just last night! The blood we have to drink is stale. Could it be that you, of all people, are showing favoritism? Mother, what if she got stuck and the sun came up? Do you think it would even affect her, especially since she isn't completely one of us?" Desmony had a sinister grin on her thirsty mouth.

"I told you never to speak of this!" Elsebeth became furious, but then startled. At that moment, Bernard burst into the room. When he would lay with Elsebeth in the day, he would see images of a man, but didn't know what to make of it. If he had any doubts, they were blocked by Elsebeth, due to her fear of him making this discovery. Elsebeth kept this secret deeper than she ever thought possible, until now.

Elsebeth needed to say nothing. There was nothing else to say. Bernard broke through her mental shield and knew the entire tale. He knew about the romance with Xavier Montez in Spain, in almost an instant. His face went from a glowing fury to a dull haze of disappointment. He thought he had always been obliged in his fidelity to a woman he risked everything to love. He risked losing her by forcing her into this life, but now, he wasn't sure that he wanted to know her, much less love her. "Was I so terrible that you felt it necessary to betray me? Everything I have done, I've done because I love you so. I love you! Why? Why have you put this crease in our life?" Elsebeth was amazed at his self-restraint.

Bernard silently wept as he probed her, wanting an answer. Desmony had long since swept out of the room. Bernard had given her a look that under no certain terms was she to be in the room during this conversation. Her job, as she saw it, was done. Elsebeth extended her arms, hoping to be able to justify, if possible, her actions. "You were born as you are. I was human. I wanted to feel that again, in some way. I know it sounds terrible, feeble. The man I was with wasn't a substitute for you, my love. I curse myself for being so weak. I've never been in control of my life, not even when I let him have me. For as much as Morgana isn't yours, she is. You have made her the person she is. Sometimes, she's bonds better with you than she does with me! Desmony does with me, because she wants me to be more like you. Please, don't hate Morgana. Punish me if you must. I know I deserve it, if I haven't hurt myself enough. I have been selfish. I am so sorry." Elsebeth was strong, but she wanted to collapse all the same.

"I can't hate you. I love you. You are right, just not justified in your actions. My absence will be your punishment. I must be alone, to think on this. I can't tell you what I will do, or where I will go, but know that you may not follow me." The fear in Elsebeth's words made Bernard not as stern as he had the power to be. His heart burned with betrayal. "I won't follow you. I can't change what I've done to you, to this family. I hope that by chance you can forgive me, before one of meets a demise. That day is yet to be determined, if ever. I just hope I won't have to wait too long for your heart to return to me." Elsebeth's emotions were a storm inside. Her fangs began to show from her sadness. "I will go with you," Blythe said to Bernard. Blythe was at the threshold of the room. She had urged Desmony to move far from that area, not knowing how Bernard would react. All of what was spoken was known to Blythe. She suspected long before this day. Desmony could hear all of the discussion that had taken place. Her family was being ripped apart, and it was all due to her exposition. For the first time, Desmony was silent, almost cryptic.

CHAPTER TEN

Nola rushed to pack their luggage. She kept all of her thoughts to herself. Bernard and Blythe would have left before Nola finished, since their last thought was to bother with any provisions. It was almost as if they were on their own, once again, as they had been several centuries before. Bernard and Blythe stopped long enough to look at everyone, remembering all of their faces. Elsebeth looked at the ground in shame. She thought it would be best to not stain Bernard's memory with her face. She wondered if even the ground repelled her visage. When Bernard saw her look away, it was more than her could bare. Bernard led as Blythe and he shattered a window as they left, with a roar of pain, hurt, and anger. Elsebeth broke down. Alec caught her as she leaned unconscious towards the ground. Bernard and Blythe had looked in on Morgana, as she slept. She was still deeply depressed over losing Victor. It was time to shed even more disturbing news on the poor girl. She was strong, but this would test her boundaries to no end.

Nola, making provisions for the evening, prepared a liquid dinner. It was animal blood, not human blood. Everyone was starving, which made everything worse.

Elsebeth was in her room, sobbing uncontrollably. Alec was her rock. Alec said nothing, he just held onto her, reassuring her. "I'm probably the only one that understands. My dear, I've kept quiet, but I have something to say to you. You love and already miss Bernard, as I do his sister. He's hurt, my love. You have devastated him. His absence, I believe to be a punishment to you. It will take a while, but luck willing, we have that. Bernard will come back, I have faith in that, if anything." Alec placed her head on his chest. "Thank you, father. You are too kind. I did an awful thing. But there's Morgana. I love Desmony and Morgana equally. I don't want either of them to suffer from this, but I know they will. Desmony knows, and she has come to terms with it. Morgana, well, I don't know how this will affect her." Elsebeth had stopped crying. She was now drying her tears.

"Morgana is a special person. Once you tell her, it will hurt, but it will make sense. I will help in any way I can." Alec looked up to see Nola standing in the doorway. She was bringing them their dinner. The house had been all too quiet. She wasn't sure what was yet to happen. Nola looked at the meal she was presented to Alec and Elsebeth. It wasn't for her. Her diet consisted of raw meat, water, and bread. Nothing cooked could be tolerated by her, much less any of them. Nola couldn't drink their brew. She didn't need to, nor did she want to be so restricted in her eating habits. She was fortunate to not be as vulnerable as all the others. Nola thought to herself, "If Morgana is half human, could she be like me? Could she live in the day light? She seems to yearn for it. Why take the chance? No, she is a vampire, her mother's child. How is Elsebeth going to tell Morgana?"

Morgana entered the dining room as everyone sat, staring at one another. "I hope you had a bite while you were out." Desmony tried to loosen the tension in her unduplicated way. Alec shot a dagger glance at her. Desmony looked down at her lap and smiled to herself. "Everyone looks so bazaar. Where is Blythe? Where is Father?" Morgana continued to look around as Elsebeth stood up from the table and approached her daughter. "My sweet, I must take you outside. We must speak, alone. It is a very important matter." They eased out of the house and strolled over to the gazebo that was near the lily pond Alec had constructed. "I'm going to miss this place. Maybe we can come back someday? You know, mother, I want a home in every continent. We just might, since it seems as though we've lived everywhere!" Morgana was bitter-sweet, thinking of Victor. Nevertheless, she was more sweet than bitter, as always. Morgana knew she couldn't return, not while Victor was there. There was no need to bring temptation to her door, and persuade her to turn Victor into one of them. It was better to just think about him.

"Darling, I need to tell you this." Elsebeth urged Morgana to sit beside her, as she studied her child. "Before you were born, your sister and I took a leave of absence to

Spain. Desmony was just companionship for my problem. I wasn't born a vampire, you know that. My destiny was altered, decided by your father and your aunt. I love them dearly, but at the time, I hadn't fully accepted who I was, what I was. While I was in Spain, I met a young human, Xavier Montez. He was so charming, alive, and passionate. I saw the life he had in him. I didn't want to take it from him. I wanted to share it; to try and absorb it. I became weak in his presence. There's no excuse for what I did, but I just wanted to-" Elsebeth was trembling while she spoke. she feared that the girl would leave her as well in rage because of her betrayal.

"Mother, this man, are you trying to tell me that he is my father? That you have been living a lie? Am I the last to know, or is that why I can't find my father and Blythe? What did you do, Mother? What did you do? I've lost so much this week. " Morgana was irretrievably confused. Elsebeth managed to hush Morgana. Morgana, no matter how upset she was, still respected her mother. Morgana saw visions of Victor. She thought of how she too had loved a mortal. The only difference was that she was not betrothed to someone. "Darling. No one knew of this! Only Desmony. She captured my thoughts when it happened. I had no choice. It is true, Xavier is your natural father. When I betrayed your father, and found that I was with child, I wanted to die for my mistake! Then, I thought about you. I couldn't deny you life. You don't know how much I wanted you to be of Bernard's blood. You still are, since his blood flows through my veins. I can't change what I've done. Just know that I love you, with my entire being. If you must hate me, do. If you must leave, I can't stop you." Elsebeth was tired. she couldn't defend herself any longer.

Deep inside, where no one was allowed, Morgana thought to herself. She really could not fault her mother too much. She couldn't condone her actions, but she could understand her conflict. Morgana was blessed with a strong sense of maturity. This was also a curse, at times. Morgana thought again about her love, Victor. She felt that she was no better. What if she were carrying his child? There was no way to know just yet. Morgana rationalized that she had also betrayed her family, her kind, with loving a mortal. But since she was not a full-blooded vampire, she wondered what was the extent of her failure? Was it even a failure? She also began to ponder what differences she might have as a part human. She continued, but didn't test any theories. Her fear was too great.

Elsebeth tried to approach Morgana later, after Morgana had some time alone. Elsebeth had been confused by Morgana's odd statement about loss. Her fear was mammoth that she would lose Morgana as well. The family was breaking apart, and it was due to a traitorous act, committed a century ago. If Morgana did in fact leave, Elsebeth resolved to find a way to kill herself.

Morgana and Elsebeth finally came back indoors. The sun was on the rise. All that observed them enter the house, surveyed them carefully. They were searching for some hint, a glimpse of some reaction from Morgana. Morgana could not bring herself to smile, but she spoke softly. "All will be well." Morgana hugged everyone, and went to her chamber. Elsebeth walked with false pride to her chamber soon after. "We must leave, without distraction, tomorrow." The next evening, everyone boarded the ship that was to take them all back to the United States. The journey was warmer than the initial trip. They left hastily, at the wrong time of year. It was difficult for them to sleep during the day with the elevated temperatures. They practiced their practiced methods of nourishment, feeding on anything that wasn't human, unless it couldn't be helped.

One evening, when Morgana was enjoying a quiet night alone, a voice crept into her mind. She wasn't sure if it was real, since she had been thinking about recent past events that had thrown her life into a tailspin. The voice was Bernard's. He was reaching out to her. "My love, it is your father. Should I say that. Yes, I will. I am your father." Bernard's voice was tense, guarded, and somber. "Father, and I mean that. You mean the world to me. No one else has the history with me that you do. You must do as you feel, but Elsebeth is my mother. I can't turn on her. I can't condone her actions, but neither can I hate her." Morgana tried to be careful with her words, but that was impossible. "I feel that this is what I must do. Worry not. It won't be forever. I need this time alone, but I will come back to you. Blythe misses everyone." Morgana's eyes began to tear up at Bernard's attempts to soften the tough blow she had received from his absence. "Heal quickly, father. We need you. Things just aren't the same." They said good-bye to one another. Morgana drifted into memories, and fell asleep.

The Mal family didn't return to their previous home. There had been enough time, but the west was expanding at an alarming rate. They relocated to western America, in the area that would become the state of Kansas. The land was filled with open and deserted places that wouldn't lend curiosity to anyone about their habits. During the end of the nineteenth century, they enjoyed some secrecy with the end of the civil war. Their old home served as a refuge for their feeding expeditions. Occasionally, they would travel to distant countries, especially when questions about missing local people would arise.

Places like Hawaii, Mexico, the Islands, even the Orient was subject to their terror, silent as it was. Often, they would wonder where all of their kind was. Even their heightened sense of smell couldn't help them. They could only hope to fall prey to another to find other vampires. Vampires couldn't advance by biting one another. Dead blood for dead blood did not help them exist. It was a weak supplement for the pure blood they needed. Discovering one another could still prove to be very dangerous. Power would be more welcome to one than another. A skillful creature could use that as an advantage, however, risking their own safety at the same time. The family had to settle for unity and longevity amongst themselves. This century was calm for them, all except for the brother and sister that was on a self-imposed exile. Blythe and Bernard had a struggle that could shatter their family like a stone hitting pond water, just after the first snow.

CHAPTER ELEVEN

When Blythe and Bernard got tired of traveling and searching, they settled down in a small Russian village. They assimilated like a chameleon when it changes colors. The climate was bitter cold and the sky was generally dark. It was a perfect setting for the two desolate and emotionally battered souls. They made home out of yet another deserted castle. It was never a problem for just the two of them. Blythe missed her Elsebeth and her family, but she began to think about how easy it used to be when it was just she and her brother. If someone had or took possession of their dwelling, they would quietly occupy the basement or dungeon. The occupants would usually not notice them, stealth as they were, decide it was a ghost or poltergeist, or become their victims if they dared to discover them. This one happened to be vacant. This self-imposed exile they had created had qualities much like the climate that had engulfed them. They missed the family, but they needed this. It was necessary. Bernard needed to heal. Blythe was the only one to help him get past this.

On an evening when Bernard had mastered the language, and felt safe to go out, as a local, he found himself in a small. but lively tavern. women laid on him like a heavy cloak, but he seemed despondent. He became bored with them and brushed them away. He only saw Elsebeth in their pale but welcoming faces. One face in particular stood out. It was a woman from Bernard's past, but he didn't recall her. She was different. She had been stalking him throughout the centuries. her eternal existence had been devoted to making him emotionally disoriented, vulnerable, and resentful as she had been. Revenge would be hers. She learned every evil and dirty trick she could. "He once thought I never would survive. Not only have I done that, I will annihilate him!" A long, ghastly creature stood beside her. "Whenever you are ready, love." He bent almost completely over before he reached the top of her head. He kissed her on her crown, leaving a small trace of saliva. He was anticipating the upcoming discovery that would undo any feelings of security that Bernard had thought he possessed.

Bernard had stripped her of her pride and her life. She loved him, yet he turned her into a cowering monster. He didn't help nurture her. He was a young immortal, and wasn't strong in patience. Inside, she believed he was more grotesque than she was. He had no remorse, no compassion for her. Furthermore, he was the instigator for her father's death. She nearly died all over again when Bernard banished her. Once it was decided by some unnatural force that she was to live, she found a creature with an even more non-existent soul than Monsieur Mal. Hlival, a Slavic that had probably been cursed by Satan himself, was her constant companion. Hlival killed and destroyed simply because he could. He exercised his powers to the limits, and beyond what was acceptable for vampires. Not even children escaped his wrath. The pure and innocent children had no meaning for him. They were merely a means to an end. *Conquer all until I am the last*! That was his creed.

Hlival must have smelled or sensed the Mal blood-bond within her. He didn't even know who she was, but he was drawn to her when he saw her. The two paired up in Budapest, where the young woman had almost given up. She was strapping herself to a tree, facing the morning sun. Her will to die was much stronger than her will to live. She could no longer fight to survive, not in the existence she was in now. The woman had almost fell unconscious, to the point where she couldn't fight, even if she wanted to. Hlival appeared out of the cold, thin air. She felt Hlival, but didn't care to explain her actions. She knew something was different about this man. He carried a dull stench, rich with a salty and bloody fragrance. The Mal family covered their dead smell with fragrances, and fruits. The woman never smelled a live vampire.

Hlival never felt like he needed to hide. He was invincible, feared by all that crossed his path. Anyone that did, and lived, did so purely out of luck. He wasn't seen or known by many people. If someone was unfortunate to meet him as he prowled, they died. Hlival made witches and other believers of the occult afraid of him. They would all run away, screaming in terror. "I'll play with you later." Hlival would yell as they bolted themselves into their shacks whenever he would raid through a town. Most thought he was crazy, and treated as such. They treated him like an outcast, but not with force. Too many people mysteriously showed up dead if he was ever made cross.

Hlival made his way over to the dying female. He hoisted her heavy and weary head up and asked her why she had put herself in such a quandary. "Leave me!" The woman growled through her fangs as her eyes made him look away. The only thing that could stir his cold heart was seeing a vampire that had given up on life. In his mind, one should be joyous to be ever-living, feeding on such a weak race of beings. It was truly sad to see her with all her spirit gone. He looked deep on her, and saw a time when she was full of life and most importantly, passion.

She heaved in sobbing breaths, which added insult to injury, in his eyes. He began to drool as he smiled. *She is so vulnerable! I could take her and create such a creature that I would be feared even more than now! She will be my minion, my tool.* His eyes began to shimmer in the marine lapis sky. "That would be such a waste. May I make a proposition? I happen to know a few things that would help you avenge your dead father and your lost mortal existence. I can do this, with the condition that you do all I say." The woman had opened herself to Hlival, even before she had realized it. Any vampire within a twenty-mile radius would have picked up on her, but Hlival was the one. Her destiny was to be with this sub-demon. He knew of the Mal family. It was in fact him that made the creature that in turn made this crippled woman. The circle would be complete. The Mal clan had deserted him, which angered him to no end. Now was the time to make them pay for their insolence and insubordination. He didn't like unity. He stopped, after he tried to bring them into his camp. He swore to bring them to ashes. With his new weapon, he would see to that.

The night was dying again. The woman would follow the same path, in a blazing furry, if she didn't succumb to Hlival's offer. Why should she give Bernard any satisfaction? She had every right to make him suffer as she had. "I thought he was my salvation. He murdered my father." She was too weak to cry. she had done much of that for many seasons. "I know child. You have opened yourself and mind to me even in these moments that we've spent together. You wanted to live, well, you can! There are a few rules that you must adhere to, but if you do, you will have a vibrant and exhilarating existence. I won't extend this offer again. If you refuse and I see you again, I will cut your existence out, understand?" He stroked her quaking throat, then her unwashed hair. He fought to conceal his anticipation of her response. He could feel her struggle. She weighed the arguments for and against self-destruction, and the impending sentence to hell. He thought she was breathtaking. He would leave her here to die however, if she said no.

He looked at her, thinking to himself what a wonderful mistress she would make, as well as a servant. She looked at the horizon and realized she must decide quickly. She really didn't have the internal fortitude to let the sun eat her alive. The sound of its rising was already deafening. She really didn't have any other choice. She knew that in her heart, she must choose life over death, no matter what capacity life came in. "Take me away!" Just before daybreak, he had her free. They sought refuge in an isolated cave. They ate on whatever ventured into "their" domain. "I will travel, work with you, and learn from you I must have revenge before I can ever have peace. Help me, and I will devote myself to you. I will do this for the destruction of our new mutual enemy, Monsieur Bernard Mal!" The woman listened while Hlival told her of his history with that family. He told her much, and she never strayed from his instruction. Her attention was fixed, like dead eyes. For the first time since her banishment, she felt alive with a sense of purpose. It was a miracle, or fate, that she had lasted this long. How long would it take for her to become ready?

On a slightly warmer night, months later, Hlival took her out to see if she had enough anger in her to apply what she had learned from him to some innocent soul. A farmer stretched as he walked towards the fields that he and his family worked on tirelessly. A storm was off in the distance, so he wanted to make sure that everything was situated so there wouldn't be much, if any, damage. The girl had stalked the farmer, learning his patterns as she waited. Hlival told her to make sure she knew what she was up against, whether it was a "mortal" enemy, or nightly prey. She was just relaxing when she finally caught a hint of the farmer's scent. She jumped up, preparing herself for her next move. She cloaked herself and maneuvered behind him in the night sky. She never had a problem with levitation and flying, but the killing, the death, that was her Achilles' heel. The farmer had finished his security check, so he turned towards home. He could smell the bread his wife was preparing for the next day.

The farmer smiled as he thought of his wife. He was almost to her. He reached the front gate when he gasped from the strain that was put upon his throat. He tried to move his head to look about, but it was impossible. He saw no one. Before he knew it, his robust body began to rise. He was levitating! This sent him into a panic so badly, he began to clutch his chest. He was sweating a down-pour. His eyes winced as his body went limp. To the girl's misfortune, the poor farmer expired prematurely from a heart-attack. She threw him on the ground, like a discarded object, previously sought after. The object was now worthless. Hlival floated down to where she was, and placed his hand on her shoulder. "Nice approach, but never get excited too quickly. Size your prey up properly. He was old, fat, and weak. He had probably never confronted another man before in his life! Don't put too much effort into certain kills. You'll continue to be disappointed, like now. When the kill is confirmed, let them see you! Let them know what exactly is taking their life. Don't overdo. It won't be a quiet, invisible killer, as you were to him and as you've killed in the past. You, my dear, will paralyze with fear! There will be such noise, such terror! Come, we must go." Hlival started off, but the girl halted his motion. "What will we do with him?" She asked as they mourned the loss of satisfaction, and nothing else. Hlival stared at her, grabbed her arm, and bluntly asked, "Who cares?" They took the form of two large birds in the sky, in search for food.

They trained for a while longer. In theory, she understood all, but when it came time to perform, she would falter miserably somehow. It was as though she was destined to fail. Hlival gave her encouragement, accompanied with discipline. Another storm was on them. It was much larger than the last one. The fire in their cave was almost like the day, so they threw snow at it. The girl found it humorous. The laughter became contagious. As it subsided, she looked at him. She had never been with a man before, not even

Bernard. She wanted to know what loving someone was like, passion or not. Hlival wasn't as good looking as Bernard, or as well mannered. He was the only choice she had. She walked over to where he was. She slapped him, then kissed him. He wasn't stunned. He was in fact intrigued. He ripped her gown. Her wings began to spread.

Hlival raised the girl into the sky. As they hovered the ground, they motioned as close together as possible. Their wings left their arms free to hold one another. Hlival was a crude lover. He was sharp and aggressive. He hit the points on her body that he felt necessary. He tried to kiss her, but the sentiment was too close to compassion. Hlival pulled at the girl's hips, pulling her close. He wasn't interested in caressing her breasts. He did not want to hold her too closely. Hlival simply took her, and forced himself into her. The movement was too awkward. It hurt the girl, more than she expected. She cried as Hlival took even more essence from her than she thought she had left to give. It almost killed her to bed this grotesque creature, in the night sky. When Hlival was done with her, they lowered down to the ground. The girl scrapped for the furthest corner from Hlival. She stayed as far away from him, in their make-shift abode as she could. The girl was consumed by rage and regret. He was ashamed, not for hurting the girl, but for feeling anything for the poor creature across from him, naked, with her back to him.

CHAPTER TWELVE

She crossed the room to where Bernard was. She interrupted the conversation he was still surprisingly interested in. He raised his head heavily, and looked at her. Even though the girl's appearance was altered, due to centuries of extreme conditions and some cosmetic alterations to her hair, and some facial features, her face sparked a glimmer of recognition. The colorless dull brown The girl had chosen for her hair made her even more pale looking than she already was. "Don't I know you?" Bernard smiled a defense melting smile at her, but without that affect, she replied, "No." "I'm sure I do. I hope you realize if your face was more kind, well, maybe that would help." He motioned to the other women not to giggle, as they had been doing. "I must speak with you, alone. I have an important message for you."

She looked at his parting company as they dispersed. She eased into the chair that was directly in Bernard's line of view. This was her moment and her teacher was watching her, almost as if he were going to grade her on this great test. "Now, my lovely, what must you relay to me?" Bernard moved to take her hand, but she jerked it away with vile disgust. A

206

flair in her smothered anger shot through the air into Hlival's senses. He gave her a cross look as she turned to him for some type of encouragement, or instruction. He had no more lessons for this one. He just pulled his hat down over one of his blood-shot eyes, shaking his head. He puckered his lips, as if to make a hushing sound. *Don't give away too much,* is what echoed in her mind.

At the new, albeit temporary Mal lair, Blythe was interrupted from her reading by an old sensation that rocked her being to the core. No one knew, but Bernard was her twin. As mortals, they had a heightened sense of one another. Now, as vampire's, it was highly acute. The force she felt was terribly negative. It was the same way she felt when That hideous Hlival took away their human hearts, and replaced them with lumps of coal. Blythe knew Bernard was not himself. The betrayal of his soul-mate devastated him, almost beyond repair. Blythe was not about to let anyone, not even Elsebeth be Bernard's undoing. "He is unaware of this danger and is in need of protection!" Blythe let her book fall as she got up. She made long and heavy strides towards the door. She grabbed a cane she had made for defensive measures in the past, but never had she needed to use it. Tonight, she felt she would. Blythe felt a hopeful sense of resolution as she moved through the air, toward her unsuspecting brother.

Bernard's defenses were taking a cat nap. He looked longingly at the beauties that had moved on to more receptive prospects. The girl, the woman before him now was struggling to keep his attention. As the fire water he was consuming took a stronger hold of him, the feat of keeping his attention on her was decreasingly difficult. He decided to make the most of the evening with her. It wasn't for want of the love-making experience. It was simply that he needed something to do. They spoke vaguely about one another until the crowd died down. Hlival ushered as many out of the tavern as he could. He wanted her odds at their peak. Blythe was stead-fast, but the weather made it difficult for her to use her top speed. Unfortunately, Bernard had chosen a spot quite distant from their home. A snow storm was growing stronger in the air. Lashing out at the poor creatures on the ground. Blythe tried to pull down the stalkers proverbial masque, to find a face to match the feeling, but it was gone. There was something interfering with her telepathic trace Blythe had on this creature. She jolted when she realized there might have been more than one danger surrounding her brother.

The girl enticed Bernard to drink, which made him more welcomed to the possibility of possibly forgetting his heart-loss. The time had come. The girl felt the resistance weakening. At the lowest point, which was upon them, she would strike. she smiled as though it was her birthday and she was surprised with a pony. A barmaid gasped as the candles were hushed by a whispering of the wind. Her rich, thick blood streaked across the window, causing the breeze. Hlival started the diversion, the attack. He was a whirlwind. He killed ferociously as he lashed out at all the on lookers. No one had time to think, do, or pray. Bernard was dazed as everyone else. Before he could bring himself around, the woman had her arms embracing his neck. "I could snap this! I want you to hurt, just as I did, when you cursed me and threw me out, nearly four hundred years ago!" The woman tightened her grip, not once breaking her concentration. "Lysa, is that you? Are you the one I had so little faith in to survive the next day rise? This is all very impressive, but you and your friend should leave now." Bernard actually smiled. He was so removed from everything, he never knew that his maker was in the same room with him, or did he?

Hlival was quietly feeding, a fringe benefit for aiding in Mal's defeat. "Damn you!" Lysa cut Bernard's throat deeply, just missing his major veins as she unwrapped her arms. This strike shocked Bernard deeply, as well as hurt him. He responded with thunderous rage. He was truly a beast. Any hesitation he had in showing his true power was dissolved at that moment. He became larger, hairier, but not as powerful as he should have been, Hlival made him, and was truly evil, but Bernard mastered his abilities. He was not dwarfed by blind evil, like Hlival. For the moment, Bernard was becoming weak, as her continued to secrete blood from his wound. The tear in his flesh wasn't heavy enough to kill. Bernard was easily strong enough to fight Lysa, but he would perish if he tried to take on Hlival as well. Hlival ceased feeding, spitting out the blood that was clotting in his mouth. He changed his form, like a mirage near an oasis, just in case his protégé fumbled, as she had in the past.

Lysa rose to the humble ceiling above. She shrieked and frothed as she chose where she was going to strike. Bernard burst out with a bolt of laughter that shook the snow off the roof. Hlival turned to Lysa, seeing that her wrath was not as traumatizing as he had hoped, took that as his queue to intercede. Hlival moved like light. He ripped his claws down Bernard's back. With his nails still in Bernard's back, Hlival picked him up and threw him across the rotted wood floor. His vulnerable chest nearly met with the wooden leg of a chair. Lysa ran over to him. "I shan't miss!" She picked up the piece of wood and stopped abruptly by a gleaming white hand, pulsating with cold, yet alert veins. With a squeeze, Lysa's arm was dangling, disconnected. Hlival picked himself up. He had been tossed aside by the flashing form that had just nearly broken off Lysa's arm. Hlival approached her, but Lysa's rage pushed caution in his face. Bernard had time to raise himself up. Then he gripped Lysa by the head. He kissed her, slowly. After he apologized to her, he snapped her neck. She never wanted to be what she had become. She had failed at it. Now, she had peace.

"I had hoped after you destroyed our lives once, that would've been enough, but I suppose nothing is enough, until you have completely annihilated something." Blythe now knew who her adversary was. It was the creature that had changed Bernard's and her mortal life to the one they had to secretly fear each night. "You should have known, I'm in this, no matter what! Destroying you two, is just like what your dear brother Bernard has to do with that little fool over there, I have to correct my mistakes. You both showed so much promise. I had hoped you would have killed much more by now. five hundred years! If you recall, I just really love a good fight!" Hlival flung his hair back and charged at Blythe. As Hlival hoofed toward Blythe, like a Clydesdale horse, Blythe unleashed a sword from the cane she had brought with her.

It was all over with one blow. His cold, pasty, misshapen head dropped, settling on the floor. The stench of old and new dead flesh spread throughout the room. Blythe sensed nothing else, except the fading odor that felt like her own from Bernard. Their scent wasn't as vile as the dead mass around them. It was one that could be confused with poor hygiene, mixed in with sickness. Blythe picked up Bernard like an infant, and flew out of the tavern. They only returned to their rented home long enough to gather what was necessary. Legend was created that night in that tavern, in that village, for as long as it stood. The legend lasted longer than the house they dwelled in. All the planning, the preparation, the work. It was all for nothing. Maybe, maybe not. Hlival never got to carry out his plan for global annihilation, much less destroying two of his brood. As for poor Lysa, she never had to fear the sun, or anything else, ever again.

Bernard healed in the cold Mongolian mountains. They had traveled far, and could go no further. Blythe couldn't take his weight on her for another yard. They took refuge in a cave that was highly secluded. Blythe fed him, and found clothing for him. She did everything she could to help rehabilitate Bernard. She wanted to reach her mind out to Alec, Elsebeth, and the girls to let them know of the great battle Bernard had fought, and the struggle he had before him. She couldn't, however. She vowed to Bernard that no contact would be made to the family until his heart healed. Now, his entire being, inside and outside had to repair itself. The healing process took longer than normal. It wasn't immediate as it usually was with most injuries. It took several weeks for Bernard to accrue all of his strength back. When food was scarce, Blythe had to feed Bernard with the blood from her own veins. This period was terribly difficult, since they both needed to regain, maintain their strength. When they were both strong enough to travel, they made their way to the Hawaiian Islands.

Bernard stayed as quiet as the moment after death, when the living isn't really sure life is over for the one they are looking down upon. He thought viciously about returning home, to where the rest of his breed was. He wasn't sure if he had purged himself of all the feelings of betrayal that tore at his conscience. He argued with himself that maybe Elsebeth was just in doing what she had, Bernard knew he was too full of passion when he fell in love with Elsebeth. He took her, without fully explaining what her life would be like from that point on. He felt guilty, which caused great torment with his damaged feelings as a sage and devoted husband. Blythe sensed his torture, and shushed his fears. She assured him that Elsebeth felt no ill feelings about the past. All Elsebeth wanted, other than having her family safe, was to have Bernard's forgiveness. At times, Blythe was surprised at Bernard's strict response to the infidelity. He was known to partake in many multiple love making sessions with maidens, simply for the experience, after Hlival had made him undead.

Bernard, before he was made, was destined to meet a vicious end, which he did. It was more of a beginning, however. Bernard ate and drank the richest of foods. He loved as many women, even at a rather young age, as he possibly could. His nature was raw and vivid. Blythe watched him, cautiously, but it was she who was taken from life first. Hlival made his presence known to her as she was just about to start her life. He destroyed her, but loved her at one time enough to leave her living undead with her only sibling, Bernard. Now, in the tropical night air, which was entirely too warm a climate for them, they talked about charting their course back to America. They arrived at the west coast of the

U.S. Their sabbatical of sorts had lasted nearly thirty years. It was now newly into the eighteenth century. The rest of the family had settled in a small isolated pioneering region.

Elsebeth tried to help Nola with the upkeep of their small, but comfortable home. They had decided to raise a few cattle, mainly for personal use, and to farm produce. During the day, Nola was a widowed land owner, which was hard for most local people to swallow, since she was not a white male. The are they inhabited was so desolate, that there weren't many people of "authority" to dispute her claims. Stray help, that didn't mind working for a *Nigress* would stay for short spurts, helping with the small amount of labor that was required to keep a modest income. They had the money to have an elaborate set up, but the need for too many people around would result in too many questions being asked.

The rest of the family kept a low profile. When nosy locals noticed the family out, they were put under great scrutiny, out of ignorance, if nothing else. When one of the townspeople became brave enough to interrogate Elsebeth one evening, she produced a story about how her father and sisters were victims of a rare skin disease that made it impossible for them to move about in daylight. Even though the story was bought, they still had to venture out with caution, and not make corpses of anyone that would be missed. It was hardly worth being in that area. There was too much to lose, too much that was already lost, or so Elsebeth feared.

Elsebeth was finishing up her chores one evening, thinking about her mate, Bernard. She missed him terribly, and thought deeply about him, nightly. She hoped he could sense her abandonment and realize that she had punished herself with grief much more than he could with his absence. At once, Elsebeth felt a rushing wind against her back. She could also smell a familiar fragrance, one that had the purpose of covering another odor. She wasn't alarmed, she was over-joyed.

"Bernard, Blythe, is that you? Please, show yourselves. I've missed you two so much! Come down, please, come down now." Elsebeth fell to her knees. She knew it must be them. She had not felt this false sense of life in her since Bernard convinced her of his love, after her transformation. "Please let it be them." She thought this, almost praying, as she looked upwards. "Are you looking for God, mon cherie? Don't bother looking for him, he's turned his back on our sorry souls." Bernard laughed as Elsebeth spun around to see the man she came to realize that she truly loved. "Bernard! Oh how I love you!" She jumped into his arms. He caught her effortlessly, with a steady embrace. He cradled her like a newborn babe. After his ordeal with his failed protégé and her heathen partner, he was genuinely glad to see the woman he wanted to spend his eternity with.

Blythe appeared behind Elsebeth, after Bernard set the trembling young woman down. It was hard to believe Elsebeth, in many ways, was still the young girl that was on the threshold of adulthood. Blythe looked at Elsebeth as she had, several centuries ago. They just continued to stare at each other. They almost simultaneously began to weep. The embrace they gave one another would break any mortals back. "I'm sorry. I will never look back at what was again. If I have the right, may I ask for both of you to trust me, please? If I should ever fail on this promise of total devotion, kill me " Elsebeth bowed her head down, expecting the worst, but hoping desperately for the best. "I shouldn't think that would be necessary, my love." Bernard faced his woman and kissed her as though it was for the last time. It wasn't. It was the first of many that would come just as passionately as that one, forever.

The family was overwhelmed to see the strayed members of their pack. The celebration was vibrant and festive, although short lived, due to the rising of the sun. At the last moments of night, Bernard pulled Morgana aside. "I must speak with you, daughter. I fear only one thing. Never did I fear that your mother didn't love me. I knew she wasn't ready to love me when I took her. I suspected something would develop, but infidelity certainly surprised me. Your mother and I have made our peace with one another. I am concerned, however, that we may never take comfort in the bond we once had. Morgana, your sister and you are my blood, my life! To most people, I have neither one of those, but with you, I do. My heart dares to beat when I am with you and Desmony. Do you understand what I am telling you?" Bernard actually held his breath. He never knew what to expect from his peculiar daughter. There were too many thoughts running through her mind for him to make any assumptions on her decision.

"I love you, father. You are the man I will always try to please, above all others. You help me bare being what I am. Everyone helps, but you dominate when I think on my family. Do I try to please you, to emulate you? Do I secretly desire to enjoy the taste of blood on my palate? Chance tells me no, but your influence makes it almost possible. Mother allows me to see myself. The time alone that you gave us was as much a gift for me, as a curse. We are strong together, but now, now it is your turn." Morgana spoke well, and without need for recourse. "Let us bed down for another day. The following night will tell much." Bernard led his daughter to her place of rest.

They all made their journey down, below Nola's bedroom floor, to their refuge. Blythe and Bernard were touched to see that among their canopy beds, there were two prepared for them. It was as though they were never gone. They were always in the hearts of Alec, Desmony, Morgana, Nola, and Elsebeth. The next evening was strange, to say the least, but the tension soon faded. No one made any mention of the reason for their separation, knowing that the issue was resolved. Everyone was comfortable with each other again. Just like old friends that only needed to reminisce for a while before they were as they once were. Once dinner was over, and everyone had their fill of the not -quite-stale blood, Desmony urged Morgana to go out with her. Desmony was still making up for lost time. Alec stayed home with Blythe, and Bernard made it perfectly clear he would be entertaining Elsebeth for the rest of the evening. Nola stayed in the parlor, playing choice classical pieces that filled the house with romance.

Bernard took Elsebeth to a desolate area nearby. He told her of the events that took place in Russia. She howled out in pain for him. They embraced each other tightly again, until their desire to be with each other took over. They made love to one another for several hours. Their need for more nourishment was abandoned for their hunger for the other's passion. Elsebeth was a gentle lover for him, since her was still not the beast that he had been. He wanted to be for her, since he knew how she missed him. Bernard winced as he became more and more excited by Elsebeth's advances. She was a clever lover. She searched out the few places on his body that she could stroke with her soft, nimble fingers. She then proceeded to use her tongue for the more tender areas. Elsebeth stroked Bernard's chest with her tongue, tasting his very essence.

Elsebeth suckled Bernard, below his waist. Bernard could barely stand having his one true love, take control of him like this. he was helpless to Elsebeth's sexual whims. After Elsebeth had awakened the essential part of her sleeping prince, she mounted him. Bernard sat up against a tree as Elsebeth did all of this to, for him. Elsebeth straddled Her love as she filled herself with him. Elsebeth pulled herself to Bernard. They were as close physically as they had become emotionally again. Elsebeth screamed as she climaxed. It was a sensation she hadn't felt in such a long time. Bernard surprised her with his response. He held onto her, like a babe. Her spilled tears as he clung onto her, kissing her breasts. He took his turn, suckling her breasts, just at the nipple, until all of their ecstasy was voided. They kissed one another, and Elsebeth placed herself next to Bernard.

After their expression of love was over, they held each other and stared skyward. "We've had enough of this mess. My love, when I wake each night, I only want to spend each night with you. I want to sleep during the day with you, near my side. I want solitude and peace for us. We will feed and we will love. That is my idea of a perfect life." Bernard smiled as he spoke these words to her. As he spoke, he slipped a jade choker around Elsebeth's throat. He kissed her neck, and her bit her, tasting just a morsel of her blood. Elsebeth leaned back, enjoying the pain that Bernard gave. she composed herself, and said to him, " I want all that you do, nothing more. I have something for you as well." She revealed a hand sewn ascot, made of lace. There were small pearls placed strategically throughout the article. They rose from their nestled position, kissed, and started their way home.

Alec and Blythe had finished reacquainting themselves with each other. They sat before the fireplace that Alec had constructed himself. The two were happy to see Bernard back with his bride. They were smiling so, that images of their love making flowed into the minds of both Alec and Blythe. Alec blushed, seeing his daughter pleasing her lord, her husband as she did. Elsebeth sensed that her father was not innocent, having taken the powerful Blythe. He touched her, and turned her into a frail woman, starved for affection and companionship. Alec made love, almost savagely to his beloved. She faced him as he pushed himself into her. He tried to be as sincere in his gestures, but his desire was too raw. He was able to hold on enough to satisfy Blythe. They came together, laughing all the while. Alec then turned over Blythe, moving his pulsating nature in her. Blythe was excited by the submission she gave Alec. He felt so good inside of her. She felt so close to him. They swore they loved each other. That was all the commitment she could muster, even though she truly loved Alec.

Alec held Blythe's breasts, supporting them as her charged her from behind. They stood together, at one point. they were one, physically. Alec placed two fingers inside her vagina, giving Blythe double pleasure. She came with such vitality. Alec turned towards him, to kiss her, fully. It wasn't possible for them to benefit from making love again. Alec couldn't muster a rise in such a short amount of time. Instead, Blythe pleased him, by bathing him. She soaked his body with a damp cloth, scented with oils. They water wasn't blessed, so he was safe, as was she. Alec smoothed the cloth over her body as well. They kissed each other all over, stopping for Blythe to kiss Alec, on the instrument that he used to please her inside. She made Alec growl as she pulled at his nature with her mouth. He tasted sweet to her. They exchanged blood with one another, to reaffirm their bond with one another. They adorned each other with fine Egyptian cotton robes, as they sat down in front of the low burning fire. the heat did them no good, but it finished the mood that was favorably set.

Bernard and Elsebeth changed into more comfortable clothes, so they all could recline into a completely relaxed state with Alec and Blythe. Nola had stopped playing, and resorted to her room. When she was certain everyone presentable, she came out. They all sat quietly, wondering what the two girls were doing. Their concern was concentrated on Morgana. She had been so quiet since her father and Aunt's return. What was going on inside her mind? It bothered Bernard greatly that Morgana hadn't come to him, to discuss her feelings. Their time was short, since Blythe and Bernard returned just before morning. Morgana knew that Bernard would need to speak with her mother, Elsebeth, before speaking with her. Morgana saw it as senseless to speak to him, if Bernard wasn't going to reconcile with Elsebeth. Her needs were secondary, as she saw it. That was simply her nature. Her world wouldn't be right until she knew her parents, the people that raised her, were back together. No one knew these thoughts that Morgana had. Desmony, in her own way, thought an adventure would help Morgana clear her mind.

Morgana's mood was unreadable. She was obviously glad to see Bernard and Blythe. She had made the time to express her love for them. She held onto them tightly, before Desmony had ruined the moment with her proposal for an excursion. With a glance from Morgana to Bernard and Elsebeth, then to Alec and Blythe, no other words needed to be said. All was understood. their love would never die. Through all phases of their evolution, their bond would always remain strong.

"You won't beat me, never!" Desmony had captured the lead in an airborne race. Morgana was close behind, but determined none-the-less. "You're cheating, Desmony!" Desmony then slowed up, just enough to bump Morgana so she would lose her momentum. "Bitch!" She pulled out her reserve energy so she could catch up with Desmony. Desmony had to swerve, so that she would miss an upcoming tree. Morgana went higher, trying to avoid any obstacles that would bring certain defeat. Crashing into a tree, and catching a tree limb in the heart at the speed they were carrying, would bring absolute death. Desmony elevated up to where Morgana was. Their desire to win was toying with the measure of time between that moment and sunrise. The more sensible Morgana realized this and yelled to Desmony that the winner would be the one to reach home without any burn marks. "You're right! We've gone too far. We'll be ashes if we don't beat ourselves back."

Morgana and Desmony hovered over a wooded area, a few hundred miles away from home, and safety. The terrain was largely a plain area, void of any real cover. Desmony looked at Morgana and said, "Next time." Their contest was put on hold, so they could attend to more important matters. They took off in the opposite direction and pulled at the air in hopes to reach their destination faster. They could see a slight change in the cloudless sky as they headed eastward. Desmony for once actually showed concern. She enjoyed living on the edge, but this was a little too much. Even though she wasn't actually alive, she still liked getting a rush. Even though she wasn't a living creature, she would perish if she continued to press her luck. It was approximately forty-five minutes to sunrise, and they had just under a hundred miles to go. The wind and trees chased after them as they shot across the air, undetectable by the naked eye.

"The sun is almost up, my love. Where could they be?" Elsebeth felt an uneasiness deep in her bones. "I feel them. They are feeling fear. I can barely sense them. They must be far." Bernard was concerned, but not yet afraid. There were only a few things that would allow Bernard to feel that uncomfortable sensation. Once, he felt it in Russia, when Hlival, the one who made him undead tried to destroy him, as he had done by terminating his human life. This would be the only other time. The words Bernard had spoken were tense and hollow. As the clock ticked, and the livestock began to make more noise, Nola awoke. She picked up on the family's tension. Nola rushed to prepare the girl's bed's, hoping they would be coming in shortly. Everyone waited, in cruel suspense.

"Hurry!" Desmony was coming undone. She felt her pores opening up. It was as if her body was drying out, like a fish without water. Her skin tingled as she felt the beginning signs of burning. It was a cloak, masking her entire body. It began to itch, and she couldn't ease the pain that was mounting up on her. The rising of the sun was almost deafening to Desmony. It banged hard. like a high school marching band kettle drum. The bravado lingered until the next rupture of sound. Desmony thought about what was happening, all around her. The day was being born, and she was about to die. She felt frail, afraid. "I am hurrying! damn it! I'm smoking!" Desmony began to cry as she saw her impending doom. she was being vanquished by the large orange orb behind her, licking at her toes. Morgana was beginning to feel weak. She felt a tingling, but not as bad as Desmony. Morgana was not experiencing the same sensations as Desmony. Morgana seemed to be under the effects of some psycho-trauma. It was true enough, she was wilting, fast. "Oh shit! There it is!" The sun? Home? Both were in reach.

Blythe saw them in the distance. "I hope no one sees this!" She took off to help them get back home, to their sanctuary. Blythe reached them just before the sun broke over the horizon. Blythe was precisely what they needed. She had with her a large blanket, thick enough to protect them from the blossoming sun. They were inside barley by the first true shinning of daylight. Nola hurried them downstairs to their beds. There was no time to undress, to prepare as they had for all this time, safely, as they should. The last memory they had was the disappointing looks on all the faces of everyone in the room.

CHAPTER THIRTEEN

The next evening was haunting, even for these creatures that dealt first hand with fear and death at all times. The two little demons were the last from their sub terrain rooms. All eyes were on them as they ascended cautiously. They both maintained very somber appearances. For each of them, goblets containing the life sustaining crimson nectar waited for them. Morgana struggled to look briefly at all of the discerning faces that glossed her over. Morgana looked away in shame as she saw their expressions. She started for the table that supported the two large pewter goblets. Desmony was used to the disapproval that was blowing on her like a fierce tempest. She walked more casually than her accomplice. Bernard broke the fog of tension, anger, fear, and disgust by bellowing, "How could you be so irresponsible? When are your insignificant little games going to end, Desmony? Morgana, I thought you had more sense! there is no measure of how disappointed I am with you. You nearly killed your mother inside. She's not any stronger than you are right now. For the duration of your lives, don't ever do anything like this to yourselves, or your family again!" Bernard was breathing down their throats now.

Morgana wept, but Desmony was angry. At what she was angry, she did not know. Desmony dropped her goblet, trembling in rage rather than fear. She retreated back to her bed. Morgana followed, apologizing for both Desmony and herself. There was just no justification for the stunt they had almost botched. After a while, all of the flared emotions were stored away and everyone reverted back to their usual characters. This sense of rejuvenated good will lasted for about one year. Another escapade was to come that would bring thrills to the memories of the girls, but of course not to the elders. The girls, with the help of Nola, planned their adventures more rationally, or so they thought. Desmony was always the miscalculated factor. Whether their stunts were smart or not, they were kept amongst themselves. None of this was to get back to the ones they respected so much.

Desmony skillfully approached Elsebeth and asked if the proverbial rope around her neck was long enough for the girls to take a short trip, via train. "Mother please! It's been so long since we rode a train. I want, we want to see how the cities have changed since we've been back to the Americas." Desmony sat at her mother's feet, looking up at Elsebeth with her doe-like eyes. Elsebeth almost laughed. The sincerity was tainted with Desmony's thirst for adventure, as well as for blood. "Well dear, you haven't jeopardized any one's life, or yours, for that matter. I'll let you go on one condition." "What is that?" Desmony seemed nervous, anxious. She hated making promises she couldn't guarantee. "Nola must go with you. She will study the train routes and stops. Someone must be with you to remind you of the difference between day and night. "Elsebeth stroked Desmony's long, dark, wavy mane of hair. "You mean death and life", said Desmony. "Respectively, dear, respectively. I don't intend to be mean, but you must never forget the basics." Elsebeth kissed her daughter on her crown and leaned back, for a rest.

A week later, the girls were on their way. It was to be a short trip to visit some of the nearby towns. That covered several hundred miles, round trip. It was amazing for them to witness the little dust bowl towns being created, constructed by men that felt they had a purpose. They wanted a better life, to leave their mark for generations to see. The girls wondered, albeit briefly, how their first American home was fairing. Was it still standing? Was it being borrowed by vagrant wanderers? The answer to both questions should have been no. The land was still being looked after, by the town officials. The law was in their favor with that acquisition.

Morgana and Nola often spoke and thought about this phrase that they kept hearing, "Manifest Destiny". It was an injustice for them to have seen what the land was like before the booming development taking place. The original inhabitants were being run out from land that they had shared with the spirits of their ancestors for centuries. It was all too sad, and made Morgana irate. "I'll leave my mark too, on the throats of those who have bullied the Natives out of the land that all should be able to share!" Morgana never had a tolerance for exploitation, of any sort. Desmony joined in Morgana's burst of emotion, but she really only paid attention to the throat part. It was almost as if she was joking with her sister, over something Morgana felt strongly about.

An argument ensued, but Nola intercepted the first strike and said, "Morgana, don't use inhumanity to justify your feeding needs. It's been a tool for you, but it isn't right. Desmony, don't taunt or encourage, all right! It makes you look like a fool." Nola was usually quiet, but a train ride with these two was enough to shake the most tranquil of souls. The train that rocked them all through the night stopped just before dawn. They departed off the train and sought solace in a cold, damp, deserted mine that appeared sturdy. The next evening, they would go investigate the city life. Desmony was anxious. She really wanted to stir things up.

The town was sparsely lit. The only building that held any life was the saloon. It looked relatively established, by age. The paint was beginning to free itself from the happy shack. People were going in and out. Most were laughing. Some were yelling and fighting. A glass shattered against the ground as Desmony and Morgana entered the saloon. Nola was not far off. She hung back, waiting to see if any fireworks would ignite, literally or just figuratively.

The shards of glass jumped up, and a few pieces nicked Desmony on her cheek. She made no motion to twitch. A drip of blood tapped the floor as she stood there, trying to contain her excitement. The bartender jumped to their aid. "Sorry 'bout that, ma'am. Didn't mean no harm. These angry curses just don't have no upbringin'!" He called himself Rawley Gibbs, a man with a limp from the civil war and a lake full of war stories. "I'm old, but I'll kick any body's ass that hurts you fine ladies." He fixed Desmony's cut, even though it would heal completely in a short while. It would've healed even sooner, if she had fed. Rawley showed them to a secluded table. "Let me know if I can fix y'all somethin' to gnaw on, all right?" "Actually, I would like to acquaint me with that young man over there." Morgana was being seduced by Desmony's spirit. She wanted to surrender to the lust, the fever she was feeling inside. Morgana wanted to see, just once if it was the instinct that she tried so desperately to hold in. She wanted to know which side of her was stronger, the vampire, or the human. Which will would win? Which would she like?

Desmony knew how to play the game, not the ones that were being played with cards or dice. The game they played would leave some random human begging for their lives in vain. Desmony was intrigued by the fact that Morgana took the initiative this time out. Desmony sat back and ordered a shot of whiskey, no ice. Rawley made his way over to the gentleman in question. He was the one who had thrown the glass that landed at Desmony's feet. The young man was in motion to hit a saloon girl that was not far from them. The girl was new there, and didn't feel ready to do his bidding. The young man settled for insulting her and bedding down with a more experienced female.

The young man was drunk, and a little tired, but he was more than willing to accept Morgana's invitation. He staggered over to where Morgana poised herself. She gave him a look that dared him to approach her. He braced himself on her table and said, "Hello there, fine lady. The 'ol man told me you would like to acquaint yourself with me. Is that so? I hope so, because I haven't seen a woman as clean and pretty as you in many a moon!" He looked over to the other woman he had spent time with, and indifferently pleaded, "No offense". He nearly plummeted to the ground as he hooted and laughed. Several other men and women were watching the spectacle. The men laughed more heartily than the women. One woman in particular was studying Desmony. Desmony did a double take, then looked around, seeing nothing but a wall behind her. Desmony thought to herself, "So, that's how it is with you? Well, it matters not to me what you do, as long as your blood is hot and sweet!" Desmony excused herself, knowing that Morgana could more than handle this mortal beast. Desmony went crossed over to the woman that was totally ignorant as to what she had gotten herself into.

"My name is Daryl Fredricksen, and you are?" He sat next to Morgana, putting his arm around her shoulders. "My name is irrelevant. It doesn't matter. You know precisely what I am interested in. Being friends would be an erroneous assumption. I want a man. You appear to be strong, with a healthy appetite. I trust you know what I want as well. Is my impression accurate enough?" Morgana felt as cold as she was portraying herself as being. The words Morgana spoke blew Daryl away. He didn't understand them all, but it all impressed his grandiose ego. He ran his hands through his sandy blond hair and cleared his throat. "You sure you don't do this for a livin'?" "Maybe I do, but it is no concern of yours. Look on the bright side, you don't have to pay, with money." Morgana unveiled an evil smile as she finished. She longed for Victor inside, which made her more determined to see this through.

As they both stood up from the table, he placed his hand on the small of her back. She giggled at his gentleman pretenses. He started up the stairs with her leading the way. Morgana paused, and Daryl inquired as to why she stopped. "You ain't goin' yella on me, are ya?" "No. Not at all. I just had to alter my plans somewhat." Morgana returned to her previous brain or soul-washed state. she was evil again, not hurt, but empty all the same. She had planned to take Daryl somewhere secluded, like usual, and take his life-blood. With the present situation, her goal would be difficult, but not impossible. They approached the door to Daryl's room. Daryl cut a glance at his mystery date. "Are you ready for this, ma'am?" He smiled smugly. "Are you?" Morgana had to hide away the humor in her response. The way she had said those words to him made his smirk retract with a feeling of unease. Daryl opened the door and spontaneously picked up Morgana. He carried her over to the bed. He laid her down and took off his coat. He smelled of sweat, dirt, and old sex. Morgana concentrated to get past that. She wondered how men, no matter how unattractive for various reasons, thought they were every woman's reason for living! She laid there, perfectly passive. He did her nostrils the favor of splashing some water on his face. He pulled off his raggedy shirt, which had concealed a lean but defined body. Daryl moved his hands across his torso with the luke-warm water, hoping to excite Morgana.

Daryl came back to where Morgana laid. He began to undo the laces of her dress. She rose up to help with her bustier. She let him get down to her silk bloomers. Right there, she stopped him. She began to, at that time, to oblige him. In no time, she had him down to his dirty white unions. One by one, Morgana unfastened each button. His smile widened as she did this. Her fangs throbbed as they searched for the surface of her gums. They penetrated through, letting her know, above all other signs, including her hunger, that it was time. Morgana held her head down, trying to conceal her monstrous secret. This seduction wouldn't work if she looked at him and he saw her black pupils and retina looking back at him, with the rest of her eyes a fluorescent flame. Morgana's nails, unsuspected by him, grew as she moved her hands down to where his navel was. This was where the last button was located. Now was the time! Morgana had to strike at that very moment! She reared her head back, hissing like a Cobra, then roaring like a lion.

Daryl's moans of ecstasy and joy suddenly turned into howls of horror. The noise down in the saloon was too great for anyone to hear his initial cry. The patrons at the bar would've mistaken his scream for a shout of satisfaction without any doubt. Morgana hushed Daryl with her left hand while she steadied his neck with her right. She nestled her teeth deep into his neck, suckling it until she was full. It never took a large quantity of blood to sustain her. If it wasn't for the nausea she experienced with most foods, she would be more inclined to use that as her source of nourishment. Morgana gently laid Daryl's body down on the bed.

Morgana wiped the blood on a sheet from her mouth. Just then, she heard footsteps. It was the old man with the limp. He was the only one that heard the yell and thought something suspicious was about. The man knocked on the door, announcing himself several times. After no answer, he became very alarmed. The old man got some help to knock down the door. When he and a few other men that weren't too drunk got the door to give way, it flew open. What they found was Daryl's dead body and curtains, motioning in the wind from the opened window that led to the alley below. The breeze kicked up the lace curtains, which gave the room a more eerie feeling. Death was taking a survey in that room. All that were in that room wondered if their name was on the list. What if whatever, whoever did this was still present? They all had questions, but no one wanted to stay around to debate the topic. That good 'ol boy's death was a freak incident, one that was tied to a very beautiful and mysterious woman that was nowhere to be found.

The next morning, the saloon girl that had taken a fancy to Desmony was found in a field, not far away. She was void of any blood, of any life. The towns people knew what had happened there. They knew something was evil there, but what it was exactly, they could not tell. Before anyone could react to any suspicions, had they the nerve, the girls were held up in a cave, more than a day's ride on any of those men's best horses. That night, they all changed their clothes. They burned the ones they had worn. They reached the next town, by flight with no difficulty, carrying Nola. They boarded the next available train, unnoticed. Desmony was spry, and spoke well into the night with Nola.

Morgana sat alone, to herself. she was mourning her actions from the night before. What she had done had a catastrophic effect on her, one she didn't anticipate having. she resolved that she wanted nothing to do with that side of her any longer. She would figure out how to sustain her life, but it would no longer be from taking blood. She felt more tranquil and at peace with herself when she wasn't stalking or feeding. Now, she was truly lost. She needed direction, but from whom would she receive it from?

After resting in a deserted mine shaft, Morgana pleaded with Desmony to cut their trip short. It was something Nola agreed to, due to the delicate state Morgana was in. Both wanted to return home. Morgana was much in need of more than Desmony's seduction into a life Morgana was ready to give up on, even Nola's unconditional love and support. "I just can't do this right now!" Morgana paced back and forth the side of some decaying dirt tracks in the road. "You mean you won't do this, anymore! There is a big difference. You can't simply ignore this very real part of you that exists. You are more a vampire than human for the simple reason that you do need blood, no matter how emotionally crippled it makes you feel. You can't survive on bread, fruit, or vegetables! Also, my dear sister, vampires are more powerful than humans, or did you forget that? There is so much appeal to being what you are, and you don't even appreciate it!" Desmony was stroking herself, proud of the speech she had just given. Vampires around the globe would've been proud of her.

Morgana pondered briefly on Desmony's statements and replied, "Then, is that why we can't worship God, or any god, even if we wanted to? My desire to not be what I am goes much deeper than whether or not I can make someone fear me. I can't let anything that might be more powerful than me know that I do fear it! I do. I can't expect you to understand. I cannot accept who, what I am. I just can't!" Morgana's face was flushed with Daryl's blood. "Every creature has its limitations. You and those fascinating spirits you search to worship can fly. Man has dreamed of that for centuries. One day, he might accomplish that, along with all the other things he has done. Men can hold roses, they pray too. Be happy with what you have, unless you can change it." Nola seldom had anything to say. She had just shared more than she probably had in her entire life. She had loved God, and spiritual things, but she made a choice, and she was *living* with it. She wanted Morgana to do the same, so she wouldn't be so unhappy.

Right now, Nola's wisdom was only a pacification, but a potential solution to a problem that had lived several life times. The problem for Morgana was deep rooted and very severe. Instead of any physical, emotional, mental attempts to bring her over to her vampire side, or verbal reasoning from others, she became obsessed with her mortal side.

Desmony was furious. All right! We go home! The next train will take us there, whether it wants to, or not. I've had enough of this. Mother, Blythe, or someone will bring your silly self around. I will never forget this trip, and neither shall you!" Just then, Desmony had a thought. She became disturbingly quiet. Morgana and Nola felt uneasy about what she must have planned. The knowledge that Desmony actually thought out her tactics was refreshing, but still not any more reassuring. They waited until nightfall. They boarded a train that held only a handful of passengers. and an engineer that would take them back, back to their reality, which was a nightmare to all else.

Desmony rubbed up against a young man gently, making him turn a bright shade of red. "I'm sorry, Ma'am, I didn't mean." Desmony interrupted the young man's apology. "That is quite all right. It was my fault." At first, Desmony was ready to dine on his thick young blood. There was something in his nature that pleaded with her strain of a conscience. Amazingly enough, she still had one. She looked for other prey as she roamed the corridors of the locomotive. Maybe, she didn't rip the young man apart because of Morgana. Desmony's temper had subsided, so there was a slight chance she wouldn't follow through with her threat to destroy maliciously. Desmony wasn't bitter or spiteful against her sibling. She was just sad for Morgana.

Morgana and Nola took comfort in their compartment. Soon, they would be close enough to home to fly back. Nola would travel on the train to make sure their luggage was returned properly. It seemed silly, but she wanted to make sure that nothing indicated their journey wasn't destructive.

Desmony changed her attire, and slid out of the misery Morgana permeated throughout the small room, keeping crude thoughts to herself. Nola watched her and waited for the next command.

Desmony worked her way to another car. Upon entering the next car, she saw a familiar face. It was one she had seen on a wanted poster. "Perfect!" Desmony thought this as she moved closer to him, forcing his focus on her and only her. The man was well groomed, but scared from a previous confrontation. He had a hard expression. Desmony all this and more as he looked up at her. His face melted from a scrounge to something more inviting as Desmony continued closer. The evil was still in him, deep under his skin, but Desmony disarmed the man, without him even being aware it was happening to him. "Are you some of the local flavor, miss?" "No, I'm from all over. You look as though you've come across some tough country though." Desmony positioned herself to her liking on a bench, facing him. "What's your name, sir?" "I'm not much for names. Listen, you don't ask me your name, and I won't ask yours." The man felt in control, as he had for most of his life. "Mine is Desmony. I'm not afraid of anything, are you?" She leaned in, looking for the fear in his eyes. Her stare at him mirrored the look of fear that she was looking for, deep within his eyes. He did a fine job of hiding it, which impressed Desmony very much. Desmony's glowing eyes helped the man reveal his fear because they shinned a luminescent black onyx. Her cool glance at him unsettled him, chilling him right to the marrow.

"Take me to your room." Desmony had appealed to every weakness the man owned. She had raped his mind and gave him no choice. His fate was in her fangs and claws. He raised himself up and took her hand. They faced each other as they stood up. Her power was working, as it always did. This routine was rather stimulating. Others looked at them as they got up. Their looks suggested they knew exactly what was going on, even though they didn't have a full scope of the scenario. The seduction had been a success. They didn't know what Desmony had in store for the grubby man. The man knew he could not break free from Desmony's charm. He knew his death, or something dreadful was afoot. The man's eyes pleaded with her, as he stared in silence. A tear fell from his quivering eye. The tear walked down his cheek, and started its descent to the floor. Desmony caught the tear in midair. It turned black when it connected with her bare hand. It was a crystal-like stone in form. It shinned brightly against the opalescent moon that shone through the open windows. "I have a chest filled with these." Desmony smiled and led him to his room. She knew precisely where it was. She knew everything about each of her victims. It was a talent that she possessed. It was a killing tool that made her very successful at what she enjoyed doing.

The man closed the door and locked it after Desmony crossed his threshold, leaving him utterly powerless. He came to her with intense haste. His mind was not his own. He wanted the passion Desmony was sure to give him. That was all she'd do for him, before she struck him dead. He cuddled her in his arms, passionately, taking control of her lips. Desmony allowed the fondling for only a short time. this was her game. She pushed back surprisingly to him with equal force.

Desmony tore his clothes off, literally. She was changing as their sexual activity escalated. With each heaving of their breath, her appearance changed. First, the claws, then the fangs. Her eyes were now a bright auburn, burning with lust for the kill. The man was emotionally numb. He wasn't even feeling the fear that by every right he should have been feeling. All he was experiencing was the mutual lust raiding his very being. Desmony nestled under his chin and slid her fangs past his dirty, oily, and musty skin. They moved past the skin, then the tissue, finally reaching the source of his life force. She found the crimson nectar she yearned for. The pain was too much for the man. He bellowed from the core of his dying soul. He mourned his own death for a short while. Desmony drank as much as she could, knowing his scream would alert many people nearby. She could feel the footsteps coming toward the room. She could also hear the voices inquiring what the noise was. Desmony released her grip and let the corpse fall limp on the floor. Blood was still flowing from the tear in his throat. A crashing bump at the door alerted Desmony. No more food for tonight. Desmony turned for the window for her escape. Just then, the compartment door flew open, letting several men in, as many could fit.

They never saw her. They only gave chase, hoping to catch something. It was difficult to see her dark form in the night. She had vaulted to the top of the train. It was effortless for her to accomplish such a task. The men had a much more difficult time trying other routes to get to the top of the moving locomotive. Desmony was feeling so cocky, she began to dance on top of the iron horse. One man in the pack had his gun with him. The area they were in was hostile, but during the ride, no one was concerned about gun play. The man with the gun was suspected to use his gun to earn his living. The man tried to steady himself for a shot at whatever, whoever was on top of the train, but it was moving too fast. Luck would have to help any bullet meet her slender, mobile frame. Desmony looked back at the other two men that were brave enough to come after the vicious killer. She gave the men a smile that made them stand erect, like ice statues. All color and spirit left them. Desmony leapt silently into the ebony background surrounding the world around them. They stared in amazement and reluctantly descended the ladder, back to the train. They wrote her off as some crazy lady that found her way on the train to kill the outlaw. She was taken for dead, throwing herself off the train, having completed her mission. That was going to be the story that spread throughout the territory, at any rate.

No one would imagine that Desmony, the woman, had landed gracefully on the ground, several yards away. She would wait, catch up with the train, and assume her identity. Desmony did all this, pasting herself against the window to the girl's compartment. Nola started, but Morgana remained calm. She knew everything that was happening, as it happened. Not so much she could read her demon sibling. She simply knew Desmony. Morgana raised herself up, then the window. Desmony crawled in. She changed clothes and leaped into bed. "Hurry, go back to what you were doing. Please try to behave innocently." Desmony merely acted as if she had pulled off a school-girl prank, with none but her confidants the wiser.

Conductors were checking the rooms, hoping no one else had become a victim of the mad woman that jumped the train. A rather young man that insisted on helping with the search came to their door. Nola answered the knock, opening the door wide open. "May we help you, sir?" She was wiping sleep away from her eyes, that actually had been there. Desmony's back was to the man. She had fallen asleep, as though nothing had happened. Morgana asked what had awakened everyone. "Ma'am, I'm sorry to have to tell you this, but a man was savagely murdered a short while ago. A wild woman did it. She climbed to the top of the train and took her own life afterward!" The man was high on adrenaline and embarrassed to be standing in front of three incredibly beautiful women.

Morgana sensed the young man's anxiety, and spoke. "We're terribly sorry to hear about that. Is there anymore danger?" Morgana was really more disgusted than frightened, but she couldn't let the man know she was sure there would be no more excitement. "No, ma'am. I think it's all over. The mad woman must be dead. Maybe it was true love gone bad. It's just awful!" Desmony got up from her conscious-free nap. A conductor passed by the room, and saw her. He turned positively ghostly when he looked at her. "Good night, sir." Morgana closed the door before either man could lace Desmony's face. All three women took each other's hands and worked an incantation, like a witch would, so that the men would not have any repressed memories come about while the girls were still on board. The charm didn't take long to perform. The hand holding was a formality at best. They were the root of all the fear everyone experienced in that train that night.

Morgana tried her best to crush Desmony's hand as she held it. Desmony only winced a bit, and laughed any possible pain she felt off. It was a welcomed response from Morgana. Morgana had cut their trip short, and Desmony had promised her she would pay. Their fight had ended, but the war raged on.

A few days later, the family was welcoming the girls back. The girls had many stories to tell of the dying 'wild west'. Towns were becoming more cosmopolitan, and talk was going around about covering up the dirt roads in some of the larger cities. A new era was starting for the country. What effect those changes would have on the family remained to be seen. The land was fast becoming less and less remote. More and more of their activities would be monitored by the nosy neighbors that surrounded them, as far away as they were. The girls talked much about their observations, but not of their experiences. Those stories would be evaded for a long time, if they were ever to be told. Hopefully, the myth of the wild woman on the train wouldn't reach their door step, or Desmony would be instantly persecuted for the stunt, no matter how long ago it would have been.

Morgana had her own secret to keep. She buried the shame of what she had done to herself. It ate at her, like a cancer, or acid. She imagined the sun feeling like that on her, the guilt she was torturing herself with. Nola shared her personal stories. She had learned much, and saw just how little so things hadn't changed. She was still a little Negro that wasn't given the courtesy of a man tipping his hat to her, or a lady granting a free smile. Nola yearned for society to change, to accept her. It wasn't the right time. At least she stood a chance to see some change in her lifetime, since hers would no doubt be longer than any human in existence. Nola felt some reassurance, coming back to a family that loved her so dearly and unconditionally. Nola had put her soul in jeopardy for these people, but to hear her speak of it, she felt her life was hell before coming upon Morgana. She wasn't a strong enough mortal to handle the life she'd been given. She wasn't hurting anyone, even though she was protecting creatures that did hurt, but for survival. They're part of a curse, seen as freaks or creatures of the devil in society." Nola thought this as she reflected on her journey.

Desmony had so much to speak about. Everything about her excursion was electric. She told them about every detail she could recall. She did keep the train sequence to herself, although the thought of it made her giggle. Desmony felt so clever. Bernard stood as she continued her tale. "I have some news of my own. My darlings, while you were away, we had some visitors. People are beginning to talk. I fear we may have to relocate. I know of no other passive way to protect us." Bernard let his head fall. His now lengthy dark hair sheltered his look of disdain.

"We should go to the mountains." Alec said only what he needed to. "There are some very secluded places up there. We can live, peacefully, for a while. Human blood will be scarce for a while. Of course we can live on animal blood. Human blood will be more of a delicacy for than ever. We have no choice, save to go underground and sleep, only to awaken weak and out of touch with this fast changing country. The thought of hiding from the life we have been given to live seems to be unacceptable. Besides, it wouldn't be fair to dear Nola. We must look after her, as she does for us. That is my thought on this." Alec sat back in the large oak chair he had made. His expression welcomed any feedback. There were only signals of agreement from everyone. The fact they had to leave was accepted, and acted upon with haste. They worked each night, making preparations for their hiatus. Townspeople would attempt to spy on them, to no avail. The family could sense them, literally, a mile away. They left one evening, during a new moon.

They were mere shadows without the light of the moon, moving with absolute stealth. The journey was made with delicate calculation. Mountains and caves were easily located with the terrain they toured. They never needed to fear the flaming sphere that could annihilate each of them. Nola made sure that all went well as a scout. She also lured in stray, unwanted loners. The family wanted them, but not for love or companionship. They needed blood. This gift was demanded and taken, if necessary. When Nola's beauty or seductive skills would fail, her strength was a sure back up.

CHAPTER FOURTEEN

They settled in a small area just before the Canadian border. The Northwest was a comfortable zone for them. The winters were cold, hard, and dark. People were scarce, which was bitter-sweet. They welcomed a rest from the hiding, the assimilation, and the fear. most wouldn't admit it, but they did possess that feeling. If they could only have one feeling, fear would be the most likely. They hid that vulnerability under their false sense of invincibility. Nola worked, existed to help them survive. She ventured out, just enough so she could find out what changes were occurring in the larger cities. Nola would bring back news of the changing world after her short trips into town for supplies. Nola soon found it ironic that her family chose to go into hiding at this time. So many changes were happening, with the industrial revolution and the first world war.

When the war came, they went to where the battles were being fought. They took advantage of their anonymity in places like Germany, England, and Italy. They feasted well, and made careful not to get close to any humans. No one was in the mood to try, having been deprived of human blood for so long. Morgana was ill at all the feeding, mostly that she had to take part in it. She thought about Victor. He would be either very old, or dead now. She missed him terribly. She tried to turn her depression into fuel to feed, but it didn't make the blood taste any sweeter. It only made her gag and curse her station in life. Morgana was happier dwelling in her solitude. She tried to feed on raw meat, but it was too much for her system to digest. She thought about her mother. She wondered what it must have been like to be human, as she once was. Morgana craved what her mother and grandfather were.

Morgana never stopped trying to assimilate. Desmony and Blythe walked in on Morgana as she was conducting an experiment. She was trying to eat cooked meat. They turned in nausea as she bit off the broiled meat. It turned her stomach once the meat touched her tongue. Desmony fainted from the smell. "Would you stop this madness?" Blythe tolerated enough of Morgana's whims and quests for the unobtainable. "We're legends! We have powers that humans don't! Why can't you enjoy the existence you have?" Blythe threw herself own into her favorite chair. "Have you ever thought that humans have powers that we don't?" Morgana feared saying those words. Blythe totally believed her existence was far superior than humans. "We all do the best with what we have." Blythe looked at Morgana so cool. Blythe's eyes said at the same time that no more was going to be discussed of this, not between them.

Morgana's thirst for mortality was almost as great as her thirst for blood. She concealed her blood-lust much more. The only difference was that if she went without blood for too long, she would allow herself to lose all strength and power. They all were frightened of her. Morgana's complexion was almost transparent. She read the newspapers, books, and magazines from cover to cover. She kept up on current events. Morgana was not going to be caught off guard when she returned with her family back into society. She certainly wasn't behaving like the phoenix that she was meant to be. She was a sad creature.

Life was hollow and empty as time passed. It did so with cryptic slowness. Many decades had passed. It was necessary to wait until a new generation of people existed, or at least until the people they had come into contact with were so old that their faculties wouldn't allow them to remember, or to be taken seriously. Bernard decided the time had come for them to venture southward, towards the pacific coast. Before he made the announcement, he discussed his plans with his mate, Elsebeth. She implored him to reason with their child Morgana. She had come as close to killing herself as possible. She was forced to drink blood when she was too weak to fight anyone off. "Of course my love, but we have virtually exhausted every facet of reasoning there is. She is trapped in a hell that we brought her into." Bernard was very alerted by Morgana's behavior and appearance, but didn't know what to do. "Don't you mean I brought her into this?"

Elsebeth bowed her head as she reminded her husband of her profound indiscretion.

Bernard nodded his head, turning away to leave the room. He went to Morgana's room, anxiously hoping to hear some form of compromise from the talk he wanted to have with her. He was hoping the news of them going back into a populated area, with many people, would bring her some joy. Would it? There was always the possibility that being around people would depress her more, since she yearned to be like them, but could only fight her desire to have their blood.

Bernard found Morgana sitting alone, concentrating on an owl in a tree some yards away. "You know, they're somewhat like us. I often wonder, who is really stronger? At those times I become frightened, vulnerable. I am alone at those times, of course. My dearest, for the better part of a century, you've been experiencing a type of melancholy, am I correct? I believe I am. You don't despise us, just your circumstances. We all want something we can't or shouldn't have. That is nature. My darling daughter, taking blood is the way we live. Everyone and everything denies another creature life, so that it may live as long as fate will allow it to. Don't you understand? Humans are just a different life form from. They eat beef, poultry, and pork. We in turn must dine on them. Some people in fact eat what others consider pets. Morgana, I care no longer to see you in such a state. I do, however, care about you. Don't enjoy feeding, that's fine.

Don't kill yourself to prove a point. Don't torture yourself. You know you can't starve yourself to death. There are only rare instances where a vampire can kill themselves. I will not share that knowledge I have with you, because I think your life is too precious to throw away, even if you don't share that sentiment." Bernard cupped Morgana's head in his hands. Both of them were trembling.

"I know, father. I suppose I'm trying to make up for murdering someone, as Desmony would. I've never told anyone, it scared me so." Morgana thought back to the wounds she had gotten during the last attack. "I'm not for this. There must be some solution. I've read and searched all this time. I've found nothing." Morgana laid her head on his left breast and sobbed. The thought that her wound had taken so long, longer than any of Desmony's scrapes had, alarmed Morgana. It gave her reason to believe there might be something more to her feelings than mere wishes for human traits. The wounds were not still there, however. They had been healed for some time now. Morgana continued to see these scars whenever she looked at that spot. They would never go away.

Bernard split open his arm and let the blood surface from his broken flesh. The fluid dripped slowly into Morgana's supple lips. She squinted her eyes and drank the nectar provided for her out of love, and a sparse amount of pity. "If you must feed, feed from me. When you are ready, I'll teach you some techniques that might suffice, right?" Bernard moved Morgana back and held his forearm until it healed completely. During the moments that process took, Morgana wiped her mouth clean. She came closer to her father, kissing him on his lips. It was a sweet kiss, filled with the gratitude of a child for its parent for a desired gift. The embrace that followed was one of surrender and acceptance. Morgana finally decided to try to be what her mother had created, a vampire.

Bernard taught Morgana self-hypnosis. It aided her when she needed to feed. He gave her a trigger word that prompted her to satisfy her thirst. It helped some, but she was much happier when her mother, Nola, and she went into town and assisted the town in collecting blood. Some of the donations went home with them, just before dawn. It wasn't a style of living a vampire could be proud of, but it was a commendable compromise. Alec and Blythe had become quite comfortable living in the high mountains. Blythe was proud of Morgana's difficult progress. Alec tried to help Blythe understand Morgana's turmoil, but it was becoming hard for him to remember his struggle with no longer being human. Alec tended to Blythe's every need, and Blythe obliged him with love and passion. Their bond was that of great works of poetry and what every mortal woman dreamed of having.

Seeing Blythe's face for all eternity was something beyond pleasure for him. Blythe had lost her blood-lust. She was becoming more concerned with sustaining her family, namely her granddaughter, Morgana. She had stopped resenting Morgana for not resolving to accept her lineage, the prevalent part of her being. Now, she wanted to help Morgana, so that she may live as long as Blythe had. Blythe wanted all of her brood to be as strong as she was. Even though she no longer fed for sport, she was fulfilled tending to her family. She fed as she needed, merely to live. Morgana respected Blythe for the gesture. It came from Blythe's own desire if the truth were to be known. Blythe was as strong as ever, and wanted Morgana to be just the same.

Blythe's heart seemed to be reborn somehow. Her main focus was on Alec. She devoted most of her time to making him content. They loved constantly. He was her idea of romance; an interest she hadn't taken part in for so many centuries. She did, however, see a great amount of honor in sacrificing her safety to help one of her family. The less she fed and focused on her family, the weaker she was. For her, this was the only way.

Desmony made the most of her seclusion from civilization. She would bitch and moan until she could sneak out and terrorize some small distant town. " I want to be the boogie man everyone fears! I want to be that shadow that follows some terrified villager home! Ha! I love it! Yes, it is true. Nothing gives me more pleasure than seeing black hair turn white. This hiatus has been torture for me! I've hidden myself long enough. I want to stretch my claws." As Desmony spoke, her words reached screeching highs, but sank to chilling deep octaves as her family looked on at her as she was losing control. Elsebeth interceded, grabbing Desmony by the shoulders. "Look, girl. You must collect yourself. This behavior, these antics won't solve anything! The time will be right, soon enough! Now, just stop it!"

Elsebeth was actually frightened by the way Desmony was carrying on. Elsebeth lightened her mood, and tone to make the announcement she had come in the room to make. "I have news. We have concealed ourselves for more than a long day. It is time to go out. We must be ready. We must be careful, as you all know, when we first step out. We must be more careful than before. Times have changed, Nola can attest to that. Horses are no longer a means of transportation. They are merely used for recreation and sport. Some people use them for work, but are small in number. weapons, like guns, are held only by the law, now called police officers. It isn't just a sheriff and a few harmless deputies. There are huge buildings, filled with them. They expand, along with the cities. There are anti-law people as well. They are groups of people called gangs. They aren't like the gangs of before that rode in outfits. These people carry guns and terrorize citizens. The military are just as advanced as everything else. Their weapons are powerful enough to wipe out entire countries! Fortunately, man has learned not to use these weapons. Instead, they threaten each other with the threat of global destruction." Elsebeth moved to sit down, so that she could continue to inform everyone.

"Many powerful leaders have risen and fallen. Not all of them were benevolent leaders. There was one that wiped out more humans than we have ever tried to, and wasn't stopped for years, even when others knew what was happening! Man kills much too easily. This is good news for you, but it sad to see any species burn itself out. As for us, we will start out small, as before, and scope out a remote area to live in. Remember, like I've said, things are different. People are not as naïve or superstitious. They're much more. and will hurt us, if they have the opportunity. I won't lose any of you, Desmony, after all this time. Blythe and I have spoken. Anyone that goes against the rules that have been established will be locked underground, if you don't try to live as you should. Anyway, there is much night life in the cities. We should blend in much better now." Elsebeth stood up and moved over to a wall, where she leaned up against. Her reluctance to step out into the new world she described was very apparent on her face as she stood there.

"When do we leave?" Nola had much to prepare. It wasn't a much as her being excited to venture out. She just focused on her responsibilities without fail. Her demeanor was very calm, conveying she was working. Nola was ready to make the move. She had been studying the changing times and new what overwhelming preparations she had to make.

She had to make sure everyone else was ready as well. "You will, with the new moon at the end of this week, Nola. We head for the pacific coast. The sun is very bright there, and the temperature is quite high, but we have found a place there with an acceptable climate. Nola will evaluate the area, which is called Northern California. She will determine what area we will occupy. After she selects the area, she will find a suitable residence for us to dwell in." Bernard concluded his part of the briefing and encouraged everyone to rest and take everything in slowly.

Nola left on the first night of the new moon, as agreed. She traveled by train, sitting far away from any of the other passengers. She wasn't sure how people would treat a single, colored female, traveling alone. There were a few friendly people that nodded their heads, but most kept to themselves. This was a blessing to Nola. She did wonder, however, what they were thinking. She didn't possess the skill of telepathy like the others did. She overheard off-color remarks, not necessarily about her. She concluded people were still seen for what they were on the outside, not what they had inside. "It is a shame they destroyed that King man. He seemed to have a lot of influence on people. I suppose that is what got him killed though. It takes more than just one man, but one man is a damn good start. " Nola thought to herself as she saw many different types of people together on the train. "Maybe things are a little better."

Nola was awe-stricken when she stepped off the train, just in time to see the sunrise. She was right on the coast line. It was fabulous. She took in all its beauty for a while, then started to work. The ocean air reminded her of home, but so much was different. That was a century ago. Nola went to a stand that had many forms of literature on it. Unbeknownst to her, this was an older method of selling these papers. The date on the newspaper she picked up was the early nineteen-nineties. It amazed her how long they stayed away. Some of the people she met were very kind, since she told them she was new to the country. Fortunately, she could tell when someone was trying to take advantage of her. "No more Neely's," she thought as she distanced herself from any unkind stranger that approached her.

Once Nola settled into a hotel, which she mistakenly referred to as an inn at first, she ventured out to locate resources to find suitable lodging for her family. She came across a Realtor that helped her immensely. He was a shrewd man, that appeared to enjoy life, not as much as his job. He was small, but extremely handsome. He had curly black hair and sexy lips, bursting with color. His walk was aided with a refreshing switch. When he spoke, he had a lovely English accent. "My name is Devon Richards. Your name is?" Devon held out his hand as he queried about this woman, rich in beauty. "Nola Paix, like peace, in French. Just call me Nola, please. I am happy that you are complying with my wishes, and asking no questions about my specifications." Nola spoke calmly, but perspired placing her warm and moist hand into his. "Well, who am I to judge really? Besides, realty is not my forté, truth be known. I really need this sale!" He laughed with desperate honesty.

Devon made Nola feel very much at ease. He spoke with her as if they were old friends. Nola knew that was just his personality, but was there something more to his effervescence she wondered. "Tell me what you would like me to do." Nola felt as though she would give him anything. Devon shrugged his shoulders and replied, "I dunno. I really like classic cars, restoring them and selling them, you know. I sing a little, but I've never really found my calling, you know?" Nola knew about automobiles, but only what she had read about. She felt inclined to have Devon show her as much as he could. Devon's stomach betrayed him with a loud growl. "Like I said, I need this sale. Would you have lunch with me?" Devon was not to be refused at this moment, if ever again. Nola instantly found herself connected to him, with utter certainty.

They ate lunch at a highly recommended bistro. "You eat like a bird, madam, you really do. I'm sorry if I offended you." Devon took Nola's hand once again. "Don't worry, I have tough skin. I'm really into fitness, so I watch what I eat. My nutritionist would kill me if I ate something I wasn't supposed to." Nola had visions of taking the unsuspecting young man, but she restrained herself. she maintained a demure, literate type. "Now it's my turn. What do you do?" Devon ignored an old, shallow, plastic friend that strolled by. "Me? Well, I am a governess of sorts. I also handle the affairs of the people I serve, sort of like an executor. Nola wondered by Devon's stare if he felt sorry for her, looking after people and using words like *serve*. Nola took great pride in her work, and it emitted through her persona.

"Well, I must bow to you as your servant. We have a lot at risk, the both of us. You must have a great amount of faith in me. I won't let your rich family, or you down." He laughed to assure her he was making light conversation, nothing she needed to worry about. If he only knew he should be the one worrying. They continued talking. They laughed throughout their meal. Devon note that Nola had no transportation of her own, so he offered her a ride home. "I would offer you a cab, but I want to make sure you make it to your room safely." Devon's chivalry was charming, refreshing. Devon let Nola out of his car, after a relaxing yet somehow stimulating drive along the coast to Nola's hotel. "I will be seeing you soon." Devon lingered, not wanting to cross the employee/ client line. "I hope it won't be too long! My family awaits patiently." Nola smiled, after having paused at just the right spot in her last phrase to catch Devon off guard. "Oh, I won't, believe me." Devon slid into his somewhat aged Alfa Romero Spider and cruised away from the hotel side walk, leaving Nola. He watched her in his rear view mirror. "She's quite lovely," he thought as he smashed down on the accelerator, peeling out to show off, just a little bit.

Devon called Nola the next day, to keep her posted on the progress of her prospective homes. They settled on one, a converted warehouse. It was freshly renovated, and suited for several tenants. Devon was floored when he learned that only one family would be occupying the entire dwelling. The warehouse was in a darker part of San Francisco. It was near the piers, which was perfect for them. It was generally quite cold, and the sun rarely shone into the area, due to the surrounding buildings. Also, the fog and cloud coverage would be an added advantage for them. Once Nola gave Devon the OK during one of their meetings, he earnestly prepared all the appropriate papers, which Nola signed. "A crew will be here on the double to make sure all of your specifications are met. Everything is put on rush, not to imply that the best workmanship won't go into this project. I'm sure your family is tired of waiting." Devon brought out a very nice bottle of wine he had been saving for his first really big sale. Nola drank with him until he was drunk. "Well, thank you for speeding up the dead line for us. My family is quite patient; I can assure you." Nola wanted to laugh out loud. but she refused to.

Devon smiled as he looked at Nola. Her skin ignited the afternoon sunset. Her wavy hair was pulled back, exposing her disciplined features. She was on the summit of perfection. Her immortality assured her of a peaked image. Devon bent over, kissing her hand. Nola touched his free hand, holding onto it firmly. He sat before her, looking at her with intense seriousness. They both moved forward, meeting at the lips. The kiss was soft, and very necessary. "How convenient," Devon said. A few pieces of a bedroom group had been left in one of the upper lofts. It was the sight of their next destination.

They both shook the dust off the sheet as they pulled them off the bed. The bed was still dressed in pure white sheets. It was almost blinding when the sun struck them for the first time in what seemed to be over a year. The crew had gone for the day. It was their mansion, for only these few hours. Devon took great care with Nola. He was frightful of making advances at a client, but Nola assured him that every move was acceptable. They disrobed each other, kissing sweetly in between each piece of clothing that was removed. Devon placed his right hand on Nola's face tracing it from her brow, down her cheek, then her jaw line. He paused at her neck to suckle her throat. He maneuvered his hand further down her lean form. He scooped her up and placed her on the gorgeous sleigh bed, done completely in oak. The sun bathed their nude bodies. They sat, facing each other, staring at each other as nature had created them. "You are truly beautiful, Nola." Devon touched her face, kissing her immediately after. His hand embraced her breast so that she jumped a bit. He moved quickly from that sensitive area down to her hand. The laid down and wrestled on top of the covers. Their kissing was abrupt, but in large quantity. He continued to search her entire body with his hands, until she became used to his touch. Soon after, he followed his path with his mouth. Nola sighed in great ecstasy. No man had ever lover Nola so gently. Nola had lived for almost half a century and had not experienced love as sweet as this.

The sun finally had reclined, giving way to the night. The had watched the sun set together. "I must have this room. I must see the sun set this way every day. This room is important to me in many ways." Nola kissed his right nipple, where she had been laying on his chest. She then kissed his stubbled face, right in the turn of his mouth. Time was escaping from them at a rapid rate. Nola was scheduled to return to her family that morning, so that she may collect them. Nola reluctantly prepared herself. Devon watched her as she slipped on a thin linen dress over a nude satin slip. Her silhouette was enhanced by the glow of dying daylight that surrounded her. Devon was mesmerized by her total beauty. Devon dressed himself, after watching this new and exciting woman he couldn't stay away from.

Devon dropped Nola off at the train station. "I don't know why you don't fly." He hugged Nola as if it was the last time her would every see her, even though her would make sure that wouldn't happen. "I almost wish I could." Nola smiled and licked his lips after she kissed him. She boarded the train and rode off. She didn't look once to see Devon as he shrank in the distance. His image was burned in her mind. Nola closed her eyes and thought only of him as she wept for missing him. She began to miss him even before she left him.

CHAPTER FIFTEEN

Nola later delighted in her return to her family. She couldn't wait to kiss and tell to Morgana. It was all she could do not to shout to the heavens about her new love. "He's so alive! I can't resist him, Morgana! There are problems, of course. I've thought joylessly about how to handle this. I am desperate to be with him, yet I don't know what to do with him! He's a mortal. I gave that up so long ago. I don't want to lose him, but what if he can't take the truth, when and if I tell him?" Nola was terribly disturbed for all her excitement.

Morgana eased her fears as they sat under the half-moon that gleamed down on them. "Nola, we must have an understanding. If he doesn't accept what you are, but doesn't want to make trouble, we can do something about that. The mind is a great toy at times. we can make it so that he forgets, so that his life may be spared. If he does understand, he will have to choose to accept us all, and live as we do, becoming as you are. I do not recommend your young man staying a mortal. It is difficult to watch someone grow old while you remain beautiful. I haven't had to witness it personally; the decision was made for me. However, this turns out, remember to take your time. Get a feel for this person. If you like, we can look deep within him and confirm your instinct to love and trust this human. If not, I trust you will judge correctly on this matter. You have always been strong in mind, and will, even if you don't think so." Morgana held Nola as she contemplated her next move with Devon.

The two women went up to the house so that Nola could tell everyone about their new home she found. "When do we leave? I am so thrilled! My things have been packed for weeks!" Desmony was practically in the car they had acquired and half way down the road. After a day and a half of packing the rest of their belongings, they were ready to send their precious antiques along, as they traveled instinctively at night. As they moved from the more desolate areas, toward the towns, then to the cities in each state they pass, they saw how much the world had changed. As they traveled, they saw how the towns were lighted with neon and false light. It was strange for them because their vision was quite unique. They saw heat and shapes when they stalked their prey. For their *normal* vision, it was similar to that of a nocturnal animal, or electric vision via infrared. The neon startled them, and frightened Elsebeth severely. Bernard calmed his wife down so that Nola could explain and answer questions as they went along.

The false light didn't harm them, it merely strained their eyes. When the light would brighten a tree, or some other object, to them, it would seem like it was on fire. The biblical analogy that Morgana gathered from the image shook her, waking up old feelings she had been storing away. From a hillside, just above a city in Washington, it gave the illusion of lava flowing from an erupting volcano in Hawaii. For them, these lights confused many vampires. The few vampires they had come in contact with during their travels spoke of how when they first resurfaced, and for a few glorious moments, saw the morning sky. It burned like sapphire and lapis at the core of a fire. The moon still shone like the sun would for humans, but as for the lights that cheated, they would need to learn quickly, or they would suffer morning burnings. All of the images they saw, but could not really see frustrated Morgana to no end. She glared at candle light while the others prowled for nourishment. The light was white, but dimmed her vision in her immediate surroundings. Morgana bowed her head and sobbed.

After tactful movements, they finally reached their new home. They were reclining comfortably in it by the following new moon. Workers had skillfully and hastily done as Devon instructed. The renovated warehouse was a large coffin for the family. No questions were asked; no answers were to be given. None of the workers really wanted to know the answers to the questions that leeched at their minds. Blythe channeled into all the people that had worked on the house. She did it by picking up each individual's scent simultaneously. She wiped away all curiosity from their minds as they slept. Her gifts were incredible. After living as long as she had, and accepting her skills as they came, she was frightfully powerful. They had all learned through the centuries as they occasioned across other harmless vampires. It was almost as if there were many secret communities of vampires. they treaded lightly, and generally kept distance from each other.

Alec and Bernard congratulated Nola on a job well done. All of the specifications had been tended to the very letter. The walls were solid concrete, reinforced with a sturdy metal alloy. It was designed to attract cold rather than warmth. The windows were framed with the same alloy that would move over the windows at a touch of a button. Air was necessary for Nola more than for anyone else, so a ventilation system was installed. The floors were done in a glossy brown linoleum. The walls were a rich beige, garnished with all of their priceless art and tapestries. There were spare placements of wall paper, only because Nola took the liberty of injecting a little color to the sublime decor. All of their furniture had been hand crafted by Alec. It was all made form rich mahogany that gave the pretense to melt like fudge, if it were touched. Nola responded, "Why thank you. I know what we all like. We've invested well, and should be safe and very happy here. I have a strong feeling about that." Nola hugged herself as she went to the large living room window that was only uncovered at night. The ventilation system blew cold air to keep everyone comfortable. The warehouse had previously been a slaughter house. Desmony found humor in that irony.

Actually, they all did. It wasn't out of character for her, but of course, when Morgana chuckled, it took everyone by surprise.

"San Francisco should be the perfect place for us. Just coming in, I saw mortals that gave even me a start! I noticed a lot of what they call disco's or clubs in the city. Maybe we could open one. It would be perfect. They are open only at night, so that is already an advantage!" Elsebeth was truly excited about the possibility of an entrepreneur ship. " We'll look into it, darling." Bernard only gave her so much rope on her leash, even though Elsebeth never gave him a reason to question her actions.

"I want to go to night school. I saw where they have teachers that work at night, not like before. I suppose they do, since they have the false light now. The classes are at junior colleges and universities. I need to do this, at least until I figure out what I should do." Morgana finally felt some direction and hope for herself. It was such a foreign feeling for her. "I guess I'll just prostitute! Just kidding. I'll find something to do. Actually, I'd like to get on television. Too bad I couldn't show my fangs on some tacky late night show! At least we don't have to hide the problem of not showing our reflections, like those vampires in the movies!" Desmony allowed a laugh to jumble out of her mouth. After a short time of planning, manipulating, and executing, all had created their characters and were playing their parts.

Elsebeth, Bernard, and Desmony created what fast became one of the chicest dance clubs in the city. Only choice people were allowed to experience the ambiance of *Eternity's Oasis.* No weapon's, drugs, or any depraved activity was tolerated. The club was original in its policy, which worked as an advantage for them. It was refreshing to know that there were some decent inhabitant's that respected clean living, as opposed to all the illicit behavior that plagued the clubbing community. Their club was a tomb by day, but at night, it's lights blinded the sky. The family's air of mystique was marveled at by their devoted followers.

Alec and Blythe guarded the warehouse, with Nola. They wanted to assure no suspicions would arise. Nola's affair blossomed with Devon with desperate affection. Alec continued to craft his furniture. That was something he did during his waking hours, when he wasn't fawning over Blythe. Nola took on the additional role of Alec's vendor. She made sure his work was acquired by the best in the home furnishing market. Nola sold Alec's pieces on the bottom floor of their *mansion en ville.* Morgana registered and began attending classes at a nearby university. This world was new and strange. Despite all of the changes and being in new surroundings, she felt safe. The assimilation was quick, as was everything with them. Morgana carried a pager with her, as did the rest, in case of any emergencies. Morgana was fascinated by all of the technology at the tip of her fingers.

The older family members hesitated, but they reluctantly followed suit.

At school, Morgana made friends quickly. People seemed drawn to her, which was not part of her agenda. Morgana was so soft spoken, so wise, and so centered. she had to be creative as well. When people asked her for functions during the day, she would have to tell them that she worked, or had extremely sensitive skin, or anything they would but that fit the scenario. Two weeks into her studies, she finally confronted the presence she could feel studying her. When the professor released the class, Morgana turned to the person that had been seated behind her. He'd been there from the beginning. The first thing that struck her was his kind, compassionate grey eyes. His dirty blond hair was uncontrolled and had just the right amount of curl. His ruddy cheeks glowed even brighter when their eyes met. Her look of intensity settled into a lazy gaze. She wasn't ready to strike any longer. She almost looked apologetic. She was consumed by his slender, but toned build.

Morgana could smell the chlorine just under his skin, which on the surface smelled of a gentle musk cologne. "A swimmer." Morgana smiled as she thought. "Hi! I'm sorry. You look really irritated. I hope I'm not to blame." The young man's voice was like cream. "You are, but you aren't anymore. I could feel you on me. I didn't know what to expect from you." Morgana felt the same way she had when she was with Victor. It startled her, to see Victor's face while she was looking at this attractive man. "Hey, I know there's a lot of sick creeps out there, but I'm not one of them." The young man tried to melt the ice with a warm smile. "I know." Morgana reciprocated the smile with one that made the young man break out in a sweat. "Do you like cappuccino? I know a java house nearby that makes incredible coffees." With his sincere invitation, they were off to the *Open Cup*.

As they walked, she stole into his mind. Images of childhood memories and events flowed out of his head and into her heart. He had always been a gentle soul. He cried when his first puppy was found out in the street, dead, after escaping from the back yard. His devastation was great when the first girl he fell in love with at seventeen broke his heart when she told him that she wanted to see other boys. A very dark image of him saying good-bye to his father made her weep silently. "Are you all right?" The young man thought he saw a tear and heard a sniffle. "I just have allergies sometimes. I just realized something, we have yet to introduce ourselves!" They both laughed at the irony of the moment. Morgana sighed as she thought of how it was more ironic for her. She knew everything about him, even his name, but he didn't know anything about her. They were strangers, but still they were going off to have coffee.

Morgana felt safe losing the frightened girl façade. "Here we are, the Open Cup, a fine gathering establishment.

The food is pretty good too!" The young man dawned that warm smile on Morgana again. She actually had to stop herself from swooning! They ate, drank cappuccino, and babbled for hours. "So, where are your parents?" Morgana needed to see his reaction to the question. It seemed cruel asking, especially when she knew the answer, but she wanted to understand the concept of being without parents. "My mom had breast cancer. My father, well he missed her. I guess he waited until I was old enough to be on my own. He died from a broken heart. I don't know if you really can, but I know he did." He lowered his head. Morgana wanted to hold his hand, but refrained. "I'm sorry, I didn't mean to bring up such a painful subject. You know, I still don't know your name!" The man's voice strengthened as he tried to find humor as an escape. Morgana gave a genuinely nervous laugh to distract him. "Luke, Luke Brant. And you are?" Luke seemingly read her mind, moving to take hold of her hand. "Morgana Mal." She smiled and took his hand.

"It's getting very late. I must be going." It was nearing one o'clock. 'I'll take you home, Morgana. Um, I've never heard that name before." Luke opened the door to the coffee house for her. "Well, I have a nice new car back on campus, yet my name is very old, ancient." Morgana had stumbled on what could be a tremendous love affair, but already she saw it ending because of her secret, her origin. Luke walked Morgana back to her car. They were very quiet. Luke kept nervously clearing his throat. "Thank you for a lovely evening. I don't get out too much. I enjoyed the conversation a lot." Morgana seemed sad to him as he stared at her. "you don't look too overjoyed!" Luke poke at her cheek to force a smile. "I'm sorry. I just have a lot on my mind. I guess I'll see you next Thursday from five-thirty to nine in English 205?" Morgana's eyes soothed his fears as she returned a gaze into his. "There's no way I'll miss it. Would you like to get together before then?" Luke was anxious as a little boy asking to go out and play. "call me, after six p.m. I'm not accessible during the day." Morgana gave Luke her number and positioned herself in her car. She started the car, and rather quickly, she was off. She left Luke with a mere good-night. He also had the memory of a very promising meeting.

The week moved at a remedial pace. Morgana was in agony. She kept it all in, no matter how painful it seemed. Bernard and Elsebeth were consumed with their new endeavor. The club was booming, with no sign of slacking up. There were many details for them to attend to. Nola helped with all of the daytime duties, such as banking, and handling any meetings that would arise. On her spare evenings, she would see Devon. Morgana and she would discuss their dilemmas with each other. Nola rested her head on Morgana's lap. "Should I tell him? I really want to, but I can't put the family at risk." Nola dropped her head in misery. "I told you, if he freaks out, I'll use my powers that I have, that I've neglected, and charm him into forgetting. At any rate, you can always visit the asylum he'll be staying at if it doesn't work!" Morgana fell back laughing. "Oh stop it! At worst, he would probably try to admit me!" Simultaneously, they said, "good luck!"

Desmony was portrayed a regular slut at all of the other clubs in town. She was known by many of the bar fly's, both men and women. If anyone wanted a thrill for the night, they just hopped from bar to bar, club to club, until they found her. She lived out those people's fantasies. She was very strange to them, but they were drawn to her. Her mystique allured them even more. Everyone wanted her, for one reason, or another.

Desmony stole about in the night, making her selection to dine on for the night, as if she was in the produce section of a grocery store. The city streets were a child's sand box for her and she controlled all the toys. Desmony toured the streets, looking at everything. She could hear multiple conversations all at once. The abilities she had were her amusement as well as her weapons. Desmony decided long ago to make the most out of being a vampire, taking advantage of her skills for a hobby. She wouldn't settle for merely using her powers to survive, she would create a volume of stories, hoping they would become stories for all to be frightened by. The thrill Desmony got from her conquests was like a drug. She always experimented with her powers, seeing just how far she could take it. She could almost hear time moving on. Desmony kept her nose alert to turn keen to the sweetest blood.

Desmony's target for the evening would be a brilliant looking model-type. "Nice butt," she thought. Desmony laughed as she glided to where he was perched. She was beyond fetching in a fluid, black velvet coat with a matching tank dress. Her stiletto pumps knocked up against the guy's Doc Martins, obligating him to acknowledge her presence. Desmony pulled her black wavy curls out of the way. That revealed her plush black lava eyes. that was all it took. The young man followed her, as if they were linked by radar.

The young man was amazed at her beauty. She knew he was hooked, that he was going to be hers. Desmony seemingly made the entire world disappear. In his eyes, she had. He almost gasped for air when she positioned herself in front of him. He wanted more than anything to touch her, but something toyed with his impulses. Something made him want to stay away. His desire was ignored by the rest of his body. His will to touch her was even stronger than his will to live. Desmony stroked his tender flesh, becoming more and more excited with each vision that invaded her odious mind. He conjured a smile and uttered his name. She pretended she couldn't hear him over the music. The truth was, she knew everything about him. She scanned him, almost like an electronic device. She determined that he was of good stock, healthy, and without disease. He was a fine choice for dinner.

That was all he was to her, nothing more, nothing less. Desmony was hungry and tired, a little cranky. Regretfully, she needed to make this one quick.

"Hello. You look like you are content with what you see. Would you like to see more? If so, speak now, or remain partially mute." Desmony didn't have a high level of wit due to her fatigue, but she managed to pull a good one out. Desmony remained direct and blunt. She had no more time for pleasantries. "Yes, I'd like to see more. I'm sorry for staring at you so much. I just have never seen someone as incredible as you. Do you want to dance, or something?" The young man was not of his own mind, playing along as Desmony conducted this intimate symphony. "Let's do the *or something.* I'm pitifully bored. Will you amuse me?" Desmony knew all she needed to know. "Why don't we go back to my place?" Desmony led the poor boy out, practically by his tongue.

The walk to her loft she had been renting was full of hopes for the fine creature she was luring in. Desmony, however, felt annoyed. A strange, but alluring odor followed her. It was old and distant, but familiar. They were started by a fluttering of pigeons resting on her stoop. "Fucking birds!" Desmony's hunger was making her more irritable by the moment. The interior of Desmony's lion den was somber with gray decor, but vibrant with pewter and silver accents. Dale, as she came to know his name. The poor boy had to offer his name, after seeing just how much Desmony didn't care. Desmony already knew his name. She supposed she forgot to ask, because she was hungry, and why should she ask, if she already knew? Desmony always remembered the names of all her victims. Dale was showing signs of coming out of his hypnotic state.

"Wow, this is a truly vicious lay out! What do you do for a living?" Dale's baggy jeans tightened, as he sat at her sterling silver bar. He had on a beautiful green silk shirt. It was more than likely one that his recent old girlfriend had bought for him, just because she loved him. Dale should've stayed around to have the girlfriend buy him more stuff, because Desmony fixed her eyes on him. All she saw was a delicious treat. An incredible human with a healthy body, and potent blood flowing through his veins to boot. The complements Desmony gave him weren't to feed his ego. They were more or less a diagnostic evaluation, like a farmer does for his herd of cattle or his chickens.

Desmony examined his earlier question with a raised brow and a crooked grin. "Well, what I do really isn't as important as whom I'm about to do." The words slipped out like cream to her new kitty. Desmony surveyed her loft again, feeling ill at ease. Of course, Desmony wasn't frightened, but she felt threatened. Part of her was regretting the acquisition of this place. Actually, she had obtained the place from a bizarre man named Lang Savant. There was something about him that had made her uneasy from the beginning, but another part of her was very welcome to do business with him.

Desmony concocted him a pitcher of Long Island Iced tea. Desmony filled him with a few, and poisoned him with her deadly poetry. He had moved over to her ebony leather divan, where he let his glass fall onto the grey wool carpet. "Oh, I'm sorry, I'll clean it up." Dale was crazy drunk as he tried to steady himself to follow through on his offer, laughing all the while, but apologetic all the same. "It's all right, Baby." Desmony began to stroke his throat. As she drew near her mark, her eyes darted over to the sky window. It displayed a brilliant view of the big dipper. "Who's there?" The same presence she had felt before they reached the loft. there was a noise in the bedroom. "I'll be back, sweetie. Don't worry, we'll pick up where we left off." Desmony eased up from the divan. The boy was too drunk to be sensible, or scared for that matter. He just laid there, stone drunk, like wet lettuce or a wilted daisy.

The bedroom was empty, as it should have been. On the way back, Desmony saw Dale preparing for their interlude. She giggled as he adjusted himself, and his position. Desmony took off her coat, dragging it a few steps as she walked. Dale was watching her, smiling. He had flirted with the idea that maybe she was a high price prostitute, which concerned him, because he didn't have a lot of cash.

The other possibility that roamed in his mind was that she was a poor little rich girl, that needed to top herself with each decadent antic.

Dale turned his attention back to Desmony. She kicked off her pumps, smiling at the thoughts that Dale was having. Desmony dragged her nails along her opaque black hose. As she unsnapped her garter, the hose fell like liquid to the floor. She then unfastened the garter itself. It sprang from around her thin waist, colliding with the floor as well. Desmony then pulled her clinging dress from her slim figure. Desmony posed where she stood, with a black silk thong on. Her jewelry was all that accented her pale olive skin. Dale pulled at his clothes obligingly with haste. They were a memory in seconds.

They charged one another, meeting in a starved embrace. Desmony had more force than he, despite her frail state. This surprised Dale. He was intrigued by this, charging back. He was determined to be the aggressor. After some intense fore play, which was more of a chore than a pleasure for Desmony, Dale was slightly sober enough to inquire about protection for their upcoming activities. He wasn't prepared. He had just planned to get obscenely drunk, then go make up with his girlfriend, maybe. Desmony's voice became shallow, almost hollow. With her already long nails, she swung her hair behind her shoulder. "I won't get pregnant, and if you're worried about AIDS, well... fuck AIDS! That's the least of your worries!" Desmony had already transformed. Dale shrieked uselessly as he took in the horror before him.

As Desmony moved to take her feeding, Lang was standing near the cold fireplace. "Don't you believe in mutual manipulation, my dear?" To Desmony's surprise, Lang was sporting piercing fangs. He had all the features she had, but his flesh was cold and grey. This suggested to Desmony that he was from old stock. Lang's skin tone briskly changed from grey to a pale ivory, since he had just fed. His cheeks were slightly flushed as well. Lang had already fed earlier that evening, but he had a large appetite. Seeing Lang for what he was made a great surprise for Desmony. It bothered her that she had no inclination that he was a vampire, as she was. That alone did not mean that she would share her meal. Dale was still alive, but in a state of catatonic shock. He couldn't move, which if he tried, Desmony would've snapped his neck, like a pair of chop sticks.

"He's mine! Get your own!" Desmony went to bite once more. Dale's screams were constant, but muted throughout the entire ordeal. He was perfectly still. Dale's blood was becoming cold. He knew there was no hope for a rescue. Desmony's strength was too much for him to handle. As many of the others before him, he wept, silently. Dale's eyes were fixed with hysterical fear. Desmony finally sank her fangs into the boy's smooth white skin. Desmony drank her fill, disheartedly until she felt his pulse stop.

Lang pushed Desmony aside to take in some, while there was a little heat to it. Desmony picked herself up, and went to put on a matching silk robe, which she often wore simply as a dress. They knew now wasn't the time to argue. It would keep. They disposed of Dale's body, not mourning the loss of the hopeful, lovely young man. Their primary concern was being seen. Their locale was rather secluded, but there were still eyes about. Deep inside, each of them celebrated their life with Dale's death.

They dealt with the body so that no one could find the source of its demise. No one saw them dispose of the body. Their secret was safe, like all the numerous others. Desmony and Lang returned to the loft. She slammed the door after they both were inside. "We must talk!" Desmony was livid. She flew up to the open kitchen window. It was the same one Lang must have used to get in. There was no need to wonder if someone could listen in on their conversation. They were far away from any residential district. Lang followed her, in almost a playful manner. "What is the matter? Are you upset I didn't level with you? Well, darling, why do you think I let you rent out this place? Why do you think I haven't tried to make you into an appetizer? I gave you your privacy. I did not care to reveal myself to you. I had to watch you, to learn you. I watched you, because I sensed you were like me. I couldn't ignore the fact you were a vampire, no matter how much I knew I needed to feed. You know, I still could stand to gain a little weight." Lang was refreshing.

Desmony was bothered because Lang could tell she was a vampire, but she couldn't sense his power. She felt comfortable when she was in his presence, but that was seldom. Lang stayed far enough away where he could watch her, without worrying whether she could pick up on him or not. What powers did he possess that she did not? Would it come in time? Would she ever have those abilities? The family never really discussed this. They never really did because they didn't know. Each one had a power that was more evident than the other, but the differences were very subtle. Their differences were more so characteristic than anything else. The family hadn't come across any other vampires, at least none made themselves apparent to them. They simply weren't aware of their limitations, or their full capabilities.

Desmony knew she couldn't hurt Lang. It bothered her that he hadn't confided in her, since he knew what she was. Desmony also couldn't pout and make Lang give in. He was the rouge Bernard used to be, still could be, but worse. "Fever, that is what I shall call you. You are similar to a rabid, fuzzy little mammal." Lang poured himself a sip of century old wine he had picked up in Italy. "How dare you judge me and hurl such insults at me!" Desmony hated the way he had treated her just then. The sad part was, she liked him. Desmony sat on an ottoman that matched a black leather recliner. Her pouting excited Lang. He wanted to possess her, be the only man in her life. Finally, maybe she had met someone that would make her father second.

My dear, we must sit down, together, and face each other. We must become acquainted with one another. It won't take long," he crossed the floor to where she was, "then we can get on with more interesting and exhausting things." They simultaneously let their defenses down. Memories, experiences, and desires were exchanged in a matter of heart beats. They felt joined by the soul by the time dawn was tearing past the horizon. The sky began to change color even as they escaped the living room, taking refuge in the customized, sun repellent bedroom. Lang had the queen sized bed converted so that under the mattress laid a cold, cemented marble crypt. "After you." Lang ushered her to the place she would occupy beside him. It was happening fast, the way she liked it.

The city awakened as Desmony and Lang fell asleep. The rest of Desmony's family did the same. Nola got up with much vigor. She had the entire day reserved for Devon and herself. It was a relatively clear spring day for northern California. Nola raced over to Devon's apartment. Devon opened his door to be greeted by a big smile and a picnic basket. Devon drove them in his sports car, to a lush park, just outside of the city. It was a slow Wednesday, so they had the bulk of the lay out to do with what they wished. They ate, talked, and drank perfectly aged white wine. She read to him under God's light. She looked at the lighted sky, hoping to be seen by her creator. Nola hoped to be forgiven, if she could be, if she hadn't been already. "Nola, I love Greek mythology. That came out of nowhere, didn't it? I just wanted you to know." Devon's cheeks were slightly ruddy at that point. "I know you do, and I think that's wonderful." Nola smiled as Devon laid his head in her lap, purring as he nuzzled his head over her thighs.

Nola laughed nonstop. Devon made jokes and funny observations without arrest. Nola couldn't remember laughing so hard in all her life, before or after she met Morgana. Nola laughed at his words. They were funny to her. His European culture was foreign to her. Nola felt as dangerous as it was, she should tell him her secret. Nola kept feeling the desire to purge her soul to him. She felt as though he was worth the risk. Nola was being unfair. She was cheating. That bothered her. "I just did. I know a lot of things about you. I can look at you, right now, and tell you about your first girlfriend. I can also tell you about the mole on your right thigh, and many other things. I'm not a psychic, or a spy. I need you to believe me, and not doubt me. I serve a small, but powerful family. I was a slave that was spared from a life of being raped and beaten to death by a girl that saw me being attacked. She is a vampire. I chose serving her family and herself instead of betraying her. She would never do that to me. She chose to give me the best of both worlds, if that is possible. They needed protection against people that didn't understand their kind. I've lived for one-hundred and fifty years. I may pay when I do go before God. less I go straight to hell, but I feel like I've done the right thing." Nola stopped. She was still, waiting for a response. Nola was hoping for her fantasy that had haunted her to come true. She didn't hypnotize him. She was hoping he would look at her and know she was speaking the truth, and accept her.

Devon couldn't respond the way he thought he might. Normally he might have laughed, guessing it was a joke, or that he had come across another freak in the city. No, he was immersed in her gaze. He rationalized everything she had told him. It amazed even him that he understood her, and didn't doubt her. "Should I fear you? I mean, can you bite, or fly, or anything like that?" Devon knew what he was being told was fantastic, but he adhered to her honesty. Nola just bowed her head with a slight grin. "No. I just live to serve them. I am abnormally strong though. Don't get me wrong, you should fear this woman as any man in love should fear his mate." Nola smiled again, this time thrusting a nervous grin. "Then, may I meet your family? From what you say, if I deceive you, I'll be dead, then and there. I won't disappoint you. This is fantastic! I feel so special, Nola. No one has trusted me as you have. All of this is crazy, but it makes sense." Devon had raised up to a sitting position, Indian style. He reached over and kissed Nola. You mean to tell me I don't have to explain my lunatic ravings to you?" Nola was truly puzzled. "Soon enough love, soon enough." Devon was eager to see if her family and world was real. In a way, something she did when she told him, made him not need much persuasion.

Devon kissed Nola again. The same urgency was in his kiss as before. Nola smiled with such comfort. Nola couldn't describe it. They relaxed and watched people as they walked by. Everyone was happy, for the most part. A couple in the distance argued fiercely. The setting wasn't as perfect as they would have liked. Nola wasn't about to have her moment ruined. Nola politely got up from her seat. She strutted over to the couple and excused herself. "I know you will mind, but I will ask you anyway. Do you love her?" The angry young man answered her, without much tolerance. "Yes, so what?" He was a little disoriented by this stranger. "Well, if that is true, then speak to her, don't yell. and as for you, listen to him, don't be too quick to retaliate. If you both have something on your mind, say it. Life is much too precious for meaningless babble. Do you understand?" Nola's voice was as smooth as butter. They both nodded their heads. They looked at each other, smiled, and commented on how Nola must have been crazy, but she wasn't crazy. Nola was simply in love. Nola returned to her lover. Devon was so proud of his woman. He felt right. He felt safe.

A week was needed to prepare for this meeting. All of the family members were joined and told of the situation. There was some yelling, due to panic, fear of their secret being sold to the highest bidder. There was much discussion and deep concern for Nola as well as the family. "How could we expect this to never happen? Not only to Nola, but to all of us. There is always the risk of one of us falling for someone that is unlike us." Blythe's wisdom and powers were so intense and formidable, that even though she spoke in almost a whisper, the entire room hung on her every word. Morgana lowered her head. Her secret was tugging at her mind, as well as her heart. For once in a long while, she was happy. The only problem was that she was guilty of exactly what Blythe was saying. Fortunately, Blythe had a reasonable outlook on the situation. Blythe wasn't clawing on to the old ways, as it was always described. The ways that their secluded family were alien to.

Morgana wasn't betraying a mate. She was betraying her family and her dominant heritage. Morgana was of her mother, and unaware of her human characteristics or abilities. Elsebeth noticed the deep concentration that Morgana was in. It was as if Elsebeth knew of all Morgana's secrets and troubles. maybe Elsebeth did. Elsebeth crossed the floor and secured Morgana's shoulders with an embrace. They smiled at one another, while everyone took their place in the center of the floor. Finally, Nola spoke. "My dear people that I love so much. I thought about all of this, all of your concerns, before I told Devon. I sought council and searched my soul. I would never do anything to endanger you all. I would die, or kill first. If Devon is worthy, he will accept this, and join us. If he has not been true to me, I shall rid us of this potential deception." Nola revealed a small vial of poison she had concocted. I've never forgotten my true roots. When I was a child, in the islands, Voodoo was very common. It was all around me. I was drawn to this world of make believe and superstition. I learned all my aunts would teach me. Sadly, I didn't have much time with them. When I came to the Americas, I wasn't allowed to practice my magic, my religion. Instead, I learned the word of Jesus Christ. I prefer him, but I do what I must to live." Nola sat down, quiet and motionless. Morgana went to her to console her. That concluded the meeting.

The following evening, Devon was driven to the house by Alec in a pearl vintage Bentley. "This is really unnecessary, Sir. I sold this place to Nola. I wouldn't have gotten lost." Even nervous and scared to death, Devon still possessed his sense of humor. He had on a charcoal grey wool suit. A slate blue shirt with corresponding tie and kerchief accompanied his attire. Devon persisted in starling himself with visions of being bitten. He jumped each time one of his fantasies brought him to that fateful moment. He also dreamt silently of participating in some dark, unholy ritual, making love with, and being converted to a vampire's slave, like Nola, by Nola. The last scenario, he thought, wasn't so bad. Devon even smiled to himself. He had nothing to lose. He couldn't make himself doubt Nola's story, as dynamic as it was. She was too logical to be mad.

The opening of the car door stopped Devon's vivid day dreams. Alec ushered Devon out of the car and into their home. Devon's first emotion as he stepped into the house where he and Nola first made love was pride. Devon was responsible for the safe environment they lived in. He executed his job with proficiency, whether it was right or wrong. The first person he saw after making his way through the hallway was Nola. She was at the top of the stairs. She stepped down as he stood in the archway of the French doors that ended the corridor's entrance. Devon's eyes were wide and his mouth was shamelessly open. Nola had been preparing the house and herself all day. Everything was done to perfection, just as she planned.

Nola's coiled hair was straight, soft, flowing like cashmere. Her skin was a glowing honey color. Her make up corresponded with her skin tone, but even richer and deeper. She had on a Mahogany colored wool suit. The curve of her calve spoke to Devon lustfully as each leg moved in front of the other. "Hello, darling. I hope you are ready for a treat." They were facing one another as she met him. Devon wanted to kiss her, badly, but remained concentrated on the reason for his visit. Devon pulled through his jet black hair, which was beginning to recede a bit, with his fingers.

The wind swirled around Devon. He surveyed the place he sold, the place they made into a home. The style that was chosen was class in definition, and state of the art. Most of the furniture was hand crafted, by Alec. The detail was so intricate; it was evident that an abundance of time was needed to accomplish all of this work. In fact, the ages of time were used. The paintings that hung on the walls were originals, purchased for an embarrassingly low amount, compared to what the acquisition value was at the present time. This home was just one of the many they had collected throughout the years. It was little more than a hobby. Really it was a necessity most of the time. It was just so easy to do. If they needed a home bad enough, and it was occupied, well, that was too bad, for the current tenants.

One by one, each family member came out from different parts of the house to greet Devon. Blythe came from the library. Desmony peeled around a corner close to the basement door. Elsebeth and Bernard acme from the opposing staircase that Nola had descended from. Morgana eased herself out of the solarium. Morgana took his hands and escorted him to the drawing room for a snifter of cognac. Devon slightly put his arm around his mate-too-be, he hoped. They each chose what area they wanted to occupy. Bernard and Blythe sat in two grand chocolate leather chairs. Elsebeth stood behind Bernard, as Alec did the same with Blythe. Desmony elected to stand near a window, in the middle of a large wall. Morgana was by the door. Nola and Devon at on an antique chase lounge that Alec had crafted. The fire emitted delicious warmth, but not too much as the heat made all, save Devon ill. Nola watched the fire, making sure no sparks would shoot out, causing any trouble.

The drinks that were served went down slow and nice. Polite questions were asked and answered. The evening was starting off quite timidly, until Desmony stirred the waters, much to her character. she hushed them all with a direct and serious question. "Nola has told us of your last rendez-vous and requested we attend this grandiose meeting to find out your intentions. As you know, we have plenty of time. You, dear boy, do not. So, tell us how we can settle this matter.

No one was really shocked. Devon appreciated Desmony's candor. Desmony hated pretense and hesitation. "I really don't know if this is a matter to be resolved. Maybe with someone else, I might question the motive for such a story, but with Nola, I can't. Something won't let me. After dinner, or before, it doesn't matter to me. We can talk more, but there's no need to explain anymore or prove anything. My loyalty is with Nola." Devon was very bold in his words. It was such a shame they all could sense his uncertainty and fear. "My sweet, I must ask you this." Nola was very hesitant now. "As I've told you, I am well under one hundred years old. I will continue to age without change. How do should we handle this? How will we live after this moment?" Anxiety was raping Nola's body and mind.

Devon moved himself in front of her on his knees. Devon took from his pocket a princess cut solitaire diamond ring and took Nola's left hand. "Nola, when I look at you, I don't see black. I don't see a monster. I don't feel fear or anything negative. What I feel is love. I see it in your eyes and it reflects on me. Really, I have no choice. I will do what I have to do in order to live my life with you. I've been alone too long." With tears in his eyes, he placed the ring on her small and soft finger. "Marry me, Nola, please." Nola replied with a quivering and exasperating "yes". Nola smothered Devon with embraces and kisses. Everyone, even Desmony was smiling and cheering. Nothing so beautiful had happened in their lives in such a long while.

Morgana made the motion after dinner to tell Nola it was time for the necessary ceremony, not the wedding, but Devon's passage into their world. "But Morgana, if we do have a wedding, it won't be of any religious significance. Shouldn't we just wait until then? Our souls may not be recognized by God, but that doesn't mean my faith should go in the opposite direction. The truth is, this all too sudden." Nola was reasoning with herself, as much as with Morgana. "That day will be for you and Devon. You need me for this ceremony. This night, I will help you with this ceremony. Someday, in the near future, you will be named man and wife by someone else. Chance might just place you in the path of a white witch that can solidify your commitment with vows. After this ceremony, you will be free to wed and truly celebrate your marriage. Right now, Devon needs my blood, along with the others, so he may be with you." Morgana's words were indeed wise.

"Everyone, after the dinner, we will conduct the ceremony. Devon will join the family tonight, before he joins the family as Nola's husband. Morgana had ushered Nola back to the group. They interrupted all the mini conversations Devon was having with each member of the house. "Are you sure, Devon? Are you ready?" Nola put her hand on his shoulder. "What exactly will happen?" Devon was a bit moist about the brow. He wanted to have his fears put to rest, if at all possible. "You will take in all of our blood,

Mine will be in a separate chalice. After you have ingested our blood, you will experience a fever and discomfort. The degree depends on how much pain you can take. Your life and health will be altered. You will feel rejuvenated, vigorous. You will have incomparable strength to other humans. You will find these and other changes, like heightened senses, after you recuperate. We vow to help you through this. When you are well, the wedding will take place." Nola was blunt, but compassionate.

Devon looked over to the shoulder where Morgana's hand was. Her nails were longer, slightly pointed. The pressure Devon felt on his shoulder from Morgana's touch was more powerful than Nola's. That was natural, and to be expected after transformation. When Devon looked up, he saw something he had imagined only in his darkest dreams. He started, gasping. Devon was like a child in a haunted house for the first time. Elsebeth and Blythe changed next. Their fangs were glistening white, and were razor sharp. Their skin was flushed, but still pasty white. All eyes were glowing in the flame lit room. Bernard and Desmony were fiercer than the others. Their violent, deep voices made their breathing shudder through the air. Saliva ran down their chins, dripping to the floor that waved as the light played with the breeze. Their hair was untamed. There was subtle howling and hissing behind all of the ghastly faces.

Alec and Nola watched all of this with Devon. "You will never see this of me. We move when they move, and we serve them, but we will never change to appear as they do." Nola was hoping Devon had not changed his mind. There was still time for him to change his mind, still time for Nola to strike, killing him. It was the one thought that passed through Nola's mind, the one thing Nola didn't want to do. "Don't worry, I trust you. I trust your family. I love you. You won't hurt me, right? You're just showing me what you're really like?" Devon turned his focus from Nola to the family as his fear kicked him in the head. "No love, we won't hurt you. You will only feel our wrath if you hurt our Nola." Desmony wiped the spit from her chin. Desmony laughed, not knowing whether or not it was from embarrassment or amusement. It was more likely amusement from her lack of manners.

Somehow, the wedded-couple-to-be, made it through dinner. They ate alone, out on the terrace. The others couldn't stand the stench of their cooked food. Nola was used to raw food, but she missed cooked cuisine every now and then. the others sipped on warm blood that they stored for nights when they didn't care to go out stalking. Blythe worked at a hospital. She worked the graveyard shift. Blythe worked for free, but not really. She compensated her volunteered time with human blood.

Everyone was a bit more relaxed after their respective meals. Devon made a feeble attempt to nourish himself, but found it too difficult. He kept trying to imagine what their blood was going to take like. He shuttered in fear. Oh how he wished this was all over. He prayed, while he could, that it wouldn't hurt, for long. He couldn't understand how they could ask him to partake in this nauseating ritual after dinner, and not before. He supposed the thought never occurred to them. Maybe, they thought he should get one last meal, as a human. The corn dog he had for lunch wouldn't define a monumental last meal. He felt like he was a "dead man walking", about to go before the gas chamber.

Despite all Devon's feelings, he still wanted this woman, that was all there was to it. Devon stopped day dreaming with the thought he had to take the necessary steps to make that possible. they gathered in the solarium, a place that was seldom visited. When it was, it wasn't for the intent of the room. Candles were lighted throughout the room. It was beautiful. the flaming lights played tricks with the pitch black night that peered through. The light also danced on the water that was in crawling distance from their home.

No one was solemn, they were concentrating intently on the future. What role was Devon going to play in their lives? Could he be trusted? Who would even believe him, even if he told? Time was silent for now. Nola kissed her man, softly on his tender lips. Nola urged him on, lovingly. Devon did not hold back. The entire process mystified him. it intrigued him to no end. His mouth was dry. Was the transformation already starting? He stepped forward, slowly. there two incredibly ornate antique chalices waiting for him. They were identical, the only two of their kind.

Soft music played in the background. It kissed the ear of everyone in the room. The breathing was light now, but everyone was tense. Devon stood in the front of the table where the chalices rested. A million thoughts passed through his mind, but he paid no heed to any of them. He lifted the first chalice, as thought it was tissue on his wet hands. No fluid was in it, yet. Bernard came closer. He stood by Devon, smiling, trying to be reassuring. he said "welcome," and cut his right wrist with his sheering white fang. The blood dripped freely into the cup. Bernard tilted his head back. Bernard enjoyed the feeling, but he kept his excitement stifled. Bernard couldn't let out a single purr. Soft fur had grown on his hands and face. Bernard stepped aside, letting Blythe come to Devon next Alec followed, as did Elsebeth, Desmony, then Morgana. Desmony shook her hair as the blood flowed. She smiled with a shameless display of sin

The cup was full, and he was expected to drink it all down, like a good little boy. Nola came to his side. She had wept silently while he drank the blood of the vampires. Now, he was to drink the blood of his beloved. Nola made a clean slit in her wrist. Her blood moved into the chalice like silk flowing in a mid-day wind. the glass was full and Nola wavered in her stance. giving her blood made her weak. Morgana clutched her, before Devon could even motion towards her. he took one last look around, as the man he was, and saw the reflection of the man he was going to be in the chalice. he looked the same, but he was different. To explain would be impossible. He brought the ornate cup to his lips.

Devon closed his eyes and said the name of his holy father. He had no one else in the world, other than Nola. He didn't want to live the rest of his life alone, waiting to be with a family that didn't show him any affection during their lives. He would spend eternity with someone that wanted to return all the love he was waiting to give. If this was what life was going to be like, then he was ready for it. Devon drank, at first quickly. His drinking became progressively slower. He began to enjoy the taste. It truly tasted like some exotic nectar. Lights flashed in front of his eyes. It wasn't from the candles though.

The next sensation was of euphoria. He remembered how he felt when he partied too hard. He felt like he had done one too many lines of coke. He began to feel so light, he leaned to one side until he fell into Alec's arms. Alec carried Devon upstairs, to the room he was able to inhabit with his love. He lingered in a deep sleep, almost in a coma state. The sleep lasted for several days. Devon went through periods of intense hallucinations when the fever and the tainted blood surged through his tender veins. His sheets were drenched with sweat. His body convulsed with the shakes. Devon became so maddened by the volatile blood coursing through his body, he continuously tore his bed clothes apart. It was a struggle for quite a while, but Devon pulled through.

The sun seemed to seer through the heavy, dark curtains, which helped keep the room cool. When the rays hit his body, he wasn't sure whether to run from the glow or not. Nola comforted his fears all day, showing him the path to recovery. Devon was thankful the sun still felt good on his skin. "Soon, you may come to not like the sun. I've never enjoyed the sun in excess. Knowing what it can do to my family makes me somewhat resentful of it, even though I know we need it for life, the ones we feed on." Nola's words were harsh, but they sounded pure coming from her mouth. Nola took exceptional care of Devon, the best she could. Soon after, Devon was back on his feet.

Devon felt magnificent. He hadn't felt so strong before. He had the motivation and energy of a ten-year-old. When his strength was fully restored, he began to improve his physical condition. His form could change for the better, however, he would not age. Working out was something Devon had avoided like the plague for much too long. In the past, he never had, or made the time. Devon was at one point in his life heading down a spiral, but Nola stopped his path of destruction. Nola inspired him to not just get by. All of the habits he had seemed to lose their allure. Nola brought Devon to a new level physically, emotionally, and in some ways, spiritually.

Morgana helped out by going on runs with Devon. They chose those times to really relate to one another. Morgana learned a lot about the human experience from both Nola and Devon. Nola's memories hadn't faded in the century and a half that she'd been with the Mal family. It was amazing to Devon. Nola assured him that his memory would improve vastly. All of Devon's senses, in fact, improved. Some were subtler, but evident, none the less. "You know, Morgana, the life I led was truly one of sin. I don't suppose to many this one would be better. I feel better though. Maybe it's because I know I won't die, or at least my chances are greatly improved. I can still be nice and compassionate, if I desire it." Devon stretched his legs against a tree as he panted heavily. "You have one advantage that some people in our family may never have. You have the power to know you can choose how you will portray the vampire persona. Well done Devon, well done!" Morgana snapped Devon's rear with her sweatshirt and took off running.

Nola ignited passion and romance for Devon by feeding him, as they read literature by Voltaire and Ben Johnson. He enjoyed the education and the company. They also read the works of Edgar Allen Poe. They couldn't help but giggle at some parts. Other parts actually made them catch their breath. "It's fiction, but it's reality for us. I've seen men buried under homes, people killed for no really good reason. I wonder, did Edgar know what he was saying? Did he know anyone in our family? Did he know any Vampires? There was so much truth in his words. It seems too crazy to believe. I guess that's what turns people on to fiction." Nola thoroughly enjoyed the books, as well as their time together.

CHAPTER SEVENTEEN

The days passed quickly as Devon healed and Nola and he grew even closer. They were certain that marriage was the right move to make. the time was drawing near for the ceremony. They were in such anticipation for the event to take place. They both agreed that physical contact wasn't going to be allowed until after the wedding. "You know, I'm only going along with this for you. I know this is your first time being married. Sadly, this isn't my first time. Alanna was someone I could've had what I have with you. I was entirely too young, and didn't appreciate her. I give her all the credit she deserves, but Nola, you embody all that any man with sense should desire. I will tell you about her more, one day, if you require it, but just know our union will be forever, in more ways than one." Devon's voice fluttered as he spoke truthfully to Nola.

Devon found Nola's request surprisingly easy to abide by. With his recent transformation, his spirit wouldn't allow him to entertain any thoughts of breaking their agreement. Devon was much too weak to exceed any basic functions. "I wonder how they can stand it? Being that close, and not doing anything, not taking advantage of it. Well, they'll have the rest of their lives for that, I suppose. As for me, I've waited all my life to find a love. Why is it I cannot find one of us?" Desmony was at her wits-end. She, after four-hundred years, finally showed that she clamored for romantic attention. Desmony only confided in Morgana, which took Morgana completely by surprise. As much as Desmony seemed to have nothing but contempt for the way Morgana chose to binge her hunger, and envy the mortals on which she fed on, Morgana was her best and only friend. Lang adhered to Desmony's mind. He was an ass, but he was all she had. It disturbed her greatly that she could not detect others like herself. Shouldn't she have another sense for that? It wasn't as though she could go up to any freaky looking guy and say: "Excuse me, but are you a vampire? Would you mind if I see your fangs?" No, that wasn't a viable course of action.

Desmony felt an intense passion for him. As she saw more of him, his appearance seemed to change. Lang became more attractive in her eyes. The change wasn't just in her mind. He was actually changing. he had feelings for her, after being alone for an entire generation, but how could he let this minx know that? They had time, and he would figure it out, for both their sakes. Lang made small changes, like grooming his mangled hair, shaving his stubbled face, and improving his ancient scent. Every time he took new blood in, it allowed him to change his appearance. The Mal family always managed to change their image, since they always hunted, successfully for fresh blood. The only time they would be stuck in the form they maintained when they were unborn, was when they were deprived of blood, as Lang had been, alone in his loft, until Desmony discovered him, saving him, unbeknownst to her.

The Mal family in their unborn state were always beautiful in their death, as they were in their life before. They would always remain beautiful, as long as they could hunt, without detection in any age, in any society. Lang had made several mistakes, but remained alive, none-the-less. Now was his time to refine his skills, so that he may survive, without hunger, with Desmony.

Everyone's agenda remained constant and calm, until preparations for the wedding were due to be made. The wedding fervor took precedence over their everyday lives. Elsebeth was in charge of the wedding gown. She revisited her gown crafting skills, using fine silk from China she had purchased over a century ago. Genuine pearls trimmed the gown. Fine English lace made the torso of the gown. No present day designer could surpass the detail and quality of the garment. The color of the dress was called "Angle's kiss". It was a cream color, with rose undertones. It played beautifully with Nola's fair, yet caramel complexion. Blythe and Morgana, even Desmony handled the preparation of the refreshments and decorations.

As expected, the ceremony was to be intimate and private. This made any preparations easily achievable. The men's greatest responsibility was to calm Devon's pre-wedding nerves. Alec was the most spiritual, so he consented to leading the ceremony. Nola felt it a shame the ceremony was essentially a formality. The noble attempt made on the behalf of her adopted family was, however, very much appreciated. There was also no need for legalities. What would the point be in drawing up marriage papers, when neither would ever produce a death certificate? Even if one perished in a reasonable time frame, Nola's birth was only documented in a Bible, long since discarded. Devon thought about the possibilities with Nola sometime before the ceremony, but none of it mattered. Their pasts were just that, better forgotten than remembered. Their futures were to unlimited to begin to fathom.

That afternoon fell into early evening. The twilight blazed across the horizon, in colors of periwinkle, and peacock blue, then to sage and indigo. The sun surrendered into the night, and the wedding finally took place. A spot was chosen far out in a secluded wooded area. The family were the only guests in attendance. The assembly was sparse, but intimate and bountiful with love. Blythe danced her bow across the strings of her mahogany, hand crafted, finely tuned violin. It was hand made from a world renown company. Devon fidgeted with his silver silk Italian tie that coordinated precisely with his charcoal hued wool suit. His crisp white shirt became limp with the moisture his body was producing at a rapid pace. It accelerated with each step Nola made towards him. His anticipation of being wed to her was mounting. Nola made her way into view from behind a grouping of trees.

Nola's skirt glistened in the early night, as the full moon shone on it. The silk clung to her curved hips, as she moved one foot in front of the other. The top of the gown was in fact made of the fine English lace, with a flesh tone lining underneath, for discretion purposes. There was a train of chiffon that trailed for nearly eight feet. Nola's veil was steadied by a simple band of material that secured her thick bun. At that moment, no one could touch her level of beauty. After a dream-like procession, Nola made her way to her betrothed Devon. Nola calmed Devon by telling him all would be well, as soon as they said yes, as long as they said yes. No other word would secure their good feelings they had been feeling until this point.

Blythe sang gingerly while Alec led a simple but deliberate ceremony. The woods were quiet, as words of love were exchanged. It seemed as though nature was behaving, just for them. Nothing seemed more perfect than that day for them all, especially Nola. After all her years as a mortal, as well as her years as a servant to the Mal's, never aging, she knew not of this joy. Time can actually heal old, deep wounds. The problem is, it takes more time than most people are allowed to live. Nola had a rare chance. She was fortunate enough to take advantage of it. Nola had spent her life trying to make others happy. As Alec said his words of praise and hope for the future, their future, Devon gazed into his woman's eyes. Nola's eyes were filled with tears so that she couldn't see her lovers tender look on her. The tears obstructed her smiling, laughing eyes. Devon never felt do alive, as the mortal life he had possessed continued to drain from his soul. He was no longer as he was, but he wouldn't trade it for anything. Devon finally felt peace. He was part of a family. This was something he hadn't had in a while.

After greeting everyone as man and wife, Nola and Devon changed their clothes and started off to a mountain cabin where they would bask in each other's love. Upon their return, rather than having a photo album, they decided to commission an artist to paint a portrait of them, in their wedding attire. That would wait, right now, they had too much urgency to concentrate on each other, rather than sit, or stand, waiting for a painter to "catch the moment". The family tearfully bid them "adieu" as they rode off into the sunset, just like an old movie from the golden age of cinema.

Morgana made her way back home after leaving the mansion. To her surprise, she was greeted by Luke, the swimmer she was falling for. The young man had followed her home once and thought her would take a chance to see if such a surprise would ignite a welcomed relationship. Luke didn't know what inspired him to take a chance on the night he did, but his timing couldn't be more perfect. "How'd you get here? How long have you been here?" Morgana actually blushed. She wasn't angry, or worried, not in the least bit. Morgana was actually happy and a little flattered. "Not long, really. I woke up out of my sleep and found myself here. I don't even remember getting dressed! I couldn't help but follow you home one night. I don't mean to keep giving you bad impressions of me, but I just can't wipe you out of my mind. Please forgive me." He looked like a shamed puppy as he approached her.

Not betraying her secret to him, she let him know she trusted him and was glad to see him. After seeing her confidant go into another life with a man she loved, she wanted to take Luke and create a story book affair all her own. "Would you like to come in? It's still a little chilly.' The cold didn't bother her in the least, but she could tell Luke was being affected by the crisp air. Sometimes, she had to remind herself about the differences between humans and her kind. Morgana couldn't believe she was taking a great risk. Dawn was upon her in about an hour. "I'd love to, but you've been up obviously for a long time, working, right? You're coming home too late to stay up with me. I just wanted to see you before class, in a few days." Luke hovered over Morgana as he spoke lightly in her ear. "Thank you. I, um, had a weird shift tonight. I am actually bushed."

Morgana felt badly lying to Luke, but it was too soon to know if had what it took to confess all to him and create a life with him, like Nola had done with Devon. "Do you work tomorrow night? There's a good movie, I hope, opening and I have tickets. Would you come with me?" Luke's cheeks turned ruddy as he asked Morgana. "I'd love to. Come to me after sundown. I'll be here." Morgana took his hand, smiled, and let go. Morgana studied him as she went inside. Luke watched until her living room light went on. "I love her!" Luke confessed silently to himself, trying to conceal his excitement as he hopped into his convertible.

Desmony's infatuation with Lang became more and more prevalent. Her presence around the Mal mansion declined with each passing week. There was little urgency to spend time with people she had spent tireless hours for several centuries. Lang was new, exciting, and a man that she wasn't related to. She was fascinated with the knowledge that she had found another one of them. No one had accomplished that before. Desmony's sister never attempted finding any others like them. It almost seemed as though she didn't care, that it was too much that their clan existed, as blood-thirsty, flesh-tearing monsters that were legendary as creatures for humans to fear, seldom to understand. That was Morgana's baggage to deal with. Desmony was falling for Lang, and she reveled in it, like a swine wallows in mud.

Desmony spent the bulk of her nights at the loft. Lang, not verbalizing his intense desire to capture Desmony's heart, his angle was subtler, looking as distinguished and desirable as possible. His grey-like hue had completely vanished. He began to hunt more, to feed on human blood again. He was determined to appear as healthy and beautiful as any vampire could. Lang was an attractive man, and before his undying, had the pleasure of knowing many women and being desired and loved by a large variety of humans, for many reasons. Some clung to him for his strength. Others wanted his company for his charm, grace, candor, as well as his polished and meticulous presentation. Lang's hair was a wavy salt and pepper combination. His eyebrows had a natural arch that made many women jealous. His facial bone structure was sharp, almost chiseled. He was tall and oppressive.

Desmony was breath-taken by his person. Lang was stern with her, very direct. He played no games with her, as most human males are known to do. These traits inspired Desmony so that her harsh attitude either began to fade, or was surrendered voluntarily. Lang treated Desmony in such a manner because he felt it wasn't becoming, that she would be more beautiful as a vampire if she had a more refined demeanor. He doubted anyone would find any fault with that.

Lang's history started long ago, before Desmony was even born. He was made into a vampire by a banished member of the German aristocracy. The individual was a lean, statuesque male of about thirty-five years. He was of questionable orientation, loving men, as well as women. Lang showed no desire in him as a lover. Lang had an expansive appreciation of women. The more liberated and affectionate, the better. Karl was considered a freak before he found his way into the *life* of his maker. Karl disappeared from the affluent life-style he had lived the night Karl made love to him, taking his essence, as well as his life, away. Karl spoke very few words. He used his gift of mind manipulation to get Lang into his feather-filled and silken sheeted bed. The death was beautiful. Not a drop of blood was spilled. Lang could not sense being violated, loved against his wishes.

When Lang awoke after being snatched from his itinerary the night prior, his perception of life was distorted beyond comprehension. Lang was soaked in sweat, convulsing, and vomiting almost incisively. He had eaten a bountiful meal of sausage, cheese, and wine. "What have you done with me? Why am I so ill? I hurt. Who are you?" Lang was shamefully pathetic. he had no pride within him. He was to find out he didn't need much blood to live for great spans of time. He would not be an effective vampire, weak and vulnerable, but he could exist, without preying on the innocent, like he had been.

Karl came towards Lang, in all his sweat and vomit. Karl kissed his glistening brow. "I have made you my friend. I saw you and I wanted you. I'm used to getting what I want. I came from a small village, two-hundred years before now. I was made by an individual that was snatched from a life of service to the great Charlemagne. Today, in sixteenth century Germany, I live a life of opulence. I have done you no harm. The pain is worth all of the greatness you shall incur. The price you must pay is never ending darkness. Your world no longer exists. I do apologize for not having a meeting with you, getting your permission. I didn't have the patience with you. I knew I needed to strike now. You have enough memories of human life to last you. If I let you get any older, you wouldn't do well as a hunter, a vampire. That is what you are. I regret I cannot tell you more of me. I am of no consequence. You may not feel that way, but what victim really gets to understand their tormentor, their attacker? Really, let's not be pretentious about this. I don't know what all of your talents will be. A vampire never really knows until they have the strength to test themselves. I picked you because I felt you were full of zest and vigor. Don't disappoint me." Karl was cleaning himself, standing next to a face bowl, naked. He was hoping to entice Lang, but there was no chance.

Karl toweled himself off and dressed himself. "Lang, the daylight will be something you will never see again. You can successfully live among humans, but I advise against it. It becomes too disturbing. You don't want to cross the line, wanting to be like them. It's as though you are a spirit, an apparition. You can't fully live as they do, so don't torture yourself. I know you will not want to concern yourself with me for a while. I promise to track you for a while, until you can fend for yourself. You love women. That's good. Use that to your advantage. Give your victims divine love, but kill them and take their blood, all the same. This is all the advice I will give you for now. Most of your life can remain the same, but I do not suggest you traveled in the same circles you recently left behind. There are more of us out there. I seldom can find them. When you do, cling to them, become mates. You have all the time in the world to find them, if you live your new life, carefully." Karl decided it was time for him to leave Lang's life, for now. He left as quickly as he came into Lang's life.

Lang had turned his back to Karl. He didn't even know the exact time Karl left him. For centuries, Lang killed, only when he had to. He usually fed once a year, feeding on some creamy skinned, ruddy mouth female. He cried as an infant does in shame and disappointment. He was alone, and stayed that way from the time Karl killed him, until he fell upon Desmony. Desmony was the first female he could have, without destroying. He took no pleasure in his killing. He did, however, become used to it. It finally was a way of life for him around the time Desmony had come into existence. Lang had a wealth of knowledge about being undead. He never made another vampire, but once he happened on Desmony, he felt compelled to use his strength and powers to groom her, since he could use her apparent attraction to him to his advantage.

Desmony never experienced this type of treatment, or love. Lang was cool, and complex. He didn't want to portray the wounded victim he once was. He had more heart than he would ever let anyone know, except for maybe Desmony. Lang did fear that if he let Desmony know just how gentle he could be, how he was without his armor, she would lose respect for him. Because Lang protected his true feelings, remaining distant, Desmony found herself falling faster for him than she could keep up with. She was emotionally drugged by him. Fortunately, he made no jokes about it, as she finally professed her love for him. "I'm glad you love me. I've looked for a spirit like you for centuries. You are wild, no doubt, but you are so innocent in so many ways. You have always been what I had to become. Much of my journey as a vampire, I have struggled. I enjoyed my life, but I lived a very decadent life. I've accepted what I am, and have at some darker points, enjoyed it. I don't want you to destroy yourself being reckless, I care for you too much. I will stand with you for as long as we can hunt together." Lang stroked her face and touched her lightly on her lips with his own.

Life missed some very important ingredients with these two. Love, compassion, trust, serenity, among other elements. When Lang and Desmony fed, they reacted with violent attacks against those they needed and envied. Lang had remembered a very sympathetic version of his existence, but he was a hunter, enjoying his kills. He had given in to the satisfaction of a kill long ago. His compassion for the human race was multi-faceted. He loved them, but when it came time to feed, he displaced his sympathy for their right to live, as they did for pork or beef. that distinction made him as cold as he was. Where Lang once knew how to feel and had forgotten how to, Desmony never knew how. They both now knew how to feel, towards each other. Lang had to pull his memories of love out to share them with Desmony, who had surprised herself with the gravity of how much she could feel. It was as though no one had ever tried in her life to make her understand vampires could love as well. Many had tried, but it took a man that had given up on love or passion to help her see that.

Many nights, Desmony spent with Lang, learning what his life was like for him all of these centuries. He was stranded, in a life he hadn't shown any concern to live in. From time to time, he thought of Karl, and how much he despised him. That freak of nature, killing him, making him a social monster! He took Lang's existence away. Lang tried to live amongst humans, but he ended up taking Karl's advice to stray away from humans. Finally, Lang stole away from his human life, not being able to take the pain. "I cannot be near my family, friends, and my many lovers. I could hurt them, of bring danger to them. Karl took my life hostage, with no ransom. They will miss me, but I shall miss them more, for I will live generations missing them, not just one life time." Lang was sought after by his family for years. With all resources exhausted, the family gave Lang up for dead. Little did they know, he was neither alive or dead.

Lang had fought his feelings about his transition period into his undead world, no longer feeling misty about his unfair hand that was dealt to him. Lang chose to try and skillfully move their conversations from him to understanding Desmony better. Desmony wasn't as complex as Lang was, unfortunately. She was born as she was, and had very little problems with her position in life. If Desmony envied any quality humans had over her, it would be the ability to stand in daylight. That would allow her to hunt all the time! Desmony tried to feel sympathy for Lang, and the life he was forced to leave behind. She couldn't, however. She saw absolutely nothing wrong with being a vampire. Her logic was unique, and she was gifted not to be bothered by a conscience.

Desmony would hold Lang, trying to help him find absolute comfort. Lang, in return, tried to help Desmony understand, or appreciate Morgana. That was Desmony's hidden Achilles heel. It disturbed Desmony to no end how Morgana couldn't just accept herself, and enjoy being what she was. It was Desmony's passion with this matter that allowed the very keen members of her family to know that she cared, and was concerned. It bothered Desmony she had no control over Morgana. Lang distracted Desmony, before she became violently evil, taking it out on her next victim. Lang couldn't bear hunting with Desmony, only to see her tear the flesh off her victims after, or even during the kill. It was so unnecessary, and ugly. Lang felt that he was more a father to her, rather than a companion, mentor. She would never heed his advice. Desmony alarmed him to be the child that would never grow up. Her hunting skills were impeccable, but her judgment was deplorable.

"Desmony, before I met you, I would feed once a year. I shall tell you why, so maybe you can understand, or even appreciate. I started out feeding every chance I got, since that was what I was told. I had immense strength, and I felt invincible. After about fifty years, after my family had been dead and gone, I lost all spirit. I began to think about what Karl had said. He told me I could test my limits, that a good vampire would do that. I was never compliant, so I decided to take his advice. I acquired a very subtle technique to my killing, but I never reveled in it. On the anniversary of my death, I would feast divinely for one night. The rest of the year, I hid, or tried to move about the living, until my complexion became so that I was noticeably different. When my flesh began to look dead, I would take refuge, until my next anniversary. I found that I could last significantly longer, but my strength would lessen greatly. Desmony, I see that I can't fully make you understand. I just want you to know, you don't have to be so dangerous. It may just be your nature, but you can control your urges. I can hope that chance will give you the opportunity to learn. As I come to care for you more and more, I hope that you will learn shortly, so that we can live in each other's company for centuries to come." That was as close as Lang could come to telling Desmony he was in love with her. Lang kissed Desmony again, hoping she understood what he was trying to accomplish.

Desmony asked if Lang would accompany her back to her home. Nola and Devon were expected back this evening from their honeymoon. Lang declined, saying it would not be an appropriate time. Desmony accepted his decision, unhappily. "Fine. That is where I will be. If you should want to collect me, I will be there for a few days. if not, I suppose I shall see you at the loft." Desmony was rejected and hurt, after such a tender retreat with Lang. It didn't end as either wanted. Desmony collected her things, knowing she would see Lang soon, but sad that he wouldn't come for her, as she had fantasized.

CHAPTER EIGHTEEN

Nola and Devon started back from their honeymoon.
They drove back home, still basking in the novelty of their
marriage. The afternoon sun sheered through the sky. Nola
was nervous about whether the alloy walls had been lowered,
assuring her, her family's safety. Nola had to remind herself
that she needed the Mal family to look after her, rather than
the other way around. Her services had been appreciated, but
not entirely necessary. Nola also had to remember the family
wasn't just hers alone. Devon knew about the Mal family, all
its secrets, all its powers, and it's few weaknesses. Devon
seemed to have read Nola's mind, sensing her anxiety. "Don't
fret, love. They are fine. I know you miss them terribly. I want
to get to know them as intricately as you do. We'll get the
chance. Listen, it's getting cold. Let's hurry inside." Devon
had found his way back to the urban mansion as he soothed
Nola's nerves. There was a nice shade over the front of the
house, from the sun just starting to set in the Pacific Ocean.
It was much cooler, but that didn't seem to truly bother the
couple. Devon unloaded the car, which was a bit heavier,
weighed down with carefully hand-crafted figurines, and
other trinkets to adorn the house with.

It had been decided Devon and Nola would remain in the mansion, *caring* for the family. The antique souvenirs of Nola and Devon's honeymoon would make tasteful and lovely additions to the house, making it somewhat theirs as well. The house was quiet and motionless. It was too soon for anyone to be awake. Everyone, even Morgana, had stayed the day at the mansion, waiting to have Nola and Devon assist them as they awoke. The day dragged itself into the horizon, disappearing for another night. Morgana was the first to rise. This was a natural assumption, for many reasons. Elsebeth, Bernard, and the others followed suit. "Oh, you two look so wonderful and happy! Please, allow us to help you for once! You must be fatigued." Morgana was right in offering the family's help. Nola accepted, only because she was terribly tired, and not quite ready to resume her life of servitude.

Bernard and Blythe initiated the conversation, asking how their honeymoon was, without prying and prodding at the new couple's intimacy. No one in the family actually knew what a honeymoon was, or what one did on one. honeymoons weren't customary when the elders of the clan had been united. Alec had been the only married soul of the group. he told his story of getting married to Elsebeth's mother on a Sunday and going back to work on Monday. They laughed, thanking everything good that society evolved to the point where common people could take retreats, celebrating the commencement of their nuptials. Nola and Devon's stories of their time alone were charming and passionate. Their looks of adoration couldn't be verbalized. If the essence of their experience could be captured and written about, it would overwhelm any romance novel advocate.

After all the discussion of the perfectly executed honeymoon, Nola assured the family that she, as well as Devon were back for good. They would resume caring for the family and the estate, assisting the family in the preservation of their lives. Their support was more emotional, protecting the family from loneliness, rather than from mere humans. It would take a great mass of humans to undo the power of the Mal family. Fortunately, Nola and Devon would continue to support the family's guise, not arousing any suspicions by being available during "business hours".

Nola and Devon found themselves providing the most company for Blythe and Alec. Their blood lust had diminished so that they barely ventured outside. It didn't seem healthy for their kind, but they had lost interest in hunting. Alec worked in his workshop. Blythe read and painted. Both spent the bulk of their time together, being in love, but never acknowledging that fact to the rest of the family. Nola and Blythe recognized Alec's talent, and assisted him with his work, when they could. Devon acquired a talent as an agent for Alec's work, selling it to the highest bidder. Buyers came from Los Angeles, New York, and many other European cities. The proceedings from the sales of the functional art work were contributed to charities of Alec's choice. Devon implored Alec to keep some of the booty from his hard work. Alec conceded, feeling as though he were a normal, working man, as he once was. Giving to the charities was his way of atoning for the victimizing he had done as a vampire, not having the choice to die as a human. It was a type of therapy for him, which no one disputed.

Blythe continued to volunteer at the blood bank, easily scamming its contents from the facility. It was too easy for her to provide for those that didn't want to hunt. the anger had left Blythe long ago. If it suited her, she could go on a rampage, consuming the entire city in fear in a night, if she saw fit. Her means of providing nourishment was not very respectable, but she chose to see humor in it. She was being evil in a very feeble sort of manner. Petty crimes to feed her craving for human blood. Blythe and Alec became like lazy lions, lying around in the Savanna. They were content just being together.

Bernard and Elsebeth made sure they took time away from the club to go far away, in order to replenish their blood supply. They enjoyed the different locations in which they hunted, tasting blood from different cultures. It was as if they were on vacation, sightseeing, and killing as they traveled from country to country. They still had the desire to keep their hunting skills thriving. It wasn't a matter of boredom or complacency, as was potentially the case the case with Blythe and Alec. Bernard wanted to create new ways to procure his *life source.* They wanted fresh human blood, as well as a change of scenery. Elsebeth tolerated the stored blood Blythe brought home, but Bernard couldn't stand it. He preferred fresh blood. There was nothing like the pulsing of the warm juice in his mouth, as it flowed down his throat. It was exhilarating, holding the prey, siphoning the life out, until the heart began to fail. They forfeited life to spare their own.

Most of the family took this sort of *healing vacation.* The only one of the brunch that refrained from these terrorizing sabbaticals was Morgana. She was the only one to not show any sign of deterioration or discontent for her surroundings, or drinking the cool, lifeless blood that came from the bank. One reason that kept Morgana going, longer than she had in a while was Luke.

Talk went rampant around the family. They all spoke of how Morgana succeeded in acquiring more human-like qualities. Morgana still had to feed, there was no substitution for that. Morgana simply didn't have to feed just as often. Morgana could last longer between feedings. She lasted longer than anyone in the family, even longer than Bernard or Blythe. That fact never inspired jealousy, rather a subtle and reserved fear. It was fear of the unknown and exactly what powers Morgana had that the other pure vampires didn't. For Elsebeth, it gave her a feeling of security, knowing at least one of her children wasn't completely subject to the rigid restrictions of being *other than human*. Morgana still refused to attempt facing what was thought to be certain death by facing the sun, or practicing any faith other than the dark one she was born into. Despite the family's speculations, it seemed more than just the end result of resistance techniques. All of Morgana's strengths seemed to be natural.

Morgana constantly thought about the things she couldn't do. It plagued her every available thought. She had to think back so far to remember how the sun looked. Most vampires couldn't recall the immense fire-ball simply because they never looked back. It was rarely a passion for a vampire to desire things from their human life. The seduction of the black power was too irresistible. It was an unwritten law that was abided by every creature that walked the earth on two legs, almost every creature. Nola would aide Morgana in her recollection by describing the sun so eloquently, utilizing words of poets to help Morgana *feel* the sun make its ascension and nightly demise from the horizon, that was as immortal as her Klan was. Nola's efforts were of little avail for Morgana. Morgana felt compelled to touch at it, to let it invade her very soul. the thought of the sun burning her skin, charring it until it ignited her entire body into something that resembled a phoenix shook her to the bone.

Morgana's school semester went on. Morgana and Luke studied together and spoke often outside of school. One evening, before midterms, Morgana asked Luke if he'd accompany her to her parent's night club. Morgana really wanted her family to see her find, her catch. Morgana felt so happy when she was around him. Morgana felt new, not centuries old. It was time for her to share more with him. She knew she could trust him with just a little more information on her vague and protected life. She sensed complete trust in him, but she didn't want to bombard Luke with too much that wasn't all that believable to any logical thinking person. Morgana, however, could tell she had invested well with Luke. He wouldn't disappoint her. He once told her he wasn't going anywhere, and she knew that to be true. Morgana was spared the ignorance that many people go through, never really knowing one can trust the other. Morgana knew, and she was determined to make their love permeate into infinity.

Luke accepted Morgana's invitation. "I'll do anything with and for you, Morgana!" Luke sounded almost as if he had won a game show prize. Morgana loved Luke as well, but resisted from telling him. If Morgana confessed her true heart, she would have to tell all.

Morgana just wasn't sure if she could confide such a fantastic story in Luke. He was in love, but would his passion for Morgana withstand her incredible secret? Friday evening came, and so did Luke to Morgana's door step. When Morgana opened the door, she saw her delicious looking man in a crushed velvet violet mock-turtleneck shirt with black baggy jeans. His hair changed into a gold color with the gel that was coating his locks. As Morgana stood at the door, she took the air in his mouth from Luke. he was ingested by the blood-burgundy calf length dress she wore with her forties inspired black velvet shoes. Morgana's hair was pulled up and away from her delicate face in a French twist with straight strands tickling her shoulders. "You look, well, I can't even describe it. Nothing comes to mind that would do justice to how you're making me feel." Luke was an exceptional male. He had never been afraid or unable to articulate his feelings.

Luke's words were anxiously spoken, almost cliché, but said with absolute conviction. "Thank you, Lucas. I hope you don't mind me using your formal name, but it suits your mature demeanor. I wish I merited such a compliment, but I really didn't spend a lot of time on this ensemble. There isn't too much to it really." Morgana smiled, almost as if she was embarrassed. Maybe, for the first time in a long time, she was. "You are much too modest, dear." Luke mirrored Morgana's startled look as his words left his mouth. Luke referring to Morgana with such a term of endearment seemed natural, but surprising, none the less. They both straightened up and came back to where they were standing. "Let's go." Morgana led Luke to his car and let her in. Luke let Morgana into his car and into his soul.

The club was near full capacity. The lights flashed from inside the huge renovated warehouse so bright that reflections shot out like flame-throwers across the bay. Every new moon was a big celebration for the club. this was because the sky was so dark and lonely. Another reason was the owners could steal about easily in the night, while the nearby crowds were distracted and fed with little worry. The coal black sky also made for a spectacular light show. There was no available space left for patrons to park, so Luke stationed his automobile in the employee parking lot with Morgana's direction. People came out from a short cut, which was an alley way. They also came out of cabs around adjacent buildings to stand in line to get into "Eternity's Oasis". The bass of the Techno beat made the hearts jump within a mile radius. Professional dancers scaled the walls, being paid for having a good time. As busy as it was, when Morgana was ushered in by young Mr. Lucas, many turned to her.

Morgana's beauty was almost unreal, surely unmatched. Her complexion was ivory, and flawless without a single blemish, anywhere. The women that analyzed her and compared themselves with her found themselves to be gracious, rather than bitchy or jealous. They spoke to her, when they were drunk enough to have nerve. They clamored after her, to find out her secrets. She never found one in the bunch that could really stomach what she had to do to maintain her level of beauty. They would have to contend with silicone and collagen, until age would refuse them any solution other than eventual death. For the fraction that weren't as vain, they were purer than Morgana could ever hope to be. Her sacrifice continued to be unbearable to her. Morgana could never bare the truth of her beauty. Morgana couldn't say, *Try sucking the lives of your acquaintances and strange victims until you can feel them trapped inside you, drinking their blood instead of Gin and Tonics*, but she would just answer with an answer of having good genes, or something like that.

Most of the men usually sat and fantasized about doing something very carnal, to the best of their abilities, which was better in fantasy rather than reality. None of the men that scanned every inch of her body could ever have the nerve to act on their perverted dreams. As long as they didn't try to, they were safe from harm. Morgana concealed her disgust for them. Some of the men wanted her, in a very pure sense. They wanted her, but their visions of loving her were sensual and if not for eternity, then for as long as she would have them. They wanted to be at her disposal. Without a doubt, Morgana was making an impact on the immediate population. Luke was extremely aware of this. Luke wondered to himself if he should even be standing next to her. There were so many attractive men in the room. Luke looked at their physical attributes, comparing theirs to his own, but Morgana was looking deeper than that. Luke continued to wonder if Morgana deserved better, if he was good enough. A million doubts ran through his mind to the point he thought about leaving her side, and running away, out of her life. Luke straightened up and stopped doubting himself, thinking just how lucky he was to be at the club with Morgana. If Morgana didn't want him there, he wouldn't be there. Morgana was very gentle, but had a great capacity to be forthright. Luke could sense how much Morgana cared about him. The only question was, how much.

A huge, hulking creature with unreal copper skin and sable hair rushed up on Morgana. He made himself available, irresistible. "Finally, a real woman to dance with." The lady that was with this beast was furious, at him. Her pride cried inside, but her grimace masked her pain. the woman looked at Morgana with hurt in her eyes. Morgana could sense the guy had been with the woman for some time. They had made love just before coming to the club. She had been satisfied, but the man's ego lusted for more than she alone could provide. the guy mistreated her regularly. Morgana felt the woman's pain and sent her a message into her mind. "Be strong. my friend. He isn't worthy of your heart." The young lady grabbed her drink and purse from the bar and eased away. The vile man didn't look for her, or miss her as time moved on. His mind was tied to the lovely twist in front of him. he smiled wickedly at her, just positive she would adorn his ego with her presence. Morgana looked over at her worried Luke, who was about to attempt pouncing this rouge. Morgana winked at him, and turned her focus back to the brawny moron. "Listen, darling. Take your steroid-infected corpse away and find someone else that would actually convince themselves into thinking they'd be lucky to be with you," Morgana expressed herself as calmly as early morning mist. Through all the noise, the man heard her clearly. Morgana spoke to his mind, as well as his face.

Luke motioned to take over, no matter how badly he would get pummeled by this old punk. Morgana held Luke's arm, steadying him. Morgana was perfectly stern as the man moved toward her. Luke wanted to jump to her rescue, but she emitted just enough strength to keep him stationary, to his surprise. Several other regulars moved in closer, ready to help remove the jerk from the establishment. The bouncers remained still, knowing Morgana's capabilities. No assistance was necessary. Morgana was in control. "I like a bitch with balls. Don't worry, I won't hurt you, now." The creep backed off and pushed several on lookers out of the way. Morgana just laughed at him, loudly, truly out of her classy character. the man turned back around, not expecting to hear laughter coming from the woman he was certain he had left terrified of his wrath, like so many others before. The obnoxious man returned, staring down her carefully angled nose. "You know what I said about not hurting you? Well, I lied." The muscle-bum charged her as if she had a red cape in front of her. Many tried, but no one could stop him. The man broke free of the many hands holding him back from Morgana's flawless face. Morgana hadn't even broken a sweat. The man was directly in Morgana's face. He stopped his attack, appearing to have second thoughts. Morgana held him by his fore arm as she put *The Whammy* on him.

The man saw detailed images of his pending death, if he tried to put a hand on her. He saw his beautiful sculpted limbs, that he spent countless hours defining, systematically falling to the ground, in a pool of blood. His tongue would be ripped out of his mouth first, so no one could hear his cries for help as Morgana picked at his bones, as if she were eating barbecue. He could actually feel his tendons being torn from his frame, unimaginable pain raped his mind. The man broke free from Morgana, catching his large head. His nose started to bleed. Most people around him knew that he did indulge in the use of steroids, so his reaction to his anger wasn't abnormal. Roaring shrieks of pain dove out of his mouth. Elsebeth and Bernard finally showed up, late from cleaning up a feeding in the nearby park. They got there as fast as they could, for potential damage control. Morgana fed them images of the incident as they retreated back to the club. Bernard was proud of his reluctant daughter. As he passed her, he whispered, "Very nice". Bernard got two bodyguards to usher the swollen freak out of his club as patrons chattered in the background.

The guards threw the man out near the garbage. He picked himself up, not knowing fully what had just happened. He staggered away, a shell of a man. Bernard turned back to the crowd after making sure he was gone. "Now you see why we don't allow drugs in such a fine establishment." Elsebeth was angry about the attack. She wanted that man's head. That was the least to be expected of someone that crossed with her flesh and blood. It was a definite maternal impulse. Elsebeth thought about feeding on him. It wasn't determined for sure if it was blood-lust, or revenge for poor treatment to her kin. No matter. Elsebeth followed through on her desire. Elsebeth recruited Bernard, and a few moments later, the muscle-bound dolt was drained of most of his poisoned blood and left in a faraway alley, near Richmond.

Bernard and Elsebeth found the fool, not far from the club, kicking in trash cans, just waiting to inflict pain on somebody. He was standing there, hitting the wall, cursing and pounding everything in sight. Bernard startled him, telling him it wasn't nice to destroy other people's property. When the guy, in his rage, told Bernard to "Fuck off", things got messy. Elsebeth set his death up to look like a drug deal gone bad. They slit his throat, letting the blood drip out into their waiting mouths. They fed like baby chicks, struggling from scraps from their mother. Of course, the crime scene, no matter how fabricated, was done to perfection. No questions were asked. the police did their thing, made up reports, and notified his next of kin.

the evening went nowhere but up for Luke and Morgana. Morgana was high on love, and adrenaline. Luke was a much more timid soul. Morgana didn't have a need for anything more than Luke was. Morgana didn't require a champion, like the Lady Gwenevere to fight for her honor. Morgana was more of a warrior than any man. Tenderness and vulnerability, but not against things like the sun were things she wanted to experience. Morgana wanted to feel like a fragile woman, not the feared killer she actually was, could be. Once before, with Victor, Morgana felt that tenderness. That was a different time, a long time ago. Morgana thought often of Victor, and missed him, but it did no good. Victor was gone forever from her life, having lived his own until death. Morgana knew Victor had kept her secret, and his love for her, and that made Morgana glad.

Morgana shook away the thought, the memory, and the feelings she felt. Morgana went onto the artificial marble dance floor to dance with Luke. From that moment on, Morgana concentrated only on him. Their interest heightened with each slower, more seductive song came on. they were feeling less and less inhibited. they held onto one another, feeling every nuance of the others body as they danced. The scene was quite mushy by many of the patrons' standards. their ambition for the night was to dance, and dance hard, partying with friends and alcohol. The ultimate goal was to get lucky, with as little risk as possible.

In Morgana's ear, Luke whispered, "You know, I can't believe what happened earlier. I mean, I was scared! You were as calm as a London palace guard, or something. I really feel bad about not being able to stop that ass-hole for you. I really should have tried to protect you better. I wanted to pound him, but I knew he would've knocked my ass out!" Luke rested his head apologetically on Morgana's shoulder. Luke half way expected her to throw him to the ground, calling him a wimpy freak, or something to that effect. Morgana was forgiving, and Luke gave a sigh of relief as they swayed to the music. "Don't worry, *Rocky*, I can take care of myself. Plus, I don't judge a man by whether he will throw his body in front of a moving train for me or not. It wasn't wise for you to try and confront him. I knew the bodyguards were near, and you don't need a prison record. the fight wasn't yours, it was mine." Morgana applauded Luke for attempting to defend her, and asked him politely to drop the subject.

Morgana and Luke eventually stopped dancing to the music, even though the pace of the music had picked up to a pulsing techno beat. They stood still on the dance floor, eyes fixed on each other. They couldn't even hear the deafening music.

They kissed. It was the first time either had shown affection for one another. It was the first kiss for both of them, in a long while, relatively speaking. The first kiss was simple. Once both of them were aware of what they were doing, they followed with a back-crushing embrace. They stared up at the sky through the large stained glass ceiling that was carefully constructed above them. The ceiling was up to code, as much as possible in the event of an earthquake, or other natural catastrophe. There was a concrete structure, woven just above the glass to protect the patrons. Morgana and Luke didn't think about that. They didn't care. They just wanted to digest the beauty of the moment.

Above, in the management office, Bernard looked on at Morgana and Luke. "She's in love. Do you suppose she will tell him? We were lucky with Devon, it was in his nature. This one, well, he's weak." Elsebeth was full of emotions this evening, good as well as bad. "He's honest and caring. Most of all, he loves our daughter." Bernard purposefully looked at Elsebeth right then. Elsebeth gave him a look that carried them into the next room that was a small, secret apartment for them. Elsebeth held Bernard, feeling the tension in his muscles and tendons diminish. He responded to Elsebeth's advances with a gentle kiss on her brow. "Thank you, my love. Morgana has been, and always will be my child. We need not ever concentrate from whence she came from. I have forgiven, as I have faith that both Morgana and you have forgiven me. I will never abandon the family, or you, ever again." Bernard was nothing like his terrifying nature was known to be. Bernard rubbed his hands through Elsebeth's black liquid hair. the soft wave motioned hypnotically as Bernard massaged her scalp.

Elsebeth responded to Bernard by tenderly stroking his taught, ivory skin, which at one time was a rich olive tone. Elsebeth hushed Bernard with a smooth kiss, one after the other. Bernard complemented her affection with caresses throughout her magnificent body. they loved each other all night long. They retired in the room until the next evening. the room was constructed as the house had been, protecting them from the sun with thick concrete and no windows.

CHAPTER NINETEEN

It was well after two in the morning before Luke urged Morgana to leave. Morgana finally gave in. The smoke or the crowd didn't bother her, but it was taking its toll on Luke. He could've stayed with Morgana there forever, or so he imagined. "You know Luke, I stay out so late with you because I hate to leave you. This is hard for me to say, but in the past few months, I've grown very attached to you. I'm attracted to you as well. It's been a long while since I've bedded someone, but I'll be ready soon, after I tell you all about me." Morgana's frankness stunned Luke, but there was no doubt both of them were thinking the same thing. Luke couldn't hide his eagerness to be with her physically. He was erect most of the night, coming down only because his body couldn't stay excited too long. As soon as he relaxed, he became erect again shortly after. It was agony for him. He didn't want to leave her, to purge his desire alone, in some cold bathroom behind a closed door. he couldn't ask for her to be with him so soon either. Morgana's words confirmed his thoughts, but gave him hope that soon, they would be together.

Morgana wanted to show restraint, but she couldn't help herself. She was feeling the same agony, burning between her legs, possibly more so than Luke. Her nipples were hard and tight. She wanted his to relieve her anxiety, but there was no way. The time was not right. Morgana was overcome by the way she was feeling, what she was saying. Morgana thought herself wicked because she knew how much Luke wanted her. Luke was about to burst and Morgana knew it wasn't right to encourage him more, until he couldn't control his actions. He coveted her. He would die for her. Morgana hoped it wouldn't come to that for them to be together.

The misty cool night air chilled Luke, but Morgana felt very cozy. They decided to walk for a while, still feeling high after the events that occurred a few minutes prior. The area had a certain ambiance, not a particularly desirable one though. Strangers and strange people eased through the night. Some tried to hide form eyes, or the elements. Some were out of their minds. They spoke to friends or relatives that weren't really there. The people that made the cold, damp streets their home, for many reasons, became savages. It gave Morgana a feeling she couldn't shake. Her heart felt sorry for these people, as is often the case. Her soul actually liked it. She felt strangely comfortable. It appealed to her dark side.

Luke held onto Morgana, wondering if she was uneasy. Of course she wasn't, but he felt better thinking he was protecting her. The echo of cars passing and sirens was overpowered by a small trampling of footsteps. "Come on, let's go. I don't like this." Luke's unapproachable charm was momentarily surpassed by his unnerving concern. Their pace picked up as they made their way back to the car. They had traveled farther than most people concerned with safety should have. Whoever, or whatever was behind them sped up their pace as well. They indeed were being followed. Luke began to feel strangely warm. Anxiety was inflaming his body. The distance back to their car was nearly five blocks away. It seemed like a country mile as they struggled to reach their destination.

"Hey man, what's up?" A dirty odious gang member jumped from around the corner of the building they were approaching. They could hear the rest of the entourage scatter around to their battle stations. They thought they'd have an easy night of a simple mugging, with a possible assault following. With the looks of this punk's lady, maybe even a rape. With their number, it wouldn't be difficult to accomplish. "What's wrong, can't talk? I ain't done nothin' to you and you bein' all rude and shit. Well, what should I do about that?" The thug gripped a shining monkey wrench he had clutched in his hands. The guy wore the typical oversized pants, sagging down to his butt-crack. His shirt was a picture of a dead rap star that couldn't get the ghetto out of him, with all his fame and glory. His jacket was decorated with his gang name and the name of all his enemies that he had slain. He had a small scar, along the side of his face. He had taken a hit in a drive by, being the only survivor. His look was finished with a rag that symbolized his gang affiliation. Soon, one by one, all his *brothers* assembled around him and their prey.

There was six of them, seven with the apparent leader. Lucky seven. "Listen Bitch, give me your money and maybe I won't fuck your boyfriend in front of you! Come on! I want your money too, beach boy!" He raised his arm to try and make them cower. Morgana reached up and grabbed the wrench from the criminal. She took the wrench out of his hand and wailed it across his head. She struck him in the temple, which would have been enough, but with her force, his skull caved in like crushed aluminum. Luke quickly became busy with two of the other hoods. "Run Morgana, run!" Luke was determined to save her. All she could think about was making sure he didn't injure or killed.

One huge guy came upon Morgana. Morgana darted around him, jumping onto a crate near the wall. He drew a bowie knife on her. As the knife came out, the tip of it cut her dress, as well as her thigh. "My dress!" Morgana felt like her wicked sister, incorporating humor in the face of danger. Morgana swung her stiletto pump at the jaw of the corrupt creation in front of her. The kick connected and his head nearly separated from his neck. Blood fell from his mouth as his body collided with the pavement. Morgana jumped down and kissed her victim. She took in his blood, letting the fluid pass her lips. She was like a striking panther. Luke fortunately didn't see the taking of the blood. She clawed the thug down his chest. He could've been gutted like a fish, if time permitted.

The next victim was grabbed by the throat. With Morgana's fangs, she stole his larynx. Even though they were evil and condemnable, their blood was sweet. The remaining gang member turned, running away, screaming. Morgana took the knife from the dead man's hand and hurled it into the back of the feeble gangster.

Luke had rallied when he found a piece nearby his hand as he laid where the two punks made him fall. After a few blows and action hero moves, the two laid on the ground, one on top of the other. his adrenaline was through the roof. He turned to see what was to be assessed, if Morgana had gotten away, and if any others were around to fight. Had Morgana fled? Was she safe? Well, what he saw when he finally found his lady, wasn't his lady at all. her eyes were a reddish-brown fluorescent. Her skin was a subtle lime-like glow in the dark green. Morgana's nails and teeth were long, extremely long and red. Blood dripped down her chin and her chest, all the way down the front of her dress.

Morgana's hair was wild and she was totally inhuman. Luke yelled in disbelief. He was afraid, but before he could react to what he saw any other way, he collapsed. Morgana calmed down, suddenly. she began screaming at herself in disappointment. She began to cry. She felt guilty for enjoying her feast. *What should I do now?* After a short while, she transformed back to her *natural* state. Morgana remembered everything, feeling horrible about the entire incident. She loathed killing, even for her own survival. If there was another way for her to survived, with total strength, she'd do it.

Morgana sat on the cold concrete, thinking about everything, fearing the future most of all. The two living gang members saw nothing of what happened, what she'd done. They were lucky. Morgana picked up Lucas, literally, and carried him through the navy blue sky, to her hideaway. The sky was changing as they traveled. The fear was in her, but she wasn't sure if it was just a reaction, from all the years of discipline, or was it from what could, should happen to her if she stayed out until daybreak. Morgana made it home, just before dawn. the wonder wouldn't be quelled that night.

When she entered the first room, it was extremely dark, black as pitch. Luke slept for nearly half a day. He came around by the afternoon, about three p.m. He felt warped. His memory was scrambled, but things came back slowly to him. As his vision adjusted to the darkness, he tried to survey his surroundings. He could barely make out a modest collection of original masterpieces Morgana acquired. There was a self-portrait on the wall over the fireplace. There was a small fire burning, which was the only illumination in the front of the house.

After all these centuries of living, the mal family had finally separated and began their own lives. Most of them did. there was always the mansion, and many homes across the world, but Morgana finally had a place of her own. She had a place to take refuge from the scrutiny of her family. No words were ever said, but the feeling was always there. All the family members went back to the mansion, to remember, but the world was so fascinating now. They made their own choices so that they could experience as much as possible. It took them several centuries to get to that point. They felt safer together in the past. things were different now.

Morgana had decided upon their arrival to San Francisco to give herself some freedom from her family. So much had happened, and the hiding period took a toll on her. She felt so paranoid about her relationship with her family. She loved them, but wasn't convinced about everyone's feelings towards her. Morgana wanted to go to school, doing things that weren't usually thought of as practical for a vampire. She tried to justify her feelings of wanting to experience all the changes, seeing if she could conform, not being detected. Morgana had her own style, one she didn't want to share with her family any longer. Morgana wanted to be around people, not to stalk them as the others did. She did not want to be on the outside looking in.

Morgana's own home had an ivory and burgundy color scheme with rose accents. The decor was antique. Mahogany wood took the shape of furniture that supported such items as vases, art, and delicate collectibles. Morgana's secret pride was a rare collection of dolls and instruments from all over the world. The newest thing in her home was a television. The Mal estate didn't have too many modern devices such as televisions or radios. Morgana didn't really have much use for electronic gadgets, but she found it a useful tool to keep up with society. The only part of the mansion that had modern appliances was Desmony's room. Desmony's room resembled any young woman's from the late twentieth century. She was well equipped with an entertainment system that annoyed the entire house when she blared her wailing music. Morgana sighted Desmony's taste in tone deaf music as one of many reasons why she moved into her own home. Morgana was on her way out of the place when Desmony had flown into her room, disturbing her, shortly after they first moved into the mansion. It was too much. They were too different to occupy the same space. Desmony claimed her fascination with the 'pop-culture' was too study her prey. She wanted to know what they liked, how they acted, how to get to them. Morgana didn't feel that television was an accurate representation of the general public. Morgana didn't really care. If she needed to feed, she would know what to do when the time was right. Morgana's passion was for peace, not anarchy.

Luke raised himself up and tried to get his barring. He made himself at home in the early evening glow, turning on her television. Luke also began to scavenge around for coffee. Morgana kept all of the necessary things around to feed others, even though she could not partake in such refreshments as coffee or any nourishment. Often, she wondered how she survived. the blood she did ingest lasted her so that she had no need for any other nourishment. She dared to try drinking wine, eating bread, but it often made her ill. After Luke successfully found makings for coffee, he made a pot, assuming Morgana would be craving caffeine as well. Luke then began his search for Morgana, his search for the truth. Luke found a cold heavy steel door. It wouldn't open, at least he couldn't open it. Memories of the night before finally came in clearly, almost breaking his mind. He wanted to believe it was some fantastic dream, ignited by drugs that were slipped into his beer or something. Luke was wrong, and he knew it. He just chose to try and not believe it. Luke looked around some more. After not finding anything, not even his girl, which alarmed him, he resolved to rest some more. He plopped down on the couch, reclining into the soft, full pillows. Luke didn't attempt to leave, he couldn't leave, not without speaking to Morgana. He gave no thought to getting a cab to take him back to his car. He wondered if that's how Morgana got him to her house. Luke had looked outside, to see if his car was outside, but the street was empty, with no sign of his vehicle.

At around six thirty in the evening, just around dusk, the huge door peeled open. Morgana pushed the vault looking door with ease. She looked like an angel. This wasn't the same woman he saw last night, it couldn't be. She leaned against the doorway with her arms crossed. She studied the floor, thinking how to phrase her following words. "Know this, my dear Lucas. Your life is in severe jeopardy. I am Vampire. I thrive on blood. I have existed this way for nearly three and one half centuries. I have told only one other that lived after my confession. He, Victor, was my first true love. I hope that you will be my last. I want not to hurt you. I feel life in my body when I'm with you. I must ask you know, Lucas. Do you have the stuff to survive with me? Might I trust you? Bring me joy, don't deny me. I won't hurt you, but you have no choice but to believe me. I trust that if you want to survive, you will hold my secret unto yourself." Morgana acted as if she wasn't there. It was as though she wasn't speaking, someone else was. It was the side of her that was doing what must be done. Morgana was prepared to do whatever was necessary. If it was needed to stop his life to save herself, she would. Morgana's air was tight as it left her body. He insides were quaking. The part of her that could love, that could care, was beyond afraid.

Luke sat as still as the sculpture that held one of her favorite hats in the living room corner. At first, he didn't know what to say. He couldn't think of any words to say. His mind hadn't taken in the full scope of the situation. He looked at Morgana, her stance unmoving. The only thing he did not question was that this was real. This staggering and incredible thing was happening to him. The woman he wanted to loose himself in was more than human, and that was something he wasn't supposed to have to deal with, but he did. This was far and beyond the most bizarre thing to ever happen to him, or anyone he knew. "Wow. I'm not sure I know what to say. I mean, what would I need to do? What choices do I have? How did this happen to you anyway? Is this real?" Luke laughed for a moment, but began crying from sadness for Morgana's obviously troubled soul, as well as his confusion.

Morgana finally moved, ready to fill in more of the holes, as requested by Luke. "Victor, my love, knew of me and who I really am. He made the decision not to be with me. He had too much to lose, too much responsibility for our love. That was two centuries ago. There has been no one since. Victor kept my secret and loved me. That is why I wear this ring." Morgana showed Luke the ring that victor had given Morgana before they parted forever. It rested on her right ring finger, and it stayed there. It was a gorgeous oxidized Marcasite band that was a braided design. It sparkled in all the right places, with an ominous beauty in the darker parts of the piece. There were also blood-colored garnet stones throughout the ring, which added a regal quality to the piece that made Morgana sure it was from nobility. Victor never told her it was a spoil from a well-to-do family that had vacated their home to elude the French rebels. For them, it wasn't "a good day to die". Luke looked at the ring, not in disgust, but envy. Luke was under a spell Morgana did not create.

Morgana continued with her incredible story. "As far as how all of this started for me, I was born this way. My mother was turned by my father that I know, he is not my biological father. My true father was a Spanish aristocrat from the seventeenth century. There is so much to tell you, if you want to know more. If you do not, or if you try to tell someone else, you can't live. Do you want to, or do you want to die?" Morgana was hollow of emotion. *What would Luke do?* Morgana held her chest tight. "I could keep your secret. I just need to understand and to adjust. I don't know what to do, Morgana. I still love you and I refuse to let you go. I don't mean that just because you'd have to kill me if I didn't want to be with you. I guess I understand that. I can see you wouldn't have a choice. From my heart, I just want to be with you. The only problem is, you scare me, you really scare me. I'm afraid of you, and I admit it." Luke wanted to go to her, but his trust in her was wounded.

"I won't harm you, Luke. I never hurt those that I love, or those that are loyal to me." Morgana's cheeks flushed from fear and embarrassment. Morgana knew Luke was hurt by her. Morgana felt badly, but what was she to do? The situation was truly fantastic, yet not to be envied. Luke came to Morgana and took her by the hand. "You're truly special, Morgana. I'm no good to you the way I am. If I were like you, I could protect and take care of you. Most of all, maybe I could make and keep you happy. You always look so sad and troubled. When you do smile, it's like a summer rain. It's so refreshing. I want to make you smile, that's all I want. If I were like you, I'm certain I wouldn't fear you. I'd understand you." Luke actually sounded hopeful in the midst of the incredible sequence of events.

Morgana smiled slightly at Luke. "Be careful. My father had a creation that didn't enjoy being what she was. Even though she was weak, she still wanted revenge on my father for cheating her out of her life, and killing her father. It consumed her, making her a true monster, worse than she already was. That woman finally died, never truly knowing love and not remembering happiness. I don't want you to not be able to support your new life. I don't want to destroy your essence. It is so beautiful, I shan't waste it." Morgana thought of how hurt Bernard was after that final confrontation between Lysa and he. "You know, it sounds like she didn't have the luxury of choice, am I right? You aren't handling our situation that way. You aren't doing that to me.

The truth is, I have no one but you, I need you as much as I love you. Ever since I met you, my soul feels empty when you aren't with me. Surely God can understand *unconditional love*? Luke saw the look on her face. That look that showed up every now and then. Morgana hungered for acceptance from God.

"My father wanted Lysa, the woman I told you of. That's all he knew. He was fascinated by her. He thought she had the fire inside her, so he took her without little thought. The entire experience was traumatic for her, simply too much I imagine. I think what hurt Lysa the most was that her father had to die in the process. Once she knew My father had killed him, there was no chance for her." Morgana finally understood Lysa, as she understood her own mother. They had to trade one life for another. Elsebeth was more willing. She wanted to survive. Elsebeth's only error was not thinking it all through. How could she? Now, all of her feelings were resolved, after five centuries of growing, living. Living as a creature other than one of God's children. It appeared as though Luke had thought this all out, maybe better than Morgana's own mother. Elsebeth had been under a type of spell, one she didn't understand at first. Luke was a bit more sophisticated, maybe a little more jaded by life. Luke gave his consent to Morgana to create him over, into another being than what he had known.

Morgana sat down with Luke. She wanted to give him a sort of heads up on what to expect before the actual transformation. "You will need much blood at first. Many lives you will need to take." Morgana touched his face. That though alone made Luke's face drop. His mind ran through images of killing another human being. He thought about his own parents. They were dead, and they certainly weren't ready to die. he would need to try and rationalize the blood gathering, but he didn't want to do that now. It was too much to take in. No matter how much detail Morgana went into, nothing would prepare him for the first time. The only thing that might help him cross that line would be his hunger for blood. At that point, instinct would override his mortal and moral hang ups. Morgana brought Luke's head to her bosom. "I will do what I need to stay with you." Luke held his face with her hand. Morgana said to Luke, "It is time for you to see my real home." They both dressed for Morgana to take Luke to her in town palace. It seemed to take hours to get dressed. The only thing they thought about was being together.

They had a lot to deal with, but the attraction and the love was still there. The same lust each of them felt jabbed at them, just as it did last night and each night before, ever since they met. Luke knew that it was important for Morgana to know that he was serious about his commitment. Luke touched Morgana's shoulder and looked straight into her eyes. "If you like, I can drive, if you don't mind me driving your car. Mine's still at the club. I may not know what to expect, but I do trust you. I hope you can trust me too. I don't have a choice, like we talked about. I love you too much. I know you wouldn't put me in any undo danger." Luke opened the door for Morgana, since she melted, giving him the keys without hesitation. Luke held onto Morgana's waist as she crossed the retreat's threshold, into the misty night.

CHAPTER TWENTY

Everyone knew to expect Morgana and Lucas' arrival shortly. They picked up on Morgana's anxiety. The family picked up on Morgana's message as Luke drove Morgana to the grand house. All family members convened there, waiting for the couple to appear at the front door. Elsebeth dropped everything, including the porcelain vase she was inspecting for flaws. She knew Morgana's companion would have to be human. "Alas, she is from my loin," Elsebeth thought as she swept up her mess. Elsebeth then volunteered her father Alec to help her make all the preparations. The air was still as Morgana and Luke pulled up into the garage. the two held each other's hand as they ascended the stairs to the front door. The door opened, even before they got to the doormat. Bernard was on the other side of the door. He possessed a very ominous look at the young man. Bernard observed Luke as if he were a newly acquired piece of art. Bernard didn't quite know what to make of Luke. Some images flashed in Bernard's mind. They were cloudy, distant. Luke's mind was on Morgana. The images of their time together were the only clear one's that Bernard could make out.

Everyone sat in the formal living room. The vaulted ceiling came in good use that night. much air was needed, even though they couldn't find much. Luke looked at them all, still not knowing what to expect. This collection of people puzzled him greatly. The people that greeted him into their home, and offered to feed him, and make him comfortable, were the same *people* that movie producers and authors make a living at, spinning tales of their horrific existence. They all looked like any family, however grossly affluent, and more savvy and educated than any group of people could ever hope to be in one lifetime.

Luke's anticipation was the worst part of all, or so he thought. The tension was too much. Those that could ate and drank. Morgana knew she needed added strength if all went well tonight. Even she drank some warm blood, fresh from flesh. the taste treated her tongue like castor oil, or oysters to someone that didn't enjoy them. A very real part of her likened the flavor to a virgin Bloody-Mary. It was soon time to get to the heart of the matter, the purpose of the assembly. Lucas took the initiative by beginning the story. "My name is Lucas Bryant. I am twenty-two years old, and I am alone. To be honest, I'm still in shock over all this. I'm very confused. This is not the usual secret your girlfriend keeps from you, so forgive me. I love Morgana, I do know that. I want her to be happy. She says I do that for her." Luke's voice rattled as he spoke. He paused to smile at Morgana.

Luke spoke of his past, something that was easy for him to do only with Morgana. No one else was supposed to know. It was Luke's way of protecting himself, since his mother and father could no longer do so. Emotions were reserved by the family as Luke spoke. It wasn't that they were apathetic, they realized the importance of Morgana's selection. they had to remain objective. They had to weigh what he said, how he said it, and if his evaluation equaled a choice candidate for the family. After Luke spoke, a conference would be held to determine what was to happen next. The family was tired of hiding, but did so for survival. to trust a human, if he remained so, would be another great undertaking in a relatively short amount of time. Blythe moved toward Luke, inspiring fear in his very being. "You are waging a great deal tonight. If we agree to trust you, you will remain safe, for now. I trust Morgana has educated you on how claiming allegiance with our clan works. If there is any trouble, anyone causing that trouble with you will certainly die. If the trouble is with you against us, you will die as well. We do this regardless of the amount of care we have for you, Morgana included. Please understand, it isn't personal." "Take time to make sure this is what you truly want. We have plenty of time." Desmony was confident in her words, but she was actually compassionate. "Well, I don't. Morgana, come with me. We'll go get my car, and we'll talk more at my house." Luke was stern and serious. He couldn't believe he was speaking in debatable disrespect in the presence of creatures that could tear his limbs out! "I must get to my tomb before dawn." Morgana never questioned that, she just performed that nightly ritual out of practice. Luke nodded comprehension. They both left, with her family spellbound, arriving at Luke's house around nine p.m.

"Your home is truly lovely. It's not terribly masculine, it's just nice. I feel very comfortable here." Morgana surveyed the area in which Luke lived. The color scheme was completely neutral. Oak wood furniture held his clothes, books, appliances, and other possessions. The light delicately touched the subtle print wall-papered walls. The trees outside made the street light dance on the wall, creating images, room for creative figures within one's mind. It was much more impressive in the day time, something Luke would have to settle with describing to his love. The hard wood floor creaked as they stepped down to his lowered living room. "My parents built this house when I was five. My mom spent endless hours decorating it. She would go to shops, looking for just the right accessories. She became ill just after she finished the house. She would tell me she wanted everything just right for me. She died shortly after." Luke moved slowly from behind Morgana and went over to the only new addition to the house, a stereo system he spent a month's salary on. The radio churned out sweet-heart felt oldies that refurbed off the walls. Morgana laughed to herself. As Luke swayed to the music, Morgana remembered when the song that was playing first aired.

Morgana remembered all of the Big-Band releases, the Ziegfield follies, Vaudville. "I adore this song. Are you OK Lucas? It still hurts, doesn't it? I'm sorry I've never really lost anyone. I never knew my real father to miss him." Morgana sat on Lucas' cream fabric love seat. It had a square shaped quilt his grandmother had crafted for him, before he was born. Luke's house had reminders all-around of how loved he was, but the pain still remained. Morgana continued to explain about Xavier. "He was a mortal, long ago. Bernard was devastated, but eventually, he healed. We all had to." Luke moved close to her. "That's quite a story, Morgana. You've been so open. I still can't believe that I'm accepting all of this! I don't have a reason not to believe you." Luke brushed her silky locks with his hand.

Morgana sipped the wine as Luke ate a steak with salad. Morgana tried to contain her nausea while she prepared the meal for him. The raw flesh didn't harm her, but as it burned, almost to a charred brown, the odor became unbearable. Morgana refused to let on to Luke, sitting melancholy on the love seat. Morgana contemplated creating steak tar-tar for herself, but her appetite for any flesh was gone. Luke ate the meal, complementing Morgana on her culinary skills. It amazed him how well she could cook, even though she hadn't eaten a meal in her life, at least since her *rebirth.* "Do you need anything?" Luke inquired as to whether or not she needed blood, or whatever kind of sustenance she required. Morgana could tell he was referring to blood, because of the nervous quake in his voice. "You need not fear me, Lucas. There's no spell for me to put on you to help. If you want me, don't doubt me. I could try and work a charm for you to forget all of this, but I doubt that it would work. You don't want it to. You can have me, if I can trust you." Morgana became very serious. "It sounds like we need to trust each other." Luke wiped his mouth as he got up from the dining table. He had just finished the last bite of what he considered a gourmet meal.

Luke took Morgana's hand, leading her to sit with his in front of a hand crafted fireplace. The attention to detail reminded Morgana of Alec. It was a shame that it was too warm for the heat, not to mention the fact that the fire would harm Morgana. Luke abruptly moved toward Morgana, aggressively. Morgana stopped Luke just before he took her in a kiss. "This is not what we will be about." Morgana refused to let their liaison be about sex, simple lust and passion without substance. "I want you, all of you. Just this moment, I thought about coming here, another night, without you, and I couldn't stand it! You have become the reason I do everything I do. I can't function without you. When you're gone, your image is in my mind. You are all I see. Your words chime in my ears. your voice is all I hear. I can't believe I'm saying this!" Luke began to laugh. Morgana joined him, joyfully. Morgana touched his strong jaw. It was ridged with his desire for her. Morgana lightly touched his chin, his nose, and finally his pouted lips. Morgana passed a delicate kiss on his mouth, taking the last piece of his soul into hers.

After a strong embrace, Luke stood up and picked up Morgana. Luke's room was very similar to the front of the house. The bed was his mother's legacy. She designed and created it. The bed was where Luke was conceived. It was the last work that his artist mother crafted. the oak canopy bed had a woven cover that made many rounded squares over their heads. There was a white colored sheer netting that hung carelessly over the canopy. Ribbons tied the material at each of the posts. Luke's mother requested in her will that if the bed should not be destroyed by circumstances beyond his control, Luke was to create his children in the elevated loft of a bed. Luke wondered if he could grant his mother's wish. Morgana told him quite honestly she wasn't sure, but they would try. Their love was pure, so it was possible. They would be children made of love, but not of a pure soul. They would have no religion, which was something neither Luke nor Morgana wanted to think about now. All they wanted was to speak to each other with panted words.

Luke laid Morgana on her back onto the bed. The sheets were white, as was the comforter. The eyelet detail broke up the monotony of the bed linen. There were forest green pillows and curtains around the room. Everything had its place. Luke respected everything about his parents. All of the pieces around the house represented them, and their memory. Morgana was filling up the empty places in his heart that went void without his parents. he had nothing new of them, except of the love he had with Morgana that seemed to be molded from the love he saw that they had for each other. The bed was soft as they lay on top of the bedding. Every move Luke made towards her was deliberate, almost as if it were choreographed. In fact, it was. Luke imagined being with Morgana, loving her, in his home. Luke knew just how she would react to each caress, each kiss, and the words he said to her. "Kiss me," was all Luke said, and she obeyed his wish.

The kisses were slow, but strong. They became more and more intense. Morgana could hardly breathe for the passion. Luke's character was meek, but he had the potential to be a great lover, possibly greater than Victor. Morgana was astounded, she never thought that would be possible. Morgana had found another knight, another warrior, quiet, but mighty. Luke clutched Morgana in his arms, until he found the zipper to the cat suit she had changed into before they left the mansion. It seemed like an eternity before the seductive unitard came off her long, lyrical body. Underneath was beautiful black satin underwear. Morgana stopped him before he attempted to disrobe her any further. "Now it's my turn." Morgana's voice was hypnotic. Lucas released his hold and let her begin her journey.

Morgana gripped Luke's shirt that in Morgana's opinion had been on his body much too long. Luke was relieved to feel the shirt leave his body, for many reasons. Luke had been in the same outfit for several days. He wasn't accustomed to going without a shower for such a long amount of time. During his earlier years, being dirty was cool, but maturity offered him the insight that being offensive wasn't advantageous in any circumstance. So much had happened to Luke that hygiene became secondary in his list of priorities. Luke couldn't stand his current state, but he didn't want the moment to be tarnished at all. If Luke couldn't have Morgana now, he would go insane. Morgana made him feel secure about his condition, which let them both continue with what they wanted most. Luke needed her, no one else could or had brought him so much fulfillment.

Morgana rolled the plush material off Luke's toned, but lean frame. His hair became a golden tussle of locks. Morgana took a survey of her *objet d'amour* and dawned a devilish grin at him. Morgana kissed Luke in the center of his chest, working her way up to his full, begging lips. Morgana took them without any apologies. Just then, Morgana surprised Luke. Morgana gently kissed his brow. Morgana unzipped his jeans slowly, feeling each groove as she pulled at the metal flap. Morgana finished, then unfastened Luke's pant button. She peeled back the jeans until most of Luke's toned stomach was exposed. Morgana moved her nimble fingers over Luke's six-pack, trying not to tickle him. She could tell Luke couldn't take much more of these idle temptations. They escorted each other under the soft white cotton sheets. Instead of acting on the rush of desire they were both feeling, they laid next to each other, enjoying the feel of one another. It was almost as if they were gathering courage to continue.

The next movements could easily be recognized from the shadows on the bedroom wall as love-making. The "beast with two backs" never looked more elusive, unobtainable, elegant. Luke hoisted his lean body from Morgana's side, nestling himself in between Morgana's legs. Morgana eased out a puff of air, as if she were exhaling a drag from a cigarette. Luke tasted each of Morgana's breasts, as if they were white chocolate, topped with caramel. Morgana arched her back, wanting to be consumed into his every pore. She wanted to loose herself in this man, with no regrets. Luke feared he wasn't pleasing such a dynamic woman, but her responses reassured him almost instantly. Luke brought himself toward, then into Morgana. He held onto her shoulder's as he fit himself inside her. It was exquisite pain as Luke filled Morgana with himself. They embraced each other as Luke brought himself closer, time and time again. After a quaking climax, the lovers positioned themselves next to each other, basking in the near opaque night.

There were candles lit throughout the room. They were the only objects revealing their secret. They resumed confirming their emotions, consummating their love and care for each other over and over, until fatigue overwhelmed Luke. They paused occasionally for a brief eating binge or listening to one of Luke's old records on his mom's Hi-Fi. "This one is great! Can this be our song? I think it describes us perfectly!" Morgana felt like a young girl once more. No amount of blood ingestion could ever do that for her, never. Both Luke and Morgana were filled with each other's passion. Both Luke and Morgana acted on whatever whim inspired them. The lovers danced nude to the dated song that crackled as it played. Neither body took notice of their unclad partner. The focus of the moment was on the eyes. Luke continued to tear into Morgana's soul, as did Morgana into his. The sensation each was filling the other with encouraged them to initiate in more love-making. After filling each other's passion again, they paused for a game of gin-rummy, then tic-tac-toe. The evening was nonsense, yet it was perfect, for them. Morgana and Luke talked and laughed for hours. Time seemed irrelevant, even though it wasn't. The carelessness of their love was setting Morgana up for a very precarious circumstance

The couple continued talking and laughing, feeling more like one than ever, not caring about any rules or conditions. Morgana was still overwhelmed by their in-between-love-making escapades. "This is so bizarre Luke! It's not totally romantic, what we're doing, but it is different." Morgana was terribly confused. "Don't you see? This is romantic! It's right. It's right for us. None of this makes sense. Right now, I'd just like to lay here, with you in my arms, feeling your thick beautiful hair on my chest, remembering every detail about us." Luke was still dripping wet from the shower they'd just taken together. The lovers stayed by each other's side, wrapped in a thick, hand woven blanket.

Luke and Morgana fell asleep in each other's arms, just before dawn. The moon rose, reaching its height, then consequently fell. Morgana's internal alarm, in all her ecstasy, failed her this one night. Morgana's hair was in her face, but she began to feel a strange sensation. The ever-young vampire's brows rammed each other in a deep frown. Morgana moved her hair out of the way, letting her lids rise with heavy weight. Just as a new born cries tears through the silence of the quiet moment before birth, Morgana bellowed a shriek, killing the beautiful moment of dawn and waking up with her true love. "What? What's wrong?" Lucas was in a semi-conscious panic. "The sun, the sun, oh God, the sun!" Morgana wept as she ran from the sun, as if it were the bad man, trying to hurt her. She made her way onto the other side of the bed, trying to stay out of the suns dangerous path. Morgana examined her entire life, all three hundred and forty-two years of it, being exchanged for a night of complete love and a painful death. She had heard about how vampires die, what they go through. Morgana knew she had only moments to envision this, and try to hold on to all the images she had stored away in her troubled heart. One thought came to her. Death for vampires in the sun was virtually instantaneous. Morgana was still alive, still waiting for death.

None of the things Morgana was told about a vampire's death was happening to her. The singeing of the skin, followed by the intense pain and burning. Being aware of total demise, until ashes blow in the morning breeze. "Morgana, stop it! Stop screaming! You're okay! Stop and look, damn it! You're not dying." Luke expected the worse, some horrific vision that was once his beautiful love. All he saw was the sun glowing against her glacial ivory skin. Morgana's traumatizing screaming decreased octave by octave. The sun was a shock to her highly intensive skin, but it soon became an enjoyable experience, knowing it wasn't pain. The sensation was the sun's heat warming her cool body. Morgana's tears and fears disappeared, slowly. Lucas came to her side, holding on to her. Luke tried to help Morgana adjust to the monumental change, the revelation Morgana was facing. "I guess a new breed has just been born." Lucas kissed Morgana, hoping to distract her. No chance, this was way too massive. "I'm alive! Luke, I'm in the sun and I'm not dying!" Morgana nestled herself in his clutch and became calm and serious.

"All my long life, I feared the sun. I was brought up never doubting that if I went out in the day, that would be my demise. I wonder if there are any more like me? This is so amazing! I wonder what else I can do?" Morgana was truly a child with a new toy. Maybe, just maybe she could finally do things she only dared to do. Morgana wanted to pray. Morgana wanted to speak with an open heart to a father that she wanted love from so desperately. All her life, she felt she had been deprived of loving God because of the un-holy clan she was born into. Morgana thought of how she felt crippled from worshipping anything holy. Terrible headaches had tormented the young woman whenever she tried to pray. What difference would it make if she could stand out in a crowd at high noon? Morgana asked the question to Luke. Her lover explained to her that there might be a chance, if she asked for forgiveness, even though what she was wasn't of her choice. Maybe God would have mercy on her, so that she could live her immortal life as a human, more than a damned creature of the night.

Morgana also wondered if she could hold wild roses, which were known to cripple, kill any vampire. Morgana pondered at what her limits were. Caution would need to be exercised to test Morgana's limits. There was a whole world out there Morgana could see, even more vividly than any human. "Morgana, I hate to steal your thunder, but be careful. You don't know how far you can take this. I do, however, want to show you what I call a little slice of heaven.' Lucas ushered his woman, his life mate to the shower, once again. The water wasn't holy, but it felt more cleansing in the morning glow. Morgana imagined this as her baptismal as God's light filtered in with the bath water. Luke bathed her, slowly. Her lover allowed her to consume every nuance of this occasion. Luke toweled Morgana off, dressing her as if she were an invalid. Morgana came to her senses, after the erotic bath. Luke permitted her to groom him, dressing him as well.

When both Luke and Morgana were done, they prepared to go out into the waiting day. The steps outside of the threshold of Luke's home could of been sheets of ice the way Morgana made her way down them. Morgana had so much fear inside her. Luke sheltered her, but it wasn't necessary. The sun did hurt her delicate, yet powerful eyes, eyes that hadn't seen the sun since her transformation so long ago. "Here, wear these." Luke handed Morgana a pair of dark sun glasses. "I can't see it all yet, like I should. Damn it all!" Morgana's frustration was quelled by a kiss from Luke. "All in due time, my love. I have an idea. Sit here with me, on these steps. We will pray, asking God for forgiveness. Maybe that will give you extra strength." Morgana took Luke's hand, and brought him down on the steps with her. Morgana didn't know all the right words. Through time, she could only pick up phrases, pieces of the whole. Luke started "The Lord's Prayer". Morgana followed in, with the parts she knew. There was some pain, at first. The tender feeling in her heart was a release of pain, a testimony to God. As Morgana spoke the words, her mind was pleading, "Please forgive me. I knew not of how my life would impair me from praising you. This is so strange. Show me your benevolence, sweet Lord. Forgive me, please." Morgana could feel an extra burst of sun rays hitting her on her brow. She felt herself being exonerated for a life she never felt love or loyalty to.

The crying Morgana couldn't help from doing made her eyes more sensitive, but she couldn't help it. Luke drove her around the city, showing her all of the things he found rare and beautiful about the city. after some hours, the two lovers ended up at a secluded park, just on the outskirts of the city. "The air is much cleaner up here. My parents used to bring me up here, years ago. I wanted you to see this. I wish you could feel about it the way I do." Lucas held onto Morgana, wishing they could remain inanimate, in that position, always.

Luke thought about how her skin felt like a newly bloomed flower. Every curve of her body melted with his in their embrace. Suddenly, Luke opened his mouth. "Make me like you, Morgana. If we can be careful about what limitations you have, we could possibly be like your friends Nola and Devon, couldn't we?" Lucas felt like he was in a warm dream. It was like looking in a room from the outside, with the window being covered in a cheese-cloth like film. Luke could almost touch the setting inside the dream, but he was still on the outside. Luke wanted to be on the inside with Morgana. He wanted to be a part of her life, to share her life. Luke was trying to sell his girlfriend on the idea of turning him into the monster she had been ashamed of being. Morgana had finally felt some release from this immortal curse by being able to move about freely in the daylight, without fear. Could she really allow herself to commit someone else to this type of existence? What if Luke didn't possess her powers? What if he couldn't survive in the daylight? Luke was in a dream, but for Morgana, it was a nightmare. Everything was happening too fast. "Luke, I'm still afraid. I know this isn't a fantasy. That's the dangerous part. What if I try something, and it kills me? If I change you, you may not turn out the same. I could very well kill you in the process! If I change you, I could make you more vulnerable than you are right now!" Morgana felt such agony over the new conflict. She feared it wouldn't go away, not anytime soon.

"Morgana, one day, I'll die anyway. My chances are better with you. We have to take the risk, before I get any older. Besides, for once, I'll be able to protect you. Do you realize you've been in the sunlight for hours now? It's almost noon, and you're fine! You may be risking a sunburn, but you're fine!" Luke was right. The tension would have to subside, and it would, naturally. Morgana was fine. She would be fine. A whole new world was open for one of her kind to explore.

One of her kind. Was she the only one? Shouldn't there be others with various strengths that others didn't have? Wasn't it possible for a vampire to truly love another human enough to create a life, after being unborn? It happened with the Mal clan, why not with some other creature in some other part of the world. The thought clung tightly to her mind. There was so much to take under consideration. What were her own weaknesses? Did she in fact have any? Damn it all! The thought of there being more than just her around was a definite possibility. How was it so difficult for her and the rest of her family to seek others out? Lang sought Desmony out. What was his secret? Would they ever know? Maybe, just maybe, there were others out there, and maybe the Mal family's senses were muted by the crossing of human blood with vampire blood. It was an untested theory, one that was too risky to test out. How would the Mal's find the others that might be out in the world? Would it be their fate to set themselves out as prey, waiting for other vampires to collide with them. Why have the experiences been so few? These types of questions didn't seem to plague the others as much as it did Morgana. The thought persisted with her that the world could be crawling with her breed of vampire. For now, Morgana just had to content herself with that possibility.

Actually, on very few occasions, unbeknownst to Morgana when Alec and Blythe would see someone that looked too much like someone they had seen before, too long to confuse with a human. The risk of approaching them, asking if they were vampire was ludicrous. Both parties would lose too much. Secrecy was their biggest weapon. Moving about in the world, unsuspected was part of their arsenal to hunt their prey, vampire against human. So much time had passed with the family keeping to themselves. It really shouldn't have mattered, but it did. It was like knowing one had family, but not knowing where to look, and making it worse by not trying. It was really too much to think about. The Mal family chose to just let it alone. If there were others out there that wanted to find them, they would. the result of any confrontation could go either way, but it would be worth it. just when would that time be?

CHAPTER TWENTY-ONE

Morgana lit every candle that she had in her apartment when Luke and she returned to her place. They were all glowing in the room Luke was dying to see. Morgana opened the vault styled door, with much ease. All was ready for Luke to enter. The room was somber, with sterling silver, pewter, and ebony with some hint of white. It was complete opposition from the rest of her apartment. The room reflected her discontent, upset, and longing desire. It was Morgana's dirty secret she kept hidden from the world. Morgana often wished she could keep it from herself as well. The room also showed her spirit and hope, with subtle optimism. The white she had in the room were statues of human women and men, in loving and sensual positions. Some had wings, thought by the rest of her family to resemble their wings. They were actually wings of angels, giving comfort to Morgana's tortured soul.

"You've been so sad, Morgana. I want to do all I can to bring the rest of your home in here. I want that smile I saw earlier in here. It made me feel like I knew what true beauty and life is. I want to put life into your life, and in your heart."

Luke surprised Morgana with these words. "You're beginning already, love. When we do this, when I change you, I believe you will be as I am. What is in my blood should be in yours. We will exchange blood. We will, in fact, be equals. I will, however, always have more power. Your life will rely on me more than it ever has. I'm giving this to you. You are not taking anything away from me. Never mind that I am a woman. You will need to remove yourself from human physiology and the belief that in the same species, the male is more dominant. Know this also, my love, I won't ever test you on my might. Our love should never come to that." Morgana's face was chilled and coarse, but her eyes still were soft.

The windows were closed, but a certain chill worked its way up Luke's spine. "Look, I know this is bigger than choosing what political party you want to join, or anything like that. To tell you the truth, I'd really like to get this over with, so I can be with you forever, or as long as it lasts. I'm not joking, I'm ready. "Luke began to disrobe, hoping to his imaginary sex-god that this woman would oblige him. "No, we must do this right." Morgana prepared an oil bath, with rose petals throughout the old fashioned iron tub. The tub itself was very old, from the turn of the century. Morgana kept it from their home in the unsettled west, when she was wild with Desmony. Wagner played softly in the background. "I adore this piece from *Tristain and Isolde*." The story was so tragic, yet so beautiful. I suppose I'm drawn to things like that." Morgana moved her way around her man and finally, slowly, removed his shirt. "I have a fine silk one, waiting for you. I've wanted to see you in it for a long while now." Morgana finished the task of undressing Luke, then undressed herself in front of him.

Morgana exposed herself to him as if it were the first time, and in many ways, it was. Luke copied every image of her bare form in his mind, never taking her beauty for granted. Morgana's sheer baby doll dress moved little by little, as she unbuttoned it. the ivory slip underneath the dress was shimmering in the candle light. Her made the material speak to Luke. The first strap was eased off by the slender fingers of Morgana, the second strap came off playfully by itself. Morgana's hair was sleek and lazy on her shoulders and face. The tresses of hair fell forward as she looked down. Morgana smiled. anticipating the first touch that Lucas would lay on her. She tied her hair up in a knot, securing it with a lace strap.

The couple eased into the antique tub together. The water was hot, but their skin gave the impression it was twenty below zero. Morgana and Luke giggled with embarrassment. After all of their love-making, they were still not used to seeing one another completely nude. The water felt like warm afternoon sunshine. An open window let in a breeze that finished the setting off just right. Both lovers breathed in the setting, mentally, emotionally, and physically. When Luke and Morgana opened their eyes, they were staring at one another. The temperature of the water was making them both sweat. Morgana perspired more profusely. Beads of moisture made its way through their pores, gliding down until each droplet came colliding down into the bath water. Morgana clutched Luke, as did he to her. They met in a solid, yet cherishing kiss. Morgana released herself from the kiss first. Without words, Morgana motioned for Luke to turn his back to her. Morgana wrapped her extensive legs around his taught waist. This position was supposed to be relaxing, but it wasn't possible for Lucas to do that. It was only necessary for Morgana to use a fraction of her strength to massage Luke's body.

Every bit of tension Luke may have felt at his body at any time in his life, even the pain he felt over the loss of his parents, left his body. Moments later, Lucas slumped back, resting his full weight onto Morgana's bosom. Morgana massaged Luke's chest and arms, not feeling any pressure from his body strewn across her own, like a strand of grandmother's pearls on a waif-sized grandchild. Morgana enjoyed the self-gratifying work she was doing, but the time was at hand. "I'm sorry darling, but you must be awake for this." Morgana began to feel the need to feed. Before Morgana took in Luke's blood, she wondered why she was lusting the blood. Was it because it was her lover's blood, and they would soon be together? Was it that excitement of finally achieving the companionship of unconditional love that

Bernard and Elsebeth finally felt for one another? Morgana feared it was her simply not having eaten in so long that her raw impulses were taking over, compensating for her new found abilities. Morgana threw the disturbing thoughts out of her head, enjoying the thought of the sensation of her fangs dipping into Luke's throat for only a little while. On the heels of the satisfaction her dark side was feeling came her old friend remorse. Morgana felt ashamed she was enjoying removing Luke's life from him. Morgana also realized Lucas wouldn't know now if he could become a father, a grandfather, if time permitted. If he did still possess the ability to create life, could he with Morgana? There were too many possibilities, too many variables, too many factors. None of that mattered in those moments. Luke never thought of the life he was leaving behind. Luke knew his parents wanted his absolute happiness, and that's what he was getting, in his mind. Luke could only hope he could be forgiven, and reunite with his mother and father in heaven, when his time came, if ever. Luke turned around to Morgana, smiling an intoxicating smile. "Finish it." Luke was truly ready. He could do as much honor to his parents by staying alive as long as he could, making their name continue to prosper, but not with him in the fore front. Luke felt natural fear of the unknown, but little else. The dream was playing itself out completely.

Morgana, the mal-content vampire traced Luke's anticipating throat with her tongue. Luke's taste was like taffy. Morgana tugged hi skin, tenderly, with her teeth. After a soft, compassionate kiss, Morgana let her throbbing fangs sink into Luke's virgin vein. Morgana drank as if she was parched, but not greedily. The glow of the candles camouflaged the glare of her eyes, which had changed. Morgana stayed in enough control so she didn't completely turn into the insidious creature she could become at will. Luke's eyes rolled back into his light head. The young man, the dying man was becoming faint. The sensation he was feeling was unlike any other he had ever experienced in his life. It was appropriate, since he was voiding his life for quite another. It seemed funny, his life, as he knew it, was ending. Everything he experienced from this point on would never be like anything her had experienced.

Luke felt as though he was submerging under the now tepid bath water. In truth, he was settling into a light coma of sorts, where his mind was to make peace with his soul. His father caught his arm, trying to steady Luke's wavering form. Luke couldn't tell who was giving him balance at first. When Luke saw that it was his deceased father, he nearly screamed, but stifled it after sensing a soothing calm as his father placed his eyes fully on him. "Your mother and I have been wanting to see you so badly, son. You must know how deeply we miss you." Luke's father was quite impressive. He had been all-state throughout his high school and college days. A man that had it all when he surrendered his heart to Luke's mother. Then, if any of himself was left to give, he gave it gladly to his son. "Where's mom?" Luke was elated to see his mentor, but his heart was begging to speak words with his mother. Luke finally was able to make her out in what seemed like a thick, web-like mist. "My precious darling! Lord knows I've missed your beautiful smile, son. Come, give your mommy a hug." Luke's mom was ever full of grace and solitude.

Luke wasn't exactly sure what was happening. He thought for a moment or two he had died during the transformation process. He thought maybe, he was in a home, not of his initial choosing, but one that would suit him all the same. "Luke, son. Your heart has spoken out to us, compelled us to come to you. We know the extraordinary situation you have found yourself in. You have chosen to forfeit all we know as immortal security with God for love with another type of being. God loves all his children, but what is the source of this creature you love? Is she from hell, trying to escape the fires that tickle her feet? Is her heart pure, encased in a horrid form? Please, don't misunderstand. If you trust this woman with your mortal and immortal life, all we can do now is trust you." Luke's father was always wanting the best for him. Luke's mother had a different approach, as do most parents. "Sugar, I have looked at the girl's heart. Where you are concerned, it is pure. She will love you an eternity as we did for just a short while. You are at a crossroads. You can allow her to perish with you, or you can live. We love you enough to bless you, if you can still be blessed. By continuing to live, you will carry us with you always. Just remember, don't lose your heart, or you will lose us!" Luke's mom knew just how to say what was concerning both parents. Luke held each parent in each arm. "Mother, father. I vow to you I will never lose sight of my love for you both. Morgana is giving me another life, just as you did. Our souls are filled with love. I have enough to give to her, as well as you both." Luke kissed both mother and father on the mouth.

Morgana shook Luke awake, out of his state of unconsciousness. Morgana turned Luke's head towards her. As she pulled her head close to Luke, she used her incisors to tear a small hole on the inside of her lip. As the blood flowed inside her mouth, Morgana kissed Luke, pushing the fluid into his mouth. Luke tasted the salty fluid and started at the flavor. It occurred to him what Morgana was doing. Luke began ingesting the liquid as though he were a child suckling his mother. Some type of instinct told him what to do, so he followed, without hesitation. The kiss seemed to last for an hour. The blood gave him the strength he had voided himself of when he allowed Morgana to drink from him. "It is done. We are each other's forever." Morgana lifted him and herself up.

Morgana escorted him to her cool bed, still soaking wet. No attention was paid to anything else except the ritual. Love was made between the two for another two hours. The ability and endurance Luke experienced now as a lover was beyond his comprehension. There was no end to the pleasure he was giving his beloved. None was needed, or wanted. The next time was as thrilling and inspiring as before. Both Luke and Morgana lost themselves in each other's stare as they smiled at one another. Both were pleased with what they had accomplished.

The sun bid a salutation to the luminescent moon as the moon glowed across from the sienna hued sky. Indigo surrounded the moon, watching the sienna fade away with each passing minute. Across town from Morgana and Luke, Desmony was just waking up. She quivered with an alarming shock through her soul. "She's done it. She's finally got what she wanted." Desmony knew it was only a matter of time before all of the family members knew what Morgana had done. Morgana didn't possess the power to mask bringing in new blood into the fold. None of the Mal family was that powerful, regardless of any unique skill or power. Even if she could, Morgana didn't even try to conceal her feelings now. Some of the day's events were able to remain in confidence, even from Desmony. The question still remained, what type of impact would this initiation have on the family?

Nola and Devon were the first to receive any suggestion as to what events had taken place between Morgana and Luke. Strange sensations coursed throughout their minds and bodies. Both of them knew the feeling was related to someone close to both of them, someone like them. They couldn't lock onto which one of the family members causing this sensation, since their powers were very limited, due to the newness of their shared power, and the fact they weren't full-blood vampires. Desmony came out of her sanctuary and met with the two to discuss the experience she had felt just moments before. Desmony was somewhat surprised to know that Nola and Devon felt anything at all, but glad since they were supposed to be the family's guardians.

The entire experience of including someone new into the family was foreign to Desmony. No one had tried since her father's "youth", when there was need for enough to guarantee safety in limited numbers. The family never believed in multiply their number for the sake of dominance. The belief was that there was a gentle balance at work between the humans and their species, half dead, half alive. Attention was not their goal, since it was understood their powers, their differences were accompanied with flaws, weaknesses they were subject to. They were as vulnerable as humans, but in different ways. Morgana was forcing the family in a very uncomfortable position, where risk was the greatest factor, and the least sought after.

"I feel a separation of power, but an increase in it as well. It's almost like the division of a cell, trying to create a life or help one grow. It feels bizarre." Desmony was bewildered by the emotions that were raiding her head. Elsebeth came downstairs slowly with Bernard. Blythe and Alec soon followed. "I sense that you know Desmony that Morgana has initiated her young man Lucas. He is now enduring." Blythe took Alec's arm. The two sage members of the clan sat closely on a love seat near a mahogany bookshelf. "I know. I knew she was going to do it. It was only a matter of time with this one. Gladly, I sense nothing negative. Morgana has, as usual, made a wise decision. It appears as though Lucas has been reborn, stronger than his human soul had been. The boy lost everything as a mortal. If chance smiles on Lucas, he'll live with more fortitude." Bernard tried to hide it, but he enjoyed Luke. Luke was refreshing. It had been almost one thousand years since, but Bernard remembered how he was as a child, before his and Blythe's life was changed by blood thirst.

Until Hlival's corruption of their souls, life had been for Bernard and Blythe as it had been for most children. Both children had enjoyed a simple and happy life. Blythe and Bernard were so care-free and jovial. They watched their parents work as they played. Later, they themselves began to work, tilling their family's land for royalty. The education they received was from the one that would undo them, destroy their human lives, but they weren't made aware of it until their parents lay dead, and they had no idea on how to continue. Bernard and Blythe were not sophisticated enough, nor did they have enough education in faith to know how to make the choice they had at that crucial time. They were manipulated by Hlival to accept his way of life, to exist as a leech in the form of a human. They hadn't appreciated their life before then, and as the centuries passed, forgot how to lament over those lost years. Nothing could be done now. Their past was a deep scar they would carry for eternity. They took Hlival's blood right away, not thinking too much of their past, not knowing it was Hlival that raided their land in the middle of the night, striking their parents dead. The siblings weren't made aware of this until they had become accustomed to their plasma depleted lives. The pain was too difficult to bare.

When the opportunity first presented itself to them, they fled from Hlival. Too much pain engulfed them to act on their rage, all of the emotions that jerked at them, tormented them. Several centuries in seclusion afforded them time to devise a definition as to whom, what they were. Enough time had passed where they forgot how it was to be humans. Hlival had told them their previous state of existing was similar to a natural metamorphosis. They were likened to caterpillars.

"C'mon Luke, let's go." Morgana had a terribly long day, but she showed no signs of fatigue. Luke was simply running on adrenaline. Luke couldn't wait to tell every detail of his experience to his new family. Luke was like a child at Christmas. Luke realized he could finally say the word family and be referencing people that existed now, not years prior. As far as Luke was concerned, he was newly married, and his bride's generous family gave the love he hoped for and needed. Luke felt calm about all the changes in his life. Luke's added anxiety was due to Morgana's discovery about her own powers. Luke put on the silk shirt Morgana had purchased for him. It was a deep forest green. He has on black jeans and some black high top hiking boots to accompany the gift he valued so highly. Morgana had noted to assist Luke soon with his wardrobe, along with all of his other adjustments after he completed his transformation.

Morgana slipped on a heather grey cashmere sweater, accompanied by some black lined linen slacks. Morgana picked up her leather pea coat and ushered her soul mate out of the apartment. Morgana motioned for Luke to relax in the passenger seat of her steel grey Stingray. The night air was still warm, but the breeze coming in from the harbor was giving a welcomed coolness. The sky had only a taste of blue towards the east, which was fading fast. Morgana placed her right hand on Luke's thigh, not for excitement as much as reassurance. Morgana knew that her actions were known by her family. Their judgment was unknown to her, since they were shielding their thoughts from her. It wasn't fair, she thought, but neither was bringing in another member without consulting the entire clan. The route Morgana took to get to the harbor side mansion was the shortest, although it seemed to take a millennium to get there. Every stop light worked against her favor. Luke was vaguely conscious as Morgana weaved in and out of each of the mostly two lane streets.

Morgana finally turned the last corner to get to the mansion. The building looked more ominous than it normally did, for good reason. The trip to the house had seemed lengthy, but was still exhilarating. The night reflected that same sensation, especially since Morgana now had the day to make that comparison with. With vampire eyes, Morgana could never see the daylight quite as a human would. It was more intense, so she would have to make an allowance for that with shades or special contacts. Luke would have to do the same, since he would no longer see the daytime sky as he had before. The sleek race car finally stopped. Luke peeled himself, barely having enough strength to do so, from the passenger seat. Morgana came around to help him come to a fully erect position. The two lovers looked on one another, taking in a deep breath. With one hand in the other, Morgana and Luke started toward the front door.

Alec met the couple at the front door. Morgana's grandfather looked much healthier, since he had gone out for fresh blood the night prior. Alec was a confessed critic of their practice of needing blood for survival, but when he needed to feed, he did it with natural skill. Fortunately, Alec required very little blood, so his hunts were seldom, which was a blessing for him, and his soul. Alec took a hold of and held onto his granddaughter in an intoxicated embrace. Another gift to Alec was that he could still consume as much ale as his body could hold. Alec didn't use the alcohol as a tamer for his disgust with his life. Actually, he had grown quite content. Alec was from an old time, he simply enjoyed drinking distilled spirits more than water. Alec's secret was that the alcohol diluted the taste of the blood, which never tasted sweet, on his palate.

The entrance into the mansion seemed different for Luke as he paced himself behind Alec, and beside Morgana. The corridor that led to an open area which beheld the library, the dining room, and sitting room seemed less foreboding than before. Lucas almost felt as though he were arriving for a homecoming of sorts. He had no idea how to initiate any powers he had inherited from Morgana, but he felt a calm that he hadn't felt on his previous visit. Luke marveled at the paintings, which were full bodied, brooding oil portraits, mainly of the family. Painters that had since died and become famous after their deaths had made the brush strokes which created the Baroque era styled works that gave the foyer a heavy and guarded feeling.

Elsebeth opened the door to the sitting room, which was prepared for the young lovers. Food awaited Luke, in the event he still craved sustenance. There were many beverages nearby. Morgana helped herself to a chilled Chablis while she surveyed the crowd. Bernard was reserved, sitting in a chair he had purchased which belonged to a Tsar some time ago. Desmony sat limp on the ottoman that matched the elaborately crafted mahogany chair. Blythe decorated a chaise lounge with her lean body, covering the full span of the piece of furniture. Alec took his place beside her, as Elsebeth did with Bernard, both standing next to their respective mates. Nola and Devon had placed themselves strategically behind a desk, hoping for the best out of this occasion. Morgana stood firm with her man, near the door. They waited for something, some word, or some movement to indicate approval or utter shame for what Morgana had done.

Desmony raised herself from the ottoman, prepared to speak. Desmony gestured to everyone that all would be well. "Morgana, we all know what it would take to make you happy. You have always been anxious for more from your life than what it appeared to simply be. All your life, you have been hungrier than any of us. Your want was never for blood, but for life. You have never wanted to consume life, as we do, no longer questioning it, if any of us ever did. Your talent lies in giving. You have desired to give love, and now it seems you have found it with someone willing to submit their life to you and your kind of spirit, totally. Luke, you have deemed yourself to be a man of substance. Your undeniable love has inspired the romantic side in all of us, even myself. " Desmony jolted most of the family with her delicate monologue. Suddenly, Desmony turned to Luke, with fangs glaring. "Welcome to the family, golden boy!" Desmony belted out a laugh that made her thought to be a witch, rather than a vampire.

The room chimed with laughter as everyone moved from their positions toward the couple. Luke was becoming weaker, but was overjoyed, none the less. Morgana had taken the initiative to make her life livable. Fate played a significant part in helping her see her destiny, seeing she had more to offer her species than miserable brooding and discontent for her life. Morgana was newly born, a new breed, unbeknownst to her clan. Soon, Morgana would share the news of her special abilities, which would rock the family even more than her taking Luke as her mate, without consent by the group. There was celebration for Morgana bonding with her mate. The night was being filled with intimate festivities. As the family reveled in the recent events, Morgana's thoughts went to her other love, her other secret. No one in her family knew of Monsieur Victor. Victor was still her secret, and always would be. At times, she had felt him, as though he was still a living part of her life. Morgana shrugged those feelings away. Morgana kept her love for Victor alive, but placed far away from prying minds. Morgana concentrated on her love now. Victor was gone, a soul unobtainable by any power known. Morgana watched as Luke blended in with the others. "Thank you for accepting this, accepting us." Luke placed his hand gingerly on Alec's shoulder. Luke's nervousness protruded from his pouting mouth with his words. Alec laughed. It was nice to experience some levity, not just boredom, or thrill of being caught or killed. Desmony, most of all, loathed the former and was intrigued by the latter.

CHAPTER TWENTY-TWO

Desmony ran out of the house, yelling with joy. Desmony was honestly happy for Morgana, not jealous as she normally would be. Morgana had finally acted on impulse, not behaved in the well-mannered fashion, which she repressed herself in. Desmony's joy could be credited to her involvement with Lang, but she would spite herself by admitting it. Morgana, Nola, and Devon followed Desmony outside. Morgana looked back, making sure Luke was still in adequate form, considering his circumstance. The young man stood tall in his boots, trying to make conversation with all that would pay him attention, mainly Alec and Bernard. Morgana gleamed a smile at her lover, and started off with the other young ones to collect Desmony. After catching up with the wild child, the four triumphantly crossed back across the threshold, surveying the expressions of the other family members. During all the laughter, it wasn't noticed that all were not content with the recent events that rippled through the family. Expressions changed as it became evident not all family members were in acceptance with the abrupt change

Nola was one of the genuinely jovial among the group. Nola was closest to Morgana, which made her privy to more information about Morgana, so Nola shared in Morgana's joy even more than Morgana's natural sister. Devon felt a special bond with Luke, being one of the newest members, adopting this family for his own as Luke had done. Alec, Blythe and Bernard remained neutral, but moved to steady Morgana's mother, Elsebeth. Elsebeth was disconcerted by the news. Elsebeth was overwhelmed with the fear of possibly losing her *special* child. There would be no way now for Elsebeth to prevent it, to share in the moments that led up to Luke and Morgana's arrival. Morgana was letting her heart run away with Luke. Elsebeth felt the invisible reigns she had placed around Morgana's heart and soul had been dissolved without the decency of a warning. Elsebeth had protected Morgana from so much, she had at least tried. It disturbed her that she could no longer protect her daughter, possibly control her. Morgana had made a move without consulting the family. Now, time could only tell if her impulsive actions would mean prosperity or demise.

Morgana walked cautiously, almost feline-like over to her distraught mother. Morgana said nothing to her. Elsebeth found herself being enveloped in Morgana's arms, seeming to give Elsebeth permission to sob. Elsebeth surprised Morgana, she did not cry. Elsebeth looked at her beaming daughter, and wanted nothing more than her complete happiness. Elsebeth's reservations were quelled before she could raise her anxiety any further. Elsebeth knew Morgana, and knew she would not endanger her family. The choice she made for a mate was a good one. Elsebeth enjoyed Luke. There was a determination that Luke was a good soul, certainly not a threat to their existence. Elsebeth stretched out her hand, beckoning Luke to approach her. Luke obeyed, coming to her side, opposite Morgana. "I hope you two are blessed by your solid love for one another." Elsebeth couldn't purge any other profound words for want of tears.

The mood of the crowd resumed some levity as the new members attempted to share themselves with one another, as well as the superiors of the clan. Elsebeth had regained her composure, seeing the love that Luke had for Morgana as they stood side by side, in total admiration for one another. "I should congratulate you, Morgana, on your union with Lucas. I suppose a ceremony won't be far off?" Elsebeth tried diligently to hide her persisting fear. There was something about Luke that made her feel uncertain. The young man appeared to be infirm, not completely sturdy in his stature. The transformation would take a toll on him. Elsebeth narrowed her fear down to his strength. The intuitive mother kept her reservations to herself, not wanting to disturb the moment. Morgana was about to take that position, telling the family of Luke and her great discovery.

"Mother, there's more. Not only is Luke as I am now, I have something in common with his past." Morgana was being evasive. Morgana created the drama unintentionally because she was still very much stunned herself. "What dear? Stop this and tell me!" Elsebeth was about to burst. Morgana took in a deep breath, knowing what magnitude her next words would bring. "I've seen the sun, Mother. Listen to me, I really have seen the sun! I was with Luke. I don't know how, but I did not wake myself as I normally had without fail. Something made this happen, and it turned out to be all right. Mother, the sun kissed my face. It didn't burn me. Oh, can you believe it? I feel so wonderful! I've not slept for days, yet I feel so alive! In a short while, Luke has shown me so much about the city that are truly fascinating in the day." Morgana's exciting story was pre-empted by her mother, who was trying exhaustibly to digest all that was being said to her.

"Morgana, I can't believe what you say to me, yet I can, or rather I should. Your biological father was human. I existed with most passion as a human, even though my outlook has changed substantially through the years. Maybe, in some way, you are actually alive. You do not live from other's death as the rest of us do, save Nola, Devon, and now Lucas." Elsebeth hid a surge of excitement and joy for her daughter, Morgana was living the experience she had wished for herself so many nights, for so many decades. Elsebeth still had her private feelings about who and what she was. These thoughts could never be spoken of or sensed by Bernard unless she wanted to be destroyed by his hand.

Eternal life had become too sweet and illusive for Elsebeth, and living for her family as she had done would be an utter disgrace to her soul, if nothing else.

Elsebeth motioned for Morgana to leave the room with her, depriving the rest of the clan from digesting the magnificent tale that Morgana was disclosing to them all. Mother and daughter left the room, arms interlocked. Luke gave a reassuring nod to Morgana as she departed with her mother. Bernard kept everyone in conversation, largely trying to summate how it was possible for Morgana to have such abilities. The questions asked were unable to be answered for many reasons. The most prominent reason was because there were no set characteristics for their breed of species. There were many tales of legend that circulated throughout each culture regarding this topic of the occult, but there were few, if any documented cases that were accepted as fact for the world to acknowledge. All stories of Vampires were disregarded as folk-lore and fantasy. Alec had taken time, with Morgana in the past to educate themselves on as many *facts* as they could about their kind, but there was no true way to verify any of it.

The occasion for the Mal family to chance upon any other vampires to date had not given them the opportunity to learn much more than what they knew about themselves. This was always a source of great discontent for them. Hlival and Lysa proved to be grossly unhelpful. There was no time, or any rapport with the vengeful duo to learn anymore about their abilities or limitations. The only certainty was there were others, but the numbers would never be able to be confirmed. Lang was there only hope for additional information, additional insight. Lang was a distant colleague for the time being. Desmony could only hope Lang could be a source of insight for the family. There was much work to do, for all involved. The knowledge of their powers was welcome, but to date not greatly necessary for their survival. however, Morgana's discovery opened many doors, wounds, and questions.

Elsebeth escorted Morgana to the rooftop of the mansion. the moon was a faint sliver in the sky, behind the fog and high clouds. The weather was cool, as the wind came in from the bay not far from their home. "Morgana, I want to say so much to you, yet I don't know where or how to begin. I can't color my words. I vowed total honesty to you from the time the truth came out about you and your true father. You never deserved that pain, and I will always be sorry for that. I've explained that a great part of me resented being what I am. My heart yearned to be human for several centuries. I grew up accepting the life I was given, and the faith I had that taught me to live as pure a life as I could, so that when my time came to dwell in the house of the Lord, I would be ready, and would go willingly. I betrayed my Holy Father when I fell prey to Bernard's charms. It has taken me many lifetimes to come to terms with that. which I keep far away from your father. I have asked for forgiveness, and can only hope my words have fallen on forgiving ears. If that isn't the case, I have also resolved to accept the consequences for my deceit." Elsebeth sat down on the edge of a cobblestone, which enclosed a tree that was planted to provide shelter for anyone who could or dared sit on top during daylight.

Elsebeth gestured for Morgana to join her, so she could finish. " I am happy for you, my dear. Your unhappiness being a vampire has out lasted my own, and has surpassed it with great vigor. You had less of a choice than I did. Legend has it that vampires aren't supposed to bear children, so the fact that I was able to have both Desmony and you is somewhat a miracle. You can blame me for the life I gave you, but I have always tried to give you enough love to mute your disgust with your abilities. Now, you are free, in a sense. You are not bound by the restrictions that the rest of your kin are secured in having. God knows your heart, so I don't figure you for damned my love. Unfortunately, we won't know, I hope you never find out." Elsebeth found joy in the knowledge her flesh and blood could now experience something she could know only faintly remember from her childhood.

Elsebeth's indiscretion with Xavier was important, no matter how shameful. It was no longer something for Elsebeth to feel ashamed of and hide away in the corner of her mind. Morgana kissed her mother on the lips, then her forehead. "I have forgiven you for some time now, mother. It makes me happy you are finally forgiving yourself. Despite the tiring headaches I suffer, I try to pray for you, and reach God. I fear my new talent of being able to walk amongst humans in the day doesn't pardon me completely, but I will continue to try, for all of us that want it." Morgana took her mother by the hand and led her down the stairwell that brought them back to the family.

It had been a while since the entire family had congregated at the main house to exchange tales of their adventures in the city. They talked during cocktails, dinner, and after dinner, coffee and tea. Those that could eat food did. The others drank their dinner, in fine crystal. The blood clung to the inside of the glasses, giving them a sinister hue. The conversation flowed, just as the wine they devoured to add to the flavor of the blood and meat. As the dark of night grew lighter, Desmony broke polite babble with inquires on any details about the ceremony expected by the family to take place between Luke and Morgana. Desmony had envisioned her ceremony with Lang, as he was now, not dull with a deathly grey complexion, but beautiful as he had become since their last meal. Desmony was explaining what she wanted, but decided to share her fantasy with Morgana, in the event Lang didn't want that type of future with her. Desmony didn't dwell on that possibility, because the remnant of the heart she had reassured her Lang was her kindred soul mate. Time would reveal the outcome of her wager she made with herself.

"Right now, I really just want to sleep!" Luke was irritable, even though he had tried to add to the good will and love that was being spread throughout the cool, yet warm home. "Oh, Luke. I know we hadn't really discussed what happens to you now. I am so sorry! My love, are you hungry yet?" Morgana had neglected to tend to her prodigy as she knew she was required to. She had sired a lover, and another vampire. No one else had done such a thing since Bernard many centuries before. Devon was sired as a servant, but not a full vampire. Luke would need blood soon to nourish his new system. Luke would now function on a completely different metabolism. The body that Luke knew and cared for now operated in ways totally unfamiliar to man. No scientist had ever come into contact with a vampire, at least to live long enough to learn from the species. Unfortunately for Luke, he would have to learn how to care for himself all over again. Luke would have some guidance, as he did as a child, but not by his mother. Morgana would educate him, take him as far as she could with her knowledge on how to survive.

Luke showed no signs of craving blood. The exchanging of blood had taken place a relatively short time ago, and it would take time. No one knew for sure how long it would take Luke, considering his circumstance with his sire not being a full vampire. "I just ate, honey!" Luke looked oblivious. The young man didn't realize what Morgana was referring to. "Lucas, I mean aren't you thirsty? Don't you crave blood?" Out of pure ignorance, Morgana began to worry. "No, not yet. When does it usually happen? I mean, am I acting abnormally?" The fast growing concern was smothered by Bernard. "Children, it takes a while before the desire to hunt blood begins. There is a process still that Lucas must endure. Morgana, with your true origins, it is difficult to say when Lucas will become fully unborn." Blythe added, "you both should stay here for the next few days, in case you need us. Don't be shy, please take advantage of our hospitality." Blythe had spoken, and that was all there was to it. Blythe's invitation was more so a demand, since her wisdom preceded Morgana and Luke's desire to share their experience intimately. Nola and Devon began to prepare what would become Luke's room, and to freshen Morgana's room.

Morgana laid down to rest with Lucas for a while in the bed Devon had made for him. Morgana couldn't rest, she was too uneasy. The fear of something going wrong with Luke's transformation was a great torment for her. What if her blood proved to be more of a curse to him than it had been to her? What if Luke became dark, evil? There were too many scenarios to run through before Morgana became completely overwrought with anxiety. Morgana dreaded thinking her gift could actually be a curse to her love, making her an instrument of destruction, or a twisted version of salvation for him, killing him, releasing him so that he might join his mother and father. The sky was dark, in more ways than one. Bernard felt Morgana's urgency and went to the room where she rested with Luke.

Morgana sat up when she felt her father approach the door. Bernard's long black hair shielded his face as he peered through the crack in the door. Morgana's father pulled his hair from his face as he asked her how she was getting on. Morgana assured him she was well, and Lucas was resting. Bernard took her words, but knew that his child was not at rest. Bernard surrendered his inquiries, bidding them a good rest. Bernard joined the family for a night of brisk conversation. No one would dare leave the house on this night for a feed, not even Desmony.

A time came when Morgana's nerves finally reclined. The placidity of the morning's rest was sheared, shockingly, by a Lucas no one had seen before. Luke was sweating profusely, tearing at his body, as if he were trying to peel out of his quivering skin. The visions that were searing through Luke's mind played with his lucidity, making him fear for his very mind. illusions were shifting his very sense of being, as though his soul was being transplanted by another soul with an ambivalent disposition. Luke saw ashen piles, shaped in the form of his loved ones. They were like snow people, but made of burnt flesh and bone. Luke motioned to touch Morgana, but she crumpled into a cluttered pile on the floor, less of a form than all the rest. Morgana had not been grey and lifeless. Luke's love had looked as she did, before he closed his eyes the night before. This vision above all others forced a high-pitched scream from Luke.

Luke was certain he was dying. The visions continued to torment the stress young man. Luke saw faces, ugly and distorted. The faces spoke, saying vile and cruel things to him. Luke felt like his soul was dying. As the voices spoke, their words hit at Luke's body, as if hands were balled into fists. Luke's body contorted as each blow hit him. The words that pelted Luke's body caused him to bruise, although no form was seen making the marks. Luke's tossing and turning gave way to a tranquil silence, for a few moments. The Demons that were trying to pull him into the dark urges seemed so real, so real, yet they weren't and Luke realized that in time. Luke envisioned himself, in his mind. Luke began to refute the demons, choosing his path for his immortality. Luke embraced the force of these beings, using their power against themselves. Luke thought of all that was pure in his life, all the things he was not sacrificing for his love or by forfeiting his mortal life.

The demons poked and cut at Luke with their spiteful words, but their words lost their potency as Luke continued to battle with the courage of a righteous warrior. Luke was appreciating the strength he now had, or had possessed all along, never realizing his full potential. Morgana, his love, had known this for quite some time, but this initiation was necessary for Luke to see and to believe.

The yelling was unbearable to all ears that were near. Luke continued to quake in his comatose state, begging to be made still. Morgana had whirled around, being jolted out of her slumber next to her lover. Morgana hadn't been able to bring herself to leave his side, nor was she expected to. Morgana struggled to an upright position, confused, alarmed, and mostly scared. Morgana gripped him, hoping her embrace would squeeze the pain away. The fairy tale solution was not effective for Luke. The young man needed blood to quell his panic. Morgana slightly in a panic herself, as she put on a robe. Morgana picked Luke up and carried him, like a sleeping child, to the bathroom.

"What am I going to do? How am I going to keep him in control? Oh shit! Everyone is asleep. Wait, Devon, yes Devon will help me. I'll get Devon to help me take Luke out, then Luke will feed. It must be time." Morgana despised not having the answers for such urgent questions. Luke's life, his existence was teetering in the balance, and Morgana was truly without a clue how to help him. Morgana sat for a moment or two, enough time to gather her wits. Once calm, she allowed her instinct to respond to the situation. Luke was like a newborn babe, needing nourishment to satiate its new hunger for sustenance. It would be risky to hunt during the day, but there were ways that would require consummate skill. "Hold tight, love. I'll care for you, I promise." Morgana bathed Luke, then dressed him. Morgana propped Luke up in bed, so she could summon Devon.

There was no scientific evidence, but the ingestion of blood seemed to reverse the natural progression of the human body after death. There was no decomposition, not for an immeasurable amount of time. The new blood aided in supernatural powers that vampires are characteristic for having. There remained the possibility that once the human body had submitted to the unborn or the vampire form newly acquired, dormant parts of the brain were made active by this process that humans have yet to discover how to use at will.

Devon heard the screaming throughout the mansion. The sound sent shivers through the course of his spine, reminding him of his transformation. Devon knew Morgana was going to need his help, for many reasons. Devon was still invincible to daylight, as all servants were. Added strength was also a benefit Devon had that would assist Morgana at this turbulent time. Devon meet Morgana in the hallway, just outside of Luke's room. The morning had just begun. The air was cool, but the silver sky was fast becoming a powder blue, intensified by the glimmering fire ball on the rise. "We have to start out early and work fast. The less people around, the better." Devon made his way into Luke's room, easing past Morgana. Devon kissed Nola good-bye as he carried Luke away from the house, putting him in the back of the family's black GMC Suburban. Morgana hugged Nola before leaving the house with Devon and Luke. Nola gave Morgana a reassuring smile which was well received. Morgana then tipped out into the sunlight. It was slightly overcast, which was normal, so the daylight wasn't as much a shock to Morgana's body. The sensation was strange, but it felt good. Morgana, however, didn't have time to enjoy it. There were more important things needing to be done.

CHAPTER TWENTY-THREE

Morgana had to finish what she had started. Devon had driven them near the wharf. It was still very early, not many people were about. Morgana tried to elevate herself discreetly, so that she might scan the area for potential prey. Morgana found out immediately that her powers were voided in daylight. The life-giving energy from the sun muted her supernatural powers, which ironically helped Morgana feel more like a human. Morgana elected to walk briskly around the buildings made of now warped lumber. The mist fell lightly on Morgana's illuminating face. The over cast clouds were burning off quickly, which meant the sun would shine brightly, making it harder for Morgana to subdue any prey she chose for Luke. Devon followed Morgana at a safe distance in the Suburban. Morgana knew if she failed to bring down her kill with ease, Devon would come to her aide. Luke lay helplessly in the back of the utility vehicle. Words failed to make it past his lips in the form of much more than a mumble. Luke was delirious, not knowing what or where he was. The demons were snatching at his ears, causing him to yell out periodically.

Morgana's tracking finally paid off. The hunter could still use her hyper-sensitive sense of smell to track down a single human. Morgana came upon a young aspiring artist. The man looked healthy, Morgana sensed that about him from his body chemistry. The artist betrayed his masculine demeanor with his naïve boy-ish charm. The young man was in his early twenties, obviously a starving student of the nearby art college. The artist was absorbing the beauty of the bay, since he was new to the city, just coming from the mid-west several months prior to prepare for the fall semester. Morgana estimated she could easily manipulate this man, without using any special powers. Once Morgana could lure the young man into a dimly lit or artificially lighted place, she would then take him, and feed Luke.

Morgana resolved she had to be dark, just like her sister. Becoming that person was hard, but she had to make the sacrifice for Luke or he would certainly perish. "Paint my picture?" Morgana opened with a strong and flirtatious line, truly out of her character. The young artist fell for it immediately. The man could have easily mistaken Morgana for one of his late night fantasies the way the haze of the behind her created a dream-like image. "Please, have a seat. If you really want me to use your likeness in a painting, I'll be famous instantly! Your beauty on canvas could make even the worst painter seem like a genius." The young man was in utter awe.

Morgana knew she had little time, but she also had to win this man's trust. "May I ask, what is your name? I think it is only proper that we introduce ourselves, especially so you can give the correct credit to you subject, after I've left your life. My name is Maureen. What is yours?" Morgana's charm was like an enchanted elixir. "My name is Justin. I'm from Omaha, Nebraska. I've traveled a lot since I left home, but I think I'd like to make San Francisco my new home." Justin was as fresh as the morning dew that was now wilting the sketch paper which was still blank, for lack of inspiration.

"Well, I think you are talented enough to do me justice. I can tell by your hands. Is this yours?" Morgana picked up a sketch Justin had done the day before for a class project. "Yes, it's mine. I know it's not original, but that's what the instructor wants. I can't wait until we get into more advanced assignments." Justin took the sketch from Morgana, touching her gracile hand purposely. "I would really feel more comfortable back at my place. I had something a little less conservative in mind, which I think you'll find quite challenging. My favorite paintings are nudes. I've always dreamt of having one done of myself. My place isn't far from here. You could sketch me, paint me, then I'll make you dinner. So, how about it? Will you paint my nude?" Morgana had him after her first sentence. "O.K., let's go. Maybe you can show me around some more, after we're done. Like I said, I'm still pretty new here, and I'd like it a lot if we could be friends." Justin was so eager. Morgana's heart began to break for Justin. It was difficult to see herself dimming such a bright light. One important rule Morgana neglected was acquainting herself with a potential kill. It undermines the purpose. Desmony would've been all over her if she knew Morgana was playing with the proverbial chicken.

Justin was in love with Morgana. The young man loved the freedom in her spirit. Morgana gave the illusion of being completely uninhibited. Morgana felt the misdirected affection Justin had for her, which made her terribly sad. Suddenly, an overbearing man came out of a store, yelling at Justin. "I told you to stay away from here, bothering my customers, you looser!" The man was balding, rotund, and obnoxious. Armed with a broom, the man continued out of his store. "As far as I am aware, this portion where my new friend is sitting is public domain. This young man is merely refining his artistic skills, and is not, as you say, a looser. You should keep your business in your business, not outside, where people are free to do as they wish, as long as it isn't illegal, which I'm sure this isn't." Morgana surprised herself. Morgana was defending Luke's breakfast, soon to be lunch if she didn't get a move on.

It was clear Justin wasn't loitering, but the man had accused him of that offense many times before. The angry bigot, whom appeared to be new to the country through the courtesy of immigration gave Morgana a stroke of brilliance at that moment. Morgana would steal *'Ol fatty* and feed everyone, not just her ill young lover. Fatty felt a rush of embarrassment come over him, involuntarily. The rotund man, whom was already sweating set his broom aside, on the face of his precious store. "I'm sorry, I was rude. You have made a point. Why don't you come inside and we can discuss an apology?" Fatty was trying his best to portray a hopeless seducer. A bead of sweat rolled down Fatty's face, more so from his lust than from the still cool weather.

Justin was confused. Morgana looked to him, smiling as if to assure him that all was well. Justin returned the smile, sitting back in his lawn chair and watched. Devon was nearby in the huge black Suburban with Lucas in the back. Lucas was getting worse by the moment. Convulsions jolted Luke's body, leaving him almost completely out of control. Morgana was running out of time, she could feel Luke's internal fire fading. A surge of strength streaked through Morgana as her surroundings became darker. Fatty glanced back at her, desperately trying to see Morgana's from behind her silk print sun dress. The pig prayed for x-ray vision, but no chance. Morgana had already begun working on his weak mind.

The glutton turned to Morgana, asking politely what he could do for her. "I have a friend that is very dear to me. My friend is in dire need of assistance. Won't you mind helping me care for my friend?" Morgana's eyes were like those of a doe, perched on a snowy mountain side, beckoning any on lookers to awe in its beauty. An irresistible fever was overcoming Fatty. "Sure, whatever you need, honey. Just let me lock up." Fatty did as he said. Both Morgana and Fatty started toward the Suburban where Devon and Luke were hiding.

Justin had attracted another customer. The subject wasn't nearly as beautiful, but the young artist was beyond confident he could do her justice. Justin had already begun working on her sketch, as if Morgana's charms had begun to ware off, bringing him back to his world before Morgana entered it. Justin looked up for a few moments. Morgana smiled, and with lips pressed together said, "You'll need not worry about being put down again by this man. After he is gone, someone close to him will care for the store. They will give you a job here, if you like. Take care, Justin. Forget all that has transpired between us this morning. Do you understand what I say?" Morgana searched for the young man's acknowledgment. When Morgana got that, she was off in a flash with Fatty.

Fatty willingly worked his way into the large utility vehicle. 'Ol Fatty was quite the zombie by now, not noticing anyone, or anything. The man had no desire, saw any need, to search for help. Morgana was the only thing Fatty could see. This woman was his salvation, as far as he was concerned. Factually, Morgana was his destruction. The area

Devon took then to was crude, dark, and damp. The surrounding appealed to Morgana in a way that would normally make her feel ashamed. Excitement swept over Morgana. Sensations of total domination of this situation overwhelmed Morgana, but she couldn't enjoy the feeling for long, she had to work fast so she could share the beauty of her being with Luke.

Fatty was the last to come out of the Suburban. The vehicle rocked with his body force as he pulled himself out of the passenger seat. Fatty took a look around. The amusement on his face suggested that a dank as this place truly was, it seemed like a field of sweet grass and heather blowing in a gentle breeze. Morgana was the first face Fatty saw as his rotation ended. Morgana had no tenderness in her face. Morgana pushed herself against Fatty, breaking his skin just above his jugular vein with her fangs. It took Morgana a few moments longer to bring her fangs out, since she seldom used them for her sustenance. Beside her encounter with Luke, Morgana couldn't really remember the last time she had killed. That gang outside her parent's club were probably the last she had killed, which was longer than anyone in her clan was willing to wait. Morgana drank. The blood was twisting in a small stream down the man's gout-like throat. Morgana had to make sure not to get too carried away. Morgana had to control herself, leaving a necessary amount for her lover.

Devon brought Luke next to Fatty. Luke was so weak now, he could barely open his sensitive eyes. Luke sensed out the blood by smell. With eyes now limp, not as much closed, Luke's mouth found the opening just near the jugular. Luke tore at the throat, until he reached the actual vein. The fluid gave Luke strength as he consumed it, pint after pint. Morgana had to pull Luke away, after she was sure he had enough to last. It was time to teach Luke his first lesson on feeding after the kill. Never drink too much blood. Too much from a feed is very much like a drug overdose. It isn't safe to consume more blood than what a vampire's body would normally take. However, a vampire can survive on that same blood for quite some time, only replenishing it with small amounts from rodents or small animals. Human blood is a delicacy for vampires. Some vampires enjoy the taste so much they would endanger those around them, as well as themselves, like Desmony. Human blood was too alluring for her to pass. Morgana was at the other end of the spectrum, denying herself even the less satisfying of blood sources.

Morgana shook at Luke to make sure he hadn't gone too far. "I'm all right darling, I'm all right." Luke was panting heavily. Luke almost choked on the blood as he tried to speak. Devon had taken hold of the body as Morgana caught Luke and helped take him back to the Suburban. Fatty was heavy, but Devon was more than able to prop his corpse up against a nearby wall. Devon emptied out his pockets, making it appear as though Fatty had been *rolled over.*

Fatty's throat was badly damaged, but Devon managed to cut his throat so that very little suspicion would arise. Unless an autopsy were performed, no one would know Fatty died before his throat was cut. Even if there were suspicious minds, a story of ritualistic cult killings would become the likely conclusion considering the missing blood from the body as well. Unfortunately, people were too desensitized to think too much on it, except they were happy it happened to someone else, and not to them. Fatty's story, his life ended as another statistic. The conclusion was that he was merely a victim of a senseless crime engineered by some gang member, an enemy, or psycho.

After Luke's debut, he rested for several days. Nola and Morgana cared for Luke more than any other family member. Luke's want of blood and yearning for knowledge of his new abilities changed him more than he ever thought a body could be capable of and still appear "normal". Luke wasn't blind to the changes that were before him, but to experience these changes first hand was truly enlightening and humbling to his mind, ego, and psyche. Blythe compensated for the demand for nourishment by depleting the blood bank of several more pints of blood than she normally embezzled. There had been questions, but with her amassed charms and powers, no one could recall her thievery. No questions were ever asked. All spent time with Luke, caching him, so that he would have control of the powers that disassociated him from humankind more and more with every passing day. It was imperative for Luke to regulate his powers, or all the sacrifice would amount to nil.

The Mal family, his new blood family were teaching him all the ways of survival they knew and had known for dozens of generations. There would be no lessons, however, of the kind Hlival had given to Lysa. The utmost care would be taken with Luke. Luke was to be a survivor. The key to the family's survival would be for their newest addition to be the strongest, especially since his ability to be seen during daylight hours had been inherited from Morgana. The possibilities were limitless. Not only for the sake of the hunt would Luke and Morgana's gift be a factor, so would it be for the family's growth in the financial world, and to eliminate the mounding suspicions about their nocturnal existence. The scheme was unfolding quite nicely, and would continue to do so, provided no non calculated errors arose.

Bernard's liking of Luke became more pronounced as their conversations became more familiar. Bernard would recite many stories, telling Luke of his many escapades and conquests, before Elsebeth and since his union with his beloved. Bernard told Luke in great detail about Lysa, and how he seduced and possessed her. The tale Bernard told was candid and unflattering, but appreciated by Luke. Luke understood that there was an immense responsibility with being a vampire, in terms of feeding, and deciding who would be and how to acquire a mate. Fortunately for Luke, Morgana found Luke, and Luke was completely willing to forfeit his soul for love. Luke listened acutely, feeling a sort of paternal bond forming between he and Bernard. Elsebeth's love for Luke was understood, but with Bernard, it was a little slower coming.

Luke felt as though Bernard genuinely cared for him, as a father would. Luke remembered how life was with his father, just how lucky he was to have a father so active in his life. Fortunately, Luke didn't take it for granted. Luke supposed he had finished grieving for his father, because he began to feel a similar closeness with Bernard. Unfortunately, no one could ever fill the void his mother left when she died. Luke was so young, all of his monumental problems and accomplishments he experienced from childhood until his tumultuous adolescence lacked the comfort and compassion a mother could give their child, and that left Luke with an insatiable desire to be coddled. At no time did Luke ever find that, until near the end of his mortal life. The irony shook him to the core. The only solace Luke could deduce for his mother and father was that they were together, his father was no longer missing his eternal mate. Luke had found the same destiny, albeit in a supernatural fashion.

One evening, shortly after Luke began to feel some sense of normalcy, Bernard came to visit him. Bernard swayed into the room, making sure his gestures kept Luke at ease. Bernard sensed that Luke still felt like the proverbial weasel in the chicken-coop. "How are you progressing, Lad?" Bernard seated himself on a chaise lounge, not far from the foot of the large canopy bed, near a beautiful cherry oak Victorian dresser. "Very well, sir. I want to thank you for taking me in and helping me survive." Luke continued to feel as though he had been saved from a seemingly eternal empty existence. The only thought that had kept him going was his parents, and living so that he might honor their memory. Luke had amended his plan, forfeiting his soul to be with another family, but he was so content he hoped that would bring no shame to the family he left behind. The change in his chemistry, his soul would eventually diminish his concern over that pressing issue, along with any others he had as a mortal. Life was new for him, even though he wasn't a living being.

Luke was able to sit up in bed by now. he was strong enough to. The over consumption of blood had actually delayed his recuperation slightly. his metabolism and other elements of his genetic make-up was still at a vulnerable state. It was only a few days since his transformation, and with the complexity of being unborn by a vampire with abnormalities, his progress was delayed. Bernard digested Luke's gesture of gratitude, becoming confused. "Dear boy, how did you come to thank me, thank us? We've turned your life into a veritable horror novel." Bernard was still amazed by Luke's statement.

Luke smiled at Bernard's disarmed reaction. "I wanted this. I truly wanted this. It wasn't something I felt I needed to analyze. It may not seem to have been a logical conclusion, but I felt, feel that it was logical, it was right. I just sensed it, just knew. You know Bernard, you remind me a lot of my father. He was strong, reserved, and disciplined. He was a very tall, straight standing man, but I guess every adult seems overbearing in stature to a kid." Lucas' head began to progressively hang lower and lower. "Luke, I sense a lot about your past. I'm truly sorry about your losses. I sense a deep sorrow entrenched in your heart, which will probably rest there forever, literally now. Know this, Lucas. You have my, our support, always. You know, you appear a little weaker than when we started our talk. I shall come to you later, when you are more able to hold a conversation without fatigue. " Bernard bowed out of the room. Luke didn't motion to stop him. Luke was extremely weak. Luke without hesitation laid back, feeling a little less lonely.

Luke's need for support was great, at first. Everyone took turns caring for the young man in his convalescence. Soon after his system adjusted to his new diet. It was theorized that Morgana's blood, diluted with her distaste for her station in life as a vampire, was working against Luke's recovery from being unborn. Morgana was in distress, not knowing how to feel about Luke's slow progression. Morgana couldn't apologize for her feelings about what she was, but she wished desperately for Luke not to suffer. None the less,

Luke became whole once more. Luke's characteristics and features altered along with his new metabolism and chemical make-up. Not only did Luke's strength return, it increased tremendously.

Luke felt some sensitivity to the sun, but not enough to deter him from letting the rays hit his carefully molded body. Luke developed an acquaintance with the sun, so that his skin felt as it did before he gave his life to Morgana and her kin, becoming kin himself. Luke did notice some slight differences when he would bask in the sun. The tolerance wasn't for nearly as long as it used to be. An uneasiness was felt in the core of Luke's being, until he became physically weak. This occurrence usually took about one hour in indirect sun light and half that time in direct light. Although the time was limited, this was still an advantage for hunting, conducting business, and making simple appearances to disprove any suspicions that he picked up on telepathically.

Among Luke's resistance to *solar combustion,* Luke had an overall sensation of feeling new, better than when he was a boy with all of that supernatural energy most kids have when they're young. Luke's vigor in bed alarmed Morgana. Morgana wasn't used to such force and desire from her partner physically. Luke in the past had been sincere, generous, and aerobic as a lover, but his performance now was on a totally higher level. Morgana found herself in a position where she had to worry about her own performance, if she was giving her man pleasure. Morgana began feeling a sense of inadequacy that she kept to herself. Morgana had never felt this emotion, and it intrigued her. Morgana played with her fear as thought it was a toy, hers alone to cherish. Ultimately, Luke interpreted Morgana's fatigue and reluctance to be intimate with Luke as having finally become her rival at something. Luke did as Morgana did, keeping this knowledge to himself until he could decide on how to best reassure Morgana of his satisfaction with her in every way.

Lucas calmly walked into the room across the hall. That room was where Morgana was keeping herself. Morgana exhausted from taking care of Luke after his transformation, and later as his lover. Luke stood in the door way studying Morgana as she sat at her vanity, brushing her hair. The long, thick coal colored strands cascaded from mid-air, collapsing on her back after each stroke. Each brushing motion revealed Morgana's long and sculptured neck, so perfect. Luke's serenity turned into a beastly panic. Luke lunged over the bed to be near his breath-taking love. Morgana had known Luke was there, all along. Luke's scent entered the room before he did. Morgana waited patiently, knowing exactly what was on Luke's mind. There had been enough time from their last romp to meet her mate head on, without hesitation. Morgana had adapted, but was welcome to know that Luke had the stamina both he and she needed and an imagination to keep them inspired for a long time to come.

Luke merged with Morgana. Morgana had arisen from her vanity, her bone straight hair swaying across her able and braced shoulders. It was as though the two lovers were preparing to spar with one another, but their passion would give that illusion to any voyeurs, should prying eyes be so fortunate to witness this quality of love-making. Morgana's breath was taken from her by Luke's invigorated desire. Morgana barely recovered from the initial blow, only to be caught by Luke. Morgana's young lover held her steadily in his solid and capable arms. There was a release by Morgana, possibly a motion to succumb to Luke's will. Luke kissed Morgana, tongue first, allowing her to melt as he developed his living fantasy.

Morgana collapsed onto her bed in a position that was to Luke's liking, so he leaned down until his body met with hers. Luke pulled at the grey silk spaghetti strap gown Morgana had adorned herself with just minutes before Luke's entrance. *Lucas'* touch was divine, subtle and enough to stimulate Morgana in the pit of her nature. Luke continued to kiss Morgana, until he reached her pulsating neck, then her luminescent shoulder, making her writhe and twist with every touch of his hand, his mouth. Luke's supple lips spoke without articulating any words. Morgana arched her back just enough so that Lucas could release her from the top portion of her gown. The kisses moved, once again, from

Morgana's delicate but firm shoulders to her breasts that adorned the same description.

Morgana composed herself enough to be aware that Luke was deserving of reciprocation for his sexual endeavors. Morgana grasped at Luke's athletic buttocks, clutching one side as his caressing of her breast with his tongue pleased her. Morgana massaged Luke's entire back area, upper and lower, in a therapeutic if not nurturing fashion. The motion of the caressing scaled up from Luke's back to his lush dirty blonde mane. Morgana secured a handful of his locks in between her fingers. As Luke moved down Morgana's body, past her stomach, her grip increased in strength to a level that Luke would have to be non-human to endure.

Once Lucas finished tasting Morgana's passion from his advances, Morgana took over. Luke found himself on his back, motionless, waiting for the anticipated suckling by Morgana. Morgana gave Luke his pleasure, nursing his nature as though she were an infant. Morgana was letting the beast inside out the most peaceful way she could. It was loving this lust that Luke brought alive in her. It was something controlled, contained otherwise. Luke was Morgana's release, if only sexually. As for the killing, nothing could bring her peace with blood-wanting.

The love-making continued as Luke and Morgana tore at the Egyptian cotton sheets that covered Morgana's lavish bed. Luke ceased his brutal motion, remembering how much Morgana enjoyed his soft, almost fragile kisses. Luke spared Morgana a few moments to wreathe in his tenderness before embarking on more carnal satisfaction. Luke proceeded to taste Morgana's skin, never receiving any indication Morgana wanted anything less than what he was giving her. Sweat had long since dripped from their bodies, expanding itself as it was absorbed through the sheets.

As long as blood flowed through the breed's veins, be it by another, less their own, sweat glands and all other organs and body parts functioned, fooling the most skeptical. The coolness of their skin from lack of blood constantly flowing was the primary distinction, which was always a problem for Morgana. Not even the stolen lab blood could compensate for that factor of the breed's chemistry. The heartbeat, although too softly for most humans to detect, unless fresh blood flowed from a recent kill. There was so much necessity for feeding, but Morgana risked all. The only saving grace was her peculiar blood mixture. Morgana always need less, which allowed her to appear more human than any of the others. A toll to be used, for sure.

CHAPTER TWENTY-FOUR

The weather was warm for northern California, and with the body heat they were capable of producing made each of them feel almost faint. The both of them ignored their weakness to bring resolution to their passion. The fine Egyptian sheets were shreds now. The pain was exquisite. Morgana revealed her elation with Lucas' performance, each thrust of his passion. No one had made Morgana feel so wanted. As Lucas gave his queen more and more pleasure, he stroked her hair. Luke told her once more just how much he loved her, how much he would do for her, anything. By giving up his soul, he had done so much already, but he was so filled with Morgana's essence, he was willing to dig new holes in his soul to fill them up with and for her.

In total exasperation, Luke and Morgana poised themselves in each other's arms, propped up against a pillow in front of the etched headboard. There was no dialogue, there was no need for any. Lucas took Morgana's hand and led her from the bed to her story book window sill. The two lovers reflected on all that transpired between them. they found fortune in the events that had brought them to that moment in front of the large stained glass window. There was added gratitude as they watched the sun rise, filling the room with the kaleidoscope of color from the windows. There was no need for the alloy plates that used to be lowered without fail, to protect their immortal, yet vulnerable flesh.

It was Sunday, which meant the early morning evangelists were on the television, spreading the holy word of God. Morgana had experimented with religion, but to no avail. Lucas remembered the word that he used to practice with his family, then by himself, mainly for comfort and guidance. Morgana had nothing to cling onto. Morgana's soul was never with God. As a consequence, she could never create a bond, no matter how pure her heart. Surely God appreciated her desire, being a just God. The painful fact was that there were certain *rules* or sacrifices to be acknowledged. Luke tried, but giving Morgana the religion she craved seemed to be the only thing he could not give her.

...By chance, could there be a ritual, a Wicca spell to amend this harsh reality? Ignorance prevented the investigation to endure...

Luke could only remember his practicing worship. This newly fulfilled soul would be subject to the same restriction as His lover in time, and time was moving fast in that regard. Morgana's soul had no choice, and Lucas forfeited his, ironically, for love.

One afternoon, a few days after, Morgana had a realization as she woke Luke from his sleep. "Luke, darling, so much has happened, I just realized we must have been dropped from our classes by now at school! I can't remember the last time we actually went!" Luke calmed her concern, "It's only been a few weeks. We have time before having to take an incomplete, or trying to pass our classes. Wait a minute, why should we care? Really! We have all the time we need. We can read an entire library if we want! As a matter of fact, I've already made use of the family library downstairs!" It was evident Luke's recovery was virtually complete. The giddy young man fell back and laughed, like a child.

Morgana snuggled next to Lucas, much like a lonesome puppy does to its new friend. "We shouldn't raise suspicion. You'll tell your teachers you had a sudden illness. It's been noticeable that we have become friends, so I will say that I've been the only person available to care for you in your convalescence. During that time, we fell in love. We spent some time debating whether or not to continue our studies, or to marry in a small family ceremony. We decided to be responsible for our futures, both intellectually and emotionally. Then, after we are told if we can finish the semester, we will devote as much time as possible to expanding our knowledge, since being a vampire doesn't mean that one becomes omniscient!" Luke stared at Morgana in silence for a few moments, looking quite like himself now.

"Morgana, baby, is this how you've kept yourself out of trouble all this time? These life alibis that you devise so easily? That is a gift, I mean that. just now, you contrived a plausible explanation that could be disputed."

Morgana paused before answering Luke's questions. It bothered Morgana not being able to be completely forthright, to consciously deceive other innocent people, but they would not be able to comprehend, much less appreciate the realty of the situation. "Our lies aren't far from the truth, you know. It isn't that great of a skill, but you must be clever, even if it means deception. It is the best way, the only way to keep our world, and theirs in balance. Hey, I love you." Luke gently touched Morgana's chin, allowing his fingers to roam downward, toward her placid chest and bosom. "I love you also, my treasure." Morgana obliged Luke, touching him on his chest, right where his heart was.

The following evening was the next scheduled meeting of Luke and Morgana's English class. Ms. James, their teacher observed them as they entered the room. They were obviously in love, more in love than Ms. James was with her current lover. The teacher knew the look, knew the body language. Luke and Morgana came early to class to speak with Ms. James. Both Luke and Morgana told their stories with total conviction, then Ms. James spoke. "Listen you two. It is quite obvious that the time you spent away from class was valid and has proven to remedy more than just Mr.

Brant's malady. That is just fine. Neither of you have missed enough to have to drop the class, but I'm telling you that you must be prepared to work very hard to catch up. The syllabus has all the information you'll need. Neither of you can miss another class meeting, or I will have to take action, which will affect your records. Please make sure you are prepared for the final coming up shortly, half of you grade is riding on it. Honestly, I enjoy seeing the love like the love you two seem to have found. Study like mad, turn in those missing assignments and start thinking now about your topic for the final. Oh, one last thing, don't disappoint me. I'm in a good mood tonight." Ms. James was a progressive teacher, which was why her classes were always filled to maximum capacity.

Morgana and Luke did precisely as Ms. James encouraged. Both eager students took their stagnate grades and carried on at the above average to excellent grade point both were accustomed to maintaining. It was amusing to Desmony how Luke and Morgana entertained so much enthusiasm over school. Were they in some fantasy world? Morgana, at the very least, was much too old and had experienced too much in life not to have already learned everything she was being taught, or needed to know. Luke, on the other hand, was newly unborn, so his desire to complete his education could be appreciated. Perhaps Morgana enjoyed watching others learn, being in a situation where she could apply her knowledge.

Morgana was very cautious about the pace at which she conducted her studies. No attention was to be brought to her aptitude. Morgana treated this opportunity, as she had with all the others in her life, to go through the entire process in all the time it would take for a normal human. That was her goal with each generation, each profession. Morgana was a chameleon of sorts, bringing a new look, a new life to her stale one. Luke would no doubt follow her method of mediocrity, but Desmony never would subscribe to such frivolity. Morgana and Luke would try to help Desmony understand the advantages in excelling in a new field, to make ease for moving in and out of human society. Desmony understood the principle, but it just "wasn't her bag".

The spring semester was drawing to a close, and the summer schedule for classes had just come out. Morgana and Luke took great pride in selecting their next classes, since they could both take day classes. Both Luke and Morgana resisted taking all of the same general requirement courses. The couple also decided not to take too many classes, so they would be available to assist in the care taking of the family members that were in need during the day. Nola and Devon continued their vigilance for the family, but it was taken as great fortune that caring for the family wasn't their sole purpose in life, and for the family.

Morgana's focus was on using this generation of life being a teacher. "I'd like to work with children, try to get them on the right track. I've seen so many changes in society, and it seems to be more and more detrimental to the young. There are values that were once thought of as second nature, that are just losing their status as a priority. Listen to me, I sound like Glenda the Good Witch or something!" Morgana, despite all her good intentions, was still a vampire, a dark soul at heart. A sensation of embarrassment had overwhelmed her as she spoke her concerns to Luke. "Yeah, I agree, on both accounts! Look, baby, do what your heart tells you, there's no harm in being constructive with your time, regardless of how you survive. Humans are existing more and more off their own because of science now every day! What about transplants, huh?" Luke bumped into his love, prodding her, hoping to secure a smile from her. Luke's mission was complete. A smile traveled across Morgana's face, assuring Luke his good intentions were well received.

Morgana was truly excited about having focus in what she wanted to do with her days, the fact that Morgana had days to do anything with was still being processed as a formidable miracle within the family. One day, as Morgana was plotting out her course schedule to get her teaching credentials, Luke said "Well, one thing's for sure, you won't have to worry about the kids scaring you on the first day of school. If they get out of line, you can just change a little, or growl maybe. That would scare the shit right out of them! Seriously, honey, I think I would like to get into counseling. What do you think?" Luke was absolutely refreshing. Luke genuinely valued Morgana's opinion, on everything. Morgana told him to search his heart. If Luke wanted to give structure to young lives, then he should pursue counseling. Luke thanked her, kissed her on the forehead, and eased into the seat next to his beloved.

Morgana wasn't just gorgeous to Luke, she was everything he, any man, would want in a woman. Morgana soared high on his pedestal. "Yes, I think you would make an excellent counselor. Your personality works with anyone you meet. Soon, my love, you will know what each person is thinking that you speak to. It will take time to control it. At first, you will hear many random thoughts. you will share their memories, fears, and hopes. You will sense their feelings, know if they are lying. That will give you an uncommon edge in your field. Use it to help, and you will be content. We can make all of this wonderful Luke!" Morgana kissed Luke and picked up her book bag. Luke followed suit as they left for their evening class.

There was no effort for Luke and Morgana to catch up. There was a need to make it appear as though there was some struggle. There was some tension because their other instructors weren't as lenient as Ms. James. The professors had no choice but to believe their story. fortunately, they returned before the deadline to drop classes, or be failed for missing too many classes. Morgana was delighted she wasn't going to have to resort to using her powers to shape the thoughts of their instructors. It dismayed Morgana a little when some instructors didn't show emotion, not seeming to care if they showed up or not. This gave her more conviction in her choice to be a teacher.

There had always been a desire to know if there were others of their species about in the world. The Mal family had the misfortune of interfacing with Hlival and Lysa, but it led some family members to theorize that there must be more. Luke took a special interest in the possibility, considering all the pros and cons of launching such a search, depending on what was found. Luke thought of taking a chance by starting a web page on the internet regarding the subject of vampires. There was quite a thriving network of charlatans, freaks, and wanna-be vampire hunters. Luke found a few "friendlies", as he liked to call them, seeming to know a little more than the usual motley crew of e-mailing macabre.

The most sizable clue to Luke was the discretion used by some. They would never give out too much information while conversing in chat rooms. Questions were responded to by vague and evasive answers. There was no cultural link from one suspected vampire to the other. Some e-mail would come as far away as Africa, Norway, the Polynesian islands, and many other, more obscure parts of the world. Holding virtual conversations with these alleged vampires was fascinating to Luke, but always gave way to doubt. Was it merely that he met some humans that were so taken with the legend of vampirism that they were delusional? There was no way to know for sure, unless a meeting was to take place.

Lucas made several offers, but none of the *night walkers* would either take the risk, or risk being unmasked as a charlatan. Blythe came to Luke one day, just as he had exhaled in exasperation. The sage matriarch of the family pulled Luke away from the computer he'd been laboring at so feverishly. "My boy, do not let this search for knowledge possess you, any more than the unnatural nature that has already possessed you. Though our lives our longer than any human, with care, we shan't waste a moment of it chasing unicorns. If there are to be others like us that we share contact with, they will undoubtedly have to come to us. This is how it has been since Bernard and my blood was taken by Hlival. That creature is precisely why we don't beckon for others. Rest now, Morgana will be with you soon. If you have any questions about what it is to be what we are, we elders can answer most, if not all your questions. You need not search for others, we are all you need to know. Keep in touch with humans, that is where the amusement lies!"

Blythe paced herself as she departed the room. There was a certainty Blythe felt when she searched Luke's mind to know if he was satisfied. Luke's door closed behind her as she thought about paying Alec some much needed attention.

Desmony literally climbed the walls. It was hot, even at night and she hated that. There was little action right now, there had to be. She couldn't go out for a while. Desmony had fed off a kid that tried to steal her purse one evening last week when she was leaving a party. Lang was ever more bored. Lang's boredom was with Desmony, however. He didn't like Desmony's lack of discipline. Desmony refused to find an interest, something that would legitimize her image. There was no more life in being what she was. Lang decided he needed a vacation. Lang wanted a break, to take a hiatus from the city, from the attention, and from Desmony. Lang had wanted to collect some eastern art, so he took off on an extended holiday to the Orient.

Desmony awoke the following evening to a candle-lit table with flowers, and a goblet filled with room temperature blood. A letter was on a black woven place mat. Lang explained in his letter where he was going and that he did not wish to be contacted. The letter left no information for Desmony to have an accurate idea where Lang was. There was a deep, dull pain in Desmony's heart. It was true, she did possess a still beating heart. The only way she truly knew she had one was the way she felt as she read Lang's letter. What hurt Desmony the most in her time with Lang was that he expressed no emotion to her, ever. Lang indulged Desmony's every whim, but he was seldom, if ever, tender. Lang never seemed to speak from his heart. They never really spoke about it, and if Desmony initiated a conversation about it, Lang would silence her with a paralyzing stare.

This personal devastation made Desmony realize that having full use of her family's unconditional love was a treasure, not something to use only in case of emergency. Desmony spent a lot of time with Blythe for the next few days. Blythe was the one female in the family that she felt close to. They were very much in tune with how they felt about their heritage, what they were. They took great pride in being *supernatural*. The time was well spent, but it couldn't fill the void in Desmony's heart that increased in size, until she felt as though her soul was being extracted. The rest of the clan tried to help, but it was of no use. Desmony felt intense jealousy and bitterness when the others were in her presence. Even though Desmony knew she needed all the family's support, that horrible, hateful part of her couldn't gather strength from those that weren't feeling her pain.

One evening, Desmony couldn't take it anymore. She jumped into her silver Porsche 944 and skidded off into the pitch black night. Her eyes were fully mounted with tears. Whether it was from the speed she was carrying, or the pain she felt, she couldn't tell. The tears streaked along her face as she blazed a trail through the factory district.

Desmony dodged pedestrians as she came closer to downtown, only as an afterthought. Why should she care about the humans anyway, especially if she is in need of attention? Desmony always needed attention, but more so now than ever. Lang has existed for so long, yet she knew very little about him. The past that Lang couldn't change had made him unforgiving of his future, and anyone that chose to live in it. The burden was still too much, even after all of these years. Falling in love with a rouge vampire was no way to heal himself either. Lang saw this, but it didn't matter as much to Desmony. It couldn't matter to Desmony, because Lang didn't help Desmony understand. Both lovers were at fault, yet neither would bend.

Desmony swerved into the mansions' drive way and hopped out of her car. She ran passed Nola, who just looked on with concern. Desmony made it up to Blythe's room, now in tears. Desmony's passion had overwhelmed her for the first time ever. She was truly lost and didn't know what to do.

Blythe had heard Desmony's cries in her mind. She was awaiting Desmony's arrival whole-heartedly. Blythe stood at the threshold of her bedroom door way with her arms out-stretched. Desmony submitted her quivering body into Blythe's. Blythe held Desmony long and hard, trying to give her the strength that was needed for times such as these. Blythe asked if she would like Elsebeth to come, but Desmony could only shake her head. Desmony knew her mother would try to make her feel better, and she didn't want that. All Desmony wanted was to be understood.

Desmony didn't really know what it was like to be in love. Actually, she wasn't really sure what the entire concept was about. Blythe had more of an idea, but failed to think anyone could understand what bond Lang and Desmony had with one another. The love Blythe had for Alec had some similarities, but even Blythe and Alec understood one another. Blythe wasn't sure that Lang would ever allow Desmony, or anyone else, understand him enough to truly love him. Lang hated himself and his existence too much. Blythe couldn't explain what she felt to Desmony in that manner, not in the state she was in. It would not be Blythe's nor Desmony's character or temperament to be frail and soft about it, but there was a need for comprehension.

"Desmony, my child. I can only sympathize with your hurt and pain. I had only loved once before I was unborn. I can hardly remember what it felt like. All I can sense about it is pain. That is only because of Hlival, taking my life away from me. I care for Alec, your grandfather, but I can never be what he would like. I feel a lot of things. I feel loyalty, anger, fear, among others. The one thing I fail to believe I can feel is love. When I think of love, I feel pity. I do this because love is abused and abandoned. Love is treated worse than any person could ever be. Love has so much of itself to give, yet we don't know how to use it in its purest form. Lang is an abuser, and yes my dear, so are you. I implore you to take this time away from Lang and try to discover love without him, in order to appreciate it with him. I myself am too old, I fear. I have no desire, never have, to investigate love. I would, however, like to see you accomplish something I never valued enough to see through." The fear that Blythe spoke of was simmering inside of her. The words she spoke could be easily misunderstood.

Blythe collected herself, and made another attempt, studying Desmony as she sat with her eyes fixed on her mentor. Through the years, Blythe had observed what love had done to and for many people. "My child, to love and to be loved is hard enough. There's always an opposing force. When one is in love, and the other isn't, or is and can't or won't show it, well, I suppose that can be or seem worse than a slow death." Blythe tried to speak with some levity, but to no avail. Desmony tried to generate a smile to show gratitude for Blythe's efforts, but she was wallowing so deeply in her own self-pity. All Desmony could muster was a whimpering growl. Desmony was committed to sulking and moping, regardless if she was at home, or at the loft.

"Why should I continue to hide the way I feel? Lang has succeeded in changing me, or at least trying. I don't like the way he's making me feel now. Everyone else is in love and happy. I've tried it, and it doesn't work on me. My life is utter shit! I've just about had it! Why do people bother with love anyway? The gamble for happiness with someone else? Well, I'm happy on my own, killing when I see fit. It's much easier

to just take care of myself than to bother with head-cases!"
Desmony laughed at her words, trying to hide the obvious
pain. Being down on herself was not Desmony's style.

Blythe had been sitting quietly, listening to the
anguished child speak her mind. Ultimately, Blythe had no
answers for her. It was ironic, however, that Desmony didn't
need love, but she wanted it from Lang. The new moon
comforted Desmony. She was in total darkness, except for the
distant city lights. Desmony could hide everything, all of her
sadness, bitterness, and confusion in the coal black sky that
enveloped her. Those night lights began to hypnotize
Desmony, even call to her. She was weak and vulnerable,
something she had never felt that she was aware of.

Desmony got up, so she could leave. She realized
Blythe couldn't solve her problems. The only thing Blythe
could really do is sympathize with Desmony. Desmony gave
Blythe a kiss and went for her car. As she drove, the cold
wind slapped her face, keeping her focused on her driving.
Visions of Desmony's enduring life and its disappointments
flashed at her, dizzying her.

Desmony pulled up to the loft, looking at it as if it
were one of her parents, waiting for it to give her a spanking
for some stunt she had pulled. Desmony stirred around the
building, imagining Lang just around the corner. It became
too much for her to take. With a deafening shriek, Desmony

broke through the sky light. She looked back at the roof as she ascended into the fleeting night. "Let him fix the damn window! Damn him!" Desmony was livid. As Desmony's speed increased, tears streaked her face. This was partly from the force, and partly from her broken heart.

It was the first time she had let anybody get that close, only to have him play with her heart and mind. Desmony had always been black and white. To Desmony, you were either a vampire, or prey for dinner. Desmony didn't play games, or so she thought. Desmony began to realize also that she did in fact play games. She would play with her prey, making them suffer at times, just for pleasure. Desmony also took unnecessary chances with her life and the lives of those close to her. Her tightly wrapped sense of self was unraveling right before her eyes.

The biggest insult Desmony had done to herself, or maybe it was some kind of supernatural discipline was when Lang entered her life, and she dared to love. She had secretly waited so long for one of her own kind to appear that she could love, as Morgana had tried to with mortals. When Lang came to her, it seemed all wrong, but he was what she wanted and damn the consequences. Desmony's wry sense of humor popped in, as usual, as a defense mechanism. "maybe Morgana has something, loving humans. I could use 'em, then suck 'em dry!" That was simply her pain talking.

Desmony's fantasy of her ideal man had now become a
haunting nightmare.

CHAPTER TWENTY-FIVE

For probably the first time, Desmony was out of control. She was completely undone. Even the ever-wise Blythe couldn't calm her fears. Desmony thought as she flew across the impersonal asphalt maze below her. Desmony's watch showed her she had precisely five hours and thirty-six minutes before sun rise. She saw something that reached inside her chasm of a troubled soul as she peered downward. A domestic confrontation was at the boiling point in a drive way. An adulterous husband had picked a fight with his wife. He was looking for a reason to leave, at least to make his date on time for the evening. "You have a date tonight you shit, don't you? Well, go! I don't even want your sorry ass anymore! You were the one who proposed to me. You asked me for my hand, to love me, and for me to have our children. You promised to love and honor me. Get out! Go to your bitch!" The woman was shaking with anger and fear. Their child was nowhere to be seen.

The husband discarded his wife, throwing her to the ground. He yelled some obscenities at her, trying to feebly justify his straying from their commitment to one another. The man paced, thinking of what to do next. The wife picked her sobbing self from the ground. She stood opposite of her soon-to-be ex-husband, moving as he moved. They were creating some kind of haters dance. None of their neighbors came outside, to see or to help. After the first few times, the neighbors lost hope, then interest. No one was ever hurt, and the wife would believe she had no choice but to forgive him. She had to think about their child and the lifestyle she was accustomed. Above all, she still loved the prick, until now.

This was going to be the last time. "What a sow! I can't believe he's treating her that way! I can't believe she's taking it." Desmony's passions made her care about that dehumanized mortal female. This was probably more so because this woman was in a way a symbol of her own pain. "It's time to eat!" The husband started for his car. He was late, that much was true. He was actually going to meet with his lawyer. Evidently, this woman he broke his vows for was worth it, or so he thought. The wife didn't beg, no. She pushed him against the car. She jammed her knee into his pride and joy.

The man grabbed at his crotch, praying for the pain to stop. "I hope she likes it soft, you prick!" The wife started away. Her husband caught her by the collar and swung her around. He raised his hand to her, but his momentum to land the strike on her was impeded by Desmony's hand. The wife was startled. She wasn't prepared for the blow, or the lack of it. "Is your life insurance paid up, laddy?" Desmony jerked upwards, carrying the woman's husband off into the dark night sky. The wife whirled around, looking desperately for him. She wondered in a panic, as if she had gone mad. "Help, help, please! Some one's taken my husband. He's gone, gone. Oh help me!"

The fog was whipping past them as Desmony flew around, aimlessly, for a while. The man was quite disoriented, still not knowing exactly what was going on. The only thing he was sure of was he wasn't on the ground anymore and that terrified him. He couldn't make any sense of this or tell his location or know how he was moving through space as he was. The man followed the tension from the collar of his jacket to the hand that held him so far above ground. Once his trail ended, he saw Desmony, clearly, for the first time.

The panic that stirred in his head was without description. Desmony was semi-transformed. Her eyes had the distinctive glow, yet her face wasn't totally disfigured. Her fangs and claws were at full length and her wings spread out across the night sky, reflecting the stars that were now visible. They were high above the fog now, flying in almost total silence. The concept of this man being led around the city, in mid-air, by this creature was enough to kill anybody. The man was surprised he wasn't dead already. He kept his eyes closed for most of the journey. Desmony saw the man was slowly accepting his present situation and gathering his composure. There could be none of that! Desmony was calling the shots and right at that moment, Desmony decided to interpret the man's composure as lack of grasping the seriousness of his predicament. Desmony swooped down, after going up a few hundred feet. The man sprayed vomit throughout the sky which pleased Desmony. Control was hers once again.

Desmony descended another time as they approached a tunnel. She so desperately wanted to take him through it. *That would be a thrill* Desmony thought as she made her way toward the empty tunnel. The velocity was so fast, the man thought Desmony might lose her hold of him. A large part of him wished she would so the nightmare would end. They made it through, undetected. No one was around to hear the screams of the man as the resonated through the rounded structure.

It wasn't long before Desmony became bored again. She tired of the tour she was taking the adulterer on. The city was still active, but not nearly as busy as earlier. Desmony decided to give the adulterer one last thrill. The bay bridge was near their final destination. Desmony darted in and out of the enormous cables that supported the marvelous bridge. "I would take you to the top of the Golden Gate bridge, but you aren't worth it." Desmony just chuckled as the man cried and screamed. Desmony set the man down on one of the large beams of the bridge. He did not find it amusing at all as he tried to steady himself. He was trembling uncontrollably and finding it almost impossible to breathe. For just a moment, he thought about jumping. He didn't whether or not it was because he lacked the courage, or he thought this beast would simply catch him and make him suffer even longer.

Desmony crouched down on what seemed to be her legs, but could've just as well been haunches. She made horrible screeching noises as her nails, or talons, stroked across the metal of the cables. Desmony sat there, thinking of what to do with him next. One was for sure, he was never going home.

Desmony picked up her baggage, carrying her passenger all the way from his allegedly safe suburb to Alcatraz prison. She felt this was a fitting place for someone of his nature. The fog surrounding the island where this institution dominated set the mood in bold letters. Desmony dropped the man on the cold cement floor, just a few feet from the ground's surface. Desmony eased herself onto the ground. She was no longer hideous to the mortal eye. She appeared forever young and beautiful now. She paced, slowly. She continued to circle him, to survey him. "You're sweating like you've just ran a marathon! Honestly, I did all the work. Funny, you look like a mountain of mashed potatoes! You smell like urine. I would tell you to clean yourself up, but the worst is far from over." Desmony was much more serious than her words seemed to be.

"Why are you doing this to me? What have I done to you? Who in the hell are you anyway? What are you?" The man tried to pick himself off the floor, but his strength failed him. His adrenaline was rushing, but his fear was overwhelming. He shivered as he lay there on the cold and wet ground. The cold wind made his pale cheeks flush. He was still very disoriented, as well as in deep shock. He felt as though he were in a terrible dream. One in which he could not wake. Memories flashed in his mind, summing up his life. He selected a few choice images. He wondered if he could have changed those, would that have kept him from being at this place, at this moment. He would never know.

The man accepted this, knowing that he had lived his life like so many he had known through the years. He was of little faith, not trying to settle for a modest life doing "the right thing". He had been ruthless, dishonest, and deceptive. He was all of these things, and had been most of them to his family and his wife. He thought of one of the eternal questions, *why do we hurt the ones we love?* He was not about to get his answer from this amazingly beautiful creature that was to be his grim reaper. He thought facetiously, *if I'm gonna die, it should be by the hand of a fetching woman like none I've ever seen!*

Desmony wanted to examine the human nature a bit with her subject, like a lab rat. There were some questions she needed answered about relationships that she couldn't get from her family. The younger ones that were in relationships had *crossed over*. They mated with the fleshy enemy. Her parents didn't count because they were from another time and were not humans. They stayed together as much for survival now than as anything else. Desmony wanted to know about the bond of a loving relationship from two like things that at least had once felt passion. Desmony also wanted to know if there were differences in the answers given by this stranger, or if it didn't matter that one's heart beat or not. The real question was, should Desmony have waited all this time for Lang? Was he worth it? Did she even need him? She had to know.

"Tell me, why do you hurt your wife? What does she actually do so wrong that you feel the need to destroy her emotionally, cripple her mentally, and sometimes abuse her physically? If, you can give me an explanation I can accept, I won't peel you inside out. Well, I'm waiting. You know, I actually think better under pressure, obviously, you don't." Desmony ran her nails along a metal rail, causing a miniature display of fireworks. The light work attracted the attention of a bay patrolman on duty, who was on the watch for drunken boaters. "Give me a fucking minute! I've been married for thirteen years! How am I supposed to tell you what is wrong in a few sentences, so that you won't kill me?

The man was truly pathetic, not because his life was in jeopardy, and Desmony knew why.

"The reason you can't supply me with an answer is because all of your motivation to ruin what both of you had built together is purely selfish. You chickened out on the deal. Having an ideal wife, life, is boring to you now, right? You still think you're that attractive, yet pimple faced, lean, full-head-of-hair puke that tried diligently to live life on the edge. You would never conform. you would have your own opinion and it would stand for something and be the only one that mattered. No compromise, no looking out for someone other than your own privileged ass! Commitment is precious. You've fucked over and on it! Your wife simply loves you. It sounds small, but it is so grand!" Desmony was on the verge of tears.

"Wait! You're telling me that you're going to kill me because I may not, well I haven't, appreciated my wife? That's my, our business! There's only one person I know of that I have to answer to for my actions, and it ain't you! "The husband's adrenaline finally kicked in, doing what it was supposed to do. Even though it was impossible to escape the fortress, he'd rather make a stand, and go on his own terms. He'd rather drown than to be mutilated by this she-beast. At once, the man began to run from her.

Desmony watched the man, admiring his delayed sense of spirit and pride. A small curl of a smile crept out from the corner of her mouth. Then, a fang slowly slipped out past her supple lips. Desmony rose up off the ground, hovering over him. She just monitored him for a moment. Desmony was still heavily outraged from her pain. Besides, she had no choice but to feed. Before the man reached a nearby ledge, she was on the other side. The shock nearly gave the man a coronary, but no such luck. Desmony grabbed him by the lapels and ripped his jacket off his robust body. She used her claws to turn his expensive shirt into rags. She attacked with such precision, she did not spill any of his blood while dismantling his garment. The man stood there, stunned, shivering, waiting for the worst. He mumbled some prayers and Desmony told him he should have thought about that while he was stroke tallying as many sins as he could.

Desmony turned the man's head away from her. She wanted to choose the puncture site well. She bit down quick, not taking her time and consequently giving him excruciating pain. Desmony wasn't being kind. She heard the sound of a motor off in the distance. The Coast Guard was checking the area before changing patrols. Desmony yanked out a huge rock from the floor and weighed down the husband's corpse with it. The young bay patrolman and a few police had rowed silently in, climbing the endless path of stairs, much like soft pawed kittens. In Desmony's triumph, her senses had somehow dulled. She hadn't picked up on the scent of other flesh about. Nor did she hear the slight noises made amidst the waves and strong gusts of wind. The patrolman saw her, just as she finished dumping the man's body. She was all set to spear herself out into the night when the men surprised her.

"Hold it, right there! Don't move! I mean it!" The patrolman was shaking, although it was undetectable with his coat rattling in the wind. The officer was terrified, but he wasn't going to blow this huge arrest. Desmony had created quite a stink. There were too many men around, with more on the way. The reports were to fantastic to disregard. Desmony didn't have time to destroy them all. She could've tried, but she thought it would be best to wait for a less attention grabbing time. There was still an opportunity to bluff her way out of this jam. Desmony concealed her laughter, even at this very serious time, playing their game. It was almost impossible not to laugh as they hand cuffed her and read the Miranda to her.

Desmony was taken to shore. Then, she was driven to the nearest precinct where she was finger printed, but there was a small revolt when it came time for her picture. The camera would pick up on her trans lucid complexion, making her appear invisible. That documentation, or lack thereof would be enough to make her a test subject, leading to a domino effect the world couldn't comprehend. Desmony resisted. "It's against my religion to have my photograph taken. I may be a criminal, but you have just told me I have these rights, n'est-ce pas?" Desmony used a thick French accent she had acquired from her many years in France and Europe. Not having any identification with her may have proved to be in her favor. She played the foreign citizen with immunity act to the hilt.

The officers persisted in trying to follow procedure until Desmony broke her cuffs and proceeded to escape. A small group of policemen gang tackled her. Desmony was beaten, even shot at. A bullet hit her in the back of her thigh. She ignored it as if it were a mosquito bite. Another shot rang out, hitting her in the small of her back. Desmony would not go down. The force jolted her, making her aware she was playing her hand. The game was nearing an end. The bright lights in the office diminished her powers somewhat. She was assumed to be a drug attic, strung out on PCP or crack cocaine. Seven police officers were finally able to take advantage of her weakened state. She was sedated, tended to by a paramedic on site, and hurried to a cell under heavy guard.

The time was three o'clock in the morning. Desmony was finally becoming nervous. She bayed and bellowed, sending out calls for Lang. The guards sedated her once again. Later, she resorted to mental communication, trying to reach Lang still. Desmony thought of her family, but she was so consumed by wanting this emotionally dormant creature, she would risk perishing in the morning sun, and possibly putting the rest of her family in jeopardy.

It was inconceivable that Desmony was putting her existence in such peril. She on purposely blocked her family out so they couldn't come to her aid. They were happy. Why should they suffer for her unhappiness? There was a chance that it would all end here, or so she thought. The thought never entered her mind that her demise could ignite a witch-hunt of sorts on all vampires, real or otherwise. Then world of the unspeakable, the unimaginable would be unveiled.

It was amazing that Desmony was even thinking that her refusing help from her family would protect them. Her actions were truer to character than it appeared on the surface, because they were selfish thoughts. How dare she think her family wouldn't mourn her dying for all the ages they had still to live. How dare she!

There were still many adventures to have, many more loves as well. None of these thoughts helped to soothe her rage. "If he won't come to me, I'll die. I can't take this anymore. I am no better than the flesh. My existence until I met Lang was a constant reaction to discontent with myself. Everyone has found love or kept it. Why not me? I must not deserve it. Morgana has had it twice! Oh how I envy her, how I love her. Morgana thinks Victor is her secret. Her emotions were so intense for him, I almost felt like I was in love with him! He was one of the very few humans I've liked." Desmony was more determined to "live up" to her ultimatum.

It was now five a.m. She was sweating profusely. She became wild, screaming at the pain her body was experiencing. "Aaaaarrrrggghh!" It's too hot! Oh Lang! Help me! Help me! Burn marks began to appear on her pale delicate skin. It changed in appearance. It looked more like rice paper than flesh.

Now, her family could sense her pain. Desmony could no longer hold up the barrier she had before. Her family knew she was dying and they were powerless to attempt anything. The ones that were strong enough to try, Morgana, Nola, Luke, and Devon were warned off. They could've saved her, but she refused. She kept her loved ones at bay by whole-heartedly promising to dash out into the coming daylight before they could reach her. That would have been better than what was yet to come. Oddly enough, they understood her. They stood together, holding one another, screaming in unison for her pain. It was not a human experience. It was the liberation of a tormented and dammed soul.

The family was nearly driving themselves mad, not fully being able to accept that Desmony's existence had come to this, that she was willing to do this. They knew, however, that this wasn't just for Lang.

Desmony was tired. She was weak and in too much pain to yell any longer. None of the injured or angered police came downstairs to tend to her cries. The guards outside of her door looked, but did nothing. They decided hours ago that Desmony was just another homicidal drug addict. As one guard turned away, Lang caught him by the throat and snapped his neck. The other guard's head fell from his body before he could collect his thoughts to comprehend, to scream.

Lang bent the bars open, like some super hero, without effort, which brought him to Desmony's cell. Desmony was almost unconscious. The daylight was piercing through all of the cells on Desmony's side of the building. It was overcast, but that only made the effect feel like being cut open with a dull knife. As painful as it was, there was thanks to be given. It wasn't too late. Desmony did not have to perish that day. Desmony wasn't aware Lang was moving toward her. She was awaiting a fabulous death, bursting into a brilliant ball of flames. She could already feel, even see the smoke. The heat and the burning was unfathomable.

Lang tore the bar doors apart like room divider beads. "Hold on my love. We mustn't lose you now." Lang picked her up, covering her with a heavy wool blanket. He carried her out the way he had come in. There were so many dead lying on the floor. They were all dead. Several never knew what hit them. Lang's fury leveled an entire squadron. No one was left to purge the miserable tale, not that it could have, or would want to be believed.

Lang shot up into the sky, hoping the morning fog would continue giving them protection. The sun's heat was already penetrating Lang's big, black leather cape-trench coat. It was the only shelter they had. Soon, the coat would be on fire, melting and burning, ignited by their flaming bodies. Morgana, Bernard, Blythe, and Elsebeth felt Lang's presence. All hoped he would make it in time, back to the house, back to safety. Now, just barely, they could too feel Desmony. Morgana and Nola waited with tears in their eyes. The waiting was unbearable. What was happening? They couldn't get a clear read on Lang and his thoughts. Desmony was too weak to form complete thoughts. There were only images of the long "life" she had journeyed through. The point Desmony never picked up on was that she was never alone, never abandoned or banished. she never went without love.

"Hold on darling. I've so much to tell you. Don't give up just yet." Lang was wincing as he spoke. The few rays of sun that tried to pop from behind the cloud cover seemed to be searching them out, like a homing beacon. Flying was almost impossible, but necessary. They would never make it in time, undetected, on ground. Lang's speed was slower than usual. The sun was draining him fast. He pushed, trying to keep them both alive. What people that were awake and about saw a flash through the air, as they looked up to evaluate the coming day. The shadow that Lang cast on the ground suggested some type of small plane or a large bird. Not so much attention was paid to the mid-air spectacle. They were closing in on the house. So close and yet so far never rang more true. A large burn had formed on Desmony's leg, unshielded by the coat. It would take a long time to mend, but if she could make it, she would live.

The pacing that was going on in the mansion was enough to make one think there was a small tremor. The elders were still powerless, even more so with the day fully erect. Their pain was as immense as their frustration. Nola had the front door wide open, hoping for a brilliant entrance and a need for her immediate care. They were all waiting, now calling out for the two. "Where could they be? Were they that far away? Oh, somebody help them!" Elsebeth was wild with fear.

Suddenly, through the fog, the black figure appeared. Lang's speed had increased since the cloud cover had thickened closer to the house. Nola and Morgana stood aside, just as Lang and Desmony broke passed the threshold. The door slammed shut behind them, shaking the entire building.

Lang whisked Desmony into the slumber chambers and laid her down, in her converted coffin. He was terribly weak and needed rest as well. Lang bided for an older coffin, previously used by Bernard. The four that were still upstairs locked the closed doors and held one another. This call was much too close. This stunt was by far the worst Desmony had ever attempted. Her motivation for the risk was different and they knew it. At that moment, the future was unclear to them. It seemed to take forever for night fall. Desmony and Lang stayed below. The elders, Morgana, Luke, Nola, and Devon slowly came up. They were heavily disturbed by the day's events.

Blythe was the first to speak. "All that we know here now is a memory. The roots we have made here must be lifted. We cannot risk anyone tracing what has happened back to us. I've seen the blood shedding that happened by Lang in order to bring Desmony back to us. All of our assets must be liquidated in haste so that we may travel. The club, your education, Morgana, the future business, all of it must be put on hold, sold, or abandoned. We take what we can now and leave. Luke, the boat that your parents left you, we will need to make use of it now. " Blythe had thought cautiously, but not thoroughly. "Madame, I had taken the liberty to look out for our finances so that we could abandon the mansion and our lives without suffering too much loss. I will be able to see to the final details with Devon's assistance. I cannot make too much of a guarantee with our material possessions, but we have many untraceable accounts throughout the globe. It may take a day or two, but I'm sure we can do it." Nola was steady now, and in her mode of preserving the family, not by hand, but by mind.

Luke responded to the requisitioning of his boat. "Of course. What's mine is yours, ours. We'll be leaving a lot behind, most of which Nola thinks we can arrange for. I believe we can do it. The world is too big, and it will take time for any traces, if any, to link us with the precinct. I only regret having to leave home, leave my parents." "If anything of ours is misplaced, we will procure it again. We always have. Nola has taken great care to catalog everything, even your family's legacy to you. One day, we will track everything down. We will seize what is ours, by any means necessary. We will try through human channels and ways. Right now, we must concentrate on our survival. " Alec rested his hand on Luke's shoulder.

It was possible the house could be closed down and protected, not to be opened. Not too many people were aware the mansion was occupied with its remote and abandoned location. They had chosen well, as they did with all their other homes. All the homes they had lived in were secure, but this time, it was different. Society was a little too jaded. Ghosts and Demons didn't scare people any longer. They fascinated them, They, were "pop-culture".

Bernard suggested Finland, by route of Alaska and Greenland. that would be a logical choice. Elsebeth added that it would take a few weeks of carefully calculated travel, but it would be the best. There were always contingency plans, ready to be implemented at a moment's notice. Now was the time. It was tragic that everything was going so well, so many wonderful discoveries had been made, such personal progress. Fate has a way of making sure the restless never really become sedentary.

The meeting was adjourned. The news casts all day long had been over the police precinct massacre. There were no leads at the time, or none that were being disclosed. Packing around the manor was fast and furious. There was no need for good-byes. the ominous sensation of danger was all around them. There was no telling what human would have the dumb, albeit, fateful luck of discovering the clan. Whatever could be brought without making the ship too heavy was brought. That wasn't very much with ten people on board. Nola and Luke made all of the arrangements with the family's holdings, while the rest labored physically. Desmony and Lang were of no use. They were still recovering into the next evening.

The police and the entire city were in a fierce panic. There were no survivors for any testimony. There was no evidence that led anywhere, not even the distorted finger prints and blurred photo of Desmony was enough to lead anywhere. It was feared that any speculation would be far too inconceivable to accept. The dead were buried, never being allowed to find peace for their brutal and unjust murders. The Coast Guard patrolman and the adulterer's wife were the only living people that saw Desmony that night. Their stories met with nothing but criticism. There was no way that woman could have done any of that carnage alone. There was no evidence to suggest there were others involved. It wasn't a terrorist attack, killing spree, or rampage. The only survivors were left to become pitied, ridiculed for their accounts of the bloodiest night in San Francisco's history.

The Mal family eased onto the water, unnoticed by anyone. Morgana couldn't believe they were making passage away from all the blood, all the death, without any consequence. Wasn't there something, anything? Why did it matter? The goal wasn't to be caught. The goal was to move on as they did many times before to settle and *blend*. Morgana still couldn't help but think they should pay for their crimes. In their world, however, they were merely surviving. It wasn't a concern for her, or anyone else on board that fishing boat.

The wind carried them away, far away. Each of the crew thought about the future, or reflected on the past. Now, right now, was exciting. They were safely on their way to another adventure. They were opening another chapter in their amazing story. Their life was decadent. They looked forward to where they were going. Where ever it was. It was a mystery. It was the best thing, the only thing they could do.

Whoever they were in San Francisco was not to be, ever again. It was shameless they were getting away, not paying for their crimes.

The night ocean breeze calmed every one's nerves. No one was following them, and no one would. This would indeed be another San Francisco tragedy, another great unsolved mystery. A new legend had been created. A film, book, and countless marches would be created to commemorate the event. The events were too bizarre to put together for anything more than fiction, except for the dead that would never be forgotten. That was the grotesque beauty of being a Vampire. They inhabit a land, live amongst humankind, cause a little misery, maybe even cause a little destruction, and leave in the middle of the night. These Vampires would only be seen again the next time and place they chose.

The waves rushed up against the modest, yet fortified vessel. Lang was back to full strength, and so was Desmony, save for a bandage around the small of her calf. "I remember, you said you had much to tell me, Lang. What? What did you have to tell me?" Desmony moved her weight onto his stern form. "I love you." Lang kissed the top of Desmony's head. Desmony smiled and said, "That's everything, my love."